Black Light

Also by Stephen Hunter

FICTION

Dirty White Boys
Point of Impact
The Day Before Midnight
The Spanish Gambit
The Second Saladin
The Master Sniper

NONFICTION

Violent Screen: A Critic's 13 Years
* on the Front Lines of Movie Mayhem*

Stephen Hunter

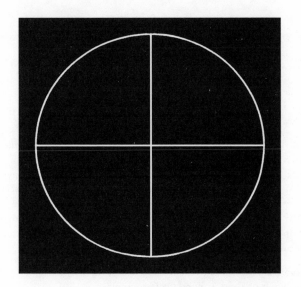

Black Light

DOUBLEDAY
New York
London
Toronto
Sydney
Auckland

PUBLISHED BY DOUBLEDAY
a division of Bantam Doubleday Dell Publishing Group, Inc.
1540 Broadway, New York, New York 10036

DOUBLEDAY and the portrayal of an anchor with a dolphin
are trademarks of Doubleday, a division of
Bantam Doubleday Dell Publishing Group, Inc.

Library of Congress Cataloging-in-Publication Data

Hunter, Stephen, 1946–
Black light / Stephen Hunter.—1st ed.
  p.   cm.
I. Title.
PS3558.U494B53   1996
813'.54—dc20   95-43079
CIP

ISBN 0-385-48042-3

10   9   8   7   6   5   4   3   2   1

For my son, Jake

And it's old and old it's sad and old and weary I go back to you, my cold father, my cold mad father . . .

—JAMES JOYCE, *Finnegans Wake*

Black Light

One

TODAY YOU CAN DRIVE south from Fort Smith down to Blue Eye in Polk County in about an hour, by way of the Harry Etheridge Memorial Parkway. It's a bright band of American road, one of the finest in America, even if it didn't quite have the anticipated effect of turning Polk County into the Branson of West Arkansas and even if some local cynics call it a porkway and not a parkway. Fast-food restaurants and super gas stations cluster at its exit ramps, pennants flapping in the breeze; the high signs of national motel chains—Days Inn, Holiday Inn, Ramada Inn—can be seen from the roadway, even if the motels are never more than half full and the anticipated Polk County land boom never quite took off. The land, especially as you near Blue Eye, county seat of Polk, becomes spectacular for the Ouachita Mountain range, the only east-west range in America, a heaving sea of pine-crusted earth and rock.

The parkway was finished in 1995, under the sponsorship of Boss Harry's son, Hollis Etheridge, then a member of the United States Senate and later a presidential aspirant. It was the son's idea to honor his father, an authentic great man, who had been born dirt-poor in Polk County and had found his fortune first in the intense ward politics of Fort Smith and then in the true corridors of power in Washington, where he was a fifteen-term congressman and the chairman of the House Defense Appropriations Committee. It was only fitting that Polk County and Fort Smith should honor a man who'd brought so much glory—and so much patron-age—their way.

In 1955 no parkway existed, nor could one even be imagined. You got from Blue Eye to the big city the way Harry had when he'd moved up there just after the Great War—that is, along snaky, slow Route 71, as piss-poor an excuse for a road as could be imagined, two lanes of shabby blacktop cranking through the mountains and the farmland, widening every ten miles but just slightly for one-horse towns like Huntington, Mansfield and Need-more or Boles or even, the poorest and most pathetic, Y City. It was just the hardscrabble landscape of one of America's most wretched states, hills too mean to be farmed, valleys where desper-ate men eked out some kind of subsistence-level survival, and now and then some cultivated land but more usually the bleak shacks of sharecroppers.

One hot morning in July of that year, a Saturday, at the Polk and Scott county line on U.S. 71 about twelve miles north of Blue Eye, a state police black and white Ford pulled over to the side of the road and a tall officer got out, removed his Stetson and ran his sleeve over the sweat on his forehead. He wore three yellow ser-geant's stripes on his shoulder and, under a gray brush cut, had the flat-eyed, incapable-of-surprise face of a noncommissioned officer in any army or police force in the past four thousand years. A whole phalanx of wrinkles moved across his leathery face, which had been baked in the sun for so many years it resembled a scrap of ancient hide. His eyes were slitted and shrewd, eyes that missed nothing and also expressed nothing. He had a voice so deep and raspy it sounded like someone cutting through a three-hundred-year-old hardwood pine with a three-hundred-year-old saw. His name was Earl Swagger and he was forty-five years old.

Earl looked about. The road was cut into the slope here, so that there was a high bank on one side, and on the other the land fell away. Not much to see, other than a goddamned billboard for Texaco gasoline: just a south-slope close-grown forest, hard to walk through, a cutting maze of shortleaf pine, black oak and black hickory with a tangled undergrowth of saw brier and Ar-kansas yucca. Dust seemed to hang in the air; there was no breeze, no sense at all of mountain crispness. You looked back toward Blue Eye and your vision was cut off by the hump of Fourche Mountain up ahead, which just appeared to be a huge wall of green. On the road, an armadillo had been smeared to meat and blood and shattered shell by a logger's rig. In the still heat, cicadas hummed, sounding like a drunken quartet of Jew's harps. It hadn't rained in weeks: forest fire weather. It reminded Earl of other hot, dusty places he'd been: Tarawa, Saipan and Iwo Jima.

He checked his Bulova. He was early, but then he'd been early most of his life. It was 9:45 A.M. The others were still fifteen minutes off. Earl put his Stetson back on. A Colt Trooper .357 rested under a flap on a holster at his right hand; he hitched it up, for the heavy weight of the big pistol was always drawing his belt downward and it was a continual battle to keep the gun where it was supposed to be. Thirty gleaming high-velocity soft-point cartridges rode in the belt loops, gleaming because unlike other officers he removed them each night from the loops and wiped them off to prevent them from corroding in the moisture the leather attracted. His fifteen years in the Marine Corps had taught Earl many lessons, but the most important of them was: always take care of your equipment.

It was a melancholy day, which, just yesterday, had promised so much happiness: July 23, 1955. Jimmy Pye was getting out of prison after ninety days up in the Sebastian County jailhouse at Fort Smith. Jimmy's cousin Bub would meet Jimmy at the jail gate and the two would take the Polk County bus. Earl would pick them up at 4:30 P.M. and take Jimmy over to Mike Logan's sawmill in Nunley, where Mike had promised Jimmy a job. That was important: Jimmy had to get off on a good start if he was to make a go of it, and by God, Earl had promised Jimmy's wife, Edie, that he would see to it that Jimmy got himself straightened out this time. Earl had reluctantly first arrested Jimmy in 1950, when Jimmy was sixteen, on a routine breaking and entering; he'd busted him again in 1952, twice in 1953. Each time, Jimmy'd charmed his way out of it, for that was one of Jimmy's gifts: he wasn't just handsome and the best high school athlete ever seen in Polk County, but he had a sweet charm; he made people care for him. He'd grown up wild: his father, after all, had been killed on Iwo Jima, and Earl had sworn to the dying man that he'd look after Jimmy, and pledges made on a battlefield have a huge weight back in the real world. Earl's wife, June, had once even said, "I swear, Earl, you care more for that wild white-trash boy than you do for your own son." It wasn't true, Earl knew, but he also knew that people might see things that way. When you looked at Jimmy you just knew he could be everything that his poor father had dreamed of: he was smart enough for college and if steered right could go on to a wonderful life. He'd married the prettiest girl in all of Polk County when he was twenty-one years old just four months ago. But it was as if he had some twisted wire in him: just when he got a thing that no one else could get—Edie White, for instance—he'd throw it away.

So it was set to be a day of celebration, on the premise that ninety long days in the jailhouse would straighten out *anybody:* a new life for Jimmy and Edie, all of Earl's obligations to Jimmy's dad taken care of and the future before them all.

Then Earl watched as another vehicle drew into sight, a black squad car rolling up 71 from Blue Eye. It pulled over and a Blue Eye deputy named Lem Tolliver, a big man, got out and Earl remembered why he was there.

"Howdy, Earl," called the deputy, "we late or you early?"

"I'm early. Besides, the damn dogs ain't here yet. I hope that goddamned old man don't forget."

"He won't," called the man, then turned and opened the rear door of the car. "Okay, boys, out you go. We's here."

In prison denims, two sunburned old boys climbed out of the back of the truck. Earl knew them: Lum and Jed Posey spent more time in the Blue Eye lockup than out of it. They were always in petty trouble with the law for every damned little thing you could imagine, usually whiskey running, which was the federal boys' problem, but also petty larceny, car theft, shoplifting, anything that'd put a bite of food down their gullets. But Earl had thought of them as essentially harmless.

"You sure you wanta go to all this trouble for a nigger gal?" said

Jed Posey. "What difference do it make? Let the niggers take care of it."

"Shut up, Jed," said Earl. "Smack him upside the head, Lem, if he gives you any more shit. He's here to work, not to talk."

"You just goin' soft on the niggers," said Jed. "Everbody knows it. The niggers everwhar is gittin' uppity. They say they got them northern commie niggers comin' on down here to stir up our niggers. It's a Jew thing. Them hebes got a master plan to take over, you watch, and give our gals to the big niggers. You watch."

"You just shut up, there, Jed," said Earl. "I done warned you, now. I don't but usually give a man a single warning. It's you I'se going soft on."

Earl was known for his courage and toughness; in a fair fight, or even an unfair one, he would have broken Jed Posey in a hundred places, then used what was left to wipe off his shoes. Jed, seeing Earl's flare of anger, knew it was time to back down; nobody stood against Earl Swagger.

"Just shootin' my mouth off, Earl. Don't you pay me no mind."

Lem used his penknife to cut a wedge off a plug of Brown's Mule. He stuck it in his mouth, on the left side, where it bulged like a sack of gold pieces, and offered the plug to Earl.

"No thanks," said Earl, "it's one goddamned bad habit I ain't yet picked up."

"You don't know what you're missing, there, Earl," smiled the swollen Lem, expelling a squirt of the sweet brown juice to explode in the dust at the side of the road.

At that moment, the third and last vehicle swung into view way down the blacktop. Pulling a tail of blue smoke and grinding through ancient gears, a twenty-year-old Nash chugged wheezily up the slope, seemed to lose its energy once or twice, but at last pulled off the road by the first two vehicles. Most of the top had been blowtorched off, forming the semblance of a pickup. Out jumped a spry old fellow, of indeterminant age, sheathed in a wad of beard under an old engineer's cap and filthy overalls. You could smell Pop Dwyer a mile downwind, it was said, and on this day there was no wind, so Pop's odor hit Earl like a blunt instrument.

But it wasn't just the odor of unwashed man, it was also the odor of dogs.

"Keep that old man away from me," said Jed Posey. "He smell like a damn sty."

"You don't smell so pretty yourself after what you been in last night," said Lem Tolliver over his plug. "Howdy, Pop."

"Howdy, all," said Pop, his nutty grin flashing through his beard. "Brought my best boys, Mr. Earl, just like you said."

"Fine," said Earl, watching as Pop went to the back of the truck, messed with the kennel cages there and leashed up three liquid, squirming dogs. Two were blue tick hounds, smooth and slick and muscley under their bright sheen, dark-gummed and eager; the third was some kind of beagle, its muzzle swathed in folds of flesh.

"Mr. Mollie's the best," said Pop. "If it can be found, old Mollie boy will find. These other pups are just along to learn the damn ropes. Mr. Mollie's getting old."

The two blues yapped and showed white teeth and pink tongues and a swirl of saliva dense and foamy; they took an immediate dislike to the Posey boys, sensing Jed's contempt for Pop. Jed Posey drew back.

"You keep that damn bitch away from me."

"Ain't no bitch. That un's got a pecker size of a corncob on him, you dumb billy," said Pop. "And I ain't wearing no chains neither, I'm a free man on a po-lice contract."

The dogs barked in the dull, hot air, swirls of energy against the dolor of the heat and the dryness of the timber. They actually unsettled Earl just a bit, though he tended to discount his superstitions. But on Tarawa, during the mop-up, 2nd Marine dog teams worked over the blown-out bunkers and pillboxes, hunting for the few living Japs among all the dead ones. To save them? No sir. If the dogs howled and came scurrying out of a bunker, it meant a Jap inside still breathed or moaned. In went two or three pineapples, followed by the call "Fire in the hole!" After the blasts, a marine with a flamethrower squirted ten seconds' worth of flaming gas into the small space, roasting it out. It was twelve years ago and Earl would remember it forever: the yapping of the dogs, the flat, anticlimactic blasts of the grenades, the stench of gas and flesh, the buzzing of the flies.

"You got something Mr. Mollie can work on?" said Pop, squinting up his eyes. "It don't work without something to start on!"

Earl nodded; now he really felt an ache. He reached into the backseat of his cruiser and withdrew the pink wool sweater.

"See if they can pick up a scent off this," he said, and watched as the dainty pink garment was seized in Pop's huge, grimy hand and dipped to the dogs, who nuzzled and rampaged with it. One of the blues got a good hold on it and shook the other two hounds away, but both shivered and closed, and got nose and fangs into it, seeming somehow to absorb or suck it in. Then, just as quickly as it had started, it was done: the dogs had beat the scent somehow into their sharp but narrow dog brains and the object itself lacked interest. It fell, moist and ripped, to the earth.

"You didn't want it back, did you, Mr. Earl?" asked Pop.

"No, no, that's all right," said Earl. "Let's get going."

"You sure it's the right spot?"

"I'm sure," said Earl. He looked over his shoulder: there, sixteen feet high, it said, "Texaco with Knock-Free Power and Sky Chief Secret Ingredient Petro X," over a vivid painting of five dancing service station attendants, currently big on some show on the goddamned television set that Earl had never heard of and didn't care about but somehow knew of anyway.

In the odd way a policeman's mind works, he'd noticed an entry in the Polk County Sheriff Department's incident log, which he made a point of checking once or twice a week, even though it wasn't in his jurisdiction proper. It simply said, "White lady called in to say late last night she was driving up toward county line when she noticed, in her headlights, a Negro boy acting strangely right there at the Texaco sign. She thought she ought to report it, since she'd heard many things about dangerous and uppity Negro behavior farther south."

It stuck, somehow, lodged there, meaningless in itself. But then last night he got home late and was surprised to see his son, Bob Lee, standing alone in the moonlight in front of his farmhouse, wearing his ever-present Davy Crockett coonskin cap. Bob Lee was a quiet, almost studious boy, but not one to panic or frighten easily.

"What's going on, son?" he asked.

"They's some people here to see you, Daddy," the nine-year-old answered. "They wun't go in the house, though Mommy ast 'em to."

Something in the boy's voice told him immediately an oddity was occurring and indeed it was: a Negro man and woman stood stiffly on the porch, evidently too frightened to take June's offer of hospitality.

Earl walked up to them.

"Hep you folks?"

It was extremely unusual for black people to pay a house call on white people, particularly strangers, particularly after dark. So Earl knew in a second something was wrong. Though it seemed ridiculous, as he approached, he let his right hand brush against the holster flap over the Colt Trooper, freeing it in case he had to go to pistol work fast.

But in the next second he realized he'd overreacted.

"Mr. Earl, I'm the Reverend Percy Hairston down at Aurora Baptist. I do hate to bother you at home, sir, but this poor lady's so upset and the town police didn't pay her no mind at all."

"That's all right, Percy. Sister, won't you sit down and git your load off?" He called through the screen door, "June, can you git these people some lemonade?" He turned back to the Negro couple. "You just tell me what it is, and I can't make no promises, but I will look into it."

But a part of him blanched: Negro problems were not a specialty of his. He had no idea how Negroes lived or thought; they seemed to happily occupy a parallel world. He also knew that they had a tendency to get into thorny problems of the sort only the lowest kind of white people ever managed. It seemed they were always stabbing each other or someone's brother was running away to the big city with someone's wife, leaving ten scrawny kids at home and an out-of-work daddy or something. None of it ever made any sense, at least to a white man, and if you let it suck you in, you might never get out. Policeman's wisdom: let the niggers go their own ways, as long as they don't get in our way.

"Mr. Earl," said the woman, who looked to be about forty, with a big hat on, in her Sunday best to come to see the Man. "Mr. Earl, it's my girl Shirelle. She went out last Tuesday night it was, and she done never come back. Oh, Mr. Earl, I'm so scared somethin's done happened to Shirelle."

"How old is Shirelle?" Earl asked.

"She's fifteen," said the mother. "Prettiest little thing in the whole town. She my sweet baby daughter."

Earl nodded. It sounded like some typical kind of Niggertown thing: the girl had been picked up by a handsome buck in a fancy suit of clothes, hauled off to what they called their "cribs" out on the west side of town where the music and the dancing never stopped and the alcohol and God knew what else were passed around for free, despite the fact that Polk was a dry county. Then the buck had the girl and left her by the side of the road. Maybe the girl woke up ashamed and left town or maybe she went to live with the buck. You never knew; it played out different each time, but it was always the same.

"Well, honey," Earl said, "maybe she met a feller and went to a party. You know these young kids these days."

"Mr. Earl," said the reverend, "I'se knowed Sister Parker and her people nigh on two decades. I know Shirelle since I baptized her. She be a good child. She be the Lord's child."

"Hallelujah and a-men, please Jesus," said Shirelle's mama. "My baby daughter be a good baby daughter."

"Yes, ma'am," said Earl, beginning to lose patience now that they were going all holy on him.

"You know, them white polices they got in town, them boys don't give no two nothings about what happens to a Negro girl, even a high-class Negro girl like Shirelle," said the minister bitterly.

Earl was surprised that Percy dared express himself so clearly; but he knew it to be true. The Sheriff's Department wouldn't do squat to help a Negro problem or solve a Negro crime.

And then Earl made the connection: the strange Negro boy out by the road, where he shouldn't have been, late at night, when he shouldn't have been. The girl who'd disappeared the same night. Who knew?

"Y'all have some lemonade, now," said June, coming out with a pitcher and two glasses on a tray.

"All right," said Earl, "as I said, I will look into it. I know some bucks who might tell me a thing or two. And—well, that's the best I can do for y'all. But I'll give her a fair shot."

"Oh, Mr. Earl, you so kind. Oh, thank you, thank you, thank you, Jesus, you done answered my prayers," said the lady, as the Reverend Hairston tried to calm her down.

Earl walked the two back to the minister's old car, a prewar De Soto that had seen a lot of miles. When he got the lady settled he followed the old man around and drew him aside.

"Percy, I may need something of Shirelle's, if it comes to it," he said, playing his last card. "You know, a piece of clothing, something she kept close to her body. Can you manage that when you drive Mrs. Parker home? I'll make some phone calls tonight about some things, get some boys I know, and I'll stop by the church early tomorrow, say, 'round nine."

"Yas sir. What you need them things for—"

But then the old man stopped and looked at him.

"I ain't necessarily saying anything," said Earl, "but yes, we may have to go to the dogs. You go home now and pray them dogs don't find nothing in the morning."

Earl was a methodical man and before he let anything happen, he carefully inscribed each man's name in big, blocky print on the inside cover of his notepad.

"Jed Posey," he wrote. "Lem Tolliver. Lum Posey. Pop Dwyer," and under that: "Search team, 7-23-55."

"Earl?"

"All right, all right," he said, hearing the impatience in Lem's voice. "Okay, let's get her a-goin'."

The old man worked the dogs beautifully. It was as if he spoke to them in a secret language, a low, soft vocabulary of mutterings, whispers, clicks and crackles and, most expressively, a kind of smooching sound. The low fat beagle seemed to understand that he was the special one; like a movie star, he didn't do much work and nosed the earth with an affected casualness, unimpressed by everything. The younger, bigger dogs were wilder and more exuberant; they seethed with impatience and immaturity. Pop took them up and down the road for half a mile in each direction, and got no response from any of them, except once one of the blues broke hunt discipline and went straining toward a coon that shimmied in panic across the asphalt. Pop gave it a mean swat and it fell into line behind the offhanded master sniffer.

At the same time Earl, Deputy Tolliver and the Posey brothers eyeballed the vegetation, looking for—well, who knew for what? Signs of a disturbance? Tracks? Articles of clothing, shoes, socks, ribbons, anything? But they saw nothing, except Lum Posey found a Coke bottle, which he carefully cleaned and put into his overall pocket for the penny it'd bring.

The sun climbed, and burned more fiercely. Jed Posey was muttering about nigger gals and how pointless all this was, loud enough to be heard, not loud enough quite to provoke Earl. Earl felt the sweat collecting in the cotton of his shirt and watched as the other men sweated through their own shirts. It was god-awful heat.

"Well, Earl," said Lem, when they'd finished trekking in each direction, "what you want to do now? Want to go into the forest and up the damn hill? Your call."

"Goddamn," said Earl. He checked his watch. It was close to noon. Jimmy Pye was out now. He'd be at the Fort Smith bus station with Bub; Earl knew the schedule by heart. The Blue Eye bus didn't leave till 1:30.

"Ah, maybe give it another damn hour or so. Say I tried, anyhow."

"Mr. Earl?"

"What is it, Pop?"

"My dogs is gittin' hot. They can't work in this weather much longer."

"Pop, you'll get your damn seventy-five cents an hour from the state, but you ain't done till I say you're done."

Shit! Earl wanted to leave too. He had things to check on. Maybe he could talk to a nigger he knew who owned a pool hall in west Blue Eye. That'd be one more thing he could check. But he still had four and a half hours till Jimmy's bus arrived.

"Let's take it about a hundred yards back through them damn trees and do a goddamn sweep," he called. "You boys keep your eyes open."

Jed Posey hawked a gob of something yellow and thick into the dust as his comment on the decision, but wouldn't meet Earl's glare. The old man yanked hard on the leashes of the three animals and the little squad set off toward the trees.

As they penetrated, the land seemed to fight them. The slope increased, to wear against their legs; no clear path yielded through the dense pines, and the saw brier slashed at their legs. The sunlight fell in slanting sheaves through the darkness but it wasn't a cool darkness, and was instead hot and close. Sweat burned Earl's eyes.

"Goddamn," screamed Jed Posey, stumbling for the tenth time in the saw brier as the frustration built, "this ain't no goddamned picnic, Earl. This ain't white man's work. Git some niggers if you want to fight your way through this shit."

Even Earl had to agree. It was pointless. You could hardly see ten feet ahead. The dust rose and swirled.

"All right," said Earl, admitting defeat. "Let's get out of here."

"Mr. Earl?" It was Pop.

"We're leaving, Pop. Ain't nothing back here."

"Mr. Earl, Mollie's got something."

Earl looked. The two stupider young dogs had collapsed, their heads forward on the loam, their pink, wet tongues spread out under half-opened jaws. Their bodies heaved with effort and disappointment. But Mollie sat quietly, his head cocked, his eyes quizzical, very calm. Then he began to keen. The sound seemed to come from some other orifice than his throat: it was pure animal, a single howl throaty with texture and meaning. Then he bobbed up, pivoted, his tail wagging smartly, and pointed with his nose.

"He's got her, Mr. Earl," said Pop. "She's here."

❏ ❏ ❏ ❏

"Goddamn," shouted Jimmy Pye. "Shoot and goddamn, boy, turn that damned dial! Git me some noise!"

Jimmy's hair was blond and longish, slick with Brylcreem, which glinted in the sun like a sheet of beaten gold above his beautiful, fine-boned face.

Bub's thick fingers worked the dial, but the trace of musical energy that Jimmy claimed to have heard as Bub slid through the possibilities seemed to vanish.

"J-J-Jimmy. I cain't f-f-f-find—"

"Spit it out, boy. Just go on, goddammit, and spit it out."

But Bub couldn't. The word hung up somewhere between his brain and his tongue, trapped in a molasses of frustration and pain. Goddamn, when would he learn to talk like a man?

Bub was twenty, a thickish, sluggish young man, who had worked as an assistant carpenter at Wilton's Construction in Blue Eye until he'd been let go because he'd never quite got the hang of it. He had grown up totally in awe of his older cousin, who was the best running back Polk County had ever produced and had hit .368 his senior year at Polk High and could have gone either to the minor leagues or the University of Arkansas, if he hadn't gone to jail instead.

But today Bub was more than in awe: he was possibly in love. For Jimmy's golden power seemed to fill the air, radiating the magic of possibility.

"Go on, boy," yelped Jimmy, his face alight with glee, "find me some music. None of that nigger shit. No hillbilly shit, neither. No sir, want to hear me some rock and roll, want to hear me 'Rock Around the Clock,' by Mr. Bill Haley and his goddamn Comets."

Bub hunted, earnestly sliding the radio dial left and right, seeking a powerful Memphis or St. Louis station, but for some reason the gods weren't cooperating, and exactly the kind of shit Jimmy didn't want kept coming up loud and clear, KWIN out of Little Rock or that nigger beam KGOD from Texarkana. But Jimmy wasn't angry. He was enjoying Bub's struggle and gave him a little pat on the shoulder.

Jimmy was driving. Where the hell had he got a car? Well, goddamn, Bub was so overwhelmed with love when he arrived at the jailhouse in west Fort Smith, he just hadn't bothered to ask, and Jimmy hadn't explained. The car was a goddamned beauty too, a sleek white Fairlane with Fordomatic gearshift, a convertible no less, looking brand spanking new, as if it'd just been driven off a showroom floor. Jimmy drove it like a god. He whipped out Rogers Avenue, zooming in and out of traffic, blowing by the slower vehicles, honking merrily, waving with a movie star's sexy confidence whenever teenage girls were glimpsed.

The girls always waved back and this was one thing that left Bub a little confused. Jimmy was married. He was married to Edie White, who was Jeff White's widow's daughter and a legendary beauty. Why would Jimmy want to go and wave at strange girls? It was all set up, it was perfect. Mr. Earl had gotten Jimmy a job at the sawmill in Nunley and Jimmy and Edie was going to live in a cottage outside Nunley on the late Rance Longacre's cattle ranch; Miss Connie Longacre, Rance's widow, had said they could have it for free if Jimmy pitched in at driving time. Meanwhile, Jimmy would learn a trade at the sawmill. He might even become a manager. Everybody wanted it to work out.

"Lookie them gals," said Jimmy, as the car sped by a Pontiac station wagon. Four pretty blond girls who looked like cheerleaders smiled as Jimmy shouted, "Hey there, pretty missies, y'all want to git some ice cream?"

The girls laughed, for Jimmy was so handsome and outrageous they knew he meant no harm, though it was Bub who noticed that he had crossed the centerline and that a truck was bearing down on them.

"J-J-J-J—"

"Or how about a drive-in movie, we could go to the Sky-Vue and see *Jail Bait,*" Jimmy hollered.

The truck was—

The truck honked.

The girls screamed.

Jimmy laughed.

"J-J-J-J—"

With just the flick of his wrist, Jimmy jiggered the wheel and stepped on the gas and with his athlete's coordination shot into the tiny space left between the station wagon on the right and the rushing, honking, squealing truck just ahead; the car dipped and swooped ahead.

"Whooooooie!" sang Jimmy. "I'm a goddamned free man."

He took the next left, fishtailing in a spray of gravel, and headed back downtown.

"You find me some music, Bub Pye, you old dog, you."

Bub caught something familiar, with at least the kind of banging rhythms he had figured his cousin needed.

"That's a nigger," said Jimmy.

"N-n-n-n-no," finally Bub got out. "That's a white boy. He sounds like a nigger."

Jimmy listened. It *was* a white boy. White boy with rhythm. White boy with nigger in him, full of piss and cum, hot and dangerous.

"What's that white boy's name?" he wanted to know.

Bub couldn't remember it. It was something new, some name he could never remember.

"Cain't 'member. Goddamn," said Bub.

"Well, you ain't no damn good, then," said Jimmy with a big old smile, in the way of saying in code, it don't matter a damn.

Jimmy looked at his watch. He seemed to know where he was going. Bub had only been up to Fort Smith a few times before; he had no idea.

Pretty soon, Jimmy pulled over.

"Just about noon," he said.

They were on a busy street, Midland Boulevard, across from a big grocery store. "IGA Food Line," it said on the sign. It was the biggest grocery store Bub had ever seen.

"Goddamn," said Jimmy. "Lookie that, Bub? Lookie all them people in and out a place like that. All of them with their goddamned money just spent on food. Hell, boy, must be fifty, sixty thousand dollars in that place."

Bub wondered what the hell Jimmy could be talking about. Something he didn't quite like about it.

"J-J-J-J-J—"

But goddamn, Jimmy's luck was good.

One, two, three o'clock, four o'clock ROCK,
five, six, seven o'clock, eight o'clock ROCK,
nine, ten, eleven o'clock, twelve o'clock ROCK,
We gonna ROCK around the clock tonight!
We gonna ROCK ROCK ROCK 'til the broad daylight!

The unleashed dogs found her. Earl heard them baying wildly, their voices a-gibber with excitement.

"Them dogs won't—"

"Won't touch a goddamned thing," said Pop.

"Over here, over here," shouted Jed Posey. "Goddamn and a half, over here!"

Earl, breathing hard, struggled uphill through the trees and saw brier and broke into some kind of clearing, where, the shade vanished, the full, killing force of the heat struck him.

Earl saw Jed standing, his chest heaving, next to a shale wash, where the earth was stony and broken, the sun harsh. On the other side of the wash, the three dogs sat obediently, barking to drive the devil away. But the devil had already been here and done his work.

Shirelle lay on her side, her pink gingham dress crunched up around her hips, her panties gone, her blouse ripped off. She was beyond shame. Her eyes were wide and lightless. Her skin was gray, almost colorless, sheathed in dust. Her body was fat with bloat so that she seemed some balloon version of herself, and the left side of her face was swollen into a massive yellowish bulge crusted with a fissure of gore, where someone had smashed her with a rock. A yard away, the rock lay stained with black.

"You can see her cooze," said Jed. "G'wan, look everbody, you can see her cooze."

You could, of course, and Earl looked and saw what appeared to be a black gruel of blood on the child's privates and what looked like contusions and abrasions. The buzz of flies, the stink of rot.

Earl had seen death in all its forms over three major island invasions. He'd done more than his share of dealing it too. But the girl looked so broken and thrown away, so blasphemed by the gases that filled her, then abandoned on the side of a rough hill, it broke a heart he thought would break no more after the long walk through the tide at Tarawa and the flamethrower work on Saipan and the up-close tommy-gun killings, so very, very many of them, on Iwo. No Jap or dead American boy ever looked so uselessly, pointlessly wasted.

Lem Tolliver spat his plug out explosively.

"Them niggers," he said. "What they do to their own kind! We never should have brought 'em over. They belong back in the African jungle."

"Lem," said Earl, "you get these boys out of here and go on down to my car. I want you to—"

"Hey, Earl," said Jed Posey. Jed's brother laughed. "Hey, Earl, you mind if I jump on for a free one? I mean, I might as well, before you close her up. She ain't going to mind none. And she sure ain't no virgin no more."

Earl hit Jed with his balled fist just under the ear, toward the jaw, a short, vicious, completely satisfying jab. He hit him so hard the man was driven backwards as he chomped on his own tongue, opening a terrible wound, and blood began to gurgle out of Jed's mouth and darken on his overalls. A storm of dust floated up as Jed thrashed a bit and then lay still, one hand raised in surrender. Earl stepped toward him as if to work on him some more. Jed scurried back on his hands and knees, his face gone to the fear a man feels when he knows he's way overmatched.

"Don't hit him no more, Earl," begged Lum Posey.

"Git this piece of shit out of here," Earl said to Lem. "I want him out of here. You go to my car, you call on the goddamned radio to the Greenwood barracks, tell 'em it's a real bad ten-thirty-nine, I want the Criminal Investigations team here as fast as they can git it. And the Criminal ID team, just in case our boy done left prints or something. You put in a call to Sam Vincent, I want him out here representing the Prosecutor's Office. He'll be the one heps me put this fucker in the chair. You call your sheriff, you tell him I want his people out here to close the site and search for evidence. You call the Coroner's Office 'cause we gonna need some real careful body work done. You got that, Lem?"

"I got it, Earl."

"Pop, you rest and feed them dogs now and git 'em into the

shade. We might need them see if they can get up a scent on whoever done that. You understand, Pop?"

"Yes sir."

"Now, go on, git."

The men turned back down the hill, Lum Posey helping his bleeding brother.

Earl was alone with the body.

Okay, baby girl, he thought, time for you to talk to me, so's I can find who done this to you. And I swear to you: I'm gonna nail his ass and watch it fry in the chair.

Earl was not Sherlock Holmes; he wasn't any kind of big-city homicide cop. He hadn't even worked a murder before, that is, as opposed to a killing, where the killer's identity was obvious from witnesses or known grudges. This was different: a body, abandoned for close to a week. It was a true mystery. It went way beyond anything Earl had ever tried before. But Earl Swagger was a serious professional law enforcement officer, committed to, perhaps even obsessed by, the twin masters of duty and justice. His mind was so rigid that he could only see one possible outcome of the event before him, the execution of the murderer, and until that happened, he would feel a serious hole had been blown into the wall of the universe. It was up to him to plug it.

He set about it methodically, oblivious first to the odor of death which attended, second to the flies that hung and buzzed and finally to the obscenity of the crime itself. First thing: drawing the scene. Let the photogs do what they would later, he wanted to record, for his own uses, the overall look of the body, its relationship to the setting. He used the triangulation method, useful in outdoor settings where no baseline such as a road could be located. He chose as his three points the closest tree, about twenty-five feet beyond the child's head, the edge of the vegetationless shale on which she lay and, off to the right, a stone humping out of the surface of the earth. Crudely, he did a stick-figure version of her broken body, placing it between the landmarks.

Then he began an immediate site search for footprints or other signs of disturbance in the earth, as well as other bits of personal evidence of the man or men who'd brought or dropped her here. But the land was so hard and dry it would register no such impression; instead a breeze kicked up, unfurling Shirelle's dress, throwing vapors of dust. Then, just as quickly, it subsided.

Earl went to the body itself. Later the Criminal Investigations team, the professionals, could make a more intense examination in search of microscopic information: fibers, body fluids, possible fingerprints, bloodstains, that sort of thing. But he wanted to learn what he could from the poor child.

Speak to me, honey, he said, feeling such an aching tenderness come over him he could hardly abide it. Something in him yearned to take her up and cradle her against the pain. But there was no pain, there was no *her* anymore, only her swollen remains. Her soul was with God. He shook his head clear and spoke again to her in his mind: Come on, now, you tell Earl who did this to you.

He looked into her blank and depthless eyes, at her utter, broken repose, at her bloodstains and bruises and cruel abrasions, and something hot and hopelessly unprofessional stole over him: he saw a vision of his own child, that serious, somber, hardworking little boy who seemed almost never to laugh: saw Bob Lee, snatched and brutalized like this, left to swell so much it spread his features over his face, and for a second Earl stopped being a police officer and became any avenging father and through a red fog had an image of blowing a shotgun shell into the heart of whoever had done the thing, in the name of all fathers everywhere.

But then he had himself back and was cool again, asking dry professional questions, things easily measured, easily known. She was quite dusty. Was it from lying here these many days? Possibly, but more likely, he now believed, she'd been murdered somewhere else and dumped here. If indeed that rock was the murder weapon, there'd be a lot more blood. He bent and looked at the bloodstain congealed under her skull. The pattern of dispersal was regular and there was no sign of spatter, only a pool: that suggested that the blood had thickened and leaked out slowly. Surely, if the girl were thrashing as she was being killed, the blood would be more widely scattered. So he thought that whoever had done this had simply bashed her dead skull with a rock in order to make it look as if he'd killed her here. But why? What difference would it make? He bent close to her throat: yes, it was bruised under the gray swollen skin. Had she been strangled, not beaten, to death? He recorded the fact in his notebook.

Then he saw on a sliver of shoulder revealed by her twisted blouse a red smear, not wet but dry. He touched it: dust, red dust. Hmmm? He turned to her hand and gently opened it. He bent and looked at her nails: under each of the four fingers was a half-moon of what might have been blood but looked more like the same red dust he'd found on her shoulder. The forensics people would have to make that determination.

Red dust? Red clay, possibly? It hung in his mind, reminiscent of something. Then he had it: about ten minutes outside Blue Eye, out Route 88 near a wide spot in the road called Ink, was an abandoned quarry noted for its red clay deposits. It wasn't so marked on any maps, but by the consensus of oral folklore, folks called it Little Georgia, in homage to the red clay state.

He wrote "Little Georgia" on his notepad, among his other recordings.

He went to the other hand, which was twisted under her, still clenched in a deathly fist. But he thought he saw something in it, a scrap of paper or something. He should leave it, he knew, but the temptation to know more was overwhelming. Gently, with his pencil as a kind of probe, he pried open her tiny hand, trying not to disturb a thing.

A treasure fell out. In Shirelle's left hand was a ball of material, crumpled and desperate, something she'd grabbed from her killer as he killed her. With his pencil, Earl opened it up. It appeared to be the pocket of a cotton shirt. And it was monogrammed!

Three letters, big as day: RGF.

Could it be that easy? Earl wondered. My God, could that be all there was to it? Finding Mr. RGF with a shirt with a pocket missing?

"Lawdie, Lawdie, Lawdie," someone was chanting.

Earl looked up. Lem Tolliver's considerable bulk was moving through the trees under the propulsion of great agitation.

"Earl, Earl, Earl!"

"What is it, Lem?" said Earl, rising.

"I called 'em, Earl, and they gonna git here when they can."

"Why, what's—"

"Earl, Jimmy Pye and his cousin Bubba shot up a Fort Smith grocery store. Oh, Earl, they done killed four people, even a cop! Earl, they got the whole state out looking for that boy!"

Two

JIMMY REACHED BACK over the seat and pulled out a paper grocery bag whose heavy contents, as he lifted it into his lap, stretched it out. But it didn't break, though when he set it down in his lap, Bub heard the dull clunk of some kind of heavy, metal-on-metal contact.

"Here you go," Jimmy said, removing a large, long-barreled revolver from the bag and handing it to Bub. "That there's a Smith .44 Special. That's a big ole mulekick of a gun."

Bub looked at the thing. It felt impossibly heavy in his hands, oily, dense, weirdly charged with energy. A gun. A pistol. He'd never had a pistol. Where he came from, everybody had guns, but not pistols. He'd seen policemen with them, that was it. He looked over at Jimmy and felt his jaw drop and the look of gaping stupidity come across his face when he didn't have no idea of what to say.

Jimmy, meanwhile, had pulled out some kind of automatic gun with gnarled stag grips and had commenced clacking and snapping it, fitting something into its handle, fiddling with a little lever.

"Thirty-eight Super," he said contentedly. "Your Colt. Goddamn asskick gun too. A lot of gun for a little package. A pro's gun."

But then he noticed the look of utter befuddlement on his young cousin's face.

"Now what's up and bothering you, Bub? What's eating you?"

Bub could think of nothing whatever to say. Then he blurted, "I-I-I-I'm . . . *scared.*"

"Oh, come on now, Bub. Ain't not a goddamn thing to it. We go in, we show 'em the guns, they give us the money and we done be gone outta there. It's that simple. Guy in the joint tole me how you take down a big grocery store. See, they put their dough in the safe every damn hour. So by now, with the morning's shopping in there, it's all in the safe in the office, right up front. Every damn IGA's the same. He tole me: nothing to it. Easiest take there is."

Bub's throat got dry and then he had trouble breathing. He wanted to cry. He so loved Jimmy but . . . he didn't think he had it in him for this kind of thing. He just wanted his old job back. He just wanted to pound nails for Mr. Wilton, every day just like the other, rain or cold, snow or frost, just pound them nails. That was enough for him.

"Look, Bubba," said Jimmy, leaning over, drawing Bub in conspiratorially, "I don't know about you, but I ain't going back to some goddamn job in a sawmill to make a Mr. Goddamned Earl Goddamned Swagger a happy man. I ain't working there. Sooner or later, you lose a finger, a arm, a leg. You seen 'em runnin' around, goddammit, no arms, 'Oh, he used to work down at the sawmill.' Not me, no sir."

He sat back, breathing hard, and checked his watch.

"Now's the time. We go, we in, we out. Nobody knows nothing. Then we got us a *stake.* Yes, we do. We can git out of shit-poor West Arkansas and head out to California. Look at me? Bub, look at me!"

Bub lifted his eyes and stared at his cousin.

"Now, do I look like a goddamned sawmill worker, making a thousand a year and living in a cottage off some old biddy lady's charity? No sir, I look like that goddamned fellow James Dean, I know I do. I am that handsome. I'm going out to California, where I aim to become a big movie actor. You can come on too, Bubba. A star, see, a star always has his Number One Man, you know, calls and makes reservations and picks up the airline tickets. That's what I got you slotted for. You be my Number One Man."

"B-but Edie *love* you." Like so many, Bub was half in love with Jimmy's young wife.

"They's gonna be plenty for Edie. You just watch, be *plenty* for that girl. We gonna take her too. She's goin' to California with us! I got me friends looking out for me out there: oh, we going to have a time, you, me, Edie, in L.A. We going to be *stars*!"

He was so ardent that Bub closed his eyes and saw it for just a second: his image of movie stars involved swimming pools, fancy clothes, little mustaches, sleek cars, all under the California sun. It seemed utterly beyond dreaming until just now.

"I swear to you, nobody going to git hurt. You just back me up in that office. You show 'em the gun, I show 'em the gun. Nobody going to fight us for some goddamned money belongs to a grocery company. Then we out of there. We swing on by and pick up Edie and off we go. Nobody going to git hurt. Come on now, Bub, I need you. Time to go."

Jimmy got out of the car and wedged the automatic into the waist of his chinos. He set his sunglasses squarely on his handsome face, then reached into his pocket and pulled out a pack of Luckys. With a flick of his wrist he snapped a butt out, picked it out of the pack with his lips and then lit it off a Zippo that had magically appeared in his hand. He turned and winked at poor Bub, who just watched, thinking, without a stammer anywhere in his mind, it already *is* a movie.

Jimmy in the lead. Jimmy walking confidently, a bebop in his step, a smile on his face. Bub is behind. Bub is scared and confused. He too has stuck the gun into his trousers but it's heavy and awkward and the barrel is so long it sticks him in the thigh, so he's walking peg-legged, like some cripple, scampering clumsily to stay up.

Shouldn't we have masks?

Suppose we get recognized?

My mama is going to be *sooooo* mad.

Why am I doing this?

Why is this happening?

Jimmy . . . Jimmy . . . *Help* me!

Jimmy just swaggers ahead, his bright face lit with pleasure. As

he blows in, he stops, gives a courtly gesture to a woman struggling
to load her car, bends swiftly and lifts her last bag up so that she
can secure it.

"Why, thank you," she says.

"Yes, ma'am," he sings, so charming she never notices the gun
stuck in his pants. This eats up a second or so and Bub catches up,
and as a twosome they enter. The store is strangely dark and vast;
Bub thinks of a church. At six counters six women are *plunkety-
plunkety-plunking* over cash registers, feeding items one at a time to
baggers as they click up the tote on the machine. It's the biggest
grocery store Bub has ever seen! He has an impression of giant
spaces, aisle leading to aisle, stacks of goods and foods. It's an
America he's never seen. Something about the order of such a
place, the hugeness and careful planning with which it's laid out,
scares him. He feels as if he's about to defile a shrine. A small voice
begins to whimper. His knees are pounding. He yearns for the
courage to scream *No! No! Jimmy, no!* But up ahead Jimmy is so
completely sure of himself that Bub's got no chance and no nerve
to confront him. Besides, it's happening already, so fast.

Jimmy has reached a kind of office beyond the last register, a
high, walled structure with a door in the center of all that space,
with a counter around it and a pleasant, red-haired woman standing there talking to a Negro lady. "Virginia," it says on her blouse,
"Assistant Manager."

She looks at Jimmy, responds as everyone does to his charm and
looks, and a broad smile begins to beam until she recognizes that
what he lifts to her face is a gun and her face melts into fear.
Jimmy shoves the colored lady to the ground and puts the gun
right into Virginia's face and is screaming, "Git into that office and
git that safe open."

Gulping poison air like a fish dying on a pier, Virginia rings a
buzzer and the door up to the office opens and a young man leans
out. Bub isn't sure what happens next. There's a *crack* that he can't
identify from anywhere, that seems to make no sense, that is un-
called-for, and the young man is on his knees and then on the
floor. He's wet. Something wet is coming out of him and going all

over the place. Bub hears screaming, shouts, yelps. He gets his own gun out slowly, and in a second they're up in the office but Jimmy is pushing him back, screaming "You cover from outside." So Bub stands guard and doesn't see or know what's going on in the little office, but that there's a terrible commotion.

Crack!

It sounds again, and Bub flinches in fear. He doesn't like the sound a bit. He knows it's a gunshot and he hopes Jimmy is shooting into the air or the ground to scare them but from the utter terror of the screaming he's begun to catch onto the idea that Jimmy is actually shooting people. Why would he do that? Why would Jimmy shoot anyone? If you ever saw Jimmy run with a football, escape tacklers, move sideways, break into the open and pump away in long, graceful strides to the roar of a crowd, you'd never, ever think such a boy could shoot people.

Bub begins to cry. He doesn't like this at all. It scares him sick. He is supposed to be on a bus with Jimmy on his way back to Blue Eye. Jimmy is going to live with Edie and work in a sawmill in Nunley for Mike Logan. Mr. Earl had said! Mr. Earl said it would happen! Why hadn't it happened? Why wasn't he on the bus?

Someone comes at Bub, some big Negro man, and has Bub down against the counter, holding his arms in. He hits Bub a hard blow in the mouth and the world bangs out of focus. Why? Why did he hit Bub? Bub launches forward with his shoulder and the man slips down. Bub points the gun at him.

"Why?" he says.

Jimmy is next to him.

"Do it," he commands. "Do it!"

I can't, he thought. *Don't make me.*

But the Negro man arises from the floor and comes at him and the gun goes off. He hasn't wanted it to. He doesn't mean to! It isn't his idea! It isn't his fault! It's the nigger's fault!

"Hoooieee, that's the boy," screams Jimmy, engorged with delight. "Come on, let's git out." Jimmy, pulling a big bag with him, leads him out. He stops once, turns, and screams, "Run, y'all!" and fires his gun five fast times over the heads of the people cowering behind the registers. They fall backwards over themselves to get away, screaming.

Suddenly it's bright. They're outside on a deserted Midland Boulevard, though Bub has the impression of people hiding behind parked cars and in shop doorways. He sort of likes this, all of a sudden. It's exciting. He feels important.

"Come on, Bub, let's am-scray the fuck outta here!"

Jimmy is pulling him across the street when a black and white police car, its siren wailing, appears far down the street and drives straight at them so fast it seems to go from small to big in but a second.

Bub is so scared. They're going to be hit. But very calmly, Jimmy takes careful aim and starts shooting.

Crackcrackcrackcrackcrackcrack!

He fires fast and Bub watches as his bullets hit and splatter the windshield of the police car, which veers suddenly to the left and slams into a parked car. The noise is terrific! Broken glass flies everywhere.

"Bull's-eye!" shouts Jimmy with a hoot. "Come on, Bub, we gotta git outta here. It's going to get hot!"

They roared along the street, then cut down an alley, spun left through Colored Town and watched as the Negroes fled. Sirens rose behind them.

"I kilt a man," said Bub.

"You didn't kill nobody," said Jimmy. "Swear to God. You gave that old boy the thrill of his life. He'll be telling his grandchildren about it for years to come."

"You sure?"

"Of course I'm sure, goddammit. I didn't put no real bullets in the guns. Those folks just lay down because they *thought* they was shot. It's a big joke. In an hour they'll be laughing up a goddamned storm. Now, I'm hungry. How's about some hamburgers?"

Bub just swallowed. He wasn't sure he believed Jimmy. He remembered stuff pouring out of the boy that fell out of the office. He hadn't seen nothing on the black man he'd shot, but it was so jangled it was all mixed in his mind. He did know the police car had crashed and that its windshield had broken.

"Here we are," said Jimmy. "You got any money? I'm flat busted."

He pulled into a giant chrome and glass structure that had a Buck Rogers look to it, where a fleet of cars was already parked at oblique angles to the central building.

Bub read the sign, his lips forming each syllable: Tastee-Freez.

"Heard this place has the finest damned burgers in the world. Let's see what they got."

"Uh, Jimmy, y-y-y-y—"

"Spit it out, boy."

"—y-you think this is a very good idea? I mean, won't the polices be looking for this car?"

"Well now, they ain't never going to think we'd stop for no burgers now, would they?"

And indeed a couple of black-and-whites, their sirens zinging, their flashers flashing, rushed on by.

"See, what I'm doing is something new," Jimmy explained. "It's called *cool*. I'm being a real cool cat."

"A cat?" said Bub. He didn't get it.

"Yeah. A cool cat is your slick customer. He don't sweat nor git excited. He's always got a laugh on his face. And he a rebel. He rebels against things, 'cause he knows things is fucked against him. But he always stays cool. Nothing gets him hot."

Bub contemplated this novel idea. Suddenly a carhop appeared.

"What's the ruckus, honey gal?" Jimmy asked her.

"Some old boys robbed the IGA," she said. "They done killed some people and a nigger too."

"Oh, you just wait," said Jimmy, giving Bub a big wink, "bet that changes real soon and you find out nobody's been shot for real."

"I don't know," said the girl.

"What's your best burger here?"

"We got all kinds. They sell a lot of the Bacon Supreme. You got your bacon and your cheese and your lettuce and tomato. They got to hold it together with toothpicks. They put a little flag on it. It's really cute."

"Sound good to you, Bub?"

Bub nodded. He *was* hungry.

"Yeah," said Jimmy, "two of them Bacon Su-premes, two orders of the fries, and you got a good milk shake? I mean, now, made out of *real* ice cream and milk, mixed up superthick on one of them beater things?"

"Yes sir. Best shakes in the town."

"You bring us two. Chocolate."

"Strawberry," said Bub.

"One choc, one straw," said the girl.

Jimmy sat back. He lit another Lucky, inhaled deeply, then looked at his watch. He seemed like a man without a worry in his mind.

"You just re-lax now," he crooned. "It's all going to be all right. It's going to be cool. We are the coolest cats around."

The girl brought the hamburgers and it was the best hamburger Bub had ever had. In Blue Eye, a place named Check's Check-Out offered hamburgers, but they was greasy wads of overcooked beef on a tough little bun, nothing like this. Heaven: the meat was so damn tender, the cheese tangy, but that bacon really made the thing sing. Who'd ever think of putting a piece of bacon on a burger?

"Damn," Bub said, "ain't that a damn burger?"

"That's a king burger," said Jimmy. "The king of all burgers. Okay, now, you just come with me." He got out of the car, taking the bag that said IGA with him ever so casually, and just began to amble along, easy as can be.

"By now, they got our car ID'd," he said. "We wouldn't get two damn blocks with it. So we'll git another car right where I got the last one. See, this is working out just fine."

They turned off the main road and walked a block or two into a nice little area with small houses neatly kept. The summer heat was lighter because of the heavy green trees that closed everything off. It felt enchanted. Water sprinklers heaved back and forth like giant fans on a few of the lawns and a couple of young men mowed their grass, the mowers sounding clackety and mechanical. They passed an old lady.

"Howdy, ma'am," said Jimmy. "Nice day."

"Nice day to *you,* young man," she answered with a smile.

Soon enough Jimmy came to an Oldsmobile parked unattended in a driveway. He turned back and smiled at Bub.

"See, you get all nervous, you can't do nothing, people sense you're up to bad. You be cool, you just smile and look like you got the whole world in your back pocket, they back off and give you all the room you want. You just watch how damn easy this gonna be."

With that, he sauntered up the driveway, opened the door and in a second had the car started. He backed up.

"Come *on,* Bub. You gonna wait for Mr. Earl Swagger himself to invite you?"

Bub got in.

Off they drove, in another nice car, tooling down suburban streets as mild as could be. Jimmy looked at his watch again, as if he had a schedule to keep.

"Turn on the radio, find us some good tunes," he said.

This felt weirdly familiar to Bub and he bent over and worked the dials and knobs as a crackle of sounds came out. But none of that hard-driving hillbilly crazy stuff that Jimmy preferred. He got some country, Patsy Kline, he got that Perry Como singing about the moon hitting your eye like a big pizza pie, he got Miss Day doing "Que Sera, Sera" and he got—

"Authorities in Fort Smith have set up a two-state dragnet to locate two armed and dangerous men who robbed a downtown grocery store, killing four men including a police officer."

Bub just heard the killing news dumbly.

"The police say that newly released car thief Jimmy M. Pye, of Blue Eye, and his cousin Buford 'Bub' Pye, also of Blue Eye, were responsible for the outbreak of violence on peaceful Midland Boulevard. They theorize that the two killers will attempt to return home to the Polk County wilderness.

"Says State Police Colonel Timothy C. Evers," and here a richer, deeper voice came across the radio, " 'If I know my bad men, they'll head to land they know. Well, they'll run into our blockades and we'll take care of 'em the way they should be taken care of.' "

"That ole boy sounds *ticked,*" said Jimmy. "He sounds like we got him out of bed or something. Jesus."

"J-J-J-Jimmy?"

"Yeah, cuz?"

"He did so say we done killed them boys."

"Well, maybe they was real bullets in *my* gun. But there weren't none in *yours.* You in the free. You was just 'long for the ride, Bub. Your cuz Jimmy wouldn't get you in no shit, that I swear. Wouldn't be cool at all. Now, we's just gonna head out to Blue Eye, pick up Edie and off we go. Figure we may lay up with an uncle I got over in Anadarko, Oklahoma. He'll—"

But Bub was crying.

"Bub, what's eating you, boy?"

"Jimmy, I want my mama. I don't want to go to no jail. I didn't want to kill nobody. Oh, Jimmy, why is this happening? It ain't fair. I never did nothing wrong, not nothing. I just want—"

"There, there, Bub, don't you worry 'bout nothing. I swear to you, you got it all up ahead: California, a job as a star's Number One Boy. You can bring your mama out there and buy her a nice little house. It's all set up. I swear to you, all set up."

Bub began to sniffle. His heart ached. He threw the gun on the floor. He just wanted to make it all go away.

"Well, lookie here," said Jimmy.

Bub looked up and saw a gaudy sign against the bright blue sky, but since it was midday, the sign wasn't turned on. It said "Nancy's Flamingo Lounge" and Bub noticed that all up and down the street were other places called "clubs," all of them with unlit signs and the sleepy look of nighttime spots. Jimmy pulled off the road and down a little driveway so that he was out back, in a parking lot area dominated by a large, blank garage.

There was utter silence.

"Hey," said Jimmy. "Guess what? We there. We made it. We gonna be fine."

Bub watched as the large garage doors of the structure peeled back and Jimmy eased the car forward. Darkness and silence swallowed them, cut only by some jangled music, far off, as from a cheap, small radio.

ROCK ROCK ROCK around the clock tonight
ROCK ROCK ROCK 'til the broad daylight!

"Cool," said Jimmy.

Three

WHEN HE GOT THERE, he thought everything would clear up, but instead—and of course—things simply got more confused. He took a room in a cheap motel near the Mexican quarter of town and spent the morning fretting in his room about his next step. Here's what he came up with: no next step.

Ultimately, he decided to go for a walk on the dumb hope that he'd just get lucky, that things would just work out, as they usually did. But of course the one fact he knew precisely and totally was that things didn't always work out. That's why he was here, because sometimes things don't work out, violence and craziness break out, people die, lives are destroyed.

It was so much hotter and brighter. It was, after all, the desert, but he'd had a different image of it, somehow. What he saw was a spine of purple mountains, or hills, actually, blocking the horizon in one direction and in all the others just low rills of hills crusted with spiny, scaly vegetation, the odd cactus pronging up off the desert floor like some kind of twisted tree of death. The color green was largely absent from a world now dominated by browns, ochers and pewters.

The town was total jerkwater; it lay along a single main street, fast-food joints at one end, trailer parks and quasi "suburban" places back a little bit farther under imported palms, and the rest scabby little shops, many boarded up, convenience stores, a grocery, a dry cleaner, cowboy and Indian "souvenir" places for the odd, lost tourist, any small town anywhere too far off the interstate. This state happened to be Arizona and the town happened to be called Ajo.

So Russ walked up and down the street and saw nothing and didn't get lucky. He found a bar-café and eventually had lunch, listening to cowboys talk in low hushed voices about nothing much. Nobody noticed him. Finally, he paid the bartender the five dollars for the sandwich and thought he caught a semihuman smile of acknowledgment.

"Say," he said, "I wonder if you can help me."

"Oh, I bet it is I know what you want, son."

"Is it that obvious?"

"It's pretty goddamned obvious."

"You get a lot of guys like me?"

"Some like you. And other kinds too. Had a German TV crew in town for close to a month. Sold 'em maybe a thousand dollars' worth of barbecue. The soundman, Franz, he really got to liking my wife's barbecue."

"But they didn't get anywhere?"

"Nope. Not them. Not nobody. Had a real slick fellow from New York. He acted like he owned the world and we was his employees. He was out here for six weeks. He'd done a lot of big business. He'd set up a deal with that fellow they executed in Utah and with O.J. himself. But he didn't get nowhere. And a French magazine writer. Some babe. Wish she'd come to write about *me*. I'd have told her all my secrets, even the secret to my wife's barbecue."

"Does anybody ever see him? Does he come out?"

"Oh, he's about. Tall, quiet fellow, keeps to himself mostly. Married a damn fine woman. They got a little girl now. But he lives a life. He does things, sees things, mixes."

"Can you tell me where he lives?"

"Can't do that, son. He wouldn't want me to. I respect him. You have to respect him. I think he just wants the world to leave him alone."

"I *do* respect him," said Russ. "That's why I'm here."

"You're probably going to fail. Everybody else has. Why should you be different?"

Why *should* I be different? Russ thought. Yes, key question.

"Well," Russ said, "I bet it's something nobody ever threw at him before. It's not even about him."

"Then just be patient, son. He'll know you're here. Probably knows already. People tell him things, you know."

"Yeah, I know. Well, thanks. I'll probably end up buying my thousand dollars' worth of barbecue too. I'm in for the long haul."

Russ went out—ouch! that blinding sun—and fumbled for his sunglasses. As he got them on, a pickup truck pulled down the road and Russ thought he saw him: a lean man, suntanned and leathery, with calm, squinty eyes. But no; it was just a fat cowboy.

He ambled up and down the street, trying for eye contact with the locals, but all he got was the grim stare of small-town America that proclaimed: No trespassing. Eventually, he went back to the motel and got out his file again.

The exhibits were tattered and dry, a few a little greasy, from being handled too much. If reading could have drawn the blackness out of the ink, then they'd be faded as well; but it hadn't and they weren't. Modern industrial printing: vibrant, colorful, indestructible.

The most famous item was the *Newsweek* cover from that month in 1992 when he'd been the most wanted man in America. "Bob Lee Swagger," it said, "hero turned assassin." *Time,* which he didn't have, had run the same shot: "Bob Lee Swagger, Vietnam's Tragic Legacy." It was an old picture of Swagger, taken in Vietnam. It told everything and nothing: a southern face, somehow, a man in his twenties who could have been in his forties, with a jaw so grim and skin so tight he looked a little like a death's head, which in a way he was. He wore tiger camouflage and a marine boonie cap; the eyes were narrow and hooded, allowing no contact with the world on any terms save their owner's; they lurked behind sharply etched cheekbones. It was almost a nineteenth-century face: he looked like a cavalry trooper with Mosby or one of Quantrill's raiders or someone who'd lugged a Colt down to the OK Corral—and come back again five minutes later, the job done.

On the magazine cover, in the crook of his arm there rested a sleek rifle with about a yard of scope atop it, and it had been well established that with that tool he was one of the world's foremost hunters of men.

Russ passed on the cover shot and looked at other photos, which had come out of the photo morgue of his recent employer, the *Daily Oklahoman* of Oklahoma City. These were shots taken at the mysterious 1992 hearing that ended Bob Lee Swagger's two months of celebrityhood and marked his return to total self-willed obscurity. He was like T. E. Lawrence hiding as Shaw the air-craftsman, a man who had an almost physical need for anonymity. He had just vanished, amazing in an America that quite routinely awarded celebrity with huge amounts of cash. But no: no book deals, no movies, no TV specials, no answers to the provocative questions some analysts had raised, suggesting that he knew things no one else knew. There'd been a rip-off novel from someone way on the outside and a number of patch-job articles in the survivalist and gun-nut press, all misleading, all vague and speculative, all, Russ knew, *wrong.* But one of them had contained one nugget of information: that Swagger had evidently come to roost in Ajo, Arizona, with his new wife, the handsome woman who had attended the explosive hearing.

Therefore, thought Russ, *I am in Ajo, Arizona, in a cheap motel, running out of money and time and luck.*

Finally, on the fifth day, as Russ chomped through his last morsel of barbecue while not facing the reality that his funds were getting dangerously low, the bartender came over.

"Say there," the man whispered, "did you know that a certain party sometimes comes to town today?"

Russ swallowed.

"Yes sir. It's Friday. He comes in to lay in supplies at the Southern States. Now, I may have this mixed up with someone else, but I'd say I just saw a certain pickup heading down in that direction and if I was you, that's where I'd relocate myself."

"Great!" blurted Russ.

"You didn't hear nothing from me."

"Not a thing."

Russ fumbled with his sunglasses and sprinted out. Southern States, Southern States? Yes, Russ remembered, two blocks down, where the ranchers gathered in the mornings before work and then returned to after work, where you could buy anything from sacks of grain to half-million-dollar International Harvester threshers. Russ was so excited he got a little mixed up, but then got himself under control and decided, rather than driving, to just hoof it.

He turned and sprinted, his feet flying, ducking along the covered sidewalk, around the odd party of tourists, past some lolling teenagers, feeling like a complete jerk. No: feeling somehow flushed and excited. Once in his career on the *Oklahoman* he'd had to sub for the vacationing movie critic and go on what was called a junket, where he'd flown down to New Orleans and sat at a table in a hotel banquet room when Kevin Costner and Clint Eastwood were paraded around the room, a half an hour per table. It was of course a completely ridiculous situation, but when he first saw the two men entering the big hotel room, he felt as he felt now: giddy, goofy, unprepared, callow as a pup, completely unworthy. And they were only movie stars and turned out to be, at least as far as he could tell in the time he shared with them at the big tables, fairly decent guys but—pretend heroes.

Now, this guy was a *real* hero: in war and in peace, he'd done extraordinary things. As Russ ran and as his excitement mounted, his concentration scattered; his mind seemed full of glistening soap bubbles.

A plan, he thought, *you need a plan.*

But before he could hatch a plan, his shoes took him around a corner and into the parking lot that lay in front of the Southern States store. It was a gravel lot and dust hung in the air; Russ stopped, and drank in what looked like a scene from some documentary on America's working habits. This would be the rural division, as imagined by someone with the mordant glee of Hieronymus Bosch and the eye for detail of Norman Rockwell: Everywhere it seemed that farmers or ranchers or cowboys milled in the yard, swapping yarns near their pickups or backslapping and grab-assing in little clots. In the background were cattle pens and there was some lowing from the imprisoned animals. It looked like Saturday night at the railhead; where was John Wayne? Well, dammit, John Wayne was *everywhere.*

These men all had craggy brown faces and seemed woven together out of rawhide and pemmican. All were encased in dusty denim and leather from head to toe in a dozen different shades, all wore boots beat to hell and gone, but the headgear was various: straw hats, Stetsons both domed and flat, brims curly or straight, baseball caps, engineer caps, even a fishing cap or two.

Out of such chaos Russ could make no sense at all, and felt as out of it as an African American at the local Klan meeting. But they seemed to be so enjoying themselves that they paid him no mind at all, and he wandered among them, looking for a set of features he could match with the features he'd memorized off the magazine cover and the more recent photos. He'd guess a man like Bob would leave a wake of wannabes, would be at the center of a circle of acolytes, so he looked for a king among all these princes. He could make out none, and now, one or two at a time, the boys would peel out and begin to leave.

"What's going on?" he asked one old-timer.

"Friday noontime, they haul in to reload on supplies. Lots of spread-out places here. More'n you'd imagine. The boys all git together for a bit of joshing time on Friday noons."

"I see," he said.

He wandered on through the thinning crowd, utterly failing to connect any of these tawny, ageless men who seemed from a different race altogether with his image of Bob Lee Swagger.

He reached at last the supply house, where some laborer was throwing sacks of feed into the back of a weathered green pickup.

Russ froze and then unfroze and just stared.

The man was tall and sweaty and had wrapped a red bandanna around his throat to soak up the sweat. He wore the faded jeans and faded denim shirt of a cowboy, but was also wearing a battered, faded red baseball cap that said RAZORBACKS.

The man felt him staring and looked him hard in the eyes and yes, yes it was him: older than Russ expected, and browner, almost

the color of Navajo pottery, without an extra ounce of flesh anywhere on his face. His skin was a nest of fissures and crags, taut yet
ruination itself. The pewter eyes were so intense they burned like
lasers. He looked not at all romantic or heroic: he looked like a hot
tired sweaty man with a lot of work still to do. He looked grumpy
as hell, and maybe mean too. He looked like he could whip Russ's
ass.

"What are you staring at, sonny?" he demanded.

Russ was overcome with shame. But also excitement, and he ran
to him and blurted, "Mr. Swagger? Mr. Bob Lee Swagger. I came
a long way to see you."

"Well, you wasted your goddamned time," said Swagger. "You
go write your goddamned book on your own. I ain't explaining
myself to a pup like you or the best writer on earth. I hate writers.
I *really* hate writers. Now go on, get out of my way."

With that, he climbed behind the wheel of his truck and headed
off.

Bob worked the horse. The horse had an eye condition, an ulcer-
ated pupil which had infected, possibly from fly contamination.
The infection had spread mysteriously and monstrously until the
eye looked like an eight ball sheathed in mildew, and terrible acne
had formed on the face all the way up to the ear and halfway down
to the nostrils. He was a beautiful gray gelding named Billy, and
the girl who owned him had done a good job building him up and
bringing him along until the eye thing.

"It's the worst disease anyone in our family has ever gotten,"
said the girl's mother. "He could *die* from it."

"Now, now," Bob had told her, but mainly told the grave little
girl who hadn't said a word, "the vet's done all he can. You got to
trust the medicine and we won't miss a night, and you got to trust
us. We'll take the best care of Billy that can be taken."

Bob Lee Swagger, having survived nearly fifty years of a life
that included various adventures in the Marine Corps (three tours
in the Southeast Asian War Games, Second Place Finish) and a
private life that was amazingly complex, had ended up the one
way he'd never thought he'd end up: happy.

Now, who in hell would have thought such a thing?

For one thing, the dry Arizona weather had a miraculously curative power over his reconstructed left hip, where a 148-grain 7.62×54 full-metal-jacketed bullet launched at over 2,600 feet per second had torn out a hideous amount of bone and cartilage. It had taken the government a long year in a vet hospital to get the thing rewired and even then, after all that time, it had been a jury-rigged job and for a good twenty years he'd awakened each morning with the reminder that if you hunt men for a living, they by God hunt you back. The pain possibly had led to the drinking, but possibly not: he'd stayed drunk and mean for nearly a decade to bury pains that maybe had nothing to do with his hip and could not otherwise be rewired, memories of young men thrown away for so much nothing, except possibly a name on a black wall. That took time to work out and make peace with and now the blessed lack of hurt down there where he was rebuilt was extra gravy every goddamned day. But that was only part of it.

The other part of it was the wife. A woman. Julie Fenn, R.N. She'd once been a picture carried between the helmet and the helmet liner by his spotter, one of the great young men who came home from the land of bad things in a rubber bag in a wooden box. Some short circuit in the universe had decreed that Bob meet Julie many years later; when he'd seen her, he'd known: This is the one. There is no other. And by the same token, she'd known that of him, and now they were married, had a little girl named Nicki who wrote her name YKN4 backwards and scrambled, the age tossed in too, on all her drawings of horses. It was so good, so many of the things he'd thought he'd never have, because he had been exiled from the rest of the human community, because he'd done his country's bidding with a rifle and gone out and officially killed 87 enemy soldiers, one at a time, over a long distance. He knew, of course, that he'd killed 341. Now all that was somehow forgotten.

And then the last thing, the goddamned frosting on the goddamned cake: the horses. This was the best work there was. There was something about a horse that he loved. They told no lies and if you handled them well, they responded. He never met one that was ambitious or jealous or hypocritical. They were honestly stupid creatures, strong and dumb as oxen, but with that magic component that he so loved in animals even when he'd hunted them, which he did no more: some magic would come over them and in a flash they'd go from grazing herbivores to sheer dancing beauty on the hoof. To watch them run—especially, say, under the tutelage of some small girl like the one that owned Billy or the one that was his own and would grow in time to be a horsewoman herself—to watch them run, all that muscle playing under the skin, all that dust ripping up beneath their powerful hooves, by God, that was a kind of happiness that could be found in no bottle and in no rifle and he'd looked for happiness in both places.

He worked Billy. It was called lunging; the horse is on a tether and if you work it around in circles, cantering twenty feet out on a lunge line, driving it with a lunge whip or, as now, if you've bonded with the horse, with voice alone.

"Come on now, Billy," Bob crooned, and Billy's muscles splayed and flexed as the horse rotated around Bob, though to Bob it was straight ahead of him, because he was rotating with it. The dust rose and clung to the gray's sweaty shoulders; he'd need a good rubdown afterwards, but that was all right, because they were coming to get Billy that afternoon.

Twenty minutes. When Billy had begun to recover, Bob had started lunging him, to get the softness and soreness out of his limbs, get those muscles hard and sleek and defined again, get him back to what he'd once been. In the beginning, the animal had balked, still unsure because the ulceration had eaten into his vision and he only saw 60 percent in the bad eye, and could only go seven or eight minutes before beginning to act out; now he did twenty minutes three times a day, no problem, and was looking as if he could show again soon.

"Okay, boy," Bob called, and began to draw in the lunge line that ran to a halter called a caveson. Slowly, he brought the horse in and at last halted him. He snapped off the line, removed the caveson and threw a halter over him. Now he'd walk the animal for another twenty minutes to cool him down; you never put a hot horse away. Then he'd wash him off. Mrs. Hastings and Suzy would pick him up at three, and it would work out just fine. Billy would be gone back to his life.

You had to do something and this was it for Bob. His marine pension still came in, his wife, Julie, still worked three days at the Navajo reservation clinic, and sometimes more if necessary, and there was just enough for everybody to have everything they needed.

"Daddy?"

Nicki was four, blond, and a tough little thing. It's good to raise them on a ranch twenty miles from town, he thought: teach them to get up early and go feed the animals with you, form their character early to hard work and responsibility, as his had been formed, and they'll turn out fine. He had been raised with a father lost to grotesque tragedy; nothing like that would happen to his child.

"Yes, YKN4?"

"Billy's sweaty."

"Yes, he is, baby girl. We got him lathered up fine. Just a good workout. Now we got to get him cooled down."

"Are they coming to take Billy today?"

"Yes, baby girl, they are. He's all better now. See, some scars, some vision loss, but other than that, he's okay. We got him through it."

"I'll miss Billy."

"I'll miss him too. But he has to go back to his life. That girl Suzy, she's missed him too the last four weeks. Now it's her turn to be happy."

YKN4 wore jeans and Keds and a little polo shirt. She was, as are all children who pass the better part of their times in barns among horses, dirty and happy. She bobbed along beside her father as he took Billy in slow, cooling circles around the corral until finally the animal's breathing had returned to normal.

"You gonna wash him down, Daddy?"

"Help me, honey?"

"Yes, Daddy."

"You are such a big girl, YKN4," said Bob, and his daughter's face knitted up and laughed.

YKN4 took the horse by the halter line and drew it into the barn, where she strained to link it to a rope. The big animal yielded entirely to her bossy directions. She didn't give it a chance and she didn't back down. "Come on, you big old dopey thing," she shouted, shoving against its shoulder to move it backwards. She brought another line over and clipped it to the halter, effectively tying the horse in the middle of a stall.

"Can I give him a carrot, Daddy?"

"Let me finish, honey."

Bob turned on the hose and fixed a pail of soapy water, then moved to the horse and began to rhythmically sponge it, neck to shoulders, shoulders to withers, down each muscular leg.

"Daddy," said the girl.

"Yes, honey?"

"Daddy, there was a man."

Bob said nothing at first. A little steam gathered behind his eyes, a little fire. "A skinny man. Thick hair, dark. Looked intense?"

"What's *intense,* Daddy?"

"Ah. Like he's galloping only he's just standing still. Not a smile nowhere on him. Face all tight like a fist."

"Yes, Daddy. Yes, that's it."

"Where was he?"

"He was parked just down the road from where the bus let me off this morning. Rosalita looked at him and he looked away."

"In a pickup truck? White?"

"Yes, Daddy. Do you know him? Is he nice? He smiled at me. I think he's nice."

"He's just a fool boy with the idea I can make him rich and famous. He'll get tired. He'll go away. I thought he got the message but I guess he's more stubborn than I give him credit for."

Would they ever leave him alone? You get your goddamned picture on a magazine cover and the whole world thinks you got enough secrets in you to write a best-seller. Over the years, no end of assholes had come at him. How did they find him? Well, it was like his address was out on some nutcase Internet, and all the losers and loonies came sniffing along. Some weren't even American. The goddamned Germans were the worst. They offered him money, anything, for an interview. But he was all done with that. He'd had the worst kind of fame, and it was enough for him. He was done with that.

"Did he bother you, honey?"

"No, Daddy. He just smiled."

"If you see him again, you tell me, now, and I'll speak to him, and then he'll go away. Otherwise, we'll just wait until he tires himself out."

Many of them just disappeared after a while. Their ideas were so absurd and ill formed. Some of them didn't even want to write about him and make money; they just wanted to see him and draw something from his presence, from the thing that his life had been. So stupid. His life wasn't a monument or a symbol or a pattern: it was his life.

It seemed for a time the boy vanished. Then he was back again one night, sitting patiently in the truck across the road. Julie was back; they'd eaten and were sitting on the porch, drinking iced tea and watching as the sun set behind the low mountains in perfect serenity.

"He *is* stubborn."

"Damn fool boy."

"At least he keeps his distance. He has some manners." In their time, people had pulled into the yard, jumped out and begun offering contracts, setting up camera lights, glad-handing, carrying on, sure they were onto something big, they'd found El Dorado at last. Bob had several times called the Sheriff's Office, the last time for the Germans, who were extremely obnoxious.

"But he won't go home. It's beginning to feel a little sick. Poor YKN4. I don't want her to think this is how you have to grow up."

"Oh, she can handle it. It helps her to know her father is an extraordinary man. It gives her a little something, I think."

Swagger looked at his wife. She was a tanned and handsome woman whose blond hair had begun to show streaks of gray. She hadn't worn anything except jeans and boots and T-shirts since they'd returned to Ajo. She worked like a dog too. Bob thought she worked harder than he did and that was saying a lot.

"How old would you say he is?" she asked.

"About twenty-two or so. If he wants adventures he should join the Corps. He could use a few weeks on Parris Island. He shouldn't hang out here, scaring the child and making me even crankier than I am."

"I don't know why he seems different."

"He reminds you a little of Donny, that's why," Bob said, naming her first husband.

"Yes, I suppose he does. He has Donny's shyness and unsureness."

"Donny was a good boy," Bob said, "the best." Donny had died in his arms, gurgling blood in little spouts from a lung shot, eyes locked on nothingness, squirming in the terror of it, his left hand gripping terribly into Bob's biceps.

Hang on, Donny, oh Jesus, medic, *Medic! Goddammit! Medic!* Just hang on, it'll be fine, I swear it'll be fine.

But it wasn't fine and there were no medics. Bob was hung up outside the berm, his own hip pulped by the same motherfucker, and Donny had come for him and caught the next round square in the boiler. He remembered the desperate pressure in Donny's fingers as the boy clung to him, as if Bob were life itself. Then the fingers went limp and the gurgling stopped.

Bob hated when that sort of thing came back on him. Sometimes you could control it, sometimes you couldn't. Blackness settled on him. In older days, it would have been drinking time.

"I'm sorry," she said. "I shouldn't have mentioned it."

"It's all right. Hell, I guess I can go tell him face-to-face to get out of here and quit wasting his life."

He got up, gave her a tight little smile and walked down the road into the place. The boy was across the road in an old Ford F-150, just sitting. He saw Bob coming and Bob saw him smile. He got out of the truck.

"Now, what in hell do you want?" Bob said. "Say your piece."

The boy stood before him. Yes, early twenties, lanky, with a thick mop of hair and the soft look of college all over him. He wore jeans and a fancy little short-sleeved shirt with some kind of emblem on the chest.

"I'm sorry," he said. "This was stupid. But I didn't know how else to talk to you. So I thought if I just showed you I was serious about all this, just let you know I was here, didn't force it or act like a jerk, they say you're a very decent guy, anyway, I thought you'd eventually let me talk to you."

"This ain't no interview. I don't give interviews. What's done is done and it's mine, not for nobody else."

"I swear to you, I have no interest in 1992."

"And I ain't doing no I'm-such-a-*hero* books. No Nam stuff. That's over and done and best forgotten too. Let the dead lie in peace."

"It's not about Vietnam. I didn't come about Vietnam. But I did come about the dead."

They faced each other for a long moment. Twilight. The sun eased behind the mountains, leaving an empty world of gray light and silence. The dead. Let them alone, please. What good does it do, what good can it do? Why would this boy come before him, claiming to represent the dead. He knew so many of the dead too.

"So, goddammit, spit it out. A book? You do want to write a book."

"I do want to write a book, yes. And yes, it's about a great American hero and yes, he's from Blue Eye, Arkansas, and yes, he's the kind of man they don't make anymore."

"No books," said Bob.

"Well, let me go on just a bit," the boy said. "The great American hero is named—was named—Earl Swagger. He won the Medal of Honor on Iwo Jima, 22 February 1945, D plus two. He went home to America, where he became a state trooper in Arkansas. On July 23, 1955, he shot it out with two armed robbers named Jimmy and Bub Pye. He killed them both."

Bob looked hard at the boy.

"And they killed him too. Your father. I want to do a book about your father."

Four

EARL ASSIGNED LEM to stay with the body until the state detectives and the county coroner arrived. He got back to the cruiser and noticed Jed and Lum Posey leaning on Pop Dwyer's hood, the three of them hooting like old drunks. But when they felt his hard glare, they dried up fast. Jed's face had swollen badly; it looked as if he'd swallowed a grapefruit, yellow and rotten. But Jed was hard mountain trash; you could bang on him for hours without really breaking anything.

"You boys stay here till the detectives come. Pop, them dogs cool?"

"Cool as they can get in this weather, Mr. Earl," said Pop.

"Good. You stay on station now, you hear."

"I do," said Pop.

Earl got into his cruiser, turned over the engine and flicked on the radio. The air was full of traffic as the state mobilized for the manhunt, led by the state police, all 111 officers of them, who would inherit responsibility for this job. He listened for a bit in disbelief, as if in disbelieving he could make it go away. But it would not go away.

"Ah, Dispatch, this is Car Two Niner, ah, we are now in blockade at 226 and I got two units arching down between 226 and 271, you got that, Dispatch?"

"Roger, Two Nine, we got the state Piper Cub working your

area, trying to cover them back roads. He's on another frequency, but if we get anything, we'll git to you."

"Got it, Dispatch, I'm holding here. Got three units, more coming in."

"Wally, the colonel says you might want to send one of your units over toward Lavca. We got good military help out of Chaffee and I think they're goin' pitch in some airborne stuff."

"Dispatch, I got a unit headed to Lavca."

"Good work, and over, Two Niner."

Earl recognized Two Niner as Bill Cole, a lieutenant in the Logan County barrack. Dispatch was talking for Major Don Benteen, second-in-command; Colonel Evers must have been calling the shots from somewhere in Little Rock, and was presumably on his way over to take area command.

Jimmy, you goddamned little fool, he thought with sudden passionate bitterness.

Where did we go wrong on you? What got into you, boy? How'd you turn out this way?

There were no answers, as there never had been for Jimmy Pye. Earl shook his head. He'd been as guilty as anybody of telling Jimmy Pye that it was okay. He'd always been there for the kid, easing the fall even as he recognized the remoteness in Jimmy and denied it, even as he began to see how different Jimmy was from poor old Lannie Pye.

He thought of Bub Pye, Jimmy's cousin, a poor dim boy who no one ever thought would amount to much, so dreary in comparison to Jimmy. Earl couldn't even bring Bub's face up out of memory, even though he'd seen him just yesterday. There was something forgettable about Bub. What would happen to him? Bub had been a carpenter's apprentice, but he just couldn't get the hang of things, and they'd let him go. He'd never found another job. He was a decent boy but without much in the way of prospects: but he was no criminal. That goddamned Jimmy had made him a criminal.

Darkness crept into Earl's mind. This poor dead colored child, Jimmy Pye, all in one goddamn day!

It was the worst day he'd had since Iwo Jima.

Reluctantly, he picked up the microphone and pushed the send button.

"Dispatch, this is Car One Four, I am ten-eight."

"Earl, where you been?" It was the major, taking over for Dispatch.

"Been at that crime scene, Major, you copy and send units?"

"Negative, One Four. Earl, you got to let that nigger gal cool till we catch up with Jimmy Pye. I seen the record, he's a Polk County boy, and you were his last A-O."

"I know the family," said Earl.

"Okay, good."

"You want me on roadblock or sweeps, Major?"

"Negative, One Four. You go cover the family. Maybe he'll make some contact with them. Don't he have a wife, that's what the records say."

"Married her a week before he done his jail time," said Earl.

"You check on her, then, Earl. You cover her and any other kin he might have there in Polk. You need help, you wire up with the sheriff's boys."

"Got you, Major. But when am I going to see that forensics team? I want them out here on the crime scene fast as possible."

"Maybe by the late afternoon, Earl. Them boys got lots of work still to do at the Fort Smith IGA. It's a bloodbath. He shot two boys in the office, a nigger outside, and he popped a city officer in a car. He's bad news, Earl."

Earl nodded bitterly, checking his Bulova.

Earl drove through Blue Eye's Colored Town, on the west side, under the bulk of Rich Mountain. It was small and scabby; why couldn't these lost people pick up their garbage, mow their lawns, tend their gardens? Everywhere he looked, he saw signs of decay and lassitude and disconnection from decent living. The children, barefoot and in rags, lolled on the porches of the shanties, staring at him with big eyes and slack faces. They wore ragamuffin clothes and their eyes were huge, unknowable pools as they stared at him, though when he rounded a corner and caught them unawares, he was able to see them playing games like jump rope and hide-and-seek with their natural exuberance; but when they saw the big black and white car and the white man in the Stetson with the harsh eyes, they immediately cooled way down and met him with those empty faces.

In time, he passed the most impressive building in Colored Town, Fuller's Funeral Parlor, an old mansion from the days when white people lived in this end of town, nestled under elm trees; and a little farther down, the second most impressive building, a church, white clapboard; and then, finally, down a tree-shaded street where the small Negro middle class lived.

The Parker house was the third on the right, also clapboard, with a porch and a trellis hung with bright wisteria, tiny but neat and well tended. Mrs. Parker led the choir in the church; her husband, Ray, was a clerk for the gas company, the only colored man employed there.

Earl was both glad and sick to see no other police vehicles; that meant he could talk alone to the Parkers without the presence of a lot of bulky white men with badges and guns, which would quiet them down and scare them or at the least drive them into the guarded conditions Negroes affected in the presence of a lot of white people; but it also meant he would have to give them the news himself. Maybe he should have called that minister.

He parked, aware of eyes upon him. The girl's mother stood on the porch. Her skin seemed not brown at all, but ashen; her features were drawn up as if she'd been stricken and she breathed heavily.

He took off his hat as he approached.

"Mrs. Parker?"

"Did—did you find my girl?"

"Mrs. Parker, you'd best sit down, now. You sit down, maybe you'd let me call the minister to come over."

"Mr. Earl, what is it, please? Just tell me. Oh, Lord, just tell me."

"Ma'am, I'm sorry. Your daughter has passed. Someone found a reason to kill her. We found her off the road, twelve miles out of town, ma'am."

"Oh, Lord," said the woman. "Oh, Lord, Lord, Lord. Oh, why

do he test me like that? He knows I love him. Lord, I love you, Lord. Amen, I loves you."

She began to sob, and rocked back and forth in the chair. It was said commonly and Earl half believed, because he'd never tested it, that Negroes didn't feel grief or pain like white folks; that there was something undeveloped about their systems. But not here: there was nothing Negro in it at all. Mrs. Parker let the power of the news have its terrible way with her. He recalled seeing men give into grief like this in the Pacific, just letting it roar out and over them. He thought of his own son, and how he'd feel if he lost that little boy. He wanted to touch the woman, comfort her somehow, but it never worked when people with different skin touched.

"I'm so sorry, ma'am."

"Oh, Lord," she said.

He ducked into the house, which was dark and neat. He found the phone and picked it up.

"Operator."

"Betty, this is Earl Swagger."

"Earl, what you doin' in Niggertown? That's Mrs. Parker's line."

"They got some trouble. You connect me to Reverend Hairston."

Betty put him through and he told the minister, who said he'd call Mrs. Parker's sister and her aunt and be over in minutes to take charge. Earl went back out onto the porch, where the woman still sat.

"How did my daughter die, Mr. Earl?"

"It wasn't very pretty. Looks to me like someone choked or beat her. I don't think she suffered long."

"Was she—you know, did he—"

"I'm afraid he did, ma'am. You know, these animals get heated up, they just can't control themselves."

"Oh, Lord," said Mrs. Parker. "He done took ever last thing from us. Every last thing."

"Your baby is in heaven where it don't hurt no more," Earl said.

"Tomorrow, there'll be some policemen to talk to you. They'll want to know what time she left, who she was with, who her friends were."

She looked at him.

"Mr. Earl, they don't care about no Negro girl. They won't ask a thing. It don't matter to them."

Earl said nothing. As far as the Blue Eye Sheriff's Department went, she was probably right.

"Well, ma'am, since this happened outside of town, the state police detectives will have to work it. And I'll make sure the work gets done. We'll catch whoever done it, you understand? I swear to you, as I live and breathe, we will solve it."

"Oh, Lord," the woman said again, knitting a tissue up against her ruined face.

"Mrs. Parker, I know it's hard now, but I want you to answer me two, maybe three things to get this all started. You concentrate on answering me and helping your baby girl."

She said nothing.

"Do the initials RGF mean anything to you?"

"No sir."

"Okay. Now exactly when did she leave and where was she going?"

"It was Tuesday night, four nights ago. She went to church meeting, that's all. She don't never come back."

"You sure she made it?"

"The Reverend say she was there."

"What kind of meeting was this?"

The woman looked at him, and Earl, who had an instinct for such things, thought he picked up a little something here.

"Just a meeting. You know, Mr. Earl, a church meeting. For the Lord."

He wrote down, "Meeting? What kind? Who there?"

"Then she left okay?"

"Yes sir. And come on walking home."

Earl looked down the street. It was but two blocks to the church. Lord, she'd been picked up on this very street!

"Mr. Earl, where is my baby now? She ain't still there, is she?"

"Yes, ma'am, I'm afraid she is. We have to wait for the detectives to come out from Fort Smith. Seems we had another crime today. A robbery, some folks killed. A bad boy from right around here did the shooting, they say."

"Lord, Lord," said the woman.

He was just about to ask her about friends when the Reverend Hairston pulled up in his old car.

"Oh, Sister Lucille," he keened, "oh, Jesus help us, Jesus help us."

The Reverend swept toward her and so did four or five large-bosomed, distraught Negro women, and Earl stepped to one side as the mourning began in earnest.

As the full weight of the melancholy fell across him, Earl drove out west of town on Route 8 toward Nunley, where the land was hilly pasturage, green and lovely. This way took him past Boss Harry Etheridge's summer home, Mountaintop, and the two stone posts that supported the gray wrought-iron gate were testimony to Boss Harry's importance in the world and how he had risen in Washington in his many terms in the House. Earl could see the road switchbacking its way up the hill to Boss Harry's compound, which in fact was on the other side of the hill. But all was quiet; Boss Harry had returned to Washington or possibly to his mansion in Fort Smith and there was no sign of habitation on the other side of the fence.

Earl caught up with the news on the radio network: just call-ins from roadblocks but nothing to report, no sightings of Jimmy and Bub.

"Dispatch," he finally called in, "this is One Four, am ten-seventy-six out to the Pye place in east Polk."

"Ten-four, Car One Four."

"Ah, Dispatch, any word yet on when that forensics team going to arrive at my ten-thirty-nine on Route 71?"

"Ah, I think they done finished up there in Fort Smith now and will ten-seventy-seven around six. They a little tired. A busy day."

"Ain't that the truth. You call me, Dispatch, if y'all nab Jimmy, 'cause I want to get back to my ten-thirty-nine."

"Okay, Earl. Good luck."

"Ten-four and out, Dispatch."

Nunley was just a few stores and Mike Logan's sawmill off the road, but beyond it was the Longacre place. He turned left, passed the big house and took a dirt road back through the pastures where the biggest beef cattle herd in West Arkansas grazed, fattening up for the slaughter just four months ahead. The cottage, which Mrs. Longacre had built for her son and daughter-in-law who had died in a car accident in New Orleans and for that reason had never moved into, was a gingerbread romantic fantasy, a mother's dream of a wonderful site for her beloved son and his wife to live while he was prepared to take over the family properties. But it was not to be.

Now before it was a sheriff's car and the lady's Cadillac. A deputy named Buddy Till leaned on the fender.

"Howdy, Earl."

"Buddy. You're a little out of your territory, ain't you?"

"Sheriff thought it'd be a good idee to keep a lookout case Jimmy made it all this way back. If he comes, by God, I'll be ready." He jacked a thumb toward his backseat and Earl looked through the glass to recognize his old pal from the war, a Thompson submachine gun. This one wasn't the military variant, however; it sported a circular fifty-round drum and a vertical foregrip underneath the finned, compensated barrel, just like Al Capone's.

"You scare me sometimes, Buddy," said Earl. "If Jimmy makes it through fifty roadblocks and seventy miles, I know he'll come in easy. Why don't you put that thing in the trunk, before you hurt somebody with it?"

"Hell, Earl, ever since you won that goddamn medal, you think everybody else is common and you can boss 'em around."

Earl never mentioned the medal and it irritated him when it was brought up to him. But he controlled the flare of anger he felt and spoke forcefully in his raspy, powerful voice.

"I done enough work with them guns in the war to know they ain't so easy to run smooth. They jump all over the damn place. I don't want to see you hurting anybody. And you don't want that. Now put it in the trunk and move a spell on down the road. If Sheriff Jacks asks why, you tell him I told you so."

Petulantly, Buddy did what he was ordered.

Earl climbed the porch and knocked once.

Connie herself answered.

"Earl, thank God."

"Hello, Miss Connie," he said. Connie Longacre originally came from Baltimore; she'd met Rance Longacre in the East, married him and come down and made Polk County and its biggest cattle spread her home. She and Rance lived the life of maharajas out here on the most beautiful spread in all Polk County, until Boss Harry bought the mountain some years back. But Connie Long-acre never quite escaped death, which dogged her like a little black mutt. Rance died at forty-eight, and just last year her only child, Stephen, had died at twenty-four along with his pregnant wife. So much death: but the woman, in her fifties, was still beautiful, in a proud eastern way that no one in Polk County could ever quite define.

"You made that awful troglodyte go away?"

Earl wasn't sure what "troglodyte" meant, but he got the gist of it.

"Yes, ma'am. He's set up down the road now. How's Edie?"

"Oh," her voice trailed off. "Upset."

"Yeah, well."

"Earl, what on *earth* happened?"

"Miss Connie, I cain't say. Jimmy, he—oh, Jimmy, you cain't figure Jimmy out, what got to him."

"I was never a great Jimmy believer, Earl. I'm old enough to look behind a pretty face."

"He never had no father."

"Yes, I know, Earl, but everyone always used that to *excuse* Jimmy. Lots of boys had no father and turned out fine."

"I should have done more for him. I could have done more. But I had my own son."

"Will they catch him?"

"Yes, they'll catch him. And make him pay. He'll have to pay. No other way."

"It's appropriate. I do feel sorry for his poor cousin."

"Bub loves Jimmy too much. Jimmy's easy to love, but dangerous. It ain't been a very good day in Arkansas," he said. "We found a poor colored girl this morning north of town. Somebody messed her up real good."

"Oh my Lord. Who was it?"

"Shirelle Parker."

"I know Shirelle. I know her mother. Oh, Earl, that's terrible."

It seemed to strike Miss Connie very hard.

"Those poor people," she finally said. "Woe is always unto them."

"They ain't got no picnic, that's for sure."

"Some black boy, I assume?"

"I hope. I don't know, though, Miss Connie. There's some monkey business going on and it's got me buffaloed."

"Earl—"

He turned.

"Honey, you shouldn't be up," said Mrs. Longacre.

Earl looked at Edie White Pye, keeping his face blank as possible. He was not an emotional man, but he had feelings, all right. He just put them away and pounded a couple of nails into them to keep them there.

Edie had been Jimmy Pye's best girl since 1950, when Jimmy had led Blue Eye High to a second-place finish in the state football classic; she was possibly the most beautiful young woman anyone had ever seen in Polk County. Her father died in the war, a few weeks after the Normandy invasion, smoked by a German Tiger in some French hedgerow. Her mother raised her alone, though not much raising had to be done with Edie. From the start, she was all right. Her nickname was Snow White, for that's who she reminded many people of; Jimmy was her Prince Charming, and charming he could be, when he wasn't being wild.

Earl drank her in for a moment and put his feelings even deeper and pounded three or four more nails into them.

"Oh, Mr. Earl," she said. "I'm so sorry."

"Don't be sorry, Edie," he said. "Jimmy made his own decisions. This is his damn fix. He's got to face the music this time. I only hope no one else has to get shot."

He imagined Jimmy running into someone like Buddy Till and his machine gun. There'd be hair and blood all over everything and God help anybody who got in between. He shivered.

"That damned boy," said Connie Longacre. "He always was too handsome for his own good. He spent too much time looking in the mirror. I never trust a man who loves what he sees in the mirror more than what he sees outside it. Edie, you needed a solid man, a real man. It's too bad Earl here is already married and has a boy. Rance used to say Earl Swagger's the best man Polk County ever gave birth to. And that was *before* the war!"

"Now, you stop that, Miss Connie," said Earl. She loved to say provocative things and watch people's jaws gape.

"Well, if *I* was a young woman, Earl's the one I'd have gone after."

"Edie, I have to talk to you. I have to ask you some official questions. They want me to stay here in case Jimmy heads this way."

"That silly boy's on his way to Hollywood if you ask me," said Connie. "We won't see him in these parts ever again. Well, I'll leave you two alone for a bit. Have things to tend to. Go gentle with her, Earl."

"Yes, ma'am," said Earl.

He and Edie went and sat by the window. Next to her he always felt cumbersome and awkward. He could feel his boots and his leather gun belt creaking. The Colt Trooper felt impossibly heavy.

He got out his notebook, turned past the ten pages of notes he'd taken on Shirelle Parker.

"Edie, has Jimmy been in contact?"

"No, Mr. Earl. The last time I spoke to him was three weeks ago. He seemed fine. He was looking forward to getting out. He was full of excitement. I got a very nice letter a week ago. He was full of excitement about the sawmill. Said he'd end up owning it before 1960!"

"He didn't say nothing about making new friends in jail or anything?"

"No sir."

"Sometimes a young guy like Jimmy, he can fall in with some hard cases and they can turn his mind. He didn't mention anybody, a new friend or nothing?"

"No sir."

"You should tell me, now. It ain't a question of betraying. He's killed some people. There's a price to be paid. He has to pay it like a man. That's the best that can be offered at this point. A safe surrender, a fair trial."

"That's what I want, Earl. I never, *ever* wanted anybody to get hurt. Oh, Earl, is it true? He killed four men?"

"They say. At least four witnesses identified him. And Bub."

Edie looked off, into the sunlight, across the fields.

"Poor Bub," she finally said. "He couldn't hurt a mouse."

Jimmy, Jimmy, Jimmy, thought Earl bitterly. *You fool. Why the hell did you have to go and do this thing for?*

"You haven't heard from him today?"

"I haven't. The truth is, Mr. Earl, I don't want to ever hear from him again. I can't have this. It's too horrible. I have to leave and start over."

He saw that she was crying.

She turned.

"Mr. Earl, I have to tell you. I married Jimmy because I was bad. I let him—"

"You don't have to tell me a thing. All that's your business."

"I was pregnant. I didn't have a choice, I didn't think. My baby had to have his father."

A single track ran down from her left eye.

"No one knows but Miss Connie. It would *kill* my poor mother."

"No one will ever know," said Earl.

"No. I lost the baby. I miscarried a month ago. The baby's gone. I lost my baby and now I'm married to a killer. Oh, Earl."

"You don't have to worry about that," Earl said. "We can fix all that."

The phone rang.

"Should I answer?"

"It's probably for me."

She went and picked it up, and no, it wasn't for Earl.

"It's Jimmy," she said.

Five

THE BOY sat on the porch with Bob and Julie.

"Can you get him something to drink, please," Bob said. "He says he wants to write a book about my father."

"Do you want some lemonade? A Diet Coke? We don't have any alcohol in this house."

"I'm a drunk," said Bob. "Can't have it around."

"A Diet Coke," said the boy.

Bob stared at him. What was he, some kind of emissary from the dead? Who could speak of his father to him? Bob found himself strangely agitated, not fearful exactly, but ill at ease, uncertain. Not that the boy looked difficult or dangerous. Quite the opposite: the boy wore wire-rim glasses and looked a little queasy. It was a look Bob had seen on boys he'd had to lead into battle. Why me? Why anyone? Why?

Julie came back with the Coke and a glass with ice. He felt that the can was cold and took a swig, bypassing the glass.

"Go ahead," said Bob.

"My name," said the boy, "is Russell Pewtie, that is, Russell Pewtie, Jr. I'm twenty-two years old and I spent two years at Princeton University before dropping out. It's possible the name Pewtie rings a bell?"

"Not yet," said Bob.

"My father is Russell 'Bud' Pewtie, Sr. Until three years ago, he was a sergeant in the Oklahoma Highway Patrol. Big guy, old-boy type. Everybody liked him a lot. Decent man. He was famous for a bit. It was in all the magazines. They say they're going to make a TV movie about him, one of those 'Line of Duty' things."

"I must have missed it."

"Well, it may have fallen through," said the boy. "I don't talk to my father anymore, so I wouldn't know. What happened was, in June of 1994, a guy named Lamar Pye led two other men on a breakout from McAlester State Penitentiary in Oklahoma. Lamar was a powerful criminal personality, tough, violent, very smart, extremely aggressive. He cut a swath through southwestern Oklahoma they're still talking about. Robbery, murder, kidnapping, the works. Now, for some reason, he and my dad—well, they were fated, somehow, mixed together. Lamar ambushed my dad, wounded him, though only superficially, but killed his partner. My dad took it personally. Twice he tracked Lamar down. He had a total of three shoot-outs with Pye. He killed his cousin, he killed a woman who'd thrown in with Pye and finally he killed Pye. Shot his face off, then shot him in the head."

"Sounds like a brave man," said Bob.

"Well," said Russ, as if judgment were still pending. "He was seriously wounded. Shot in the lung, broke his collarbone, nerve damage crippled his right arm. But he recovered, and then one day he says to my mother, 'I love you, I always will, goodbye.' Leaves flat cold on a Wednesday morning. Moves across town to a little house near the airport. He was in love with and was carrying on with the woman who was his partner's wife. Closer to my age than to his."

"Excuse me, Russ," said Julie, "where is this going? What does this have to do with my husband?"

"I got to thinking how much we lost to Lamar Pye. And we were *lucky*. We got out alive. Lamar Pye killed two men during the break out, he killed Ted Pepper, my dad's partner, he terrorized a farmer and his wife and the woman died soon after, he kidnapped and terrorized a young woman, he killed seven people in a robbery before my dad finally ended it. We were lucky. There's eleven people in the ground because of Lamar Pye. That was three months' work. But Lamar took my family. He broke it up. Whatever happened, he enabled my father to leave my mother. It nearly killed my mother. I should tell you, to be quite honest, that I now truly *hate* my father. How he could do that to her after all those years he gave her? And so if all the Pewties survived Lamar, Lamar still killed the family. He couldn't have done a better job with a shotgun."

He paused, took a swig on the Coke. Now it was dark.

"I got curious. Where does a Lamar Pye come from? What so fills him with anger and hatred and fury, what turns him that way? So I thought: There's a book. There's a great book. The story not only of how my dad got Lamar Pye but what created Lamar Pye."

"Russ, we still don't—" Julie said.

"Honey, let the boy finish," said Bob. "I know where he's going."

"I thought you would," Russ said. "So I contacted the McAlester prison authorities—I'm a journalist, used to be assistant Lifestyles editor of the *Daily Oklahoman* in Oklahoma City—and I got to look at his records and the stuff he left behind. I found his reform school records, his criminal rap sheet, the prison records and I found—this."

He reached into his wallet and unfolded a document and handed it over to Bob.

"What is it, honey?" Julie asked.

Bob recognized it immediately and shuddered.

It was from the *Arkansas Gazette* of July 24, 1955.

HERO TROOPER SLAYS TWO BEFORE DYING, ran the headline.

> A state trooper sergeant shot and killed two suspected murderers on Route 71 north of Fort Smith yesterday evening before dying himself of gunshot wounds inflicted by the two men.
>
> Dead were Sergeant Earl Lee Swagger, 45, of Polk County, a marine Medal of Honor winner in the Pacific; and Jim M. Pye, 21, of Fort Smith, and his cousin Buford 'Bub' Pye, 20, also of Polk County.

Bob's eyes ran down the account of the long-ago gunfight.

He handed it to his wife.

"See," he said, as she read it, "this Lamar Pye that shot all them people in Oklahoma. He was the son—I guess that's it, right?"

"That's it," said Russ.

"—he was the *son* of the man who killed my daddy."

"So you see—" started Russ.

"Incidentally," said Bob dryly, "the papers then weren't no better than the ones we got today. The *Gazette*'s a big Little Rock paper: it don't know shit about West Arkansas. They got a fact wrong. They said north of Fort Smith. It was south of Fort Smith. That's why I don't trust 'em."

"Well," said Russ, a little nonplussed, "uh, yes, mistakes do get made. Uh, but you see if I wrote a book about Lamar Pye and what he took from people and where he came from, well, it has to start on the night of July 23, 1955. It *all* starts that night: Lamar's life, and what became of it. Is it some genetic thing: like father like son? Well, maybe it is. Jim Pye was a criminal and a killer: his son was a criminal and a killer. On the other side, there's Earl Swagger, war hero and man of honor. And there's *his* son. War hero and man of honor."

"My father was a man of honor," said Bob. "I was just a marine."

"But it all begins on that night. All of it: your life, Lamar's life, what you did, what Lamar did. What happened to all those people in Oklahoma, people who never heard of Jim Pye—"

"Jimmy Pye," said Bob. "They called him Jimmy."

"Yes, well, anyhow, people who just walked into the fury Jimmy passed on to his son and died for it. It could be a great book. Too bad a great writer didn't see it. But I'm the guy that saw it, and so I'm going to write it. I'm going to call it *American Men*. It's a study of the life of Jimmy Pye and Earl Swagger and it's the story of Jimmy's son, Lamar, and poor old Bud Pewtie, the cop who ran into him and chased him down. The parallels are so *unbelievable*. Two bad boys just out of prison, father and son. Two state police sergeants. Two violent robberies. Gunfights, close up and scary and dangerous. It's—it's a great book."

Bob just looked at him.

"It won't have a thing to do with 1992 and what happened to you and the *Time* and *Newsweek* covers and all that," Russ said. "It's not about Vietnam. It's about a legacy of violence handed down through two generations and the two lawmen who stopped it, who stood up and said, by God, no more, it stops here, tonight. Your dad who gave up his whole life and my dad who got his head all messed up because of it."

Bob doubted that at any moment during their long and violent nights either sergeant had said, "By God, no more, it stops here, tonight." That's how the movies would have it. More likely, each man had thought, "Oh, Jesus, don't let me get killed tonight," but the movies never got that part right.

"Bob," said Julie, "it would be so nice to give your father his due. He could have some measure of the respect and honor he deserved, even now, forty years later."

"What do you want from me?" Bob said.

"Ah. Well, I suppose, fundamentally, your blessing. And in small ways, your help. I was hoping to interview you on the subject of your father. I was hoping you'd share your memories of him, not just of that night and the aftermath and what you remember or know of it, but generally, what sort of a man he was, that sort of thing. Then I guess there might be some documents you'd still have: photo albums, maybe some more articles, letters, I don't know. Anything to build it up, to recall it, to help me re-create it."

"Umh," grunted Bob noncommittally.

"And finally, some kind of help, you know, in getting others to talk. I know how reluctant people can be to open up to a stranger, particularly a younger man from a different part of the country, though Lawton, Oklahoma, where I'm from, isn't all that far from Blue Eye and Fort Smith. But a phone call, a letter of introduction. See, it has to be all oral recollection. One of the first things I learned was that in 1994 the Polk County courthouse annex burned down, and that's where all the files and exhibits from the hearings were stored. The after-action reports, the medical records, all that. I have secondary sources from the newspapers but I want to talk to people. I even wrote the Arkansas congressmen and both senators and some other people in hopes of opening doors. I just got generic replies, but with Bob Lee Swagger helping me—"

He stopped. He was done.

"That's it. That's all I have. I'm finished. Uh, why don't you, you know, think about it? Give it some thought. I'm no salesman. I hate selling things. I want you to be comfortable too."

"Well," said Bob. "Look, I could lie to you and say, yep, you let me think about it and we could play this game out. But here's my answer, straight out: No."

"Bob—"

"Julie, no, you let me talk. I can't have it. That's all over. I buried my daddy and went on and made my way. I can't be talking it up into some tape recorder. Those memories—you don't give them away for someone else's book. It seems—indecent."

The boy took it well.

"Yeah," he said. "Well, you're consistent, at least. Just let me say, I'd try to do honor to your father. To me he's a hero. He never left his family. But going back is painful, what's the point except to make some kid you never heard of a published writer? Okay. Uh. I'll probably still go ahead, somehow. I'm sort of committed. I actually quit my job and I'm determined to take it the whole way. So . . . well, I'm sorry. I appreciate your time and your honesty."

"I wish you luck, Russ. You seem all right. Your dad seems like a hell of a man. I'm sorry he did what he did."

"Sure. Uh, I guess I'll be going now."

He stood and tentatively put out a hand, which Bob shook, and then turned and stepped out of the porch and began to walk up the road to his truck.

"Bob," said Julie. "Are you sure—"

Bob turned and his wife saw something on his face she'd never seen before. It was, she realized, fear.

"I can't go back there," he said. "I can't face all that. It nearly killed me then. It killed my mother. It's better off forgotten."

Six

"OH, GOD, Jimmy," she said.

The voice came from far away but as Earl drew near he could hear it increasing in clarity and the familiar rhythms of the young man he'd watched grow up became evident.

"Honey, oh, God, I am so sorry," Jimmy was saying, "I have made such a mess of things, oh, Lord, it just got out of hand."

Earl hovered over Edie, feeling huge and helpless and enraged at what Jimmy was doing to her.

"Jimmy, please, don't hurt anybody else."

"I swear to you I won't."

Earl tried to fight his way through his anger: What should I do? What's the smart move? He was always so certain, he always acted decisively and correctly, in every situation from a hunting camp to a battle to any of a hundred police dilemmas. But now he felt sluggish, stupid, lost. He tried to get his mind working.

This was almost a jail breakout, and in almost all jail breakouts, standard operating procedure was to wiretap the homes of those the escapee would most likely turn to, then raid them when contact was established. But would the department have had time to set up a wiretap? The robbery was around noon; it was now four, that was a few hours. He didn't think so.

More to the point, though, Betty Hill, the operator, was known to listen in as she threw wires into jacks at the Polk County switchboard. She might be listening. And if so, who would she call, the sheriff? She might even call Earl himself!

"Find out where he is," he mouthed to Edie.

"Jimmy, oh my God, where are you?"

"I'm at some general store up near Mulberry on the public phone. It's around back, ain't nobody can see us. We done dumped two cars and picked up another one."

"Oh, Jimmy. They'll get you. You know that."

"Honey, listen. It's all over for me. I got to face up to it, I'm finished, I'm over. You're a free gal. I love you but you can't stick to me from now on. Ain't nothing in it for you. Honey, I crossed the line and can't get back over."

"Oh, Jimmy, Jim—"

"But listen here, the problem is Bub. Christ, that boy didn't do nothing but what I told him. He's out in the car crying for his mama. I cannot have it said that I got Bub killed or sent away."

"Jimmy, I—"

"Honey, I want you to get Mr. Earl. Mr. Earl will know what to do."

"Honey, he's here."

"Oh, thank God! Put him on!"

Earl took the phone.

"Jimmy—"

"Earl, don't waste your breath telling me how I done messed up. Lord, Lord, I know."

"What the hell happened?"

"Earl, I wanted a stake. I wanted to go to L.A. and be a movie star. I didn't want no job in no sawmill living in a cottage off some rich lady's charity."

Earl could only shake his head in dismay.

"Now I got a mess," said Jimmy, "and I got to fix it up. I got to save Bub. Can you git me a deal?"

"Best just come in and face up to it."

"Here's the deal, Earl. I go murder in the first, and if the state wants, it can fry me. And it'll probably want. In exchange for my plea, Bub gets maybe accessory to armed robbery, manslaughter two at the worst, he gets out in a year or so, no hard joint neither, one of them work farms where nobody going to bother him."

"I can't get you that deal without talking to the Sebastian County prosecutor. Best thing for you to do is to surrender peacefully to the first law enforcement officer you see and then tell them you did all the killing. I'll call Sam Vincent down here and—"

"No!" screamed Jimmy. "Goddammit, Mr. Earl, these boys is loaded for bear. They got machine guns and shotguns and deer rifles and dogs. I killed a cop. They got a taste for blood. I walk in there hands up and by God I end up on a slab with dimes on my eyes next to some tinhorn deputy smiling for the camera and thinking about how famous he's gonna be. Poor Bub too!"

Jimmy was right, of course. Earl knew it. Too many hotheads with guns, too many chances for a slipup, a mistake. He thought of the fool Buddy Till with the big tommy gun and the fifty-round drum, just itching to cut loose and make himself a state hero. The man that got Jimmy Pye! Jimmy would die certainly, poor Bub probably, as well as whatever citizens happened to be standing around. Shit, Jimmy, what'd you do this for?

"Mr. Earl, I'll surrender to you! You can put us both in cuffs. Please, please, please just give me a minute or two with Edie afterwards, one last time with her, and promise me you'll call Sam and help out with Bub. That's a lot, I know, but please, Earl, please, Mr. Earl, I know you got it in you, help me clean up my mess."

"How the hell you going to get up here?"

"I can make it up there okay. We won't move till after dark, and I know the back roads like the other side of my hand."

"Jimmy, no one else can die! Do you understand? Do you swear it?"

"I swear to you, Earl. I swear to you. I got it all figgered out, how we can work it. I'll meet you at ten. Swear to you."

Earl thought darkly. He didn't like it at all. Jimmy crossed the line, you couldn't cut him that slack. It went against so many principles. Be rigid, he told himself. Live by your rules. You have rules, now live by them.

But Lannie Pye, Jimmy's dad, begged Earl to look out for his boy, help his boy. That cut to the quick. He gave his word on Iwo and it wasn't a thing he could walk away from, goddamn his own soul.

"There's a cornfield just below Waldron, maybe ten, twelve miles," said Jimmy. "It's right off 71."

"Which side of Boles?"

"The Fort Smith side. Just beyond Boles. On the right as you're coming up. Beyond the mountains."

Earl had lived the past ten years on Route 71.

"I know it."

"There's a cornfield road. I'll pull in maybe a hundred or so yards."

"No, I'll pull in first, Jimmy. I want to see you approach and throw the beam on you. You git out of the car with your hands up, you and Bub both. You show me your guns, then throw 'em on the ground."

"Okay, Mr. Earl. That sounds square. Ten."

"Ten. If you get jumped or chased before, you throw your hands up, you hear? Nobody else can die!"

"Tell Edie I love her."

"I'll have her waiting in town. We'll take you boys into Blue Eye. I'll be with you every step of the way."

Jimmy hung up.

"It sounds like he's trying to do right by what he done wrong," he said.

He looked at Edie, who'd gone over back by the window. In the distance, they could see Buddy Till, arms folded, leaning against his fender, chewing a long stalk of grass.

Earl picked up the phone and pushed the button a couple of times.

"Operator."

"Betty, it's Earl, calling from the Longacre cottage."

"Why, Earl, you do git around."

"What you hearing?"

"The coloreds is all excited about that poor little gal. They're blazing away on the line. Them people really talk a lot. There's talk too about Jimmy Pye, and what he done. The coloreds don't care about him, though. They only care about their own, just like people everywhere."

"Is there any talk about Edie and Miss Connie?"

"Folks wonder about how they'll take it when Jimmy gets his reward. Pity, lots of pity. Pity and palaver. And a little about you, Earl."

"Me?"

"Earl, you are a mighty man, but there's an element that don't care for you. They think you're too big for your britches, ever since President Truman hung that ribbon on your neck. There's talk that if you'd taken a hard hand with Jimmy when he was young, he'd not have turned out as he did. There's talk—Earl, do you want to hear this?"

"I suppose."

"There's talk it'll serve you right and bring you down a peg or two. You tried to *invent* some fairy-tale life for Jimmy and that poor girl who maybe didn't love him as much as you told everybody she did. You and Miss Connie, you got together and wrote a fairy tale and never really knew what was going on."

"And what was that?" asked Earl.

"The Pyes are trash and always will be. It's as wrong to mix trash and quality as it is to mix black and white. It's not meant to be and there's consequences. Earl, sometimes as smart as you are, you can be a very thick old boy."

"All right, Betty, thanks."

He hung up. There was no news there, nothing he hadn't felt or suspected before. What was important was that Betty couldn't have gotten through that performance if she'd just heard Earl talking to Jimmy; she'd been too busy eavesdropping on the others. He felt safe at least; if the sheriff and his machine gunners showed up when Jimmy came in, it could be a disaster.

He went over to Edie, who simply sat and stared out the window.

"You all right?"

She smiled and put a hand on his wrist.

"Yes, Mr. Earl. I am fine."

"Some are saying Miss Connie and I tried to set up a life for you and Jimmy out of something of our own. I never thought of that. If it's the case, I apologize. I tried to help. Sometimes helping just makes it worse."

"Mr. Earl, you did what you thought was best."

"I swore to Lannie Pye I'd help his boy. That's what it was. I went too far."

"Jimmy is no child anymore, Mr. Earl. He's twenty-one. He made up his own mind. But he does have a gift for selling. I bought because I wanted to buy. Except for the poor folks in the store, maybe this is best for all of us down here in Polk County. Now we all have a chance to start over."

"That's the smart way to look at it. Okay, you're okay, then? I'll be moving out. I have other places to cover before tonight. I'll—"

"Earl?"

"Yes?"

He was aware she'd never called him that. It made him slightly uncomfortable.

"Earl, if I was you, I'd call in your buddies. If Jimmy gives you even a twitch, I'd have them shoot that boy down like a dog. And Bub too. Earl, I don't trust him. In honest-to-God truth, I don't trust him a bit."

"Edie, I have to give the boy a chance. And on top of that, I don't trust my own people. They might shoot no matter what. I can bring this thing off, you watch."

"Earl, Miss Connie would tell you your word to a killer doesn't matter. You look out for Mr. Earl first."

"This is the best way," he said. "I know it in my heart. We can set this thing as right as it can be set, and then we can go find whoever killed that poor little Negro girl."

A weird light shown in Edie's eyes. He'd never seen it there before. She was gazing at him with such admiration.

"Earl, Miss Connie says no man ever carried more of the world around on his shoulders than you do. You're going to carry this whole thing around until you set it right. Where do they grow men like you? I never met a one."

"They grow us on trees, in the thousands. Don't you put no

account on it. You're still young. You'll meet plenty now. You have some great things ahead of you."

She looked at him as he'd never seen her look at him before. Late in a very long afternoon. Her face was calm, grave, lovely in the serene light. She was so young. He'd never let himself look at her before. She was someone else's daughter who grew to be someone else's wife. The most beautiful girl in the county, and so what? He was married to a good woman, had a son, enough responsibilities to choke a cat, a goddamned duty that would never, ever stop.

"Earl," she said.

Put it away, he told himself. Put it far, far away.

Seven

SOMETIMES the thirst for whiskey was so palpable it ached. This was such a night. He lay in the bed, hearing the warm desert breeze run through the night and the low, even breathing of his wife. In a room down the hall his daughter slept.

He dreamed of whiskey.

In whiskey was the end of pain: whiskey blurred the images of boys shot in the guts crying for mama and mama wasn't there, only Sergeant Swagger screaming *"Medic!"* at the top of his lungs while pouring M-16 fire off into the paddy breaks. Whiskey banished the stench of the villes after the Phantoms had laid down napalm, the odd blend of burned meat and scorched straw and fried water buffalo shit. In whiskey disappeared the emptiness of emotion when the recoil spent itself against one's shoulder and the rifle settled back and the crosshairs reimplanted themselves on a man so far away, who was now horribly altered, his posture destroyed by death arriving in packages of 173 grains launched at 2,650 feet per second. Sometimes they staggered, sometimes they instant rag-dolled. Always they went still forever.

Gone too in the whiskey was this one:

He woke late, to a lot of commotion downstairs, the sounds almost of a party or meeting. He blinked sleep out of his eyes, confused, a little scared.

"Daddy," he called. "Daddy?"

Outside another car pulled up and then another. He was wearing underpants and a Davy Crockett T-shirt which he had got by sending fifty cents and six caps from Mason's root beer off to Chicago. It took weeks for it to arrive and he wore it every day and every night. He was nine. He heard his mother crying downstairs and listened to a man's footsteps on the stairs. He heard creaking leather, the sag of the floorboards, the squeal of the stairway banister, all familiar from a thousand times his father came home late as he always did, letting the duty day stretch out sometimes for eighteen and twenty hours. But there was a heaviness to the tread which he knew was not his father's. He sat up as the man entered and it was some other state policeman. The crickets were chirping desperately in the dark just beyond the open windows and outside it was a clear night, glittery with starlight.

"You're Bob Lee, is that right?" said the man in his daddy's uniform, the flat-brimmed, round-topped hat, not quite a cowboy's hat, and the big gun in the holster, not quite a cowboy's gun. He stood in the doorway, just a silhouette, the light behind him blazing.

"Yes sir," he had said.

"Bob Lee, may I come in? Have to talk man-to-man to you."

Bob nodded. He knew something was wrong. Another police car pulled up out front of the house.

"I'm Major Benteen. You're going to have to be a man now, son," the man in his daddy's uniform told him.

"What you mean?"

"Son . . . son, your daddy was killed in the line of duty this evening. He's in heaven now, where all the good soldiers and policemen and men who do their duty have to go eventually."

"What's duty?" Bob said.

"I can't explain it. I don't even know. It's what special men like your dad lived by and for," said the major. "It's the best thing a man can have. It's why your daddy's a hero. It's—"

But the man stopped and Bob saw that he was crying too.

Now Bob shook his head; that big officer bawling away in the dark over his father's death, trying so hard to be manly but so destroyed by the bitter futility of it he had no chance.

That was a whiskey memory. You wanted to soak that motherfucker in amber fluid that roasted your tongue as it went down your gullet and sent its radiant message of hope and love to the far precincts of your body and numbed out your mind with the buzz of alcoholic bliss. That's what whiskey was for, to kill those lost black memories that when they came out from hiding would try and kill you like this one was now trying to kill him.

Bob sat up in the bed. He was glad there was no whiskey in the house for if there were he knew he'd grasp it and drown himself in it, going down so far there'd never be an up. He could hardly breathe.

He rose, a tall, thin, strong man, graying, but still with a gift for silent movement and a face famous for the little that it showed. He had slept alone for so long: now he wasn't alone in the bed anymore and he looked at her, dozing softly under the sheets, such a beautiful woman. Who'd have thought it?

He slipped down the hall and pushed open the dark door into the next room, hearing the child's breath. He snapped on the light. YKN4 was curled up, her little nose fluttering ever so gently. She stirred, disturbed by the light. She looked as if she were made of candy, a moist, perfect little thing, her wide lids enveloping her wide eyes, her curled lashes as perfect as the tracing of a doily, her tiny little nose cusping her tiny perfect seal of lips. She rubbed a hand against an eye, shivered in some sort of animal delight, pushed some hair off her face, and pulled the blanket tighter, dreaming, no doubt, of horses. He wondered if he would ever be the mystery to her that his father was to him. He hoped not. Bob turned off the light, bent to her and kissed her smooth cheek gently, feeling a radiance much stronger than whiskey's and much truer.

That's worth getting through it all, he thought.

Suddenly, he felt a bit braver. Resigned almost, steady at least, and aware at last of what must be done.

He walked down the hall, pulled a lanyard so that a section of the ceiling pivoted downward with a groan, and a section of wooden ladder slid out. He climbed into the attic, pulled the light switch. It was any attic: jumbled trunks, racks of old clothes, sheaves of pictures, most of it Julie's. But a small portion of it was his, loaded into the trailer for that drive out from Blue Eye years ago, after he'd buried his guns. He climbed and looked toward his small claim of the space. He saw an old seabag full of marine utilities, boots, the like, his dress blues hanging off a rack, a leather shooting jacket with its many buckles and straps, a few old pieces of luggage.

And at last, what he was looking for. It was an old shoe box, with a red ribbon tied prettily outside it. The label on the box said "Buster Brown, Size C7, Dark Brown Oxfords," the container for his Sunday shoes sometime in the fifties. Though it was sheathed in dust, he could make out handwriting, his mother's ornate script: *Daddy's Things,* it said.

He tugged on the old ribbon, which, easily enough, gave up the ghost and popped. Dust stirred like vapors of lost memory. He carefully lifted the lid off, and there, kneeling in the yellow light in a pair of sweats, he began his exploration.

This is what remained of Earl Lee Swagger, USMC, Arkansas State Police, killed in the line of duty, July 23, 1955. First, Bob saw old brown photographs on stiff, slightly wilted papers. He picked them up to enter an alien universe that seemed built around a little farm boy with a chubby face that showed but a trace of the bone structure that would eventually yield the face he would recognize as his father's. In this brown world, there was a farmhouse, a trellis, a scrawny old goat in a straw hat, a three-piece suit even in summer's full blaze, a bow tie and starched collar, a face chipped out of granite who must have been a father, that is, Bob's grandfather; he also wore a circled star on his chest that was a sheriff's badge and a wide belt festooned with cartridges and a holster that swallowed up all but the Colt Peacemaker's curved grip. Next to him was the grandmother, a dour woman in a shapeless dress and a face that looked as if it never had worn a smile. He turned it over and in faded ink read the date: 1920, Blue Eye, Ark. There were others, various arrangements of the same three people, sometimes together, sometimes alone or in twos. None of them had ever gotten fat off the land, Bob saw. A final shot showed Earl in his twenties, in a marine olive-drab service uniform, with that tight tunic collar, a glistening Sam Browne belt diagonally transecting a manly chest and a sergeant's three stripes on the shoulder, looking proud and ramrod-straight. He'd joined in 1930, at twenty, and had made his rank fast: turning the picture over, Bob saw in his grandmother's flowery penmanship the inscription "Earl home on leave, 1934." Earl's hair was slicked back over white sidewalls and he looked dapper as possible.

Next he found the medals. There was a nest of them, police marksmanship badges (his father was a natural, extraordinary shot), Pacific Battle Star and campaign ribbons, the Purple Heart with four clusters, a Presidential Unit Citation for the 2nd Marines, another one for the 3rd Marines, a Distinguished Service Cross, a Silver Star and of course, the big one, the Medal of Honor, a chunk of metal in the configuration of a star that hung on a necklace of now faded but once sky-blue ribbon. He hefted the ornament: it had weight and density, gravity almost, dignity perhaps. Its gold plating was grimy from years of neglect and he realized that he'd never seen the thing itself before; his father never had it out or displayed it and his mother must have dumped it in this box sometime after the funeral, and sealed the box and herself off from the pain.

He held it in his hand for a few seconds, waiting to feel something. It was only a chunk of dirty metal, a trinket. He'd won medals himself and knew the odd distance a man feels from them, looking at them and thinking, so what? They explain so little, they have no connection with the reality of what they signify.

The citation was there too, on official Department of the Navy paper, a fancy-looking, thick piece of paper dated 10 December 1945, that had the look of formal ostentation that he despised. It could have hung in a dentist's office.

He read it, wondering if he'd ever read it before or only heard it told by other men. His father never spoke a word about the war.

> On 21 February 1945, on Charlie-Dog Ridge two miles inland from Beach Red 2, Platoon Sergeant Swagger's unit from E. Co., Second Battalion, Ninth Regiment, Third Marine Division, came under intense fire from several enemy machine-gun positions. All his flamethrower opera-

tors dead or wounded, Platoon Sergeant Swagger led a squad off on a flanking maneuver, but only he reached the ridgeline in sufficient condition to continue the attack, the others having been killed or wounded. Wounded himself three times, Platoon Sergeant Swagger climbed into the first nest from the rear, killing the enemy soldiers with his submachine gun.

He continued to work his way along the line, silencing two other positions in the same fashion, by rolling over the parapet and spraying the enemy with gunfire. In the third nest, his gun jammed and he killed two enemy soldiers with the butt of the weapon. Advancing on the last position, a concrete bunker, he realized he was out of ammunition. He returned to the previous machine-gun nest and removed the enemy weapon and several grenades. He blew open the steel door of the emplacement and leaped inside with the light machine gun, killing thirteen more enemy soldiers.

In the seven-minute engagement, Platoon Sergeant Swagger killed over forty enemy soldiers while sustaining five wounds himself. His actions saved the lives of thirty men in his platoon. For conspicuous gallantry in action against the enemy above and beyond the call of duty, he is awarded the Medal of Honor.

Somewhere Bob had seen a picture, though it appeared not to be here. He remembered a yellowed scrap of newsprint, almost delicate to the finger in its crumbly dryness, and on it the image of his much younger father, flat-bellied and stoic of face, in dress blues, as the President of the United States, behind bifocals and a folksy Missouri face, laid the ribbon over his head. Again, it was nothing: the ceremony was for other people, not for his father, who kept his feelings to himself about what he'd done and why he'd done it.

At last Bob set the medal down. He knew enough of war to know that the description of his father's action was antiseptic to say the least. In the nest with the Japs, working them over with a tommy gun, he must have watched them disintegrate under the heavy impact of the .45s. The air was sulfurous and full of lead and smoke; mortars exploded everywhere, sucking the oxygen from the surface of the planet. Exhaustion, stress, dirt and filth, grime, the gritty volcanic soil of Iwo, the hundreds of scrapes, cuts and abrasions from low-crawling, the utter terror, maybe some bloodlust, some pleasure in watching the enemy's head torn off or limbs blown away, fear that the gun would jam: all that, and much more, was left unnoticed by the citation.

Hell of a fight you made, Daddy, he thought.

Next his eye caught on something unusually regular and a pull yielded a thick wad which turned out to be an old tablet of Arkansas traffic violation citations. An amazement! There were at least twenty unused citations with their triplicate carboned forms left flat on the pad, but curled back over the spine of it were five or six carbons on tickets already handed out. Bob saw in a second that they were the tickets his father must have issued that last week and was unable to file with the court before his death. He shuffled through them, seeing his father's own handwriting recording a series of meaningless misdemeanors against the Arkansas Standard Traffic Code in the second and third weeks of July 1955. "Driving with left taillight disabled" was checked on one citation, and the driver's name and address and license number and below that, under the rubric "Issuing Officer," the scrawled semisignature "E. L. Swagger." A couple of speeding violations on Routes 71 and 88, a DWI, the small beer of a rural highway patrolman's life. He felt his father so powerfully he almost doubled over.

And then, next, a notebook. Evidently, Earl's pen had broken or some such, for it was spattered with brownish fluid on the cover, and a discoloration had worked under the cardboard and bled through the pages. Bob peeled them, one at a time, trying to make sense of it. He saw a list of meaningless names inside the cover, like Jed Posey, Lum Posey and Pop Dwyer. He saw a stick figure crudely inscribed and lines radiating off toward landmarks that indicated distances; and a variety of other unrelated facts or observations: "Was she moved?" it said at one place. "Little Georgia," it said at another. "Cause of death," it wondered, "blunt force or strangulation?" "Meeting at church? Find out what?" He could make no—

A sudden sense of profound unease hit Bob. He turned back to the cover of the notebook and felt the thing burn in his fingertips. It occurred to him that the brownish stain that had seeped through to discolor the pages must be blood. It was his father's blood. His father had been holding this or had it in his pocket when Jimmy Pye fired the fatal bullet and the wound had emptied on this document.

It had the sense of something religious to it, something from an ancient saint's reliquary, like a blessed chard of bone or a fragment of hair or cloth. Its power overwhelmed him, and he put it down, feeling somehow as if he'd blasphemed. It was almost too much.

He suddenly had a need to put the lid on the box, stuff the box back into the slot where it had rested beribboned and sheathed in dust, and flee back to the good life he'd finally built for himself. He had horses to care for, a daughter to raise, a wife to support. In the box was only pain and black memories.

No, go on, he told himself. Go on, do it, see every last thing.

Next came some news clippings of the event itself, the various rags' account of the events of July 23, 1955. He slipped through them, uninterested in details. Only one caught his attention: HERO TROOPER BURIED, it said, July 26, 1955, the *Fort Smith Southwest Times Record* front page, also brown and crackly with age. He saw himself as a small dour boy standing next to his poor mother, surrounded by a sea of uniforms and suits under a spreading elm tree. A minister seemed to commandeer the most attention; the casket was aligned next to the hole in the ground under the tree where it would go. At least Daddy had some shade. A marine honor guard stood on the right, ramrod boys with no hair and severely raked white dress hats, bills low over their eyes, their gloves white, the high-necked dress coats severe as any Puritan's frock. Bob glanced at what the picture showed of himself, and saw only pudge and softness, as if he were out of focus, which he was. He could barely even remember the event itself, though the photo brought something back: his mother would not stop crying, though by this time he himself had been fully cried out. It was hot, the speeches seemed to go on forever. Someone called Miss Connie was like the dowager empress of the event, the Mother Courage who took over and got everything organized and done. He remembered her smell and beauty and how strong she'd seemed. But she was not in the picture.

Bob put the clipping down, passed through what little was left. Letters of condolence, official and otherwise, testifying to his father's greatness, from, among others, the commandant of the United States Marine Corps, two men in the platoon who could write that day only because his actions had saved their lives, one on Iwo, one Tarawa, testimonials in inflated language from the commanding officer of the Arkansas State Police and the governor of Arkansas and a final crude letter from someone called Lucille Parker, telling his mother what a wonderful white man Earl Swagger had been, the only white man who'd listened to her pain over her daughter, Shirelle, and pledged to help. What on earth could that mean?

So many mysteries, so many unconnected elements, unfinished bits of business, the stuff of his father's life. Not much to show for forty-five years on a planet where you'd done so much good work, and only a shoe box was left to testify to your existence.

That was it? Would the boy find such material interesting? Possibly. Bob made his mind up that in the morning he'd call the boy and arrange to let him borrow the stuff. Possibly some good would come out of it, after all.

There was a last scrap of paper. Bob picked it up, curious. It took some effort to get it figured out. It was the last page of what may have been an autopsy or a hearing report. In fact, lodged under the staple at the left top was the mulch of other pages that had been torn away. Bob understood that it had been the necessary, clinical, appallingly unemotional and excessively professional description of the wounds his father had suffered. A copy had been sent to his mother and when she discovered its meanings—Bob guessed it would have read something like "translateral passageway from under left nipple at 43-degree angle to sternum led to severe and catastrophic destruction of left ventricle" or some such—she'd just been unable to face it and had ripped it up and destroyed it. Why had this page survived? He couldn't guess; it couldn't be explained. Maybe she'd gone back and pulled it out of the garbage can and remorsefully tucked it away in the box. Her own sad decline had just been initiated; she would not live much longer herself, bent under grief and regret and finally alcoholism.

So this alone remained. Bob glanced at it and saw that it was a partial list of exhibits pertaining to the ballistics evidence of the hearing or autopsy or whatever. Because he knew a great deal of such matters, he read onward and saw what state police detectives had recovered at the scene.

"1) Colt .38 Super Government model, serial number 2645, with staghorn grips, four cartridges left in the magazine in the pistol." That was Jimmy's gun, slick, flashy Colt automatic shooting high-velocity bullets, vest-penetrating, shock-inducing, meant only to kill. Very professional choice.

"2) Fourteen cartridge cases bearing headstamp COLT .38 SUPER—WW," the spent casings that Jimmy had ejected in the fight, meaning he'd fired fourteen times, he'd reloaded once and was halfway through the reloaded mag when his father took him out. He was a shooter, that boy. Bob wondered which of the fourteen rounds had been the fatal one, whether his father took it early or late. He shook his head. A fleeting wish came to him that he could reach back through time and deflect that bullet or maybe improve Earl's aim just a bit on an earlier round; who knew how differently it might have turned out? But no: Jimmy fired the last round; he killed Earl even as Earl was killing him.

"3) Smith & Wesson 1926 Model .44 Special, SN 130465, with six unfired WW .44 Special rounds in the cylinder." Bub's gun, Bob guessed. Unfired. Hadn't got a shot off.

"4) Colt Trooper .357 Magnum, SN 6351, with three loaded cartridges and three empty in the cylinder." His father's gun. Bob had seen his father clean that big piece of machinery once a week and after every firing session. Most of his memories of his father, in fact, were connected with firearms and his father teaching him how to shoot, how to hunt, how to clean, care for and respect the firearm. They were the lessons he'd never forgotten.

"5) Six cartridge casings bearing headstamp REMINGTON

.357." His father had reloaded himself, a speed reload under heavy fire from a guy with a semiauto and plenty of ammo. Good work, he thought, the best kind there is.

Only one label remained on the sheet. It bore the depressing title "Bullets Recovered" and he knew it meant recovered from bodies. The coroner's last connection to the physical mechanism of death.

Did he have the courage to read on? With a sigh, he discovered he did. There were three "exhibits," that is, bodies, and under each of them was listed the items recovered. Nothing in it surprised him, except that he learned that Bub had a bullet in him from Jimmy's gun, probably delivered in the excitement of the action, a friendly-fire accident of the kind that was distressingly common in battle.

At last he read of the bullets taken from his father.

There were three.

"Two (2) misshapen (calibration impossible to determine) bullets, copper clad, weighing 130.2 grains and 130.1 grains."

Then "One (1) misshapen (calibration impossible to determine) bullet, metal clad, weight 109.8 grains."

Bob looked at it, not quite sure what he was reading, then he read it again and a third time. It did not go away. 109.8 grains.

"I thought I'd find you here," Julie said.

He turned, startled.

"Yeah, here I am. Going back through it."

"Bob, you ought to help that boy. It would help *you* more than anything. You've been angry ever since 1955. You should face it."

"I'm going to do more than face it," he said.

Eight

IN THE GLOOM OF TWILIGHT, Earl drove swiftly down Route 88 until he passed beyond Board Camp and came to his own mailbox, turned in and followed the dirt road to his own house. He picked up the microphone and called in.

The news was not good at all. The state detectives had not been able to get to the Shirelle Parker site yet and wouldn't make it until the morning. Only a one-man shift from the Polk County Sheriff's Department could be assigned to secure the crime area overnight, though a coroner's assistant had come out to make a preliminary investigation.

"How long was he there?" Earl asked over the radio.

"Ten minutes."

"Ten minutes!" Earl exploded to the sheriff's dispatcher. "How the hell could he learn anything in ten minutes?"

"Come on, Earl, you know we goin' to go to Niggertown to-morrow when all this about Jimmy is settled, and sooner or later someone goin' to talk to us. That's how it works down there. Them people can't keep no secrets."

Earl thought: Suppose it was a white person who killed Shirelle?

"Okay. Tell them I'll be out there first thing in the morning, and to keep the site as clean as possible. I hate to think of that little girl lying out there all alone another night."

"It don't matter to her none, Earl."

Earl signed off.

All sorts of things weighed on his mind; he tried to will them away.

You got to stay sharp, he told himself. *You got lots to do.*

But he wanted more than anything to sleep, to end the day and hope that tomorrow would be a better one.

He reached the house, which had once been his father's, low but surprisingly gracious, a white place with a porch and green shingles in a grove of elms. Out back there was a rope swing and a creek. The barn held four good riding horses and the fields were Earl's for two hundred acres all around. His son came running off the front porch.

"Daddy, Daddy, Daddy, Daddy!"

"Well, howdy there, Davy Crockett, how's Daddy's best boy?" he said, his heart swelling at the sight of the kid running toward him, the ever-present coonskin cap clutching his head, its tail bobbing on his back. Damnedest thing Earl ever did see, but all the kids wore them.

Bob Lee was nine and had never given anybody a lick of trouble. He was all the son a dad could wish for; all boy, but a hard worker too, and he had something of his father's natural ways with a firearm. For a nine-year-old, he could fire a .30-30 lever gun with amazing accuracy and last year had bagged a deer, though he'd shot it too far back and Earl had to track it all the way into the mountains of Scott County to finish it. Earl picked his son up and gave him a swirl up to the sky as if he were a bag of feed, swinging him till his little feet swept upward.

"Whoooooooooo!" screamed the boy.

"Best hope I hang onto you, Bob Lee, I let you go, you'll end up on the moon!"

The boy laughed as Earl set him down.

"Mama's up the road a piece," he announced. "Mrs. Fenson felt poorly and mama said she'd take over some dinner."

"Umh," said Earl, recognizing his wife's behavior in the gesture. "I'm just gonna git me a sandwich and an iced tea and be on my way."

The disappointment was ripe on the boy's face.

"You going out, Daddy? You go out *every* night."

"Tomorrow, I swear to you, I'll stay in. Got me one little thing to do. When that's over, I'm going to take a rest. Come on, boy, let's see what she's got in the kitchen."

In they went, and in no time, Earl had slapped some ham on his wife's good bread and opened two root beers. He took it all out on the porch, and Bob went with him. They ate in silence. Earl looked at his watch. It was now 8:30 and he had close to an hour's drive up to near Waldron and the cornfield. He finished the sandwich, took a last gulp on the root beer, draining it.

"Walk me to the cruiser, Bob Lee."

"Yes sir," said the boy, adoring the private time with his father.

They got to the car. Earl opened the door, ready to climb in and pull away. The sun was setting. It was the gray hour of perfect stillness and clarity in the world; here in eastern Polk County, the Ouachitas changed subtly in character and became lower, rounded hills, crested with pine and teeming with game, like islands rising out of a flat sea. Earl didn't do much farming, but it was nice to have some land to hunt and to shoot on. He'd made a good life for his family, he thought.

An immense melancholy and regret suddenly flooded him; there was a kind of hole in his mind where he'd exiled his most recent memories and focused instead on the perfection of the here and now. He reached down and grasped his son and gave him a crushing hug.

"You be a good boy, now, Bob Lee," he said. "You tell your mama how much I love her. I just have this one last little thing to do, you understand? Then maybe we'll take some time off. It's been a rough summer. Time to go fishing, you understand."

"Yes sir."

"Got a surprise for you. In a month or so, the Chicago Bears goin' come down to Little Rock and play the New York Giants. Saw an ad in the paper. They call it the Football Classic of the South. War Memorial Stadium, September 10. You send off for tickets. They're pretty expensive, three-eighty apiece, but what the heck. Figure you, me and Mommy'd go down to Little Rock, have us a nice dinner and see that game. How'd you like that?"

"At night?"

"Yes sir. They rig these big old lights and it's bright as day."

"That'd be *great,*" the boy said.

But he had picked up the strangeness in his father.

"Daddy, you okay?"

"I am fine," said Earl. "I am—" He paused, perplexed. He felt he had to explain something to his son.

"I'm going to arrest a bad boy," he said. "A boy who made a big mistake. But there's two kinds of bad, Bob Lee. This boy's bad was he just decided to be bad. He said, *I will be bad,* and he did bad things and now he's got to pay. See, that's one kind of bad."

The boy looked at him.

"But you ain't ever going to be like that. Most nobody's ever like that. That other kind of bad, see, that's the kind that a good boy like you or any good boy could fall prey to. That's the kind of bad that says *I will be good* but somehow, not meaning to, not facing it, not thinking about it, lying to yourself, you just sort of find yourself where it's *easy* to be bad and you don't have the guts or the time or whatever, maybe you don't even *realize* where you are, and you just do it and it's done. Then you know what?"

The boy's vacant eyes signified that he was lost.

"Well, anyway, someday you'll understand all this. What you got to do next, you got to *clean up* your mess. You got to make it right. If it's busted, you got to fix it. You got to face the consequences. Do you see?"

The boy just looked up at him.

"Well, so you don't. You will, I know, and you'll be a fine man and not make the mistakes your poor, stupid old daddy made. Now I have to go. You tell your mama that I love her and I'll see y'all tonight, do you hear?"

"Yes, Daddy."

Earl got in the car, took one of his swift, practiced U-turns, the maneuver of a man who drove beautifully and with great confidence, and pulled away. As he drove he saw his son in the rearview mirror, standing there in the fading light, one arm lifted to say goodbye. He put a hand out the window and gave a little waggle of acknowledgment, hit the main road and sped off.

❑ ❑ ❑ ❑

"That was the last thing I remember," Bob said.

"The wave?" Julie asked.

"Yep. He just put his big old arm out the window and gave a little, you know, a little wave. Then the car turned and off he went. Next time I saw him, he was in a casket with a pink-frosted face and a smile like a department store dummy and all these grown-ups were saying sad things."

He paused, remembering the wave, not the man in the casket. It seemed to sum his father up, a little masculine salute from an arm thickened with muscle, hand big and loose and square, three yellow chevrons gleaming in the failing light, hat set square on his head in silhouette as he went off to do something—no one could ever tell Bob what it was—called duty.

"Would you let me be, please," he said.

"Are you all right, honey?"

"I'm fine. I need to be alone a bit, is all."

"I'll be downstairs if you need me," she said, and departed softly.

When she left, Bob cried hard for the first time in his life since July 23, 1955.

Nine

RUSS HAD HIS Lamar Pye dream again that night. As they usually did, it started out benignly. He was sitting in a Popeye's, eating greasy chicken and red beans, and Lamar walked in, big as a house, friendly as life itself. The fact that he had never seen Lamar but only pictures of him freed Russ's subconscious to invent interesting details for Lamar. For example, tonight Lamar was wearing a clown suit and had a bright red Ping-Pong ball for a nose. His teeth were bold and shiny. He radiated the power and the glory.

As he saw Russ sitting there, Lamar came over and said, "Are you a spicy kind of guy or a regular kind of guy?"

That was the key question for Russ. And it was another test and he knew he'd fail it.

Bravely, he said, "I'm a spicy kind of guy."

Lamar's mean but shrewd eyes locked on his, squinting with intellectual effort. He looked Russ up and down, and then he said, "The hell you say, boy."

"No, it's true," Russ argued through a tide of liar's phlegm rising in his throat. "Really, I'm spicy. Been spicy all my life."

A rhinolike flare of rage blossomed behind Lamar's clown makeup and the urge to strike viciously displayed itself in the narrowing of his pupils to pinpoints, but he controlled himself.

"I say you're regular and I say to hell with it." Only he said it "reg-lar," two syllables.

Russ cowered in Lamar's force. Lamar was huge and strong and knowing and decisive, unclouded by doubt, untainted by regret. He was definitely a spicy kind of guy.

"All right," he finally allowed, "we'll see what kind of guy you are."

With a magic wave of his hand, the clown-god Lamar made the Popeye's disappear. Instead the two were deposited on the front lawn of Russ's family home in Lawton, Oklahoma. It was a small rancher on a nice piece of land, a well-worn house where Russ and his brother had been treated to stable, loving childhoods by their parents. From the smoke curling out the chimney (though it was full summer in the dream), Russ understood that the family was home. Lamar willed it and in the next second he had some kind of tacky X-ray vision, as if he were looking into a house onstage through the old invisible fourth wall.

His brother, Jeff, was in his room, lacing up a baseball glove with the intensity that another boy might spend jacking off. Not Jeff. Jeff just poured his whole heart and soul into the effort, trying to get the glove just right, limber, supple, soft but not too soft. It was the central issue of his life.

In the kitchen, Russ and Jeff's mama, Jen, a handsome though somewhat hefty woman in her early fifties, slaved over a hot stove. Mom was always cooking. He had a sense of his mother as cook to the world. That's how he would think of her always, having traded all chances at happiness and freedom and self-expression to spend her time instead in the kitchen, whaling away at this dish or that, concocting elaborate dinners, never displaying an iota of disappointment or despair, rage or resentment. She just gave it up for her family.

Downstairs, his daddy was doing something to a gun. His dad was always doing things to guns. He was in his trooper's uniform and totally lost in his own world, as he usually was, just working away. There was a young woman with him, nude, watching him and asking him to hurry up, please, goddammit, she was getting tired of waiting and he kept saying, "Just let me get this bolt oiled up, and we'll be outta here."

Finally, Russ saw upstairs again and saw himself: a grave boy, as

usual doing nothing but reading. By the time he was fifteen he had
read everything there was to read, twice. He read like a maniac,
soaking it up, trying to draw lessons from it. He had a freak gift
for the written word, which, when regurgitated crudely, became in
turn a crude gift for his own writing. He had a small fluency, a big
imagination and enough doubt to sink a ship. Why did he work so
hard in this area? To escape Oklahoma? Was there some sense that
he was too good for Oklahoma, for this little life of homey plati-
tudes and small-beer deceits and easy pleasures? He, Russ, he was
too good for it? He deserved such wonderful things in his life? He
deserved the East, he deserved bright lights, fame, adoration? No
little-town blues for him, no sir.

"See, that ain't healthy," Lamar said. "You just a-sittin' up
there. You oughta be out doing things."

"My brother's the jock," Russ said. "I had a mind. I didn't want
to waste it."

"Well, here's the deal," Lamar said. He drew a chain saw out of
nowhere and dramatically pulled the ignition cord, and it leaped to
churning life, filling the air with that high, ripping scream. "The
deal is, I'm going in there and I'm going to kill all them people.
You go stand by that tree. I'll deal with your sorry young ass when
I get out."

"Please don't do it," Russ said.

"Oh, and who's to stop me?"

"My dad will stop you."

"Your dad. All that old bastard cares about is fucking that girl
and his guns. He don't care about you or your mom none."

"No, he'll stop you. You'll see. He's a hero."

"He ain't no hero, sonny. Just you watch."

And so Lamar walked to the house and commenced an atrocity.
It actually duplicated several such episodes that Russ had seen on
the silver screen, and thus it unfolded according to the rules of the
movies. Lamar kicked down the door. The young woman
screamed, Russ's dad reached for his gun but this time Lamar was
too fast for him. The saw dove through them each, and they fell.
Behind each, on a far wall, blossomed a blood spatter like a red

rose opening to the sun, aesthetically perfect, showing the devotions of a supremely gifted art director.

"See," Lamar called back, "he weren't no trouble at all."

Lamar climbed the stairs. Jen looked at him and said, "Don't hurt my boys. Please."

"Lady, I'm hurting *everybody*." Lamar instructed her laconically in the second before he swiped at her with the saw, driving her backwards into the refrigerator which had been rigged to collapse as she crashed into the jars and cartons and cans. She died in bloody splendor amid a smorgasbord of brilliantly conceived food effects, with mustard and ketchup and Coke flung every which way by the grinding chain of the saw.

Jeff, a hero, heard the noise, picked up a bat and came running. But a bat and heroism are no match for a chain saw, no sir. Lamar got Jeff on the stairs, and the camera, which loves the destruction of the young and tender best of all, zeroed in on the poor boy's face, flecked with his own blood, as the life in his eyes shut down into blankness. That left Russ, reading something obtuse and meaningless, as the killer stalked him. Russ had no defense when Lamar kicked his way into the room. He begged, he sniveled, he quivered, he raised two trembly hands.

Lamar turned away from begging Russ weeping for mercy by his bed to the Russ who watched from outside.

"Should I do his young ass?"

"Please don't kill him, Lamar. Please."

"Can you stop me?"

"No, I can't."

"Then you ain't worth a turd on a hot day."

He stepped forward with the chain saw and Russ awoke.

It was really not one of the truly bad ones, an essay more in dream-state illogic and pernicious movie influence than in sheer vomiting violence. He'd had those too, though not so bad lately. One night he'd awakened screaming and someone thought to call the Princeton cops, who took him in for drug testing. Another time he'd evidently rolled off the bed in stark fear and badly bruised himself. Once he cut himself thrashing in the night and awoke in his own blood.

This one: not too terrible. Survivable, at least. Were they getting easier? He didn't know. You just couldn't tell when it was going to explode over you, and to his knowledge nobody in his family, not even his father, suffered the same.

But perhaps he alone had worked out the logic: Lamar Pye was coming to kill them. That is, the family: to punish Bud Pewtie for his crimes, he would kill Bud's family. It was only a twist of fate that the drama played out elsewhere and that only Lamar and his minions died. But the weight of it settled on Russ for some reason: the idea that, not randomly, not accidentally, not out of whimsy or malice or the sheer force of the universe's irrationality, Lamar Pye had targeted the Pewtie clan for extinction.

It sat upon Russ like a fat black cat in the night. So do not send to know for whom Lamar comes: he comes for thee.

Russ blinked. He was still in the motel room, daylight showed wanly through the cheap curtains. He felt hung over but he hadn't been drinking. Rather it was the caffeine he'd had in the Diet Coke at Bob Lee Swagger's that had kept him awake, full of ideas and theories and arguments that he hadn't made, until well after four. Finally, he had been permitted to sleep. He checked his watch. It was close to eleven.

Nothing to do. He tried to figure out his next move but there was no next move. He thought he'd go back to his apartment in Oklahoma City and maybe work something out. But that idea filled him with boredom. His big book was going the way of all flesh: that is, toward lassitude and indolence and ultimately nothingness.

Russ showered, dressed, checked his wallet. He had less than fifty dollars left. It was about a ten-hour drive back to Oklahoma City, through New Mexico and across Texas and half of Oklahoma. It filled him with despair and self-loathing.

He threw his dirty clothes in the suitcase and went out to dump it in his car. Then he settled up with the motel—his credit card didn't bounce, not quite yet—and gassed up. Driving through Ajo, he pulled into the little cantina where he'd had so many lunches.

He went in, took his familiar seat at the bar, and without even having to order it, the usual plate of excellent barbecue was served, with a draft beer. Russ ate, enjoying it. That woman sure could cook.

"Well," he said to the bartender, "I didn't quite spend a thousand on the barbecue, but it's pretty damn close."

"You did okay, son," the bartender said. "Now I take it you're moving on."

"Yep. Gave it my best shot. Got to the man, put it before him and maybe for just a second I saw something in his eyes. But no. He said no."

"You worked as hard as any of 'em. But he's a tough nut to crack, that one."

"That he is. Well, anyway, I really enjoyed your barbecue. No kidding, it was the best. I'll miss it. I—"

But then he noticed how quiet it had become in the bar and that the barkeep was standing almost gape-mouthed and goofy. He looked left and right and there was only silence and men staring quietly. Then he looked in the mirror across the bar and at last saw the man standing behind him, tall and sunburned, with a shock of tawny hair and gray, narrowed eyes.

Swagger sat down next to him.

"Howdy," he said.

"Er, howdy," said Russ.

"Barbecue's pretty good here, so they say."

"It's great," said Russ.

"Well, one of these days I'll have to get some. You still interested in writing that book?"

"Yes, I am."

"Nothing in it about Vietnam? Nothing about 1992? That still the deal?"

"Yes sir."

"You all packed?"

"Yes, I am."

"Well, then," Bob said, "you and me're going to Arkansas."

Ten

THE CORPORATE HEADQUARTERS for both Redline Trucking and Bama Construction are located in a suite of offices in a flashy modern building on Rogers Avenue in east Fort Smith, Arkansas, as befits firms which annually bill over $50 million. In fact, it was Bama Construction that, on a federal contract, built the Harry Etheridge Parkway, which runs between Fort Smith and Blue Eye, seventy miles south, in Polk County.

The offices, which occupy the top two floors of the Superior Bank Building right across from Central Mall, are everything one might imagine of dominant prosperous regional corporations, complete to potted palms, soothing wall-to-wall carpeting, leather furniture and exposed brick in the public and presentation areas, all of it designed and coordinated by one of the finest (and most expensive) corporate interior design firms in Little Rock, no Fort Smith firm quite being up to the owner's tastes. In these offices, lawyers and secretaries and engineers labor intensively on Bama Construction's far-reaching plans, such as the Van Buren Mall or the Planters Road residential development; meanwhile trucking executives supervise the hundreds of routes and accounts that Redline controls, as Fort Smith is ideally located for east-west commerce, given its central location on the huge U.S. 40 route between Little Rock and Tulsa. It all hums along perfectly. The only oddity is the huge corner office, jammed with antiques, with two vivid picture windows that yield powerful views of the city. From here, one can see the old downtown, the bridge over the mighty Arkansas River and even a little of Oklahoma.

It's a beautiful office, some say the most beautiful in Fort Smith. It displays on one wall civic awards and family mementos, pictures of visiting dignitaries and political figures, examples of philanthropy and civic involvement, all signifying a solid career and a solider place in the community. Yet the office is almost always empty.

Rather, Randall T. "Red" Bama prefers to spend his time in the back room of Nancy's Flamingo Lounge, on Midland Boulevard in north Fort Smith, on an uneasy tribal border where the black district spills into a poor white one, where the city's surprisingly large Thai population has begun to contest its more lengthily settled Vietnamese one, where a workingman can get an honest but tough game of pool and a shot and a beer, all for under five dollars, and a stranger can get a steely look that tells him to get lost fast. Perhaps such quarters are an unnecessary indulgence. To keep his empire running—or at least that part of the empire which the newspapers so regularly chronicle—Red must make dozens of calls a day to his middle managers, for of course he makes all decisions himself. It helps that he has a supremely organized mind and a special gift for numbers. It's said he can add as many as eight three-digit numbers accurately in less than ten seconds, which qualifies him not quite as a prodigy but certainly as a man with a flair for integers.

Red arrives at ten, parking his gray Mercedes S-600 on the street where it will not be molested, stolen, ticketed or even touched. He always drives himself, enjoying the time alone on his spin down from his family's complex on Cliff Drive above Fort Smith, clearing his mind for the day's tasks. But he's preceded by two extremely professional men in a black Chevy Caprice who are authorized by the state of Arkansas to carry the SIG-Sauer P229 .40-caliber semiautomatics they wear in shoulder holsters under their jackets. They are tough, calm and decisive, excellent shots. Each wears Kevlar Second Chance body armor, capable of defeating all handgun and most shotgun ammunition. They are never far from Red.

Red doesn't say hello to Nancy because there is no Nancy and nobody can remember or cares much if there ever was. He makes his way to the back room, where he hangs up his expensive suit coat, sits at a navy-surplus desk and begins to drink black coffee out of Styrofoam cups from the bar while a continual stream of supplicants, acolytes, gofers, errand boys, emissaries and the summoned go before him for judgment or assignment. It is here that he receives reports on his nineteen pawnshops, his seven porno stores in the greater Fort Smith area, on his heroin dealerships and his crack franchises, mostly located in the black section of town, his six brothels and his seven rural gambling cribs, located across the river in Oklahoma, and the jewel of his night empire, the Choctaw Gentleman's Club, in Holden, Oklahoma, five miles west on Route 64, where rubes pay five dollars admission and sit there drinking overpriced beer and slipping one-dollar bills between the plastic-engorged breasts of the strippers, who must give forty-five cents on the dollar to the boss man.

His enforcers and district captains report in, with good news or bad, usually good. Occasionally, Red must order severe consequences for an infraction, not a pleasant task but a necessary one and one from which he has never and will never shrink. It is here that he conducts meetings when necessary with Armand Gilenti, the crime boss of Little Rock and Hot Springs, or with Jack Deegan, who runs Kansas City these days, and sometimes with Carmen St. Angelo, of the New Orleans organization and sometimes Tex Westwood, of Dallas.

It is said that Red sticks to the old room in the back of the old bar and billiard parlor because that is where his father, Ray Bama, did his business and built, on a smaller scale, the brilliant organization which Red inherited upon his father's death (car bomb, culprit uncaught, 1975) and so vigorously expanded upon.

Perhaps, perhaps not. Red in other ways does not seem a man given to sentiment, being noted far and wide for shrewdness, sagacity, persistence and toughness, though he indulges his three children from his first marriage and his two from his second grotesquely. Yet his father is something of a holy relic to him, that brilliant, tough man who fought his way up from the mud of Polk

County to the heights of Fort Smith in a single generation, building an empire but, more important, creating a vision which would sustain the empire. Red has called him, to each of his wives, "the redneck Joe Kennedy."

"Well, you ain't no JFK," his first wife shot back, "except when it comes to screwing around."

"Never said I was," said Red. "Just said I wouldn't let my daddy down."

At fifty-one, he's short and powerfully built, with a faint spray of freckles, stubby fingers, deep blue eyes that are said to be able to see through anybody's lies and a bald spot that he vainly tries to minimize by wearing his reddish-blond hair crew-cut. He favors gray suits with pinstripes, blue button-down shirts, red ties (Brooks Brothers, usually) and black Italian loafers. He wears a gold Rolex and never carries less than $5,000 on him in small bills but other than the watch wears no jewelry. He doesn't carry a gun, never has. He loved his first wife, and loves her still, even though he divorced her when she got a little too old. She was the third runner-up in the Miss Arkansas contest of 1972. He loves his new wife, who is thirty-seven and blond and was the authentic runner-up in the Miss Arkansas contest of 1986. And that was back in the days when beauty contestants had real tits and beauty contests were about beauty, not about saving the whales and feeling the pain of the homeless and all the other feeble liberal do-goodisms that were ruining America. Ask Red about this one: he'll tell you all about it. It's a real sore spot.

He loves his children. He loves his wives. He gives his wives and his children and himself anything he wants.

On this day, a sullen man sits before him in the uniform of the Polk County Sheriff's Department, as Red's eyes hungrily eat up data from the gambling chits before him.

Finally, Red looks over. What he sees is what he was, what he escaped from, what his father heroically rose against and conquered. But Red knows it well. Some would call it white trash: dead eyes, a narrow, ferrety face, a lanky, still body, too much hair, the whole radiating both danger and craftiness and best of all, stupidity. Red knew that men with gifts for the larger issues were seldom any good in getting the nitty-gritty work done.

"So, Duane," he finally said, "I got reports here both good and bad on you."

Duane Peck said nothing, but made a small clicking sound, tonguing his dentures so that they crackled and snapped. It was a nervous habit, disgusting, but no one had ever had the nerve to straight up tell him about it.

"You do like to gamble, don't you, Duane, and Lady Luck hasn't been holding your hand of late."

"Don't suppose she has," Duane said.

"I see you got paper out in most of the cribs in eastern Oklahoma. You owe Ben Kelly twenty-one thousand. Keno, Duane? That your weakness?"

"No sir," said Duane. "More to any card game."

"Duane, you got a card imagination?"

Duane's narrow eyes squinted as he contemplated this notion, failed to get a grip on it and then emptied of emotion as he dispensed with any more thought on the issue.

"I mean," said Red, "do the numbers or the faces stick in your mind? Are the suits very vivid? Do you sense the deck charging up or closing down? A feeling that what's left is in your odds or against them. Not counting cards, that's only for the pros, but just good card instincts. A feeling. Most good card players have a gift for that sort of thing. They also may have a good head for numbers. Duane, what's 153 plus 241 plus 304?"

"Ah—" Duane's eyes narrowed. His lips began to move.

"Never mind, Duane. Now, on the plus side, I see you did some associates of mine a favor now and then."

"Yes sir," said Duane Peck.

"You did some collecting and some enforcing?"

"Yes sir." Sometimes Duane moonlighted on his debt problem by collecting for Ben Kelly, who ran a gambling crib in the back room of the Pin-Del Motel over in Talihina, Oklahoma.

"Hmmm, that's good. You hurt anybody bad?"

"I busted some jaws and heads, nothing nobody couldn't walk

away from a week down the line. I had to break one boy's leg with a ax handle. He got way out of line."

"You kill anybody?"

Duane's eyes went blank.

"No sir," he said.

"I don't mean since you joined the Sheriff's, Duane, and I don't mean headbops on crib debtors. No, I mean *ever?*"

"No sir," said Duane.

"Now, Duane, one thing you must learn, never lie to me. Ever. So I ask you a second time. You kill anybody?"

Duane mumbled something.

"Arco Service Station," Red said. "Pensacola, 1977, June. You were just a redneck kid with a drug habit. A few quick hitters to raise the cash. But that night you popped a boy, right, Duane?"

Duane finally looked up.

"I forgot that one," he finally said.

"Well, Randy Wilkes didn't forget. He works in New Orleans for some people now. You do a job like that, you better come to an understanding with your partner. You don't, it seems sloppy. You are sloppy, aren't you, Duane?"

"Six ninety-two," said Duane. "It's 692."

"No, Duane, but close. It's 698."

"Damn," said Duane. "I can do it on paper."

"This isn't an arithmetic test, Duane. You're clean now? You're straight?"

"Nothing with real buzz," said Duane. "I do like my bourbon on a Saturday night."

"I like it then too, Duane. All right, now: I got a job for you. You interested?"

"Yes sir," said Duane, who had been wondering why one so lowly as he had been summoned before so powerful a figure.

"A private job, just for me. That's why you're talking to me, Duane, not Ben Kelly or anybody in between you and me."

"Yes sir."

"Duane, your twenty-one thousand could disappear, you play it right."

"Sir," said Duane, stirring from his phlegmaticism, "I will play it right. You can count on that."

"Duane, I'll be honest. Wish I had a better man. But you got one thing I need and it makes you valuable to me."

"Yes sir."

"Not your big dick, Duane. Not that fine-tuned brain of yours. No sir. Your badge."

Duane gulped a little.

"I need an inside boy to keep eye on a little situation that may be developing down in Polk. I send a stranger down, in that little place, people will notice. I got to have an insider, a man with the state's authority who can go places and ask questions without attracting attention. You game, Duane?"

"Yes sir, Mr. Bama. You just say what it is."

"It could get dicey," said Red. "I might have you get your fingers dirty for me. I have to have your ultimate loyalty if I'm to give you mine."

"Yes sir," said Duane.

"You understand, I'm a fair man. If you end up doing joint time, it'll be *good* joint time. You don't have to be any big nigger's fuck boy. You'll be protected. Fair enough?"

Duane could do prison, he knew. For a shot at a place with the Man, just about anything was possible.

"Yes sir."

"All right, Duane, you listen up. Many years ago there was a tragedy in Polk County. A heroic police sergeant shot it out with two very bad boys, killed them both. They killed him too. Mean anything to you?"

"No sir."

"Not a history buff, eh, Duane?"

Duane's face remained stolid: "history buff" as a concept was unrecognizable.

"Anyhow, I now have it on good authority a young Oklahoma journalist has decided to write a book about this event. You know, Duane, true crime, that sort of thing."

Duane nodded dully.

"Ah—this is something that must be looked at."

"Should I whack him?" Duane wanted to know.

Interesting question: key question, and Duane with his primitive's craftiness got to the heart of it. The boy could be dealt with harshly, killed, destroyed, and things left as they lay. But that very act, by the law of unintended consequences, could bring catastrophe itself, an investigation, the asking of questions that had so long gone unasked.

"No, Duane, but let's not rule it out. Let's leave it at this. You are to keep me informed on what's going on: who he sees, what he asks them, what he finds out. This may involve documents. Which documents? You may have to do very little except arrange for certain documents to disappear. It may involve more dramatic countermeasures, and if so, manpower won't be a problem. But for reasons you needn't know, and Duane, I suspect you wouldn't understand, it's important that this boy learn very little and that his book go unwritten. Do you understand?"

"Yes sir."

Red looked at poor Duane. He felt like a general sending a Boy Scout against the German Army. He had much better people. He had access to ex-CIA operatives, ex–Green Berets, longtime underworld troubleshooters, extremely competent, aggressive, experienced professionals. But all were outsiders and they wouldn't know a damned thing about a dense little universe like Blue Eye's and they'd stand out hugely. Duane, the most brutal and sociopathic of Vernon Tell's deputies, was also the most corrupt; he would attract no attention and much respect. So: Duane it had to be, Duane carefully controlled and directed, Duane in the game of his life, and Duane capable, if handled correctly, of anything.

"Duane, I've got here a list of people this boy may consult and offices he's likely to see. You'll monitor them. Also here is an 800 phone number. You can call it free from any phone in America but I will get you a secure cellular with that number preset so all you have to do is hit one button. I want a detailed report every day. Then you will get further instructions from me. Do you understand?"

"Yes sir," said Duane. "But I heard they can git taps on them cellulars easy. The Feds do it all the time."

Good point. Red was impressed.

"No, this one's secure at each end, can't be intercepted without a preset descrambler. What they can do is subpoena the records so they can find out who was talking to who. But I don't think the cellular company would cooperate with them, at least for years and years."

"Why?" asked Duane.

"Because I own it," said Red. "Now, Duane, be delicate. No bullyboy stuff. You have some charm, I'm told. You can be a backslapper, a laugher, a regular guy? Those are the colors I want you showing in this first phase."

"Yes sir."

"Now you must go. I'm behind schedule," said Red Bama, looking at his Rolex, "and I want to get to my son's soccer game."

Eleven

IN THE LATTER HALF of the nineteenth century, it was not uncommon for armed men to ride into Fort Smith, Arkansas, the bawdy, bustling city nestled on the confluence of the Arkansas and Poteau rivers. Founded in 1817, it boasted a population of thirty thousand by 1875, perched as it was at the head of the long valley between Ozark and the Ouachita Mountains, and perched again on the border between Arkansas and what in those days was called Indian Territory and is now known as Oklahoma.

In those days, the city was nicknamed Hell on the Border. Fort Smith was the gateway to the savage and untamed West. In those days, civilization tried mightily to enforce its will upon the lawless, and the enforcers were federal deputies to the hanging judge, Isaiah J. Parker. Between 1875 and 1896, the judge sent his men into Indian Territory to carry out the law. They were of a type: lean, slit-eyed, exquisitely practical, without much in the way of larger views. All could shoot; all would shoot. For two decades Fort Smith was the gunfight capital of the world, sending its men out to bring back the desperados and outlaws who roamed Indian Territory. Of the marshals, 65 were slain in the line of duty; of the 172 men they brought back alive, 88 were hanged by the judge; no one knows how many outlaws perished in the territory at the hands of the deputies. In those days, such facts weren't worth recording.

Now, of course, all that has changed: there are no gunslingers, no bawdy houses, no rigid judges. Instead, Arkansas's second largest city is a bit shopworn, its downtown, once the most sophisticated urban thoroughfare west of the Mississippi and east of Denver, fallen on hard and empty times, with the action having moved out to the suburbs where the Central Mall and the Wal-Marts are. Its skyline is dominated by two large grain elevators. City fathers have tried gamely to reclaim or re-evoke the glories of the past, and the old fort, Parker's courthouse, a brothel called Miss Laura's and many fine homes in the stately Belle Grove District of Victorian Houses have been restored, but they do little to disguise the fact that history has moved elsewhere. Now its parade-widened Garrison Street, a reminder of the days when it was an army post sited to keep the Cherokee and the Osage from tribal war, has the look of a beautiful mouth that has lost too many teeth to gingivitis. The most prominent downtown landmark is, in fact, the Holiday Inn on Rogers Avenue, a mock Hyatt with a nine-story atrium and a disco that blows loud, bad rock into the night. It is partially owned by the Bama group.

So the men who come to Fort Smith from Indian Territory these days are unlikely to be federal marshals or gunfighters. But still, some come on missions, and some are slit-eyed, hard and practical. One was Bob Lee Swagger, accompanied by his new young partner, Russ Pewtie, driving east on U.S. 40 in Bob's green pickup truck. They reached the city near twilight. The lights were coming on as they approached it through the rolling land of Sequoyah County, Oklahoma, though they couldn't see the Arkansas River off to their right, broad and flat but invisible behind a train of trees.

"See," Russ was saying, the folder of old articles from 1955 on his lap, "it just shows how crappy the newspapers were back then. We're *much* better now," he insisted, though Bob only grunted noncommittally.

"These stories," he argued, "they just don't tell you enough. No reporter ever *went* to the sites, they just took the police handout and reprinted it. Jesus, I can think of a *hundred* questions I'm going to have to figure out how to answer. How do Jimmy and Bub get all the way from Fort Smith down to Blue Eye through the largest manhunt in Arkansas history? How do they just *run* into your father? Is it coincidence? Yet there's no speculation here on these issues at all. Also, the bigger question: *why?* Why did Jimmy Pye on his first morning out after ninety days in jail go off on this thing, and why did poor Bub, who had no criminal record, why did he go along with him? And this bit here, stopping at a drive-in and eating a burger and flirting with the waitress? What was *that* all about? It sounds like someone who wants the world to think he's cool. Also, why—"

"Say, you do talk a mite, don't you?" said Bob.

"Well—"

"It ain't like *I* haven't thought about this, you know."

"All right," said Russ. "One of my least lovely characteristics. I am a talker. I can't shut up. I don't *feel* things, I yap about them. And you're the original Wyatt Earp and you're stuck with me."

"Son, I ain't no Wyatt Earp. I'm just a beat-up old marine trying to stay on the goddamn wagon."

Russ said nothing. In the fading light, Swagger's face looked as if it were carved out of flint; his eyes hardly showed a thing. He hadn't said a word in hours, and yet he drove with the perfect adroit grace of a race driver. He just swung the truck in and out of traffic, smooth and light as could be, hardly moving himself. He was the *stillest* man Russ had ever seen; no man seemed to care less what the world thought of him.

"I've worked out a plan," said Russ. "I want to approach this coherently and methodically. I know where we'll begin and—"

"The plan," said Bob, "is that we go grocery shopping."

It was full night when they got there, but the store was still open. If once it had been the flagship of a national chain, that identity was long since faded, though if you looked, in the neon you could make out the silhouettes of the letters when they removed the "IGA" from the big sign. It just said "Smitty's," hand-painted on plywood, nailed halfway up the big struts of the old sign. But it was still at 222 Midland Boulevard.

Brown light sustaining a cloud of insects beamed down from the pylons installed as a crime deterrent. The store looked ratty, even threadbare, and through the broad windows, Russ could see a few shoppers rushing among junky, sparse shelves. It occurred to him that the neighborhood had changed in forty years: everybody he saw in the store, everybody going in and out, was black or Asian or Hispanic.

"So," Bob said, "you're a writer. You figure things out. You tell me: why here?"

"Huh?" said Russ.

"Begin with a beginning. That day, it starts here at this grocery store at about eleven in the morning. Now: you tell me why."

"Me?"

"Yep, you."

"Ah, maybe they just fell into it. They were—"

"Russ, they'd stolen a car and somehow come up with two guns and ammunition. They were fixing to rob something. Now, if they went to all that trouble, you think they'd just walk into it? First place they saw? The jail is downtown. Blue Eye's the other way, south, out of town. Why'd they come north to this place?"

"Ahh—" Russ had no answer. It shocked him, though. Clearly, Bob had mastered the material at a much deeper level than he'd expected, surprising from a man who seemed as far from formal intellectuality as he could imagine.

"Look at it as a military problem. What is it about *this* place that recommends it for an operation?"

Russ looked around nervously. It was on a long straight stretch of road, a main drag into and out of town from the north, but now looking grim, three or four miles removed from downtown proper. There wasn't much to be seen. Long, straight road leading off in both ways, trees, a commercial strip full of bars and car dealerships and decaying retail outlets. Now and then cars moved up and down the block just by them, but there wasn't much.

"I don't see a thing," he admitted.

"Or, consider this way," Bob said. "There were two *other* big grocery stores in Fort Smith in 1955: Peerson Brothers, on South Thirty-first Street, and Hillcrest Food Market, on Courtland, in Hillcrest. Do you want to drive there and see what's different about them?"

"Er," said Russ. Then he asked, "Do you see something?"

"I didn't go to no college or anything," said Bob. "What would I know?"

"But you see something?"

"I see a little thing."

"What is it?"

Bob looked up and down the road.

"Now, I'm no armed robber. But if I *was* an armed robber, what I'd be most afraid of is that while I'm in robbing and before anybody even got an alarm out, a cop might come along."

Russ nodded. It seemed logical.

"Now, what's different about *this* block?"

"Ahhhh—" He trailed off in acknowledgment of his stupidity.

"It's long. If you look at the map you'll see that it goes for an unusual length. Look, no side streets and there ain't a stoplight in either direction for more than a bit."

Russ looked. Indeed, far down in each direction a stoplight glowed, one red, one green.

"Now, if you looked each way, and you knew no cop was in sight, you'd have about a clear minute or so to git in and out and you'd be guaranteed no cop could sneak up on you. In fact, a cop *did* come, but the boys were out and old goddamn Jimmy Pye had plenty of time to set up a nice clear shot. That cop didn't have a chance."

"Wow," said Russ, surprised. Then he added, "Jimmy was smart. He wasn't just improvising, he'd worked it out. It figures. His son was very smart. Lamar was very, very clever when he set up his jobs, and he always knew exactly what to do. That's something he got from his old man."

"Yeah, he was a regular genius," said Bob. "But how could he have scouted it out if he was in jail for three months?"

"Uhhh—" Russ let some air out of his lungs but no words formed in his brain.

"Now, let's consider something else. The guns. All the newspapers say Bub brought the guns. They was planning a job, Bub got the guns together, had plenty of ammo, they went right into action."

"Right."

"But Jimmy's was a Colt .38 Super, not a common gun, a kind of special gun, very few of 'em made. I'd love to find out where that gun come from. The .38 Super never really caught on; it was invented by Colt and Winchester in 1929 to be a law enforcement round, to get through car doors and bulletproof vests. But the .357 Mag come along a few years later and did everything it did better. So the Super just sort of languished. It wasn't your street gun, the kind a punk kid like Bub would come up with. It's not a hunting gun. It was never accurate enough to be a target round. It's not a nineteenth-century cartridge, a .38-40 or a .32-20, say, that could have been lying around a farm for sixty years. No, it didn't have its day until the eighties, when the IPSC boys begun loading it hot to make major. But in 1955, let me tell you, it wasn't something you'd just find. You'd have to ask for it: a professional's gun, real good velocity, nine shots in the mag, smooth shooting. If you were a cop or an armed robber, it's just the ticket. How'd Jimmy know that? He a gun buff? He into guns? He a hunter, an NRA member, a subscriber to *Guns* magazine? How'd he end up with just the *right* gun for that kind of work?"

"Ah—" Russ flubbed.

"And how'd Bub get it?"

"Stole it, I guess," said Russ.

"Guess is right. But no one ever reported it stolen, not so's I'd know. What's that tell us?"

"Ah," said Russ, not quite knowing what it told him.

"It tells us maybe someone's putting this thing together who knows a little bit about what he's doing."

Russ said, "Like I say, Jimmy was smart, like his boy, Lamar."

"Not *that* smart" was all that Bob said.

Where is this going? What's this guy up to? Russ wondered.

The next morning, they took the new Harry Etheridge Parkway down toward Bob's hometown. It was a strange experience: the road was not yet built when he left Blue Eye, seemingly forever, three years ago. Now it seemed so permanent, he could not imagine that it hadn't been there forever, four wide lanes of white cement gleaming in the sun. The road, however, was practically deserted. Who went from Blue Eye to Fort Smith and back again? As a recreation area, Blue Eye had yet to be developed.

It was strange, almost dislocating. He'd walked these hills and mountains daily for the seven years he'd lived alone on a mountain in a trailer with the dog Mike, just forgetting the world existed. He knew them a dozen different ways, all their trails and switchbacks, their enfilades and shortcuts, the subtle secrets of terrain that no map could yield. Yet penetrated from this angle, they gave up visions before unseeable as the highway almost seemed to rearrange the mountains themselves in new and unusual ways. It troubled him, announcing the mistake of going back thinking that things have stayed the same, for they always change and must be relearned again.

A part of him hated the damn road. What the hell was the point, anyhow? They say Boss Harry Etheridge never forgot he came from Polk County and he wanted to pay back his home folks, give them some shot into the twentieth century. They say that his son, Hollis, when he was in the Senate before he began his presidential quest, wanted a monument to his father. They say that all the politicians and businessmen wanted a free feed at the expense of the U.S. government, which is why so many people called it the porkway and not the parkway. But it was meant as a monument to a father's love of his home and a son's love for his father.

"This Etheridge," Russ asked, "is this the same guy that's running for President? The guy that's finishing third in all the primaries?"

"Same family," Bob said. "The father was the big congressman. The son was a two-term senator. Handsomest man that ever lived. He thinks he can be the President."

"He'll need more than pretty looks," said Russ.

"Umm," grunted Bob, who had no opinions on politics, or particularly on Hollis Etheridge, who was only an Arkansas fellow by political convenience. He'd been raised in Washington, been to Harvard and Harvard Law School and only came back during symbolic trips with his father when he was a youngster. In Arkansas, he was a tribute to name recognition. His two terms in the

Senate were marked by obedience to the rules, blandness, party-line votes, rumors of a flamboyant adultery habit (and if you saw his wife, you'd know why) and a great willingness to siphon funds back to the statewide political machine that had put him in office.

Whatever, the road he built got Bob and Russ to their destination in less than an hour where by the old twisty Route 71 it was a close-to-three-hour trip.

"That's a hell of a road," said Russ. "We don't have anything in Oklahoma like that. Too bad it doesn't *go* anywhere."

The end of the highway yielded a futuristic ramp that swirled in streamlined hurry to earth—but it was the earth of beat-up old Blue Eye, depositing them quickly enough in the regulation strip of fast-food joints: McDonald's and Burger King but also some more obscure regional varieties. Bob noted there was a new place called Sonic, a classic fifties drive-in that boasted pennants snapping in the breeze, clearly a hot dog joint, but it didn't look like it was doing too well otherwise. The Wal-Mart had moved across the street and become a Wal-Mart Super Saver, whatever the hell that was, and it looked like some kind of flat spaceship landed in the middle of a parking lot. A few blocks on they came to the same scabby, one-story town hall and across the square, the razed remains of the old courthouse, which had burned in 1994 and had simply been flattened and cemented over, until someone figured out what to do with the property. Some Confederate hero stood covered in pigeon shit and graffiti in the center of the square, saluting the empty space where the courthouse had been; Bob couldn't remember the Reb's name, if he ever knew. Off the main drag, the same grubby collection of stores, general merchandising, men's and women's clothing stores, the life sucked out of them by Mr. Sam's Wal-Mart. A beauty parlor, a sporting goods store, a languishing tax accountant's office. And, to the left, the professional office building where two doctors, two dentists and a chiropractor had an office, as did one old lawyer.

"We'll start here," Bob said. "Good to see this old dog again. Hope he can still hunt."

"Is this the great Sam?" Russ asked.

"Yes, it is. They say he's the smartest man in the county. For close to thirty years Sam Vincent was the county prosecutor. In those days, they called him Electrifying Sam, because he sent twenty-three men to the chair. He knew my daddy. I think he was assistant state's attorney for Polk in 1955. We'll see what he has to say. You let me do the talking."

"He must be in his eighties!"

"He's eighty-six now, I think."

"Are you sure he's even *here*? He could be in a rest home or something."

"Oh, no. Sam hasn't missed a day since he came back from the war in 1945. He'll die here, happier than most."

They parked and got out. Bob bent and reached behind the pickup's seat and removed a cardboard box. Then he led Russ up a dark stairway between Wally's Men's Store and Milady's Beauty Salon; at its top, they found an antiseptic green hallway that reminded Russ of some kind of private-eye movie from the forties; it should have been in black and white. The lettering on the opaque glass in one of the doorways read SAM VINC NT—Atto ney a L w.

Bob knocked and entered.

There was an anteroom, but no secretary. Dust lay everywhere; on a table between two shabby chairs for waiting clients lay two *Time* magazines from the month of June 1981. Cher was on one of the covers.

"Who the hell is that?" a voice boomed out of the murk of the inner office.

"Sam, it's Bob Lee Swagger."

"Who the hell are you?"

They stepped into the darkness and dank fumes and only gradually did the shape of the speaker emerge. When Russ got his eyes focused, he saw a man who looked as if he were built out of feed bags piled on a fence post. Everything about him signaled the collapse of the ancient; the lines in his baggy face ran downward, pulled inexorably by gravity, and his old gray suit had lost all shape and shine. His teeth were yellowed and his eyes lost behind Coke-bottle lenses. He was crusty and unkempt, his rancid old fingers blackened from long years of loading and unloading both pipes and guns. A yellowed deer's head hung above him, and next to it some kind of star on a ribbon and a couple of diplomas so dusty Russ couldn't read the school names.

He squinted narrowly.

"Who the hell are you, mister? What business you got here?"

"Sam. It's *Bob*. Bob Lee Swagger. Earl's boy."

"Earl. No, Earl ain't here. Been dead for forty years. Some white-trash peckerwoods killed him, worst damn day this county's ever seen. No, Earl ain't here."

"Jesus," whispered Russ, "he's lost it."

"Sonny," said Sam, "I ain't lost a thing I can't find soon enough to whip your scrawny ass. Go on, get out of here. *Get out of here!*"

Bob just looked at him.

"Sam, I—"

"Get out of here! Who the hell do you think you are, Bob Lee Swagger?"

"Sam, I *am* Bob Lee Swagger."

The old man narrowed his eyes again and scrutinized Bob up and down.

"By God," he finally said. "Bob Lee Swagger. *Bob,* goddamn, son, it's great to see you."

He came around the desk and gave Bob a mighty hug, his face lit and animated with genuine delight.

"So there you are, big as life. You on vacation, son? You bring that wife of yours? And that little baby gal?"

It was a little awkward, the sudden return to clarity of the old man. But Bob pretended he hadn't noticed, while Russ just looked at his feet.

"She ain't so little anymore, Sam," Bob said. "Nicki's big as they come. No, I left 'em home. This is sort of a business trip."

"Who the hell is this?" demanded Sam, looking over at Russ. "You pick up a long-lost son?"

"He ain't my son," Bob said, "he's someone else's."

"My name's Russ Pewtie," said Russ, putting out a hand, which the old buzzard seized like carrion and crushed. Christ, he had a grip for a geezer!

Bob said, "Here's the business part: this young man is a journalist."

"Oh, Lord," said Sam. "The last time anybody wrote about you I sued 'em for you and we made thirty-five thousand."

"He says he isn't going to write about me."

"If you don't have that on paper, you better get it there fast, so that when his book is published we can take him to the woodshed."

"It's not about Mr. Swagger," said Russ. "It's about his father. It's about July 23, 1955."

"Oh, Christ," said Sam. "That was the longest goddamn day I ever lived through, and I include June 6, 1944, in that reckoning."

"It was a terrible day," said Russ. Leaving out the personal connection, he tried to explain his book but Bob had heard it and Sam appeared not to care much.

"So anyway," he concluded, aware he had not impressed anyone and getting a headache from the plummy odor of the tobacco, "that's why we're here."

"Well, goddamn," said Sam, exhaling a burst of smoke that billowed and furled in the room. "Probably a day doesn't go by I don't wonder why all that had to happen. Lots of good people all messed up. Your own mother's decline begun that day, I believe."

"I believe it did also," said Bob.

"And poor Edie White. Edie White *Pye.* I always fergit she married that piece of trash. Her decline begun then, too. Nine months later she gives birth and in a year she is dead. Whatever happened to Jimmy Pye's son, I wonder."

"He continued in his father's footsteps," Russ said. "They were two of a kind."

"That I don't doubt. So what is it you want from me?"

"Well, sir," Russ said, "I hope I can re-create what happened that day in a sort of dramatic narrative. But as you know there was a fire in 1994, when the old courthouse burned. That's where all the records were kept."

"I don't have a thing, I don't believe. Maybe a scrap or two."

"Well, did the papers have it right?" Russ asked, fiddling with a small tape recorder. Sam eyed the little machine warily.

"Bob, this is under your say-so? You're letting this boy ask questions because you want the answers too?"

"He says it could be an important book."

"Well, I've read enough books not to give a hunk of spit and a quart of whittler's shavings for any of 'em. But go ahead, young fellow. You ask 'em and if I don't fall asleep, I'll answer 'em."

"Thank you," Russ said. "I wanted to know, did the newspapers have it right? Their accounts?"

"Wasn't much to get wrong," said Sam. "In my business, you get to a lot of crime scenes. Oh, I've seen death in bathrooms and kitchens and basements and in swimming pools and outhouses, even, and sometimes there's a mystery to it, but most often not. Mysteries are for books. In life, you look at the bodies and the cartridge cases and the blood trails, or you look at the knife and the spatter pattern and the fingerprints, and they won't lie. They'll tell you all you need to know, or at least the whodunit part. In this case it was pretty open-and-shut. Whydunit, why it happened? That no one ever can truly know."

"Is there some account somewhere of the movements of the day? I mean, how and when Jim and Bub got down here, how Earl ran into them in that cornfield?"

"No sir. As I say, the event explained itself. No other information was really important."

"Was there any kind of legal resolution?"

"In the case of unlawful homicides in which there are no survivors, the state of Arkansas deeds all power to the Coroner's Office to hold an inquest. I represented the state and all agreed with the finding: the death of Earl Swagger was murder in the first degree, the deaths of Jimmy Pye and Bub Pye were justifiable homicide by a sworn law enforcement officer in the course of his legal duties. So it went into the books."

"Is that document worth chasing down?"

"For your purposes, probably not, though I bet I have a copy of it at home. It contained a diagram of the bodies' locations, a list of the recovered exhibits, testimony of the first officers on the scene, that's all. But I'll find it for you."

"That would be very helpful. As I break this down, I'd like to try and acquire material in four other areas," Russ said, consulting his notes and trying to sound important. "Witnesses. Maybe *talk* to the first people on scene. Then relatives of all concerned, that is, Jimmy and Bub. Next is secondary accounts. News media coverage, but maybe there were other accounts in true-crime magazines. Of course we ought to walk the site too, don't you think, Mr. Swagger?"

"Hah," said Sam. "Walk the site! I believe the famous Harry Etheridge Memorial Porkway buried it under a ton or so of concrete in memory to the greatest man Polk County ever produced. Son, you're looking for a past that ain't hardly there no more. There's no Pyes left in Polk County. I heard that Jimmy's father, Lannie, had a brother in Oklahoma."

"Anadarko," said Russ. "He was murdered in 1970, by parties unknown."

"Miss Connie Longacre knew Edie the best. But she left town after Edie died and the child went to some Pye kin. She tried to get that baby herself, but they said she was too old. Nineteen fifty-six, I think."

"Was there an autopsy?" Bob asked.

"There was," said Sam. "State law in the case of unlawful deaths. Paperwork all gone, however, in that courthouse fire."

Bob nodded, chewing that one over.

"A long and terrible day," said Sam. "It has always seemed to me a tragedy of the Republic that it can no longer produce men the caliber of Earl Swagger. I've said this to you many a time, Bob Lee. He was a quietly great man."

"He did his duty," said Bob, "more than some."

"Fortunately, Polk County has never had such a day since. Four dead. It marked the community for many years that followed. In some places, the pain even yet hasn't—"

"Excuse me," said Russ. "You mean three dead. Or are you counting the victims in Fort Smith? Then it would be *seven* dead. Just a little—"

"Young man, where did you go to college?"

"Ah, Princeton, sir."

"Did you graduate?"

"Er, no. I, uh, left after two years. But I may return."

"Well, no matter. Anyhows, Princeton? Well, if you want to climb up and blow the dust off that picture frame"—he gestured to the wall—"you'd see old Sam Vincent, the country rube lawyer from Hicksville, Arkansas, *he* went to Princeton University too! And if you blow the dust off the *other* frame, you'd see he went to Yale Law School. And though he's old, he's not as dim as you seem to think, at least on good days. And if he *says* four, he goddamn-your-soul *means* four."

Russ was stilled.

"I'm sorry," he finally said. "I meant no disrespect. But who was the fourth one?"

"Earl's last case. A poor girl named Shirelle Parker. A Nigra child, fifteen years old. She was raped and beaten to death out in the Ouachitas, and it was Earl who found her that very morning and made the initial reports. I felt it was his legacy and I pursued it with a special attention to duty. Fortunately, it was open-and-shut too. In that one, there was some justice."

"I think I remember," said Bob. "Some Negro boy. Wasn't he—"

"He was indeed electrocuted. I watched him die up at the state penitentiary at Tucker in 1957. Reggie Gerard Fuller, it was a terrible tragedy."

"You going to put that in your book?" Bob asked.

"I don't know . . . it is very strange, isn't it?"

"Earl spent the morning out there. Possibly he was still thinking of that case when he ran into Jimmy and Bub and that's how they got a jump on him."

"It was open-and-shut?"

"Like a door. The poor girl had ripped his monogrammed shirt pocket as he had his evil fun with her. We checked among the colored folk for the proper initials, and when we found one that matched, we raided. I'm happy to say that even in those benighted days, I arranged for the proper warrants to be issued. Here in Polk County, we run it by the goddamned rules. We found the shirt stuffed under his bed, the pocket missing. It was smeared with her blood, by type. She was AB positive, he was A positive. The boy made a mistake, he got carried away, he couldn't stop himself. She died, he died, both families devastated. I don't hold with the theory Nigras can't feel pain as white people do. The Parkers and the Fullers felt plenty of pain, as much as I've ever seen."

Russ shook his head, which now profoundly ached. He wanted to get away: this was like something out of Faulkner or Penn Warren, blasphemed southern ground, soaked in blood a generation old, white trash and black, white innocence and black, all commingled in a very small area on the same day.

"Sam, we've tired you. I may have some things I want you to do. You'll take my money, I suppose," Bob was saying.

"Of course I will," said Sam.

"Here's a box," he said, handing over the cardboard container. "You have an office safe, I guess?"

"I'm so old I may have forgotten the combination."

"Well, can you keep this stuff here? It's my father's effects. For some reason, I thought it might come in handy. I don't want to be carrying it about."

Sam took the package and they all rose.

"Tomorrow," Bob said, "I think we may go see where it happened. Sam, could you come? You were there?"

"Oh, I suppose."

"In the meantime, you'll look for that document and any others?"

"I will."

"This afternoon I think we'll go to the library, see what the old papers said."

"Fair enough," said Russ.

Sam shook Bob's hand and ignored Russ, leaving the younger man to face the fact that nobody gave a damn. He thought he could live with it.

The two went out, down the dark stairs, and stepped out into bright daylight.

"He seemed a little daffy there at the beginning," said Russ. "I hope he's up to this thing. What did he call them? *Nigras? Colored folk?* God, what Klan klavern did he come from?"

"That old man is as tough as they come. Not only did he keep my bacon out of the fire a few years back, he was the first prosecutor in Arkansas to try a white man for killing a black man back in 1962, when it wasn't the easiest thing in the world. He may say 'Nigra' where you say 'African American' to show everybody how wonderful you are, but he risked his goddamned life. They shot up his house, scared his kids and voted him out of office. But he stuck to it, because he knew it was right. So don't you go disrespecting him. He's solid as brass."

"Okay," said Russ. "If you say so."

Then they saw a big deputy sheriff looking into Bob's cab window.

"What's *this* all about?" Russ said.

"Oh, just a small-town cop who noticed an out-of-state plate." He walked over to the cop.

"Howdy there," he said.

The cop turned, flashing pale eyes on Bob; then those same eyes hungered over to Russ and ate him up. He was a lanky, tan man, with a thick mat of hair that was maybe a bit too fussed over, hipless and lean and long-faced, with a Glock at a sporty angle on his belt. He looked mean as a horse whip.

"This your truck, son?" asked the cop.

"It is, uh, Deputy Peck," Bob replied, reading the name off the name tag. "Is there some kind of problem?"

"Well, sir, just checking up is all. We got a pretty nice little town here and I like to keep my eyes open."

"I grew up in this town," said Bob. "My daddy's buried in this town."

"Bob Lee Swagger," said Peck. "Goddamn, yes."

"That's right."

"I remember—"

"Yes, all that's finished now. You want to run my tag and name you go ahead. I come up clean, you'll see. That was all a big mistake."

"You back on vacation, Mr. Swagger?"

"Oh, you might say. Got a young friend here with me. It's just a sort of a sentimental trip. Looking at my old haunts and the places I went with my father."

"Well, sir, you got any trouble or need any help, you come see me. Duane Peck's the name."

"I'll remember that, Deputy Peck."

Peck drew back, let them pass, but Russ had an odd feeling of being sized up, read up one side and down the other. He didn't like it.

"Did that guy seem a little strange?" he asked. "I've been around cops all my life and that guy couldn't keep his eyes off us."

"You think so?" said Bob. "Seemed like a pretty nice feller to me."

Twelve

I T WAS OPENING NIGHT. A road company *Cats,* fresh
from Little Rock and due in Tulsa in a week, had booked three
days in Fort Smith, five performances only. Good seating was
available on subsequent nights, but not tonight. It was SRO and
the Civic Center seethed with the town's most raffish and self-
assured men—the Rich Boys Club—and their families, the manu-
facturing, poultry and corn elite of western Arkansas and eastern
Oklahoma.

Red Bama sat with his slim beautiful second wife, Miss Arkansas Runner-up, 1986, his two new children and Nick, the youngest
of his children from his first marriage. He waved, chatted, took
homage calls and genuflections from others as the excitement built
and curtain time approached. Then he saw his first wife, still
beautiful but not so young and not so slim anymore, sitting with
his only daughter on the other aisle.

"Honey," he said to Beth, "there's Susie. I'm going by to say hi."

"Go on, baby," said Beth, smiling, showing her perfect teeth.
Before she was the Miss Arkansas Runner-up, she had been the
1985 Miss Sebastian County.

"You boys and girls, you don't give your mama no hard time,
now," he warned in his humorous trashy tyrant-father voice.

He rose, said hello to Jerry Flood, regional vice-president of
Hoffman-Prieur & Associates, passed between Nick Conway of

Harris-Ray Furniture, Bill Donnelly, who ran the Shelter Insurance Companies, and finally made it over to Susie.

"Hi, doll," he said, leaning to give her a kiss. She wore a diamond necklace that had cost him $52,000 in 1981. "Jeez, don't let Beth see that. She'll want the same damn thing. How are you, baby?" he added to his snooty oldest child Amy, who attended Smith and taught tennis at the club during the summer.

"Hi, babe," Susie said. "That gal of yours just gets prettier every time I see her."

"She is a peach, I agree, but she ain't half so much fun in the sack as you were!"

"Daddy, don't be so gross," said Amy, making a face of disapproval.

"Amy, when you going to come down to the truck depot? We could get you a nice Peterbilt 16 and give you the Macon run for Tyson's. You'd like them chickens shitting up the rig!"

"Daddy!" said Amy prissily.

"Red, you shouldn't tease the girl."

"I've spoiled her, like I've spoiled all my children, can't I have some fun teasing her? Honey, why don't you quit teaching that silly tennis and come down to the office. We'll find something *useful* for you to do."

"No thank you. You *overmanage*. That's why everybody hates you."

"They don't hate me. They love me. They only *think* they hate me. And they fear me, which I like a lot."

"Red!"

He turned from provoking the young woman he loved so much and returned to Susie.

"Well, anyway, I think, no, I *know* we're going to get Tyson's new regional headquarters, plus I have it on good authority that GM is thinking about Greenwood for its new Blazer plant. We'd get that job too."

"Honey, that's the best news. And everything else, it's going—"

"It's fine, sweetie. Oh, it's just—"

He felt something like a sting at his hip, jumped a tiny bit, then recognized it as his beeper's vibrator. But it wasn't the office beeper, it was the new one. It was the Blue Eye 800 number.

"Red?"

"Just got a message, no big deal," he said, taking the little cellular out of his pocket. "I'll call in a sec. Amy, honey, haven't you had that Rolex three whole weeks? It's gotten boring, hasn't it? Why don't you let Daddy buy you a new one?"

"Daddy, you suck."

Red laughed. Good-naturedly tormenting his children was one of his deepest delights. Amy knitted her fierce, bright little face up into something like a fist, and if it had been possible, she would have smacked him with it. A wave of deep and uncompromising love poured over and through him. The way a man feels about his favorite daughter who goes her own way, takes nothing and makes good on everything. The watch was presented to her not by Red at all but by Maryvale Prep, for graduating with the highest accum in its history.

The lights began to dim.

"Okay, got to get back to family number two," Red said cheerily to Susie.

"You'll bring Nick home tonight?"

"He can stay with us if you want."

"No, that's fine. He's got practice early. I know *you* won't get him there."

"We'll take him for ice cream after, and bring him by."

"Great, honey."

"See you," he said, as the overture came up, hot and pounding.

But Red didn't return directly. He walked back to the rear of the house, paying no attention as the curtain opened to tumultuous applause, revealing what looked like a back alley populated by sleek, sinuous feline shapes that one after another began to shimmer to life.

Red dialed his number and listened.

"It's Duane Peck here," the voice came, telling him what he already knew and impressing him with nothing. "Anyhows, uh, this kid is in town, and I got him nailed and I'll stay with him.

First stop, old Sam Vincent. Is that a problem? Should I take care of that? Let me know. Also, uh—"

Someone was singing.

> And we all say: OH!
> Well I never!
> Was there ever
> A Cat so clever
> As Magical Mr. Mistoffelees!

"—ah, he ain't alone. Tall guy, lanky, looks you up and down real fine. I thought it might be. Yeah, it was. The son. The guy in Vietnam, called him Bob the Nailer. He's along with the kid. Don't know why, but he's here too. Bob Lee Swagger, Earl's boy."

No emotion showed on Red's face. He just cleared the call and, standing there in the back of the house, dialed another one.

"Billy, Red here."

"Hey, Red, what's on your—"

"Listen here, got me a situation. You put me together a team. Very tough guys, experienced, qualified on full automatic, professionals. I don't want to use my boys. Got that?"

"Red, what—"

"Shut up, Billy, and listen. I want no less than ten. I want good weapons, good team discipline. I want 'em all to have felony records, preferably as drug enforcers. Get 'em from Dallas, get 'em from New Orleans, get 'em from Miami. Out-of-town boys. I want them to have records, in case we lose a few and bodies start showing up in Polk County, the newspapers will start calling it a drug war."

"How much you want to go, Red?"

"I want the best. The best costs. You get 'em here, get 'em here fast. Good boys. Shooters. I want the best shooters. I want an A-team."

"We'll get working on it right now."

"Good work, Billy," Red said, then returned to his seat for the rest of *Cats*.

Thirteen

I T TOOK THREE HOURS, not at all helped by the fact that
Sam's old eyes weren't as good as they once were and that he
had to stop twice to go to the bathroom. Then he got irritable and
hungry and they bought him some pancakes at the Waldron exit
Denny's. But there were no more episodes of strangeness, where
Sam forgot who they were or who he was.

Then, once, Sam said, "Here, here, I think it's here!"

"It *can't* be here," Russ, the navigator, exclaimed. "We just
passed 23 and the papers say it was *south* of 23. We're heading
north toward Fort Smith. We must have gone too far!"

"Goddammit, boy, don't you tell me where the hell we are. I
traveled all this on horseback in the thirties, I hunted it for fifty
years and I've been over it a thousand times. Tell him, Bob."

"It's the new road," said Bob. "I think it's throwing us off."

For old 71, with its curves and switchbacks, slalomed between
the massive cement buttresses that supported the straight bright
line that was the Boss Harry Etheridge Memorial Parkway. Sometimes the huge new road would be to the left of them, sometimes
to the right of them and sometimes above their heads. There
would be times too when it disappeared altogether, behind a hill or
a screen of uncut forest. But it was always there, somehow mock-
ing them, a symbol of how futile their quest seemed: to recover a
past that had been destroyed by the coming of the future.

But at last the two points of their peculiar compass jibed to form some sort of imaginary azimuth to where they wanted to go: Sam's memory and Bob's to the corrected version of the *Arkansas Gazette* of July 24, 1955.

They had just passed an odd little place set by the side of the road called Betty's Formal Wear, in a ramshackle trailer a few miles out of a town called Boles. It was Sam who shouted, "Here, goddammit, here!"

Bob pulled off the side of the road. A little ways ahead, an Exxon station raised its corporate symbol a hundred feet in the air so it could be seen from the parkway, the inescapable parkway, off to the right. The roadway was thirty feet up, a mighty marvel of engineering, and even where they were, they could hear the throb as the occasional car or truck whizzed along it.

"Aren't we looking for *corn?*" Russ asked. "I thought it was a cornfield."

"Ain't been no corn or cotton in these parts for two decades," said Sam. "All the land's in pasturage for cattle or hay fields. No cultivation no more."

They were parked next to a GTE relay station, a concrete box behind a Cyclone fence.

"Back there?" said Bob.

"Yeah."

Someone had planted a screen of pines in the sixties and they now towered about thirty feet tall, as if to block the ground from public scrutiny. Bob could see the flat, grassy field through the pines, however, shot with rogue sprigs of green as small bushes fought against the matted grass for survival.

"Yeah," said Sam. "Corn, it was all corn then. Couldn't hardly see nothing. I was the fifth or sixth car out here, but it was getting busier by the moment."

Bob closed his eyes for just a second, and he imagined the site after dark, lit by the revolving police bubbles, punctuated by the crackle of radios, the urgent but futile shouts of the medics. It reminded him somehow of Vietnam, first tour, 1965–66, he was a young buck sergeant, 3rd Marine Division, the aftermath of some forgotten nighttime firefight, all the people running and screaming, the flares wobbling and flickering in the night the way the flashing lights would have ten years earlier, in 1955.

"You okay, Bob?"

"He's fine," snapped Sam. "His father died here. What do you think he's going to do, jump for joy?"

Russ seemed stricken.

"I only meant—"

"Forget it, Junior. It don't mean a thing."

Sam opened a flask, took a tot.

"Believe a man named O'Brian owned it, but he tenanted it out to some white-trash families. Over there, where that goddamned highway is, that was the crest of the ridge, woods-covered then. Took a deer there in 1949, and one of the white hags without teeth came out and gave me hell, shooting so close to her cabin where her damn kids were playing."

"She was right," said Bob.

"Yes, goddammit, I believe she was. Buck fever. I had to shoot. Silliest damned thing I ever did—that is, until today."

"Where were they?"

"The cars were back through there," Sam said, lifting a blackened claw and pointing. "I believe you can see traces of the little road that ran between the cornfields. About a hundred yards in. Your daddy's cruiser was parked slantwise of the road, Jimmy's twenty yards farther down."

"The bodies were where they were in the diagrams?" said Russ.

"Yes, they were. Believe I answered that one yesterday. No decent lawyer ever asks the same question twice. He *remembers* the question he asked and the answer."

"I couldn't remember."

"All right," said Bob. "I want to go back there, look at the land."

"Believe I'll rusticate here," Sam said. "You boys go on ahead. Sing out if you get lost or need me to haul you out of the mud. And watch out for snakes. Mac Jimson killed a big rattler in the road the night your daddy was killed. Scared the hell out of us. Shot it in the head. Had to. Just crossing the road. Never saw no snake act like that before."

"A rattler?" said Bob.

"Big goddamn timber rattler. Strangest goddamned thing. All the cops around, the rattler skedaddles across the road. Mac had to shoot it."

"I hate snakes," said Russ.

"Hell, boy," said Sam, "it's just a lizard without legs."

Bob and Russ left the old man, cut through the trees and headed across the overgrown, weedy ground. It was field now, no corn anywhere, junk land that crouched in the shadow of the highway. Bob made it to the trace of road, not road so much but simply an opening where the vegetation hadn't grown so high because it had gotten a late start. The trace went back toward the big highway, then began to curve around. Bob got about a hundred yards back.

"Here?" asked Russ.

Bob took a deep breath.

"I do believe. Ask the old man."

"Sam! Here?" screamed Russ.

Bob watched the old man, who studied them, then nodded up and down.

"Here," said Russ.

Bob had never been here before. So odd. He stayed in Blue Eye eight more years and he'd never come out here and stood at the spot. Then he went away to the Marines, and then came back and went up in the mountains, and never once, either before or after, had he been to this spot.

Never laid any flowers or felt the power of the blasphemed earth. Why? Too much pain? Possibly. Too close to going under with a poor drunken mother who just could not hang on and the terrible, terrible sense of it all having been taken from them. The bitterness. It could kill you. You had to let the bitterness go or it would kill you. He knew he'd been by, though. As he remembered, Sam had driven him up U.S. 71 to Fort Smith to join the United States Marine Corps on June 12, 1964, the day after he graduated from high school.

"Here," said Russ, consulting the diagram from the newspaper. "Here's where Jimmy ended up parking. Now"—he walked past Bob, hunched in concentration, nose buried in the clipping before him—"here is where your father's car was. And your dad was found in the driver's side, sitting sideways, fallen slightly to his right and hung up on the steering wheel, his feet on the ground, the radio mike in his hand."

"Bled out?" said Bob.

"What?"

"That was the mechanism, right? That's what killed him. Blood loss. Not shock to his nervous system or a bullet in a major blood-bearing organ?"

"Ah, that's what it says here. I don't—"

"Russ, how does a bullet kill? Do you know?"

Russ didn't. A bullet just, uh, *killed*. It, uh—

"A bullet can kill you three ways. It can destroy your central nervous system. That's the brain shot, into the deep cerebellum, two inches back from the eyes and between the ears. Instant rag doll. Clinical death in less than a tenth of a second. Or it can destroy your circulatory and arterial system, depressurize you. The heart shot or something in the aorta. That's fifteen, twenty seconds till clinical death, your good central body shot. Or, finally, it can hit a major blood-bearing organ and you essentially bleed to death internally. A big stretch cavity, lots of tissue destruction, lots of blood, but not instant death. Say, three, four, sometimes ten to twenty minutes without help. Which of those?"

"I don't know," said Russ. "It doesn't really say. It just said he bled to death. The latter, I guess."

"It would be nice to know the mechanism. It would tell us a lot. You write that down in your book under things to find out."

"Where would we go to find that?"

Bob ignored him, just standing there, looking about. He tried to read the land, or what little of it was left. This was a hunter's gift, a sniper's gift: to look at the folds and drops and rises in a piece of earth and derive meanings from them, understand in some instinctual way how they worked.

The first thing: why here?

Standing there exactly where his father had stood, he realized that in high corn, this spot was invisible from the road. Moreover, it took just enough delicate driving to steer back here without losing control and careening back into the corn; there'd been nothing in the papers about a high-speed chase. There couldn't have been a chase! His daddy's car would have been behind theirs, not in front of it, unless Bub and Jimmy were chasing *him*!

He looked about, trying to imagine it in high corn.

"You run back to Sam," he said to Russ. "You ask him about the moon. Was there a moon? We can check, but I don't think so, not from my memory anyhow. Ask him about the temperature, the wind, that sort of thing. Humidity. Was it heavy?"

The boy looked at him vacantly. Then puzzlement stole across the delicate features.

"What is—"

"I will tell you later. Just do it."

"Okay, okay," said Russ, turning away on the errand.

A wind rose. The sun was bright. Now and then a car rushed along the parkway, whose buttresses were about a hundred yards farther back. Bob turned in each direction, trying to feel the land. To the south, there was an incline. His father would have come that way. To the north, at least now, the bright roofs of the highway service buildings, the motel and the gas station, and the restaurants. But in those days, nothing but wild forests; the town proper of Waldron still lay eleven miles ahead. To the west, more incline, as the other side of 71, the road fell away toward the prairies of Oklahoma. He turned back to face the east, to face the parkway. But it hadn't been a parkway then. It had been a ridge, obliterated in the building of the road. How high? How far? The road was a hundred yards off, but possibly the road builders hadn't placed the road at the center of the ridge; maybe it was at its highest even farther out.

"He says no moon," said Russ, breathing heavily from the jog. "He says stars, but no moon. No humidity. About seventy-five degrees, maybe eighty. A little breeze, nothing much."

Bob nodded. "All right, now ask him two more questions. The first is, where were all the tenant farmers' shacks? Were they right here, did this road run back to them? Or were they farther along? Where did this road go then? And second: ask him which direction my father's car was parked. He said it was aslant the road and the body was behind the steering wheel. I want to know on which side of the road that was, which direction it faced."

Russ took a deep breath, then turned and ran back to the old man.

Again alone, Bob turned to face the highway that towered above him. He walked back through the weeds and came at last to stand next to one of the mighty concrete pylons upon which the road rested. It was cool here in the shade, though the road rumbled. Someone had painted POLK COUNTY CLASS OF '95, and beer cans and broken bottles lay about on the gravel. Beyond the parkway Bob could see the land fall away into forest and farm over a long slope of perhaps two miles until a little white farm road snaked through the trees.

He looked back and saw that the action had played out halfway down just the subtlest slope. He saw Russ standing big as day where he had left him. He walked on back.

"Okay," Russ said, breathing hard, trying to keep it straight. "The road evidently was an old logging trail and it ran back and up and over the ridge. This area used to be logged back in the twenties. The 'croppers lived another mile or so down U.S. 71 away from Waldron, toward Boles. *That's* where Sam shot his deer and the lady yelled at him."

"It wasn't here?"

"No sir."

"Okay. And my daddy: he was on the left side of the road. Facing east. Facing the ridge, right? Sitting sideways in his seat, with his feet on the ground, not as if he were about to drive away, is that right?"

Another look of befuddlement came across Russ's face.

"How did you know that? It wasn't in any of the newspaper accounts. Sam says the car was parked on the left side of the road and the door was open and your daddy—"

Bob nodded.

"What's going on?"

"Oh, just seeing the place gets me to thinking. I got a question or two."

"What questions?"

"How'd they get here? Through the biggest manhunt in Arkansas?"

"That was *my* question! Remember, *I* asked that question. When we were driving in the day before—"

"But when you asked it, it was a stupid question. It was stupid because we had no idea of the layout of the roads that led to the site and the kind of terrain it was. It could have been there were fifty obscure country roads, far too many for the cops to cover, all leading here. But there weren't. There's only Route 71, a major highway, well covered, and this little logging track that don't go nowhere. So now it's a smart question."

Russ didn't get the distinction, but he didn't say anything.

"Then," Bob said, "how come here? You tell me?"

"Ah—" Russ had no answer. "This is where he ran into them. He chased them, they turned off the road, he got by them and blocked them, uh—"

"You think that little road is wide enough for him to get by them? It's night, remember, and if he slides off the road into the soft soil of the cornfield, he's fucked. No, he was waiting for them. He was already here. And it's off the road, out of public view, so they wouldn't get surprised by someone coming along. How'd he get jumped by them? Hell, he was a salty old boy. He'd made two thousand arrests, he'd fought in three major island invasions, he was nobody's fool. Yet they open up and hit him bad, first few shots? How?"

"Ah—" Russ trailed off.

"Maybe he was the mastermind of the job. Maybe he had come to get his payoff and split the take."

Russ looked at him in horror. "Your father was a *hero,*" he said.

"That's what it said in the papers, isn't it? He was just a goddamn man, don't think of him as a hero, because then you don't think straight about it. No, he wasn't in on it. He didn't trust 'em. But he knew they was coming. Reason he swung around to park in the direction he did was so he could use his searchlight, which was mounted outside the driver's-side window. He had to cover 'em. Hell, they were *surrendering* to him, that's what it was. How'd he know where to go, where they'd reach him? Why would he believe them? What was it really about?"

Russ had no answers.

"Come on," said Bob. "There's only one man who can tell us."

"Sam?"

"No," said Bob, leading the way, "Daddy himself. He wants to talk. It's just time we listened."

They walked back and found Sam sitting on the open tailgate of the truck, his pipe lit up and blazing away. It smelled like a forest fire.

"You boys didn't get lost? That's a surprise."

"Sam," said Bob, "let me ask you something. Suppose I wanted to exhume my father's body? What sort of paperwork is involved?"

Sam's shrewd old features narrowed under his slouch hat and grew pointed.

"Now, what the hell you want to do that for, boy?"

"I just want to know what happened. The diagrams may lie and the newspapers may lie and all the official documents may be gone, but the body is going to tell the truth."

"Bob, it was forty years ago."

"I know there's not much left. That's why we need a good man. Now, what's it going to take?"

"Well, I file a Motion of Exhumation with the county clerk and the Coroner's Office and you have to find a good forensic pathologist. Get a doctor, not an undertaker like they got in too many counties down here."

"Someone from Little Rock?"

"There's someone in the medical school up at Fayetteville who's well thought of. I could call him. Then I suppose you have to make an arrangement with a mortuary to clear out a place for him to work. Bob, you want to go to all that trouble? It was open-and-shut."

"It's the only way my daddy can talk to me. I think I ought to listen to what he has to say. I have to find out what happened that night."

❑ ❑ ❑ ❑

Sam slept on the way back and when they pulled up to the old house where he'd lived and raised his kids and married his daughters and his sons and buried his wife, they waited for the stillness in the car to wake him. But it didn't.

"Sam?" Bob finally said softly. It was twilight, with the sun lost behind Rich Mountain, which towered over Blue Eye from the west.

Sam made some wet, gurgling sound in his sinuses, stirred a bit but then seemed to settle back.

"Sam," said Bob a little louder, and Sam's eyes shot open.

He looked at each of them.

"Wha—where—what is—"

"Sam, Sam," said Bob, grabbing the old man's shoulder. "Sam, you been sleeping."

But Sam's eyes lit in panic and his body froze in tension.

"Who are you?" he begged fearfully. "What do you want? Don't hurt me!"

"Sam, Sam," said Bob calmly, "it's *Bob,* Bob Lee Swagger, Earl's boy. You just done forgot where you was."

The old man was shaking desperately.

"You're okay, Mr. Vincent," said Russ. "Really, it's fine, you've forgotten."

But Sam's eyes flashed between them, wide with horror.

"It's okay," said Bob. "It's okay."

Fourteen

EARL EASED into the cornfield road. The dirt felt soft, and he progressed slowly. Around him, illuminated in the shafts of his headlights, the stalks of corn towered, eight feet tall and quivering ever so gently in the breeze.

Off the shoulder of the road, in the field, the earth looked loose and he was afraid if he got off into it, he could get stuck. Wouldn't *that* be a goddamn mess!

The road curved a little to the left, until eventually it paralleled what, from the darker texture of the night, had to be the rise of Ferguson's ridge. He'd taken a deer on the ridge, though several miles away. That same day, some sharecropper woman had given Sam a tongue-lashing for shooting so close to her children. Served him right, though to hear him tell it, Sam'd never made a mistake in his life.

When he was about a hundred yards in, that is, so far in he couldn't see the U.S. 71 for the thickness of the corn, he halted the car and tried to think. He wanted to be able to put the light on Jimmy and Bub. That meant he had to turn the car. He got out, looked around, kicked at the shoulder and the dirt off the shoulder to tell if it would support the weight of the Ford. It appeared that it would. He climbed back in and painstakingly ground the wheel toward the left, cranking the car in a tight turn until the front wheels were just about off; then he spun the wheel in the opposite direction, backing slowly. This put him on the left side of the road, pointed outward. He turned off the engine, then leaned out the window and tried his spotlight. It threw a harsh circle of white light down the road that collected in a vivid oval a hundred feet out. With one hand he pivoted it, tracked it up and down like an antiaircraft searchlight, then turned it off.

He looked at the radium dial of his Bulova. Nine-fifty. Ten minutes to go.

Why am I so nervous? he wondered.

He'd been nervous in the war, or at least on the night before an amphibious operation.

Reason to get nervous. Amphibious operations were tricky and dangerous. At Tarawa, the Traks had run aground on coral a thousand yards out. It was a long walk in through the surf laden with equipment, with the Japs shooting the whole way. You get through that, you could get through anything.

But just some little goddamn nervous thing was flicking at him. He felt cursed. He'd made a big mistake today. He hadn't meant to but he'd sure as hell wanted to and so he did it and now what? So he'd clean it up tomorrow. He'd clean up the mess he'd made, he'd be a man. These things could be handled and to hell with everything else. He knew he'd do it. He just didn't know what it was to do.

It was all running together on him, the whole goddamned, messed-up day. *Shirelle Parker Jed Posey Pop Dwyer Jimmy Pye Lem Tolliver Bub Pye Miss Connie Longacre Sam Vincent Buddy Till Edie White Pye Edie Edie Edie his son Bob Lee Shirelle dead missing her underpants her eyes eternally open the barking dog Mollie "He's got it, she's here."*

Forget about it, he told himself. *Concentrate on the job.*

He got out of the car when he could feel his limbs begin to tingle with lack of circulation. He stood, breathing in the country air. It was so incredibly quiet. But no, it wasn't: just as a man in war learns the darkness isn't really darkness, but a texture of different shades that can be learned and read, so quiet wasn't really quiet. He heard the snapping of the cornstalks as they rustled in the hiss of the breeze. He heard crickets off on some spring by the ridge, and bullfrogs too, low and mournful. He thought he heard a man cough far away. No, couldn't be. Nobody out here. Some goddamn frog thing or something, or maybe some freak of nature carrying a real cough miles and miles. It happened all the time.

Up above stars, not like the Pacific, but still towers and piles of stars, almost a smoke of stars. Constellations that he had showed his son, trying to remember the stories that went with them and feeling he wasn't doing a very good job. There were no city lights out here to bleach them out; the closest town was Boles, a good five miles back, and in Boles they closed up for the night around nine.

"What's that one, Daddy?" someone asked.

No, no one asked. It was his son's voice, but it was only in his mind; he remembered the question from a hunting trip last fall.

"That's the North Star, Bob Lee. Always find your way home with that one. Secret to night navigation."

"What's night 'gation?"

Damn kid had so many questions!

Concentrate on the job, he told himself.

He checked his watch. It was ten o'clock. Nothing.

THE MONKEY TOOK

ONE LOOK AT JIM

AND THREW THE PEANUTS

BACK AT HIM

BURMA SHAVE

Bub drove. He couldn't hardly see nothing. Just corn on both sides of the road, and now and then a rhyming set of Burma Shave signs or on a barn a MAIL POUCH or a COPENHAGEN or even a JESUS SAVES. He felt lost. It was so dark. He was very scared and also very tired. He was hungry. Hadn't eaten since the burger.

Jimmy looked out of the car, peering intently.

"There it is," he said. "Right up there, on the left, you see it?"

"Yes sir," said Bub. He saw a gap in the corn and what looked to be a road leading back. Far off was a ridge.

"You ain't forgot what you're going to say?" he asked. It was very important that Jimmy tell him again. It stopped him from getting so scared.

"No sir, I give you my word," said Jimmy. "This one was my deal the whole way. It was all my fault. Old Bub had nothing to do with it. We'll git you back to your mama in no time. You might even get to go home tonight."

"Do you think? do you think? I miss my mama."

An image of his mama came before Bub. She was an immense woman, usually harried, sometimes quite mean, but he loved her just the same. He remembered a time when he and some other boys had set fire to a cat after dousing it with kerosene and it had run just a little bit, screaming horribly, before it collapsed into a smoking heap, and he had felt so bad, and his mama had pulled him into her arms and rocked and rocked him and in her abiding warmth and under the ministrations of her calm heart, he had fallen asleep. That was his favorite memory.

"You just do what Mr. Earl tells you," said Jimmy. "It's going to be all right."

Bub turned onto the dirt road. He paused, feeling the car slip a little into the soil.

"Go on," said Jimmy. "Just a bit farther. I'm afraid old Earl missed it, goddammit."

They edged ahead until they were swallowed by corn, the corn seemed to lean in from each side, like it was attacking them, and Bub had a brief spasm of fear.

"Jimmy?" he asked plaintively, feeling his voice rise just a bit.

"There, there," said Jimmy.

The headlights prowled ahead on the dirt road, and in time they came to the state police cruiser resting on the side of the road.

"Here we are," said Jimmy.

Earl watched as the car came slowly into view, swung around the curve, then pulled off to the side of the road fifty or so feet away. Whoever was driving switched off the engine. A little gray dust still floated in the air. The car, cooling, ticked and creaked a bit but neither of the two men inside moved.

For maybe thirty long seconds it was quiet. Then Earl switched on his spotlight, throwing a circle of illumination in the front seat of the automobile. He recognized Jimmy Pye, raising a hand to block out the harsh glare. Jimmy was blazing in the beam, his natural colors turned flame-white, his thick locks of hair golden.

"That's bright, Earl," he called.

Jimmy! Earl thought. Goddamn you, Jimmy, why'd you go and do this goddamned thing?

"All right now, Jimmy," Earl called out. "You move real easy."

"Yes sir," said Jimmy. "Can Bub call his mama? He's awful upset about his mama."

"We'll take care of that in a little bit. Now I want you to come out first, Jimmy, I want to see the gun held by the barrel in your left hand and I want to watch it tossed until it lands in the dirt. Then I want you, Bub, I want to see hands, I want to see the gun held in the left one by the barrel, I want to see it in the dirt. You got that? This is going to happen nice and easy."

"Yes sir, Mr. Earl," called Bub.

"Okay, let's do it."

"Hey, Earl, you sound like Joe Friday. This ain't *Dragnet*. Hell, Earl, it's only Jimmy Pye and his little cousin," said Jimmy. He unlatched his door, then, showing his hands, kneed the door open and stepped out. His hands were high and empty.

"I'm going to get the gun now, Earl," he called, and reached down with his left hand and removed a pistol from his belt. He threw it forward, where it landed in the dust, kicking up a little puff.

"Okay, Bub, you slide over, and out you come, the same way."

Bub scooted forward along the seat and pulled himself out. Where Jimmy's posture had been nonchalant, even arrogant, Bub was tight with tension. Absurdly, his arms flew straight up like a grade school boy aping an angel's flight. Earl could see his knees shaking.

"The gun, Bub. Did you forget the gun, Bub?"

"Oh-unh," came a little choke of despair and terror from the big boy, "it's still in the car. You want me to get it?"

"Turn around, so's I can see you're unarmed," said Earl.

Obligingly, the big youngster pivoted and Earl saw his belt was empty.

"Okay, Bub, you turn back around and set them hands against the roof of the car, next to Jimmy."

"Y-yes sir," came the plaintive cry, as Bub turned and leaned.

"Now, y'all stay like that real steady. I'm coming across, I don't want any sudden moves."

"Hurry up, Earl, the damn skeeters is eating me alive," called Jimmy.

The spotlight locked on the two boys, Earl reached down and unsnapped the flap over his Colt Trooper. Then he reached back and removed the pair of handcuffs from his belt case and another that he'd stuck into the belt.

He started to walk across.

"Damn!" said Jimmy, slapping suddenly at his neck where he'd just been stung. "Goddamn *bugs*!"

It happened so slowly yet so fast at the same time; Earl's eyes followed as Jimmy's hand seemed to go back to the car but at the same time, in a maneuver that made no sense at all, Jimmy was curling, pivoting, turning and he felt himself say "Jim—" when he saw the gun and he couldn't figure it out because the gun was on the ground, he'd seen it hit, and he saw the—

FLASH

—before he heard any noise and he felt the—

WHACK

before he heard the noise too, and then he heard the noise and saw the flash again and

WHACK

from so close, so very close, and the next thing he knew he was on his knees and somebody was running at him and he heard the noise again and it was Bub.

Bub ran at him and seemed to stop as a red spider crawled across his T-shirt front and his face was drawn and terribly tense with fear. But still he came crazily at Earl, like some kind of monster, his arms outstretched, his mouth working, his eyes wide like big white eggs, coming on as if to crush the life from Earl.

Earl fired. He couldn't even remember drawing.

Bub went to his knees.

FLASH.

Earl turned as Jimmy fired again, then again, both misses as he slipped back into the corn. Earl imagined a sly grin on Jimmy's face and more than anything to wipe that terrible grin away, he squeezed the trigger four more times, four booming blasts, the gun bucked in his hand, the four shots as fast as any that ever came out of his tommy gun, until the gun clicked dry.

What the hell is happening? Earl thought, not in words so much as in bright flashes, spangles, fragments of light and hot metal that danced through his mind.

Then he saw he was still in the light, still on the ground, and around him the cars towered and beyond the cars the corn towered. He slithered backwards, out of the light, waiting to be shot, but no shot came. He heard steps, the rush of corn being shoved roughly aside, the sigh of the breeze, no other sound.

He got behind the cover of his cruiser. Bub lay on his back, covered in blood.

"Mama!" Bub screamed. "Oh, *Mama,* hep me, please, oh Jesus, Lord, I don't want to die."

There was no sign of Jimmy.

Reload, he told himself, putting out the gun before him and reaching over with his off hand to unlatch the cylinder and reach for ammunition.

But he had no off hand. Or at least it didn't work.

He looked and saw he was covered with blood. An angry black pucker oozed black fluid just below his elbow, the blood coursing down to his fingers where it dripped off. He couldn't move the fingers. The arm was dead broken. His left side was covered in blood too, his uniform and trousers soaked in it.

Am I going to die? he wondered.

Well, if I am, goddammit, I better reload just the same.

With his good thumb, he managed to pull back the cylinder latch and shake the cylinder out. Turning the gun upward, he shook and shook until one at a time all six shells fell out. He wedged the gun between his knees and, again one by one, picked shells out of his cartridge loops and threaded them into the cylinder. Big .357 soft points. With a snap of the wrist, he flicked the cylinder shut.

The pain started. It howled in his arm. His side was numb and wet. He wanted to sleep or scream. He didn't want to go after Jimmy in the corn.

Gun loaded in his hand, he slipped the Colt into the holster and crawled into the car and picked the mike up.

He was way out in the country with no relay stations close by but the radio was a powerful low-band AM. Could he get through? He should be able to.

"Any cars, any cars, trooper down, ten-thirty-three, repeat, ten-thirty-three, any cars, please respond."

Dead air answered him.

Shit.

A sparkle caught his eye; he looked up to a blur of fractured glass in the windshield, where one of Jimmy's shots had flown and then beyond that his aerial, snapped in two by a bullet.

Goddamn.

Lucky little prick. That would cut the range way down. No backup.

He slid back out of the car, took a look around. Bub was still, though Earl could see he still breathed. Nothing could be done now. Earl certainly wasn't going out there in the light.

He figured Jimmy was somewhere close by, maybe circling, just getting closer. For one thing was dead clear: Jimmy was trying to kill him. That's what this goddamn thing was all about.

Jimmy was so hopped up he could hardly hold still. He knew he'd got him. He got him good, Earl was probably dead. He'd seen him fall, seen the blood all over him, and when Earl, normally a dead shot with any kind of gun, had fired at him, he'd missed by plenty.

Jimmy crouched in the corn, still as a sleeping cat, though he was breathing hard. From his low angle he couldn't see much through the stalks, which even now wavered and clicked in the low breeze. Somewhere far ahead was a blaze of light that told the location of the two cars. He was going to wait to catch his breath and then begin the slow crawl back. He knew he had to make sure. Then he was out, he was gone, he was done, a whole new world lay before him. He had done it!

Rocking round the clock till the broad daylight!

But abruptly the light vanished.

He contemplated the meaning in this. Had the light gone out on its own? Had Earl turned it out? Had people come and turned it out? No, it couldn't be people. There'd be cars, dogs, airplanes, maybe them helicopters, the whole goddamn shooting match.

It was goddamned Earl. Earl hunting him. Earl turning out the light so there wouldn't be any backlight to throw up a silhouette.

He knew he should just be quiet another few minutes. Earl had seen him go, so if Earl was coming after him, he'd know which side of the road, and he'd come low and fast, and he'd make noise.

He'll make noise, he thought.

He didn't doubt that Earl would try such a thing; the man was a bulldog of guts. But he was old, he was wounded, he probably lost a lot of blood.

Just stay still, Jimmy told himself.

So of course he yelled, "Earl! Earl, you coming for me? Goddamn Earl, I'm sorry. I thought you was fixing to kill me and be a big hero!"

There was no response.

Then he heard a yell.

"Goddammit, Jimmy, you are a fool and you done shot me good. I am a dying man. You come on and surrender now because ain't no way you're getting out. Help is on the way."

"Nobody's gettin' way the hell out here in time for this," Jimmy yelled, laughing, for he knew it was true, just as he knew Earl wasn't that bad hurt but was lying to set him up. Earl could be a tricky devil.

But that didn't really scare Jimmy. In fact, nothing scared Jimmy. His mind was ablaze with ideas of glory and fame, with adolescent notions of toughness and reputation, and he wanted to assert himself over the man who had loomed above him half his life like a dark cloud. He loved Earl. He also hated him. He wanted to save him. He wanted to kill him. Most of all he wanted to impress him.

He had just reloaded his clip from the pocketful of bullets and slammed it back into the .38 Super. His trick had worked. He threw a wrench and Earl thought it was a gun. Ha, Earl, fooled you!

He started to crawl toward Earl. He knew the man would be there soon and he'd get the jump and the first shot and he'd say, Hey, Earl, ain't I the newest thing, ain't I *cool?* and kill him.

Now the pain. The pain so bad it went up and down his arm looking for new places to hurt. The hand was numb. He was still bleeding. He'd seen somebody literally shredded by a shell blast on one of the islands—couldn't remember which one now—literally turned into a confetti of flesh and blood, and that's what his worthless arm looked like now.

Next, fatigue. So utterly tired. Why was he so tired? He wanted to sleep. Was he bleeding to death? Possibly. There just came an urge to lie down and sleep it off.

And finally, melancholy. Why oh why was this happening? What had gone wrong? Who made such a thing happen? Goddamn Jimmy Pye or what?

Sadness too for Bub, whom he now realized was not trying to kill him but was running to him in panic for protection. Bub stopped the bullet that might have killed Earl, and for his trouble, Earl shot him in the chest with a .357 Magnum soft point, blowing a hole in his heart. Bub was dead, sure enough, for no man can lie the way Bub had unless he was dead.

He felt the Trooper in his hand, his finger taut against the trigger. He yearned to fire but at what? He simply moved ahead, not crawling because crawling was too slow and hard with the broken arm, but walking sideways, crabwalking, down the side of the road, deeper and deeper into the corn toward the direction of Jimmy's last yell. It would come down to one shot, he felt. Jimmy might get him, but he knew if he didn't do something fast, he'd just bleed out and that would be that. Jimmy would be even more famous than he was now.

He had no hat. He'd taken off his badge. He was just a wounded man with a gun hunting an unwounded man with one.

He was old, he was slow, he was very scared. He thought he might never see his son or his wife again. Above him the stars were distant, unblinking, completely neutral. All around him the corn shivered and clicked and far off the insects and the frogs wailed away. Why was he doing this? For what? For some goddamned civilians who'd never know his name and would call him too big for his britches behind his back?

He'd never wondered such a blasphemy before, not on any of the islands or in any of the scrapes or near scrapes as a law officer. Why? Does it matter? No, not really.

He went to his knee, the big pistol heavy in his hand. He felt now that Jimmy was close. Then he knew it. Jimmy wouldn't be ahead of him, Jimmy would be behind him. Jimmy would let him pass then come from behind. That's how Jimmy's mind would work because Jimmy was an athlete, who had been schooled in the arts of feint and attack.

"Jimmy!" he called. *"Jimmy,* come on now, boy, this don't have to happen."

No answer.

Earl stood by the side of the road and made as if to look forward, peering into the corn.

Jimmy watched him come. Earl wasn't *in* the corn so much as half in the corn, clinging to the edge of the road. He moved not fast but not slow either, with grim determination. Even in the dark Jimmy could see Earl's face tight and clenched. It was a father's face, the face of a man who knew what to do next or maybe the face of a man who told you what was wrong with what you were doing.

Jimmy raised the gun; Earl would pass within a few yards of him. But then he paused. There were a thousand stalks of corn between him and Earl; who knew if the bullets would deflect or what and who knew if he could shoot that accurately in the dark? He could fire all his shots and miss. No. Better to let Earl pass him by, then snake over and come out on the road behind him. Get close. That was it. Get real close and just shoot and shoot and shoot. Show him who's best.

❑ ❑ ❑ ❑

Earl listened. Nothing. He edged forward farther.

"Jimmy, come *on!* I don't want to have to hurt you."

Nothing. Then he heard the click of a pistol safety snicking off.

"I got you beat, Earl."

Earl straightened and turned, the gun at his side.

Jimmy was twenty feet behind him, the Colt automatic out and pointed straight at him.

"I win, Earl."

"Jimmy, for God's sake. Put it down. It's all over."

"It *is* all over."

"Jimmy, it ain't worth it."

"Earl, put the gun down and I'll let you live."

"I cain't do that, Jimmy. You know that. This is the end of the line. Another second or two and I can't cut you no more slack."

"Earl, I don't hate you. But it ain't my fault."

He pulled the trigger.

The gun flashed and bucked and smoke swirled about.

Earl stood straight as a goddamn rail.

"You missed, Jimmy. It's too far, you ain't a good enough shot. Son, you're overmatched. Put it dow—"

Jimmy fired, sure he'd hit, but astonished at how fast the older man was as he dropped to one knee, the gun rising in a blur. He wasn't just fast, he was some other kind of fast, his arm a whip, a smear, a flash, and the two shots were almost one, so swiftly did they come.

The next thing he saw was Earl over him in a fog.

"Earl?" he said.

"Yes, Jimmy."

"Earl, I cain't see nothing. It hurts." Something with his head. It was like in a vise or among broken boxes or pieces of glass or something. Fog everywhere. Never seen nothing like it.

"It's all right, Jimmy. It's all going to be all right."

Jimmy breathed the last time and went still. There was no death rattle, final gurgle or twitch, as there sometimes was. It was as if his soul simply departed, leaving only a cask behind.

Earl could see that one shot had torn through his left eye and exited the side of his beautiful head, destroying it. The second had hit him just above the heart. He lay as calm as a young king, soaking in his own blood, utterly motionless, one eye beautiful and blue with its perfect curl of blond lash, the other eye shattered pulp, leaking black jagged streaks into the earth.

Earl looked away and found the strength to rise. He stood on groggy legs, dizzy and unsure. With an act of will, he took a step and then another, and walked back to the car, feeling as old as the mountains. God, he felt so awful. No man should have to kill a boy he'd known for twenty years.

Why hadn't Jimmy told him what was going on?

What was going on? What got into Jimmy?

I will by God find out.

His arm was still bleeding. It only hurt like the goddamned devil himself was beating away on it. His left side was completely numb and he was sopped with his own blood. He realized he would die if help didn't get there soon enough.

It all came down to the radio with the broken aerial.

He bent over, retrieved the mike and pushed the send button.

"Any cars, any cars, goddammit, trooper down, ten-thirty-three, please respond, please respond."

Silence.

He looked up into the sky. Stars, piles of them, against the dark. He felt so goddamned alone. He tried again.

"Any cars, any cars, this is Car One Four, is anybody out there, trooper down, ten-thirty-three, ten-thirty-three, Jesus Christ, I am losing blood."

So. On a road in a cornfield, bleeding out. After so many chances in the islands. Bleeding out in a cornfield.

"Any police cars, any tow trucks, any band jumpers, please help, trooper down, ten-thirty-three, please acknowledge."

Nothing.

It ends. It's over. It's finished. I didn't make it. He closed his eyes. His son's face floated before him, and he felt himself reaching out, but it vanished.

"Ah, Trooper One Four, this is a commercial aviation flight, Delta One Niner Zero up here at twenty-seven five and vectored southbound into New Orleans. I'm hopping the frequencies and I happened to pick up your signal, son, where the hell are you?"

"Delta, Delta, I am eleven miles south of Waldron, Arkansas, just off Route 71 in a cornfield, one hundred yards off the highway. I have been hit twice and I am losing blood."

"You hang on, son, I am going to shift frequencies and put the squawk onto the Little Rock emergency frequency and the boys on the ground will ASAP it to your local authorities and you will get assistance and if they can't make it, I will set this buggy down on the goddamn highway and pick you up myself, Trooper."

"Thank you, Delta One Niner Zero, ain't you a Good Samaritan?"

"And ain't you a tub o' guts, Trooper? Good luck, son." He signed off.

Earl set the radio mike down and sat in the dark. The world seemed suddenly full of possibility.

Then he heard the sound of death; it chilled him. It was the dry, raspy, spastic crackle that signified the presence of a rattlesnake.

Great, he thought; that's all I need.

Fifteen

J UDGE MYERS was going to beat him. This was very frustrating for Red because Judge Myers never beat him. Nobody ever beat him, goddammit.

Red was the best sporting clays shooter in West Arkansas, and maybe the whole state; he'd placed high in several national tournaments, including the Big Pig in Maryland, the NSCAs in San Antonio, the Seminole Cup Challenge in Orlando. He had a gift for the game, a natural grace with the shotgun and a kind of geometry-instinctive mind—his arithmetic gift again, perhaps— that let him solve complex problems of deflection with an almost eerie confidence.

But even the good shooters have the odd off day, when the birds come from the trap not as they should but by freakish chance too close, too far, or caught and toyed with in a burst of random wind, lifted oddly or squashed oddly, faster, slower; when, for whatever reason, the eye isn't seeing with quite the clarity it normally does, or the brain isn't reading and solving with quite the same power, the hands are slow, the gun never gets mounted right: so many little things that begin to erode at whatever it is that makes you hit. So it was today with Red.

The judge, who had never broken 45, was standing at 45 now on the last station. Red was standing at 43. If he ran five, the best he could do would be to top out at 48, so the judge could beat him with a five or even a pussy four and the man was so confident and feeling so full of himself, the five looked possible, the four positive.

"This isn't my day," said Red.

No, it wasn't. He hated the last station, not the two oblique outgoers that came low off the trap, easy for a shooter at his level, but his worst damned shot, a far teal, straight up and way out, first a single then a goddamned simo. He should have it changed; after all, he owned the course.

The judge stepped into the cage. Before them the beauty of the state's wildness displayed itself, for the course was a good one, with shots hard enough to keep it interesting. The trap was to the left; the first two outgoers sailed low and dropped as they fell into a valley amid dogwoods, crossed a pond and disappeared in the vegetation. The teal were the bitches. They looked like dots, popped straight up from a remote on the other side of the pond, bare against the sky only momentarily, so dark and far you couldn't even see their orangeness. You wanted to catch them as they paused in equipoise at the cusp of their rise; if instead you tried to take them going down, you'd run out of shot before you could pull the trigger.

"I'm feeling strong today, Red," said Judge Myers, of the Fort Smith Myerses, who was also chairman of the Sebastian County Party and a close personal friend and campaign fund-raiser of and for Senator Hollis Etheridge, and if Hollis's campaign ever got into gear, the judge would be headed for a Big Job in Washington, all of which pleased Red no end.

"Well, Judge, if you want, I'll just write you the check now. We don't even have to shoot it out. The better man won today."

"Oh, Red, you sly damned dog you, you really are Ray Bama's son! But that kind of psych job won't work on me." The judge laughed; Red's gamesmanship was a legend in Fort Smith's raciest poker, golfing, and wing-shooting circles, which, essentially, were the same circles, and only one circle, the Rich Boys Club.

Red and the judge went way back; when, in 1991, a Justice Department attorney working for the Organized Crime Strike Force, had petitioned for a wiretap, someone Red knew had tipped him with the information and it was Judge Myers who'd granted

Red a temporary enjoining order. That case would come up to decision sometime soon too, possibly by the second or the third decade of the next century.

So the judge owed Red, who contributed money by the gallon to the party, and Red owed the judge. That's why Red loved to shoot against the judge: it was even.

The judge slipped two ACTIV 8s into the chambers of his Perazzi, snapped the lovely gun's sleek barrels into the receiver with the solid thunk of a bank vault closing and took up a nice loose ready position, the gun tucked under the right shoulder, the weight forward on the balls of the feet.

"Trapper ready," came a call from the bush.

"Pull!" the judge called, and obediently the unseen trapper launched the disks, two orange saucers which in a blur flashed into the valley, sinking, skimming, diminishing all at once. The judge's gun spoke twice, fast, and two orange puffs marked the hits as he swung through.

He opened the barrels, let the empties pop out and slid two more ACTIVs into the over-and-under chambers.

"Pull," he shouted, and quickly enough, from beyond the pond, a bird the size of an aspirin screamed into the sky, paused ever so slightly, and the judge stayed with it, followed through and killed it.

Except he didn't.

"Goddamn," he said. "Now I'm spooked."

"You're not spooked," said Red. "Not you."

"Damn!" said the judge.

He reloaded for the really hard simo: two birds launched at once, inscribing arcs away from each other. You couldn't get them both with one shell; you had to take one early as it rose, then swing to the second one, before it fell too far and you lost it in the vegetation, tricky as hell because you had to trust your instincts as far as finding the line, and if you came down through it and were off center, there was nothing to be done.

He steeled himself, took a swallow, tried a hundred ready positions, then found one to his liking.

"Pull!" he shouted.

And missed both.

"Goddamn!" the man screamed. "Son of a bitch," he muttered, as he stepped away.

"Well, well," said Red. "Lookie here."

"Red, you ain't never run this station and I don't believe you're going to now."

"Jack Myers, you are probably right, but we shall see what we shall see."

He stepped into the cage.

The test was concentration. Thinking too hard about the teal that lay ahead could cost him the easier outgoers that he had to deal with first. Visualize, he ordered himself, and in his mind he watched a movie of himself, mounting the gun smoothly, coming up on line with the two birds with no excess motion, not even much gun movement, killing them fast and getting out of there.

He slid two shells into the gleaming chambers of his Krieghoff K-80, $12,000 worth of poetry and grace assembled lovingly by the best gun makers in Germany. He locked the gun shut and just felt himself leaning ever so slowly forward, letting the shot assemble in his mind, letting his emotions calm, his heart still and his concentration begin to gather.

"Pull!"

You don't want to look as the birds come off the trap, because they move too fast; you'll be late. As Red smoothly pulled the gun up and into his shoulder with an economical, practiced placement until it naturally found itself pointing exactly where, also by long practice, he was already looking, he watched the birds come into the window of his sharpest vision. There was no time for thought or consideration, for things happened faster than words could be arranged to record them: the birds were there, falling, diminishing, but etched in his focus, the barrel was a blur beneath them, the gun seemed automatically to fire twice as he swept along, and the orange smears where the birds' ceramic was dissolved by the force of eight hundred pellets of bird shot driving through their center marked his hits.

He popped the shells out, reached into his shell bag and took out a No. 7½ Winchester Heavy Trap load, and slipped it into his lower barrel, where the tighter of his two chokes was screwed, the Improved Cylinder.

He set himself again. Oh, he hated these far teal. It was so easy for the bird to find a hole in the shot pattern and so distant it was also possible for the bird to take a bunch of hits and yet not break or chip. It happened all the time.

"Pull," he shouted.

The bird rose, the gun rose and as these two things happened, yet another did: the vibrator on his pager went off, momentarily disconcerting him.

He lost a tenth of a second and when he got up to where the bird was supposed to be paused as gravity overcame its upward velocity, he was late; it was already falling.

But Red didn't panic.

He punched the gun downward hard, caught up with the falling orange disk and fired as he passed it.

Goddamn, he missed.

"No, you hit it, Red," said the judge. "I saw a chip. Not much of one, but by God a chip. Great shooting, damn you."

"Do you mind if I make an emergency call?"

"Sure, go ahead. It's your concentration."

Red leaned the Krieghoff against the cage, stepped outside and pulled his folder off his belt. He punched the key that accessed Duane Peck's hot line for the recorded report.

"Ah, sir, here's the latest. Yesterday, I followed 'em out Route 71 toward Waldron and then lost 'em. I went back and forth for a coupla hours and finally I picked 'em up at some field out near, uh, Waldron. They never saw me. They were there until dark. That was the kid, you know, and that Bob Lee guy, and they got old Sam Vincent with 'em. Uh."

The man paused, seemed to lose track, then got himself settled down.

"So anyway, today, *today,* early, Sam trots over to the temporary courthouse and files some papers. He files what's called a Motion of Exhumation, to get county permission so that they can dig up Earl Swagger and perform some kind of autopsy on the body. Uh, what's your thought? They don't got no idea I'm interested, except for that fucking kid looked at me smart when I first bumped into 'em. I could deal with it now, before it gets too much."

It was like the sun breaking out on a cloudy day. It was like finding a million dollars. It was free sex with a beautiful woman and no consequences.

He pushed the button to reach the recorder.

"Don't do a thing. I think we got 'em flummoxed. We may git out of this one without a real problem. Things are looking very, very good."

They were. This one was covered.

"You look as though you've had extremely good news," said the judge, as Red returned to the cage.

"You know sometimes how a deal looks like it's going to fall apart on you with all kinds of difficulties? But then something you did years ago, because you were smart and thought about it, clicks in, and it turns out just the way you figured."

"Well, I can't say I've had *that* exact pleasure."

"Well, it feels great," Red said.

He picked up the gun, popped the breech and dropped two more 7½s in.

"Pull," he said, feeling wonderful. The birds shot upward and he killed them both.

Sixteen

HE REMEMBERED IT as somehow more beautiful. In his memory he saw a rolling green meadow mostly in shade from the stately black oak that stood nearby. The tombstones had a grandeur to them; it was like a parade of the honored dead, a mini-Arlington where an honor guard would keep eternal watch.

But if that Polk County veterans' cemetery ever existed or if it was only an imaginary place, like an Oz for the dead, it was certainly not the bitter reality: blasted by sun, parched and treeless and very shabby and as flat and banal as a pancake, the cemetery stretched to the empty horizon. It wasn't even really a veterans' cemetery, it just had a veterans' section in it, but beyond the crooked fence the civilians lay just as dead as the vets.

"You never came here?" Russ asked.

"Oh, a few times. When I was small. That was before my mother got what we called 'sick,' meaning drunk. She was better off not coming. I just remember her crying like a baby. Her sister had to drive us home. Then I came the night before I left for the Marine Corps. Drove myself. I came once more on liberty but by that time my mother was dead and there wasn't much else to come back to. I never came when I got back from the war. I just stayed on that goddamned mountain."

"Is it the same?"

"I remember more trees. Hell, though, I was just a kid. A bush looked like a tree."

"Is this it, Mr. Swagger?" cried one of the gravediggers hired for the occasion.

"Well, let's see."

Bob walked over to the simple stone. It looked no different from the hundreds in here, the war dead of West Arkansas dating back to the Civil War. He bent and squinted in the sun and read off the corrupted limestone:

EARL SWAGGER
U.S.M.C.
ARKANSAS STATE POLICE
1910–1955

And then:

Husband, Father, Marine, Police Officer
UNCOMMON VALOR

"Yes sir, Mr. Coggins, that's him. Now, if that damned doctor would just get here."

"We may as well get started," said the old man.

"Why don't you just."

The crew—three black men, two young and the older Mr. Coggins—set to it with solid work. Bob watched them cut into the earth with their spades, slice the turf out and then really put their backs into it. Swiftly, the dirt mounded up on the tarpaulin they had set out for that purpose.

"Lot of dirt in a hole," Bob said.

Russ, watching the black men dig, felt a bit uncomfortable. The whole thing was so matter-of-fact. Nobody at the cemetery office had seen anything remarkable about the paperwork served, but it seemed there were no records left, as the cemetery had changed administrations many times since 1955, and somewhere along the line, the record keeping had grown sloppy and the actual physical materials had somehow disappeared. But it was no big deal: Bob found it easy enough.

"I feel guilty with them doing all the work," Russ said.

"They're professionals. They're doing a good job. Let them earn their pay. My father loved a job done well and by God them boys are doing it well."

Through the morning the men dug, without much in the way of rest. Two in, one out, the shovels a steady machinelike attack against the ground, and the hole widened and deepened.

Bob just watched. He could be so still. Russ, bored, ambled around, trying to think of something to do that would be helpful but which wouldn't require his actual presence. But then he thought: This is my party. I have to be here.

"You remember that cop?" Bob said.

"Yes."

"You said to me there was something fishy about him, right?"

"Yes."

"What? Be specific."

"Ah—" Russ's mind seemed to fill with light. Another test which he would fail. But then he remembered.

"Well, I've been around cops my whole life. My father, you know—"

"Go on. Get to it."

"Well, here's how a cop's eyes work. He stares hard at you and makes a reading. Reads you up and down. It's how a cop's mind works. He's comparing you to type. He's got fifty types in his head, and three or four of them are dangerous. In his first few seconds, he eyeballs you to try you against type. But then if he determines you're not dangerous, he loses interest. Then you're just an irritating problem for him. He fills out the ticket, he gives you the directions, he takes the statement, whatever: but he's not interested in you, he's not really paying attention to you, he's looking around for other threats."

"Ummm," said Bob, considering.

"This guy," said Russ, "he *kept* eyeballing. Unusual cop behavior. Because any cop could tell in a second that a twenty-something yuppie in Reeboks and a polo shirt wasn't dangerous. But I puzzled him. Odd."

"Maybe he thought *I* was dangerous."

"But he wasn't looking at *you*. He was looking at *me*."

"Well, we could ask him about it. He's been staring at us from behind the trees for ten minutes. Now here he comes."

"Jesus," said Russ.

"And he drove by us three times while we were in that field yesterday." Bob smiled at him. "You be cool, now."

The deputy sauntered up, lanky and tawny, his big hands hooked on his belt, his hat low over his eyes, shades on, bright, reflective lenses that sealed the world out.

"Howdy there," he called, smiling.

"Deputy Peck," said Bob.

"Well, I see you boys are making good progress here on this thing."

"We think we might learn a bit from the body. Though it grieves me to disturb the dead."

"Well, sometimes you got to do what you got to do."

"That's true enough."

"You know, Mr. Swagger, I done some thinking. I could *help* you. Like, fer instance, I could fish them old records out of the sheriff's files from 1955. I don't think nobody's looked at them in years. Maybe I could help you find witnesses, and the like? There might be old-timers around from them days be of some help to you. I could help Sam. He don't git around much; he might need an extra pair of legs. Be my pleasure."

"Well, that's damned nice of you, Deputy. Fact is, right now we're just sort of grasping at straws. We don't know if there's enough here. Things change, people forget. Ain't much of 1955 left. We may not be around much longer if we don't get some better stuff."

"Well, that's how I could help," said Peck. "You let me know you come up with something I can help you with. Meanwhile, I'll pretty much look for them files and see what I can dig out."

"That'd be great, Deputy Peck."

"Call me Duane. Everybody does."

"Duane, that'd be—"

"Excuse me."

This came from a new voice, and Russ turned to see a bearded man, possibly fifty, in an open-collar shirt and a pair of slacks, holding a heavy leather satchel, which looked like a doctor's bag. Wasn't this growing into some big party?

"Would somebody here be Mr. Swagger?" the newcomer asked.

"I am," said Bob.

"Hi, I'm Carl Phillips. Dr. Phillips. I teach forensic pathology up at Fayetteville in the medical school and I'm a board-certified forensic pathologist. I was called by Sam Vincent."

"Yes sir."

The doctor stepped up, gestured to the work party a few feet away.

"The remains, I assume?"

"Yes sir," said Bob.

"All right, I arranged with Winslow's Mortuary. They're going to give us a workroom. You'll have to pay them, I suppose."

"Sure," said Bob.

"And I assume all the county paperwork is in order? Sam said he'd take care of it."

"Yes sir," said Bob. "Here, you want to look?"

"Yes, I do. The state is very particular what can and cannot be done with remains. It has more to do with the funeral industry lobby than anything. For example, the remains must be transported via hearse, you're aware of that?"

"Sam told us. I called and set one up. It should be here shortly."

The doctor took the papers and made a quick appraisal of them. They seemed to satisfy him.

"All right, everything's in order. I suppose you'll want to go to the mortuary with me?"

"Yes sir. He was my father."

"Look, let me be frank with you. I know you're an experienced man, been in combat."

"Some," said Bob.

"So you've seen what high explosives and machine-gun fire can do to bodies?"

"Yes sir."

"Well, there's nothing that you've seen that can prepare you for the effects of time upon a cadaver. Forty years after the fact, what comes out of the ground is unrecognizable. That's why it's fine for you to come along, but I want you nowhere near the actual work. I can't let what his body has become represent what your father is to you. When I do these private jobs, that's my rule. It's my neck of the woods. You let me do the navigating."

"Sure, Doctor," said Bob.

"Okay, we're all set."

"Mr. Swagger?"

It was Mr. Coggins, who stood by the grave, gleaming with sweat. He was wiping his forehead with a red bandanna.

"Mr. Swagger, we're ready. He was a long way down."

The doctor went to the edge of the grave and looked into it.

"Mr. Coggins, you'll rig the block and tackle next?" he asked.

"Yes sir," said Coggins.

Bob and Russ went to look into the grave. The men had done an excellent job in the excavation; the grave's walls were hard and straight and black, the dirt heaped in perfect mountains. Russ looked down, unnerved. But it was only a long wooden box, caked with mud, completely exposed, five long feet down.

The doctor turned to them.

"A cedar coffin? That's very interesting. I'm going to have to ask you to leave. I have to check something out. Mr. Coggins, you help me down."

The two young black men, gleaming with sweat as well, helped the doctor into the grave. There was just enough room for him at one end. He reached into his pocket and pulled out a surgical mask, which he donned. He asked the black men to leave the hole too.

Bob and Russ wandered away. They heard the sound of wood being pried.

"Mr. Swagger," called Dr. Phillips.

"Yes sir."

"I'm afraid I have bad news for you."

Bob and Russ looked at each other.

"Yes sir?" said Bob.

"This man was killed by gunshot wound, I can see it clearly in the remains. But from what I can tell from the condition, it happened in around 1865."

"Damn!" said Duane Peck. "Don't that beat all?"

Seventeen

THE OLD MAN was on a goddamned rampage. Where the hell was it?

Sam had torn his office apart in the morning and now he was at his home, tearing it apart.

Goddamned sonofabitching bastards had done it again on him!

They'd hidden something. They were doing it more and more these days. They'd sneak in, late, while he slept, and hide things, steal things, move things. They'd rearrange his drawers, so that one day his socks would be in the third one and the next in the top one. Sometimes his hairbrush and razor were on the left side of the sink and sometimes on the right.

The fury was like smoke, hot and bright, and it seemed to fill his veins so that a ropy blue Y stood out on his forehead and his temple throbbed strangely.

The other day they hid his pipe. His pipe, his meerschaum, picked up in Germany after the war, he'd smoked it every night for close to fifty years and it was gone. It had vanished. They changed the names of his grandchildren on him and they even mixed up two of his surviving daughters.

They moved his car when he drove to the store. They changed the stoplight on him as he accelerated through an intersection and then they honked or yelled rudely to him. Sometimes they confused him as to what side of the road he was supposed to drive on.

It was enough to make a man seriously angry, but this one, their last prank, was the worst.

For so long he had been such a methodical man. He was the kind of American who believed not in law and order but that order *was* law. Thus he carefully cataloged or recorded his materials, he took infinitely detailed notes, he went over testimony forward and backwards, he mastered evidence forward and backwards and he never, ever asked a question twice or to which he did not know the answer.

He had outargued them all, until these new invisible devils had come gunning for him.

But he wouldn't let them win, or if, by chance, they won, if someone finally beat him, by God they'd know they'd been in a fight.

He looked around the carnage of his basement. Someone had literally dumped his files out of their cardboard boxes onto the floor in a frenzy. Who would do such a thing? Then he remembered: *he* had done such a thing. Just a few minutes ago.

What was I looking for?

Yes: a copy of the report to the coroner he had put together in 1955 on a wrongful death hearing in the case of Earl Swagger. He knew he had it. He had to have it. It was in here somewhere. But where?

The box marked 1955 was empty and he'd emptied 1953 to 1957 as well, in the thought that maybe sometime when he left office and was transferring these boxes to his home, he or one of his secretaries—he'd buried more secretaries than he could even remember—had misfiled it.

Or maybe he didn't even *have* a copy. It was a report on an investigation, but it didn't lead to a prosecution or a decision not to prosecute, but only to a dead end in the Coroner's Office, so possibly even back then he didn't file it with his regular case files but in some other file, some annex or something.

It wasn't like he couldn't remember now. It wasn't his memory that was going. No sir, not him. It was instead a sense of fog drifting through his mind. The memory was still there. It was a vision problem: he still had all his books organized just so in the library of his mind, but for some reason he had trouble reading the names on the spines and he couldn't get them out without groping. It made him furious!

He hated the idea of going to that smug kid Rusty or whatever his goddamned name was and saying, "You know, I can't find that document. I told you I could, but I can't. I must have misremembered."

Rusty would look at him as a few of his grandchildren did: their eyes would behold a relic, a living fossil, something that belonged behind glass in a museum.

Well, goddamn him anyway! Sam felt an eruption of anger so intense it was physical; his knotty old hand formed into a fist and he imagined smashing Rusty or whatever his name was in the mouth. That would satisfy him so.

He bent, but discovered his back too stiff to allow him to stay in such a position. So he knelt, and began to scrape the files up, to try and get them into some semblance of order.

A name leaped out at him.

It was like a musical tone or something, soft and vague but oddly familiar. What was it? What did it connect with? What could it mean?

Nothing. He had it, it tantalized him, then it was gone.

Goddamn them, they were doing it to him again!

He got the files together and saw from the dates they were all 1955s, and so again he slipped through them one more time and by God no, no Earl Swagger anywhere. Where did it go? Where had it—

Parker!

He held the Shirelle Parker file in his hand. It was quite thin, not much to show for such a horrible crime, though it had been an open-and-shut case.

Why was this important?

Yes, Earl's last case. That day: July 23, 1955.

He opened the file and a picture greeted him: Shirelle at her eighth-grade graduation. He remembered some policeman had given it to him before the trial. He looked at it now and saw such a pretty girl, her eyes so lit up and full of hope. She was a colored child in the Arkansas of the fifties and she was full of hope! Now, wasn't that something! She must have been a wonderful child, but he realized he had no evidence about her. He knew nothing about her, except the facts of the death, which are all that matter to a prosecutor. It doesn't matter if they're good, bad, wonderful or evil: if they've been killed you try and put the killers in the chair or at least in the house.

The next picture was more familiar. It was marked POLK COUNTY SHERIFF'S DEPARTMENT PROPERTY, JULY 24, 1955—EVIDENCE. The crime scene. Shirelle, on her back on the hard shale wash of the hillside, her dress up, her privates violated, her face still and swollen, her eyes wide.

He put the photo down. He could not look at it.

I got him for you, Shirelle, he thought. *Yes, I did. I got him for you and Earl. That was my job.*

He remembered. It was so easy.

He'd gotten to the scene late the day after, having been devoured by the terrible mess of Earl Swagger's death in the cornfield, by the grief and the rage and all the long and terrible ceremonies to go through.

Now, finally, at 4:00 P.M. on the twenty-fourth he arrived at Shirelle's site. He could see in an instant that it had been hopelessly contaminated. Footprints scalloped the ground around her, the litter of candy bar wrappers and pop bottles lay everywhere, one lazy Polk County sheriff's deputy lounged under a tree, smoking a cigarette.

"Has the state police forensics team been here?" Sam demanded.

"No sir. They ain't a-coming, I hear. Too busy with Mr. Earl."

Sam shook his head, but realized it didn't really matter. There was no evidence left to be gotten here.

"It looks like the goddamned army's been here."

"Well, folks heard about the dead nigger gal. They come to look. I tried to keep 'em away but you know how word git around."

This enraged Sam but he saw the pointlessness of exploding at this dim fool. Instead, seething, he walked to the body. By now

Shirelle was gray in color, almost dusty. Her negritude had all but vanished. She was simply a dead child, puffed up with gas that almost took her humanity away.

"You heard about the pocket?" the deputy asked.

Sam hadn't.

"Earl done found it yesterday, put it in an envelope for Lem to give the state police boys, but when they done never showed, he gave it to the Sheriff's Office."

"Pocket?"

"I hear. Ripped from a shirt. Monogrammed. Said RGF on it, pretty as you please."

Amazing, thought Sam. He'd been investigating and prosecuting murder for thirty years, with five years off for the war, and he'd never come across anything so lucky. But murder was like that: it defied rational explanation and was full of crazy things, coincidences, freaks of happening, the sheer play of the irrational in the universe. A Baptist, he hated murder because it always made him doubt God's wisdom and even, if he pressed too hard, God's existence, though he would never utter such heresy.

"I'm going to call the coroner," he told the deputy. "It's time to git this poor little girl out of here. Now, you listen to me, you see anybody else pulling up for a free look at the show, you chase 'em goddamn away, you understand? I don't want to hear about people coming up here no more. It ain't right."

"Sam, she's only a nigger gal."

Sam turned away.

By the time he got back, the raiding party was already to go. Five sheriff's deputies with shotguns and rifles and clubs, the sheriff himself already to lead the outfit in search of glory and headlines.

"No," Sam told them. "Not yet. You boys can be cowboys later."

But the evidence was undeniable. A quick scan of tax records in the County Clerk's Office, happily segregated by color, had turned up but one Negro with the initials RGF. His name was Reggie Gerard Fuller, he was eighteen and the second son of Davidson Fuller, the most prosperous Negro in town and owner of Fuller's Funeral Parlor, which buried all the Negroes. Reggie had a driver's license on record, and access to an automobile, the hearse, or more likely one of the two smaller black Fords the parlor used to transport mourners. On top of that, Reggie was known as a sharp dresser: his shirts *were* monogrammed.

High school records indicated that Reggie was a studious though not overbright boy who placidly accepted that he would work for his father in some clerical capacity, lacking the grit and smarts to take over the business himself. He had no incidents on his record, but he was, after all, colored and young, and therefore by inclination more inclined toward deviant behavior. Most sensible people realized that in each Nigra there lurked the secret potential of the rapist and the killer; it had merely to be brought out by liquor or jealousy and knives would flash. The deputies even had a name for the crimes such behavior inspired: they were called "Willie-thumped-Willies" as in, "Oh, hey, I hear you caught a Willie-thumped-Willie the other night." "Yeah, goddamned coon cut up his old lady with a whiskey bottle. Bitch died before the goddamn ambulance came. I don't blame the ambulance. I wouldn't go down there for nothing." In this one Reggie thumped Shirelle.

But Sam was a stickler. After examining the evidence, he personally called Judge Harrison and personally drove the eighteen miles out to the judge's farm to get the search warrant and the probable-cause warrant signed.

"This ain't goddamn Mississippi," he said. "Or goddamned Alabam. We do things by the law here."

And he went along on the raid. He knew his presence would considerably lessen the thunder and the fury of the event; white deputies kicking down black doors in the middle of the night, no, not in his county.

So instead of kicking in doors, the deputies waited outside while Sam and the sheriff knocked on the door of the biggest, whitest house in what was called Niggertown but was actually a six-block-square neighborhood in west Blue Eye.

It was four in the morning. Groggily, Mr. Fuller opened the door with a shotgun in his hand and Sam was glad he had come along; the deputies might have opened fire.

"Mr. Fuller, I am Sam Vincent, Polk County prosecutor, and I think you recognize the sheriff."

Automatic race fear came upon the man's face: he saw stern whites in his doorway, and behind them, parked at the curb, four police cars, light bars flashing.

"What is this about?"

"Sir, we've come to question your son Reggie. And to serve papers on a search warrant. I've instructed the boys to be courteous and professional. But we do have an investigation to run. Could you please bring Reggie down to us? Say, the living room?"

"What is—"

"Mr. Fuller, I know you've heard, there was another terrible crime yesterday. One of your own kind. Now, we have an investigation to run."

"My boy didn't do nothing," said Mr. Fuller.

"You know me to be a fair man, and I swear to you nothing will happen here tonight or any night except what the law decrees. That's how I run things. But we have our duty to do. In the meantime, the deputies will search the house. I have a legal paper here which says it's all right. The deputies won't break anything and if they do, they'll pay for it out of their own pockets. But we have to do what we have to do."

Eventually, the sleepy Reggie was brought before Sam. He could have taken him to headquarters for questioning, but he elected, out of respect for Mr. Fuller's position, to do the initial here.

"Reggie, where were you five nights ago, that is, July 19?"

"He was here," said Mrs. Fuller.

"You let him answer, ma'am, or I will have to take him away."

Reggie was an almost fat boy, with pale skin and an unfocused quality about him that had nothing to do with the late hour. His eyes drifted, he fidgeted. He smiled and no one returned the smile. He blinked, and seemed to forget where he was; for a while he stopped paying attention. He was wearing pajamas with butterflies on them. He betrayed more confusion than fear; nothing about him suggested aggression or tendency to violence. But Nigras were strange that way: they looked calm one second and the next they could go amok.

"Sir," he finally said, "I don't 'member. Just around. Maybe in my room. I can't say. No, I think I went for a drive in daddy's big old wagon."

"The hearse?"

"Yes suh. I went for a drive, that's all. Listen some to the radio, you know, from Memphis."

"Anybody see you? Got people who can testify to where you were?"

"No sir."

"Reggie, were you near the church? Did you go to the church and that meeting they had there that night?"

"No sir."

"Reggie, you listen to me. If you were someplace you don't want your daddy to know about, you have to be a man now and 'fess up. You were at a crib, drinking? You were gambling, you were with a woman?"

"Sir, I—"

"Mr. Sam, my boy Reggie, he's a *good* boy. He's not no genius, but he works hard and—"

"Sam."

It was the sheriff.

"Sam, the boys found something."

That was it, really. Sam walked into the bedroom and watched as one of the deputies pointed to a little corner of blue shirt that peeked from between the mattress and the box spring of the now stripped bed. Sam nodded, and the deputy separated the two: the corner yielded to a larger mass of material. Very carefully, with a pencil, Sam nabbed it and lifted it off the bed. It was a shirt, with the pocket missing, blue cotton. It was streaked with rust, which Sam knew to be the color of dried blood.

"Think we got us a nigger," someone said.

"Okay," Sam said, "mark it and bag it, very carefully. People are going to be looking at this case and we can't afford to make a mistake."

Then he headed back to the living room to arrest Reggie Fuller for murder.

The trial, three months later, was over in a day. The Fullers were willing to spend their life savings to hire a Little Rock lawyer, but Sam looked at the evidence and suggested that they'd do better to have Reggie plead guilty and throw himself on the mercy of the court. A Fort Smith lawyer told them the same thing: the shirt was indeed Reggie's, as laundry markings subsequently proved and nobody ever bothered to deny. The pocket matched perfectly with the ripped seams on the chest. The blood was AB positive, as was Shirelle's. Reggie had no meaningful alibi; he had taken the hearse that night and just "driven around."

No bargain was ever offered, because there was no cause to. The evidence was such that a confession had no meaning. Sam made the melancholy but firm decision that Reggie, though he was young and somewhat distracted, must die. It wasn't that Sam was a cruel man but he felt the simple rhythms of the universe had been violated and must be forcefully returned to normal. An eye for an eye: it was the best system, the only true system. He spoke for the dead, and it only worked if he spoke loudly. Besides, it was Earl's last case: Earl would have wanted it that way too.

The Fullers finally found a lawyer who would take the case on appeal, and though Sam warned them not to throw their money away, they did so anyway, on a desperately vain attempt to save their son. For over two years Mrs. Fuller wrote Sam a letter once a week begging for mercy as the case dragged through the courts and Reggie moldered at the Cummins Farm at Gould, where the Negroes were sent. When the Fullers ran out of money, they sold their house and moved into a smaller one; when they ran out of money again, Mr. Fuller sold his business to a white man and went to work for that same white man, who called him, behind his back, "the dumbest nigger in Arkansas for selling a business that did sixty thousand clear a year for sixty thousand!" Then Mrs. Fuller died, Jake Fuller, the older boy, went off to join the navy and the two daughters, Emily and Suzette, moved to St. Louis with their aunt. But old Davidson Fuller took up the letter duty and wrote

Sam every week and tried to talk to him, to get him to look at the evidence one more time.

"You a fair man, sir. Don't let them do this to my boy. He didn't do it."

"Davidson, even your own Nigra people say he did it. I have sources. I know what's being said in the churches and the cribs."

"Don't take my boy from me, Mr. Sam."

"I am not taking your boy from you. The law is following its course. This ain't Mississippi. I gave him a fair trial, you had good lawyers, the reason he is going where he is going is because he has to pay. You had best adjust to that, sir. I know this is not easy on your family; it wasn't easy on Shirelle's either. The balance has to be squared off and restored, and we can go on from there."

"Tell them I did it, if they want a Negro to die. I'll go. I'll confess. Take me. Please, please, please, Mr. Sam, don't take my poor little boy."

Sam just looked at him.

"You have too much love in your heart for that boy," he finally said. "He's not worth it. He killed an innocent girl."

There was but one act to be played out and it occurred on October 6, 1957, at the Arkansas State Penitentiary at Tucker, where they'd removed Reggie from the Cummins Farm when his last appeal was finally denied. It was the day of the fourth game of the World Series, and Sam listened to the game that afternoon as he drove the hundred-odd miles to Tucker, just southeast of Little Rock. It was not his first time to make such a trip, nor would it be his last. On the other hand, he didn't make it automatically; of the twenty-three men he sent to the electric chair, he only watched eleven die. Tonight it was Reggie's turn.

Simply in terms of convenience, it worked out. He was able to get a clear signal from Little Rock and listened numbly to the baseball all the way over. Warren Spahn was on the mound, mowing them down. Sam hated anything with the word "Yankee" in the title just as he hated anything with "New York" in the title, so he lost himself in the baseball, hoping the upstart, uprooted "Milwaukee" team—really, just the old, pitiful Boston Braves—would triumph. Sam stayed rooted in the drama the whole way, even as the game went into extra innings, even as the Yankees tied the game in the ninth on Ellston Howard's three-run homer and then scored the go-ahead run in the top of the tenth *(goddammit!).*

It looked over for the Braves, but somehow they clawed their way back into the game, when Logan doubled to left, scoring Mantilla to tie again, and Sam had the sense that something very special was about to happen. It did, shortly thereafter: Eddie Matthews's two-run shot over the right-field fence, Braves win 7–5.

Sam looked up: he was at the prison. He'd driven straight through town, forgotten to eat dinner. He doubled back, found a diner, had roast beef and mashed potatoes.

Eleven P.M. He pulled into the parking lot of the penitentiary after a nodding acknowledgment from a guard. He was known: there was no difficulty getting in, and getting through the checkpoints, until at last, with twenty-some others, he found himself in a little viewing room that opened on the death chamber. He recognized a couple of Little Rock newspaper boys, somebody from the Governor's Office, the assistant warden, and a few others. It was an odd group; one could listen to the determined banality of the conversation, most of it now turning on the great game that afternoon and the Braves' chances against the pinstriped colossi of Gotham, with the mighty Mantle, Berra, Larsen, McDougald and Bauer. In the chamber, a few guards were making last-moment adjustments; the electrician was tightening circuits on the chair, a sturdy oak thing that was so well made and severe it could have fit into a Baptist church.

"You must feel pret' good, Sam," said Hank Kelly, of the *Arkansas Gazette.*

"Not really," said Sam. "You just want it to be over."

"Well, I'll be glad when it's over too. I mean, he is just a nigger and he killed a girl, but now they got us believing niggers are human too. We had all that trouble with 'em this summer, the goddamned army and everything. Mark my words, it's just the beginning."

Sam nodded; Hank was probably right, though old Boss Harry Etheridge was raising hell in the House, aligning himself with the

Dixiecrats and swearing to gut the army appropriation in the up-coming budget to make Dwight Eisenhower pay for sending the 101st Airborne to Little Rock and humiliating the great state of Arkansas before the nation. But everyone knew that Boss Harry would never do such a thing; it was all show for the folks who elected him with 94 percent of the vote every two years.

None of that had anything to do with tonight's drama, however, which was simply the squalid end of some very squalid business, which nobody could really remember except Sam, and in which nobody had much vested interest and emotion. As ceremony, it was banal and flat; the Masons understood ritual much better.

He pulled away from the milling gents and went up to the glass window, where he got a better look at the engine of destruction: a chair, solid but upon closer inspection much worn, somehow insti-tutional and bland for all its presumed meaning. Sam stared at it as he always did: heavy cables ran from behind a screen (where the executioner would do his business in private) to one leg, were bolted to the leg and pinned up the strut of the chair, rising to a sort of Bakelite nexus. Smaller wires extended from it, two down the front, one down each arm and one to lie across the top of the chair, which ended not in a wrist or ankle bracelet but a little cap. It looked very thirties, Sam thought, assigning to it the style of the decade that had spawned it.

A phone buzzed, the assistant warden picked it up and listened.

"Gentlemen, please take your seats. They're bringing the con-demned man up from death row."

Sam looked at his watch. They were late. It was 12:02 A.M. He found a seat as the lights dimmed; around him, as in the theater, people squirmed and made ready, then fell silent. The minutes ticked by; the assistant warden lowered the lights until they sat in darkness, and then he too sat.

In the chamber, the door opened. Two guards, followed by the warden, followed by a priest, followed at last by Reggie Fuller, nineteen, of Blue Eye, Arkansas, Negro male, 230 pounds, eyes brown, hair brown, though it had all been shaved off.

Reggie was weeping. The tears ran down his eyes and his face was puffy and moist. A little track of glistening mucus dribbled from a nostril, and Sam watched as his tongue shot out to lick at it. He was manacled, walking in little stutter steps, talking to himself in a desperate stream of chatter. His eyes were out of focus. He was still fat; prison had not slimmed him down or, apparently, toughened him up.

They led poor Reggie to the chair and sat him down in it, though his body appeared stiff and he had trouble understanding what they were saying to him. At last he was seated; then came a horrid instant when one of the guards stepped back quickly, out of reflex: a stain of darkness blossomed at the crotch of Reggie's prison denims.

The priest whispered something to Reggie but it did him no good at all; his face seized up and his eyes closed; he continued to mutter madly. The guards moved in to secure the boy to the chair: one of them applied a slippery saline solution to his bare ankles, his wrists and the top of his head, where the electrodes were to be tightened—that would get all the electricity into him and prevent his skin from burning, although in Sam's experience this didn't always work out. Two others tightened and buckled the straps after the liquid had been sloshed on. Finally, they strapped the little leather beanie atop Reggie's round, shaven head though they got it slightly skewed, so that it looked like a dunce cap.

Quickly, a little man emerged from behind the screen and checked all the electrodes a last time, the sure professional, making dead certain that all would work. He pointed to one problem area, and a guard bent to make an adjustment. Then the little man stepped back and disappeared.

Sam looked at his watch. It was 12:08 A.M., eight minutes late. The warden seemed to be choreographing things. He gave a nod, and the guards left the room, leaving him alone with Reggie. He gave another nod and apparently a microphone was switched on because he now spoke in a grave voice and his tones were amplified into the witness chamber.

"Reginald Gerard Fuller, the state of Arkansas, in full accordance with the laws thereof, finds you guilty of murder in the first degree and sentences you to death this sixth, uh, seventh, day of October 1957. Reggie Gerard Fuller, do you have any last words?"

It was silent, though the mike caught Reggie's ragged breathing. Then he took a deep breath and spoke through sobs: "Sir, I apologize for wetting myself. Please don't tell nobody I peed my pants. And I am sorry for Mr. George if I got pee on him as he always done treated me nice."

He broke down, losing his words in a string of choking sobs. But then he breathed deeply, fighting the anguish. A dribble of snot ran out his nose, irritating his lips, but he could not do a thing. He looked out to the men behind the window. He took another deep breath: "And I miss my mama and my daddy and love them very much. I didn't kill Shirelle. God bless all the people who was nice to me and I hope someday somebody be able to tell why this had to happen."

"Are you done, Reggie?"

"Yes sir. I am ready for Jesus."

"Jesus probably ain't ready for him," said a man next to Sam in the dark.

The warden leaned over him, unsnapping something in the top of the beanie, and a blank mask unfurled, sealing off Reggie's features.

The warden left the chamber. Reggie sat still in the chair and for a second there was no change. Sam almost thought that—but no, the first charge hit him.

From his experiences, Sam knew it was a cliché of the movies that the lights dim in prison when an electrocution takes place: the chair and the prison lighting systems draw their power from separate generators. What happens is that witnesses involuntarily flinch, for to watch the cold extermination of a man, no matter how evil, is not an easy thing; and in memory, they recall the diminution of illumination and ascribe it to a power drain. But Sam didn't flinch or look away and had no illusion of flickering lights; he watched the whole thing, because that was his duty. He represented Shirelle and he hoped that by witnessing he was in some way liberating her soul from the agony of her death.

Reggie stiffened against the restraining straps as two thousand volts hit him. The shot lasted over thirty seconds. A vein on his neck bulged. He fought like a bull. His hands seized up into fists which held so tight Sam thought they'd explode. He seemed to pivot in the chair, just a shade, as if he were daintily trying to sidestep his fate. A small wisp of smoke rose from his skull and another from one of his wrists. His head lolled forward, but then somehow picked itself up again. He coughed and a spasm of vomit, mostly liquid, spurted out from under the mask to cling in globules to his naked chest. Huge crescents of perspiration blossomed moonlike under his arms.

"Another," said the warden into the phone.

The second surge bucked through Reggie but beat him down. He was limp by second 10, but the executioner held the circuit closed for another twenty, and by the small vibration of Reggie's now limp fingers could Sam tell that he was riding the bolt still. But then it ceased.

The odor of electrification reached Sam when the warden, two guards and a doctor entered the chamber. It wasn't the smell of burned meat or hair, but rather connected with Sam's memories of Christmas, when he'd given various of his boys Lionel train sets and usually set them up and ran them for a bit, until the kids tired of them: but they had an odd, metallic odor to them, heavy and pungent at once.

Sam flashed back from Christmas: in the room the doctor took out a stethoscope and pressed its cup to Reggie's chest, bare because the buttons had been ripped off his shirt. He stood and shook his head. The four retreated so that the executioner could hit Reggie again. It took five charges before the heart finally stopped beating.

"That boy just didn't want to die," said somebody.

The last official document in the file was the certificate of execution, meant to close the file out, mark it as justice delivered. Sam stared at it numbly.

Reggie, boy, why did you do it?

It was one of the great mysteries of the human heart, why one person will up and kill another. Sometimes it's money, sometimes sex, sometimes anger, sometimes simple meanness. Sam had studied it for most of his life and didn't know, not really. In this one, it seemed so simple: He figured Reggie must have picked the girl up after the church meeting and asked her for a kiss. She gave him the kiss. A young buck, a kiss, maybe he'd had a bit to drink at an Oklahoma Nigra crib, though no evidence as such was ever produced, and off he went. The more she fought, the more he wanted it. Finally, he did it and once he did it he was afraid she'd tell. So he drove her out Route 71 and smashed her over the head with a rock, just not noticing she was ripping at his shirt while he was smashing her. That simple. Usually when a Negro killed a Negro in those days, nobody much cared. Under usual circumstances he would have gotten away with it. It just happened to be Earl's last case and *that* made it important to white people like himself, nothing else.

The remaining documents in the file were the letters crazy Mrs. Fuller had written him until her death. They arrived, sometimes three and four a week, as the woman fought so desperately for her son's life before a brain aneurysm killed her. He had stopped reading them quite early and evidently a forgotten secretary along the line—he could never remember his secretaries' names—had just taken to dumping them unopened in the file. Fool woman! What was the point? If she were here and he could remember her name, he'd yell at her, like he did all his secretaries, which is why he had so damned many of them over the years! Most hardly lasted a year.

Sam looked at the letters. Now they seemed strange to him. He was on his knees in his basement looking through an old file. Why? He couldn't remember. Goddamn, it was happening again!

He looked at the file name. Parker. Parker. Oh, yes, the girl, Reggie, now it came back. Earl's last case.

All the letters from Reggie's mama, on their pink stationery. But why was one of them on blue stationery? Hmmmm? He plucked it from the stack, saw that it was in different handwriting. He had no memory of ever seeing it before. The date was September 5, 1957.

He turned it over and looked at the signature.

Lucille Parker.

It took him a second to realize that it was the dead girl's mama.

Thirty-nine years late, he opened the letter at last and started to read.

Eighteen

S O WHO would have moved your father's body?" asked Russ. "Stupid question," said Bob.

He stood up. They were bunked in Bob's old trailer on land he still owned seven miles out of Blue Eye on U.S. 270, abutting Black Fork Mountain. In the years since he'd left, the souvenir hunters had taken their toll and so had the graffiti writers, but his keys still opened the padlocks. In just a little time they'd restored the place to livability, though of course there was no phone and no electricity. But a fire kept the water hot and Coleman lanterns kept the place lit at night. It was a hell of a lot better than camping and a hell of a lot cheaper than staying in the Days Inn.

It was dark outside and the drive back from the cemetery was bleak and silent. Bob wasn't talking. He'd paid the laborers, and the doctor said he'd bill him for expenses but not for professional services. They'd stopped at a diner and eaten and now they were back.

"Why is it stupid?" Russ asked.

"Don't they teach you nothing at that fancy university? I thought you were supposed to be smart."

"I didn't say I was smart," said Russ. "I said I wanted to be a writer. Different things."

"I guess so. You can't ask who until you first find out if, and then how. *Who* don't have no meaning until you have figured out that there *was* a who. Got it?"

"Well—"

"Well, yourself. Think about it. How could it have happened?"

"Could the ground have shifted in some way?"

"No. The earth doesn't work like that. I thought you grew up in Oklahoma, not New York City."

"I did, but not on a farm. Anyway, they could have come at night and made an exchange with another body somewhere in the cemetery and—"

Russ paused.

"You saw for yourself how hard it was to excavate a body," said Bob. "It took three strong men the best part of a morning to uncover one. We didn't even get to the moving. It would involve block and tackles, a hearse or some kind of cart or something. Then you need the same thing with the other body. Then you got to patch up all that dirt so nobody would notice. Couldn't get all that done in a single night. Too much to do. So they'd have to do it in the day, under some kind of legal guise. But that wouldn't do 'em no good neither. You'd have to have lawyers, you'd have to concoct some kind of legal justification, it would end up doing exactly what maybe it was trying to avoid, and that is draw a lot of attention to itself."

Russ nodded.

"So what do you do?" asked Bob. *"Think,* son. Either come up with it or call that Princeton place and get back the half million or so your poor dad spent to get you educated."

"He didn't spend a cent," said Russ.

"Oh, that's right, I forgot your dad was such a bastard. Anyhow, *think.* Think!"

"I can't—"

It came from nowhere. Hooray, humiliation momentarily avoided!

"The stones. They move the gravestones! Two men could do it in a few hours under the dark of night. No problem. Especially since the original records have long since disappeared and whenever they did it, no one was there to give a damn."

"Not bad," said Bob. "But you are ahead of yourself. Maybe some night in the sixties a bunch of high school kids got drunk and went gravestone tipping. And maybe they was caught and maybe some judge made 'em replant the stones. But they were kids, they didn't give two shits. So they just stuck 'em in any which way. So what does that leave us?"

"Fucked," said Russ.

"Yes, it does. On the other hand—well, well, lookie here."

Russ saw headlight beams sweep across the windows and heard the car engine.

Bob opened the door.

"Howdy, Deputy," he called. "Come on in."

He stepped back and Duane Peck entered. Without his sunglasses, his eyes were small and dark.

"Mr. Swagger, I just wanted to tell you something. Remember I told you I'd see about getting the sheriff's records?"

"Why sure, Duane. You want a cup of coffee? Russ, put some coffee on."

"No, no," said Duane, then paused quickly to look around and up and down the room. "I'm on duty, got some patrol patterns to run. I just wanted to say they moved them records over to the courthouse basement. That's where most of the municipal records was stored. You know, it burned down in 1994."

"Damn!" said Bob. "I knew the court records were lost but I was hoping maybe the sheriff's records were different. Damn!"

"I'm real sorry."

"Duane, don't you fret on it. So far we got pretty much a big zero. With the body lost and no cemetery records, the whole damn thing is falling apart on us. We just may have to hang it up."

"Okay, I just wanted to tell y'all."

He gave each man a hearty smile, then backed out.

They waited until they heard the car pull out.

"Now, where were we?" Bob asked.

"You were saying that if it was kids who messed up the tombstones we were screwed. On the other hand . . ."

"On the other hand, if just for the hell of it we figure someone did this on purpose, then don't it follow only two tombstones were exchanged?"

"Yes."

"And we know the wrong one belonged to a twenty-five-year-old fellow killed in the Civil War?"

"I got it, I got it. We try and find records—in the courthouse, dammit, burned again, no, no, the historical society—on deaths in Polk County during the Civil War. Maybe we can find the names of the young men who fit that category. That would cut *way* down on the possible alternative grave sites. But what—excavate ten or twenty of them? I don't—"

But Bob was fishing through the familiar manila folder of clippings and soon enough produced the front page of the *Southwest Times Record,* July 26, 1955.

HERO TROOPER BURIED, it read.

Under a spreading elm, on rolling fields filled with trees, a group of mourners stood, somber people putting a good man into the ground.

"I don't—" Russ said. "The trees are all gone. You couldn't get much out of that picture. It's just a field."

"The trees are gone but the land's the same. Look at the rolls in the earth, the orientation to the sun, the mountains in the distance. I'm betting I can read the land from the photo and pretty much triangulate on that part of the graveyard. We link that with a name and bingo."

"You're not thinking of giving up?" said Russ.

Swagger fixed him with the sniper's glare.

"Not hardly," he said.

Duane Peck drove away from Swagger's, then, a mile or so down, pulled over. He snatched the little cellular folder from the glove compartment and pushed a button.

When the phone beeped, he made his report.

"Swagger and the kid seem stuck. They got nowhere to go 'cause they couldn't find no body. I went over to see 'em tonight and they were both down in the dumps. I think they may be moving out or giving up. So far they have nothing.

"Also, I went over to Sam Vincent's. I knocked on the door and he wasn't there. So I went around back and looked into his basement. Goddamn, he was sitting there, reading some old file.

Couldn't tell what it was but I seen a picture on the floor of some nigger gal. I knocked and knocked. I yelled, I did everything. That old goat's losing it big-time. Wherever he was, he sure as hell wasn't on this earth. Didn't even *hear* me, though I was but ten feet away. Maybe he's going deaf."

He hung up and started to drive home. But in ten minutes the phone rang. He picked it up.

"Duane?"

"Yes sir?"

"Duane, you keep an eye on Sam Vincent. He may be old but he's sharp."

"Yes sir."

"You may have to break in and find out what file, do you see?"

"Yes sir," said Duane.

Bob stood in the sun in the field of the dead. Around him, neat as Chiclets in a child's game, the gravestones fell away in rows. So many dead, from so many American wars.

He took a look at the picture. In the light it seemed to fall apart on him. He'd stopped that morning at a photography shop to inquire about a more useful enlargement but the man pointed out that without the original negative, he'd simply be enlarging the dots of which the photograph was composed in the old hot-metal rotogravure technology: the bigger the photo, the bigger and farther apart would be the dots. It was at its clearest as it was in the paper.

Russ had a thought about computer enhancement and thought they could FedEx it back to Oklahoma City, where a friend on the staff of the *Oklahoman* might be able to do more with it. But Bob said no, that would take too much time and he wasn't letting it out of his hands, so he would make do with what he had. So he sent Russ to the historical society in search of names that might link up with Bob's efforts in the boneyard.

He turned to the four compass directions, hoping to identify the mountain silhouette in the background, but it was difficult to make out, because only fragments of the line could be seen in the photo and even then he wasn't sure that it was mountain or some imperfection in the photographic process. And he didn't want to look too hard at the photo: the more he looked at it, the more the details disappeared among the dots. It was like a magic photo: it was only potent in small glimpses. To study it was to destroy it.

He looked up from the picture to the stones.

Martin.

Feamster.

O'Brian.

Lotsky.

Kummler.

Kids' names. Lost boys, what did it earn, what did it matter? Why? A darkness settled over him. He could remember still the name of the boys in his first platoon, 1965, or at least the thirteen out of the twenty-six that didn't make it back. And the five that lost limbs or the ability to walk. And the one that went into the nuthouse. And the one who shot himself in the foot. That left seven who made it home exactly as they'd gone, or some reasonable facsimile thereof. Those names he could not remember at all.

He looked about: so many of them, a starry skyful of them. Too many of them. Maybe coming to this place by himself in the middle of the morning was a mistake. He yearned to talk to Julie or to YKN4, to someone human and whole and normal. Get me off this frozen star, he thought, let me back in the world.

Bensen.

Forbes.

Klusewski.

Obermeyer.

As he moved, his perspective shifted and it seemed almost that the parade of white gravestones was itself moving. He thought of old Roman armies, phalanxes they called them, which moved in steady company formations against hordes of savages, calm, determined, believing in the unit concept and the spirit of the legion. That's what it felt like: moving through phalanxes of the dead, who stared at a living man and wanted to know: Why aren't you among us? Why are you special?

Gunning.

Abramowicz.

Benjamin.

Luftman.

Because I was lucky, he answered. Why did a line come at him? It was some poetry thing he'd read years back when he tried to understand what a war was and read every goddamn thing on it there was: the orient of thick and fast.

That's what it was too: an orient of thick and fast, a total world where one damn thing after another happened, and maybe you got out and maybe you didn't, and not much of it had to do with skill. His daddy, now maybe there was a man with skill. His daddy was a hero. His daddy killed the Japanese on Iwo Jima and Tarawa and on Saipan. His daddy must have killed 200 men. He himself had killed 341, though the official fiction read 87. So much death, their boys and our boys, marines and Japs, marines and gooks or slopes or whatever they called them back then. He shuddered. So many men who could have had children or written poems or become doctors.

Bergman.

Deems.

Ver Coot.

Truely.

It was a great puzzle. He stood and realized that he was on a ridge, one of the folds in the land that wasn't really visible until you actually walked it. He stood, now a little higher, and unfolded the photograph and compared what he saw with where he was.

The site in the photo seemed to be on a ridge too. Could he make out other ridges behind it, all the way to the trees? He could not. The background was lost in blur, as the dots became nonsense. He saw that the key had to be the trees, now gone for whatever reason. His daddy lay under a big tree. Maybe one hundred yards behind it was another tree. And that smudge in the dots, was that a tree? If so, that meant three trees in a rough line heading—in which direction? Couldn't say.

Hey, boys, help me. Help the one among you who should have been with you, help him.

But the dead were silent.

Feeling lost and a complete failure, he took another step to leave the ridge and find another, when in his far peripheral vision some anomaly registered. He turned to track it down and saw nothing. He turned back, moving, and again there came a signal from his subconscious that something should be noted.

Were the dead speaking in some odd way?

Come on, boys, tell me. Give me your message.

No, nothing, only silence. Far off, the sound of a power mower. Above, a jet glinting high in the sky, a commercial job leaving a fat contrail. A white car in the distance.

Duane Peck's, of course. Keeping watch.

Duane, who *are* you working for?

Someday soon, we may have to have a discussion with you.

He turned again: another strangeness assailed him.

He tried to sift through it. What was he feeling or noticing? It seemed only to come when he moved and in his peripheral, as if in focusing on it, it went away. He set out to duplicate the phenomenon.

He stepped, turning, trying to keep his eyes focused straight ahead and his mind emptied. Nothing. Did it again. Nothing. Felt like an idiot.

Did it the third time.

Now he had it. Far off, in the orthodox line of gravestones, was a gap. No, not a gap, an irregularity. One stone was slightly out of line. Why would that be?

He sighted on it and walked. It was 150 yards away.

Mason.

Mason, what's your goddamned problem? You a fuckup, Mason? You a mama's boy, you think the rules don't ever apply to you? That's how a sergeant would talk to a man out of formation. Why are you buried about a foot to the right of Shidlovsky and Donohue? Isn't Murphy pissed, you moving in on his territory?

Was it a mistake or—

A tree.

It was gone now, but when poor Mason went into the earth back in 1899 with a Spanish Mauser bullet in his heart, a giant tree must have been right here on this spot, and so they made a slight adjustment. Later the tree died, but Mason stayed out of whack until eternity.

Bob took the picture out.

If he looked hard, he could force himself to believe that if this was the spot for the tree, and since this spot was quite close to the boundary of the cemetery, then maybe this was the third tree in the line.

He looked again at the picture. What time of day was the picture taken? He ransacked through forty long years of memories, putting aside much that was not pleasant, and a little that was, and at last he remembered a formidable presence named Miss Connie rushing him through breakfast and dressing him because his mother kept breaking down. That put the funeral in the morning, before noon in any case. Figuring then that the photographer would have moved until the sun was behind him, and that it would have been reasonably low, Bob guessed that the photographer was facing west, his back to the east. So if this was the last tree, then the other two in the rough line would be to the east.

He orientated himself that way and saw only crosses. But he took off his blue denim shirt and draped it on Mason. He didn't think Mason would mind. Then he turned to the east and began to walk the line.

He found the second gap fifty yards beyond and rushed ahead. But where the first one should be, according to his reading of the photo, he found nothing, except a damned sidewalk that led to a little park of what appeared to be abstract statuary a little bit farther out. The rows were nice and even. He looked, uncomprehending how such a huge tree, had there been one, wouldn't have thrown the lines of graves out of whack. What the hell was wrong?

He looked more carefully at the picture.

Sidewalk, he thought. Where the hell is it going?

He found it, walked to the little garden. Some Confederate thing? No, dammit, Vietnam. The county had erected a little memento mori to the boys of Nam, a plaque, inscribed with words like *honor* and *duty* and *sacrifice* and of course the names. He looked, then looked away. He knew Harrison, and Marlow, he

knew Jefferson too, though Jefferson was black. Jefferson was Air-
Cav, right, a brother of the Black Horse? What about Simpson?
Straight-leg grunt, draft bait, caught a booby when he was down
to days until DEROS, the town's favorite hard-luck story.

Now Bob's head ached and he couldn't deal with the problem
any more. He turned to leave, and as if in giving up, he got it.

The tree comes down for whatever reason, but it was so imposing that its very presence had intimidated the gravediggers, so
they'd never gotten near to it. And when it came down, *that's*
where they build their garden to the Vietnam War dead, and that's
where they build the sidewalk. So that would make his dad's now
hidden grave somewhere along the sidewalk, probably to the right
of it. He thought it made sense too. If some guys were exchanging
gravestones that probably weighed two hundred to three hundred
pounds apiece late at night, they'd need a wheelbarrow or cart and
the sidewalk would be helpful. He walked a bit until he reached a
halfway point and then just turned west. He saw nothing, then
moved up and back and at last up a bit more. He was on a ridge.
He could see two gaps in the line before him to the west, one of the
tombstones by the farthest gap the blue of his shirt.

"Hey."

He turned. It was Russ.

"Those old records were miserable, but I got at least thirteen
names. Man, it's amazing the records that place keeps."

Bob looked to his immediate right.

"I bet one of them says Jacob Finley."

Russ dug out his paper, looked them over and then said, "Yeah.
Jacob Finley. Fifth Arkansas Light Infantry."

Bob looked at the grave marker, limestone corrupted by the
passage of time, untended, leaning ever so slightly to the right.

He knelt and put a hand on the cold stone.

Hello, old man, he thought. *I've come. It's time.*

This time it was easy. They went back to the County Coroner's
and refiled the exhumation papers for poor Jacob Finley, according
to them Bob's long-lost cousin. No lies had to be told regarding the
reasons for changing the request, because, the first paperwork al-

ready in order, nobody in the Coroner's Office particularly cared. Sam wasn't even necessary. A few phone calls later and all the mechanisms of the day before were reinstalled.

Mr. Coggins and his two boys were luckier this time. The grave site, being accessible off that helpful sidewalk, was now approachable by backhoe, and Mr. Coggins was an expert with the machine. In less than an hour he excavated the coffin, and just as the machine uncovered the box, Dr. Phillips showed up.

"How did you find him?" he asked.

Bob explained.

"Well, maybe you're right and maybe not." He went and looked as the quickly erected tackle drew the box from the ground.

"I will say this, that's a metal casket, circa the fifties. Do you remember the funeral home?"

Bob said no and then a name shot into his memory like a flare out of the void.

"Devilin's," he said.

"Yep," said the doctor. "And your father's name was Earl Swagger."

"Yes sir."

"That's what it says here. That's him. Okay, boys, load it into the hearse and we'll be off."

It didn't take a long time at the mortuary.

Bob and Russ waited outside, while a funeral procession formed up in one of the viewing rooms and people filed out to cars. The hearse that took Earl to the mortuary took some other poor joker back to the boneyard a half an hour later.

"I feel soaked in death," said Russ.

Presently the doctor came out. They went over to a little shady remembrance garden tastefully sculpted into the earth near the funeral home. Beautiful day late in the afternoon: the sun was just setting.

"I can put this in writing for you, but it'll take a day," he said, lighting a cigarette.

"Writing's not necessary. The boy'll take notes."

"Fine. First of all, then, I found the physical remains of a man in his midforties in a state of some advanced decomposition. What that means is that little tissue remains, which in turn means that some pathological determinations are impossible. Bullet tracks, for example. We can't tell which directions the bullets went through the body and what damage they did to soft-tissue elements like organs and the central nervous or respiratory system."

"Damn!" said Bob.

Speak to me, Daddy, he thought. *This is your only chance.*

"But," the doctor continued, "the skeletal remains were in good shape and the marks of the wounds were recorded there."

"Yes," said Bob. "Go on."

"I initially noticed two wounds. The first was on the left-side ulna, the outermost bone of the forearm, just down from the thickness of bone we call the olecranon, an inch or so beneath the elbow. I could tell from impact beveling that a bullet struck and shattered that bone; there was a traumatic ovoid indentation visible on some of the fracture segments. This is characteristic of a high-velocity solid-point bullet delivered at close range."

"Thirty-eight Super."

"A jacketed .38 Super would get the job done nicely, yes. The bones were in such fragmented disarray that, pending further lengthy examination, I couldn't rearrange them to get a caliber reading on the damage."

"Not necessary," said Bob.

"The second wound resembled the first. The same shattered bone, the same fragment presence, the same ovoid groove in some of the pieces, again characteristic of a smaller-caliber, high-speed bullet. This was observed at the frontal curve of the third rib of the left-hand side of the cadaver."

Bob mulled this over.

"Could he move, hit like that?"

"If he wanted to."

"Both wounds were survivable?" he finally asked.

"Well, that's a subjective judgment, dependent upon the subject's viability. Given that your father was in extremely robust health, that he'd been hit before and understood that getting hit didn't automatically equate to death, and given that he stanched his blood flow and that help arrived within a few hours, and given that there were no serious soft-tissue wounds not registered in the skeletal system, then yes, my judgment is that those two wounds were survivable. But there was a third wound."

"Go on," Bob said.

"I missed it at first," said the doctor. "Some tissue remains were present and the condition of the bones was not pristine. Of course I'm not in my lab working under the best conditions."

"But you found something?"

"Yes, finally, I did. In the sternum, a frontal plate of bone that shields the heart and anchors the ribs. There's a very neat round hole, or almost round. Ovoid actually, suggestive of a downward angle, that is, a high to low shooting trajectory. There's impact beveling suggestive of an entry wound. If you extrapolate from the placement of the penetration of the sternum on that angle, you get a real solid heart shot. The bullet path leads straight into the right ventricle where the pulmonary artery pulls the deoxygenated blood in. That artery and the ventricle would have been instantaneously destroyed. Brain death would have followed in, say, ten to twelve seconds."

"So he couldn't have been shot in the heart and walked three hundred feet back to where he was found?"

"He couldn't have moved a step. I doubt he was conscious much more than three seconds after impact."

Bob nodded and turned to Russ.

"So how's goddamn Jimmy Pye hit him a hundred yards out in the corn and he walks all the way back to the car?"

Russ just looked at him.

"You measured the hole, I take it," Bob asked the doctor.

"Yes, I did."

"I'm guessing it wasn't .357 or .429, right? It was, what, .311, .312 inches?"

"Good. Actually, .3115."

"As I understand it, the impact beveling always widens the diameter by a couple of thousandths of an inch?"

"Typically," said the doctor.

"So the bullet that killed my father, it was, say, .308 in diameter? That would make it a .30-caliber rifle bullet?"

"That's what every indicator says," the doctor replied.

"I don't get it," said Russ. "What's all this with the numbers?"

"It tells me who killed my father," Bob said, turning to look at him. "It sure as hell wasn't no Jimmy Pye."

"Who killed your father?" asked Russ.

"A sniper," said Bob.

Nineteen

THE SNAKE rattled again in the corn. The arm hurt. The side had gone to sleep. The legs ached.

Earl, sitting sideways in the front seat of his cruiser, straightened his legs out before him. He was all right. He would make it. A little smile came to him.

If that goddamn snake don't bite me, I made it again.

His radio crackled.

"Car One Four, this is Blue Eye Sheriff's Department, Earl, you hang on, goddammit, we are inbound and closing fast and I have an ambulance a minute or so behind. You hang on, son, we are almost home."

There was always that moment in the islands when it finally occurred to you that you had somehow made it again. It was like a little window opening, and a gust of sweet air floating through the room, and you experienced the simple physical pleasure in having escaped extinction. Other things would come later: the guilt you always felt when you thought of the good men lost forever, the endless dream replays where the bullets that missed you hit you or your own weapon jammed or ran dry. But for now it was okay: it was something God gave to infantrymen, just a moment's worth of bliss between the total stress of battle and the dark anguish of survivor's guilt. You just got one moment: Hey. I made it.

Earl thought of the things he had to do. He made a list.

1. Take Bob Lee to that football game. The boy had never been.

He himself hadn't been since 1951, on a visit to Chicago, when he'd seen the Bears play the Rams. It was a lopsided game. He wanted Bob Lee to see a *good* game.

2. Buy a Remington rifle, Model 740A, the new autoloader, in .30-06. He'd read about it in *Field & Stream*. Said they were building them even more accurate than the Winchester Model 70s, and you had that second and third shot automatically, without a recock.

3. Kiss his wife. Tell her how much he liked her strawberry pie. Buy her a present. The woman needed a present. Hell, buy her *two* presents.

4. Face it out with Edie. It had to be dealt with. Do it, put your house in order, clean up your mess.

5. See Sam Vincent. A policeman had to have a will. Sam could recommend a lawyer. Get a will, figure it all out.

6.

But at 6 an odd thing occurred. It seemed like time stopped for a second and Earl's soul flew out of his body. He imagined himself floating through space. He watched from above as the black Arkansas woods and hills flew by. In the distance, beyond Board Camp, he saw a well-lit little house off by itself. He descended and flew through the window. His wife, June, was there. She was doing something in the kitchen. She was dutiful, erect, a little irritable, in an apron, looking tired as usual, and not saying much. He floated up to her and touched her cheek but his finger had no substance and sank through her. He stroked at her harder, but could make no contact.

Puzzled, he flew up the steps. Bob Lee sat in his room, trying to put together a Revell model airplane. It was a Bell P-39 Airacobra, very dangerous-looking, but Earl knew the pilots hated it and that it never flew after 1943. Bob Lee, still wearing that damned coonskin cap and that Crockett T-shirt, was bent earnestly into the effort, trying with clumsy boyish fingers to cement the clear plastic cockpit bubble to the cockpit frame, a tricky operation because too much cement could smear the transparency of the ersatz glass, ruining the entire illusion of reality. Usually, Earl did this job himself, though the boy glued the bigger pieces together and was getting better and better at it. Earl reached to help the boy, but again his fingers were weightless; they touched nothing.

Bob Lee, he called. Bob Lee, Bob Lee, Bob Lee, but Bob Lee didn't hear him and struggled with the cockpit and somehow got it mounted. Earl watched as his boy's face knitted in disappointment and fury, and he beat a single tear away. But Earl knew too the model was ruined. He ached now to take the boy into his arms, and say, now, that's all right, maybe you didn't do so good this time, but there'll be other times. But when he reached he touched nothing.

7. Stop vomiting blood.

The blood was everywhere. What was happening? It spread across his chest and poured from his absolute center. When had this happened? It must have occurred in that split second when Earl went out of his body. It occurred to him that he had been shot and he looked out into the goddamned darkness and heard only the hooting of the owls and the stirring of other animals. It was so dark.

He had the consciousness of it all slipping away. He thought of a drain, of being whirled down a drain. His mind grew logy and stupid. He yearned to see his son again and his wife and his father; he yearned but it did no good.

Twenty

RED WAS AT AN EXECUTIVE MEETING for Redline Trucking when the call came, and he was almost happy, because Thewell Blackwell II, of Blackwell, Collins, Bisbee, over from Little Rock, was halfway through his briefing on potential complications if Interstate Commerce Regulatory Bill H.355 got out of the House Interstate Commerce Committee without serious reconfiguration, namely that the requirement for weight inspections at interstate borders be open on weekends as well as during the week, which had a long-term downsizing application in terms of routes serviced for out-of-state clients. It was all very interesting but Thewell was hardly the world's most commanding speaker and somewhere in paragraph 13, subsection II, subpoint C, Red began trying to decide whether he should go to a No. 8 shot for the long floater at Cherokee Ridge, where next year's nationals were slated.

The buzz against his hip shook him from his reverie. He leaned over to Brad Pauley, his vice-president for legal affairs and liaison with Blackwell, Collins, Bisbee, and whispered, "Be back in a sec."

Brad nodded, and Red smiled tightly and slipped out of the meeting, walking through the quiet hush of the suite that everyone assumed was the hub of his empire. He knew the name of everyone and everyone knew his name and as he moved toward the executive washroom just outside his fabulous corner office, he nodded and exchanged pleasantries with his employees.

But at last he was alone and punched in the number on his folder.

"Uh, sir, uh, I don't know what this means," the dull voice of Duane Peck, spy and idiot, reported, "but, um, I found out early this morning that Bob and that kid done reapplied for a Motion of Exhumation. I got to the cemetery and found out that they removed the body they wanted and it went to Devilin mortuary. They had that doctor come on down from Fayetteville to look at it. Don't know what he told them, but he told them something. I don't rightly know where they went. I drove by Bob's place just a few minutes ago, but it was deserted, though the truck was there. Maybe they was out in the woods out back or something. So anyway: that's what it is. I'll spin on by the old man's place later and see what's going on."

Red didn't curse or stomp or do anything demonstrative: he was too disciplined and professional for such exhibitionism. But now he knew he had a serious problem and it must be dealt with swiftly, or the time would pass when it could be dealt with at all.

His first call was back to Duane.

"Yes sir?"

"Where are you?"

"Uh, I'se headed back to town."

"All right. I want you to back off from Swagger and the boy. You'll have no more business with them, for now."

"Yes sir," said Duane.

"Someone else will deal with them. Now, you concentrate on the old man. I have to know what he's up to. You find that out, do you understand? But you have to do it easily; you can't carry on like a goddamn hog with a corncob up its ass."

"Yes sir," said Duane. "I'll be gittin' right on it."

Red disconnected. He didn't like what came next. This business was tricky and always involved the immutable law of unintended consequences but thank God he'd thought ahead and had good people in place and it could be done neatly and professionally, with maximized chances of success. He thought his father would be proud, for this was an old Ray Bama trick: Avoid violence, avoid force, always negotiate. But when violence is unavoidable, strike fast, unexpectedly and with total commitment and willpower.

He dialed a number. A man answered.

"Yeah?"

"Do you know who this is?"

"Yes sir." The voice had a familiar Spanish accent to it, Cuban probably.

"The team is ready?"

"The guys are all in. It's a good team. Steady guys. Been around. Solid, tough, know their stuff. Some are—"

"I don't want names or details. But it has to be done. You do it. I'll get you the intelligence, the routes, and you clear everything through this number. When you're ready to move, you let me know. I'll want a look at the plan, I'll want on-site reports. No slipups. You're being paid too much, all of you, for slipups."

"There won't be no slipups," the man said.

The man on the other end of the phone, in a farmhouse just outside Greenwood in far Sebastian County, let the dial tone come up and then he consulted a card and began to dial pager numbers.

Nine pagers rang. Two, one right after another, went off at the Blood, Sweat and Tears Gymnasium on Griffin Park Road in Fort Smith, where two immense men with necks the size of lampshades were hoisting what appeared to be tons of dead weight at separate Nautilus stations. Each was olive in skin tone, with glistening black hair and dark, deep, watchful eyes, identical even to the tattoos that festooned their gigantic arms, though one had a crescent of puckered, bruise-purple scar tissue that ran halfway around his neck, evidence of some grotesque encounter about which it would probably be better not to ask. They had bodies of truly immense mass, not the beautifully proportioned, narcissistic sculptured flesh of bodybuilders, but the huge, densely muscled bodies of men who needed strength professionally, like interior linemen or New Orleans mob drug enforcers and hit men.

Another pager rang in the back room of a crib just across the state line in Sequoyah County, Oklahoma, where a sleek black man was enjoying an act of oral sex being committed on him by a blond-haired woman of about thirty. He knew that she was really a man, but he didn't care; a mouth was a mouth.

Another pager buzzed on the firing line at On Target Indoor Firearms range over in Van Buren, as its owner stood with a customized Para-Ordnance P-16 in .40 S&W, calm and steady as a rock, blowing an ever-widening tattery hole in the head of a B-27 silhouette hanging from a pulley-mounted wire twenty-five yards out. He finished the sixteen-round clip, pulled in the target and examined the orifice he'd opened. Then he smiled, returned the gun to its case and checked out. In the parking lot, he made a show of putting the case in the trunk, but adeptly slid the .40 into an Alessi inside-the-pants holster, after, of course, inserting a fresh sixteen-round clip and cocking and locking.

Other sites: Ben & Jackie's Harley-Davidson shop, on 271 South, where a huge man in black leather and the lush hair of a rock singer, drawn into a ponytail, contemplated a chrome-plated extended muffler; the Central Mall Trio Theaters, on Rogers Avenue, where two rangy men who could have been ballplayers but weren't sat watching an extremely violent but idiotic movie; Nick's Chicken Shack on Route 71, where a large, pie-faced black man with a great many rings and necklaces ate a second extra-spicy breast; and finally at the Vietnam Market on Rogers, where a snake-thin Asian, also with a ponytail and a webbing of tattoos that ran from his neck down one arm (and scared the hell out of the proprietors), was trying to decide between diced mushroom and dried asparagus for the three-color vegetable salad he was contemplating for that night. He was a vegetarian.

The team leader, a Marisol Cuban with a gaudy career in Miami behind him, was named Jorge de la Rivera. He was an exceptionally handsome man and spoke in his vaguely Spanish accent to the assembled unit before him.

"We're thinking mainly of going for the kill from cars. Not a drive-by, not this guy, but a setup assault off a highway ambush, coordinated and choreographed, with good command and control. Three cars, a driver, two shooters in each car. Body armor. Lots of firepower up front. You want to go at this guy behind a fucking wall of nine-millimeter."

He waited. They were assembling their weapons, a selection of submachine guns stolen in a raid three weeks earlier from the New Orleans Metropolitan Police Property Room. He saw a couple of shorty M-16s, three MP-5s, one with a silencer, another with a laser sighting device, a Smith & Wesson M-76 with a foot of silencer, and the rest that universal soldier of the drug wars, ugly and reliable as an old whore, the Israeli Uzi.

Those who had satisfied themselves with their weapons loaded ammunition into clips: Federal hardball, 115-grain, slick and gold, for the subs; or Winchester ball .223 for the 16s.

"You been paid very, very well. If you die, money goes to your families you got families, your girlfriends otherwise. You get caught, you get good lawyers. You do time, it's good time, no hassle from screws or niggers or dirty white boys, depending on which color you are. Good time, smooth time.

"That's 'cause you the best. Why do we need the best? 'Cause this fucking guy, he's the best."

He handed a photo around: it passed from shooter to shooter. It showed a thin man who might have been handsome if he hadn't been so grim, leathery-faced, with thin eyes, squirrel shooter's eyes.

"This guy was a big fucking hero in that little war they had over in fucking gook country."

"Hey, Hor-hey, you not be talking about my country that way, man," said the ponytailed Asian, as he popped the bolt on a 16 and it slammed shut.

"Hey, we can be friends, no? No bullshit. I'm telling you good, you listen. Nigger, spic, cowboy, motorcycle fuck, wops, slope, fucking southern-white-boy asskickers, we got to work together on this. We're a fucking World War II movie. We're America, the melting pot. Nobody got no problem with nobody else, right, am I right? I know you guys have worked alone mainly or in small teams. If you want to go home in one piece, take it from Jorge, you do this my way."

"I don't like the gook shit."

"Then take it out on this boy. He killed eighty-seven of you guys. That was back in '72. They even got a nickname for him; they call him Bob the Nailer, 'cause he nails you but good. You think he forget how? In 1992, bunch of fucking Salvadorean commandos, trained by Green Berets even, think they got his ass fried on the top of a little hill? He kills forty-four of 'em. He shoots down a fucking chopper. He sends them crying home to *mamasita*. This guy is good. They say he's the best shot this great country ever produced. And when it gets all shitty brown in your underpants 'cause the lead is flying, they say this guy just gets cooler and cooler until he's ice. Ain't no brown in his pants. His heart don't even beat fast. Part fucking Indian, maybe, only Indians are like that."

"He's a old man," said the lanky cowboy. "His time has passed. He ain't as fast or as smart as he once was. I heard about him in the Corps, where they thought he was a god. He wasn't no god. He was a man."

"Were you in Nam?" asked Jorge.

"Desert Storm, man. Same fucking thing."

"Yeah, well," said Jorge, "whatever. Anyhow, we tie the whole thing together on secure cellulars. We move south this afternoon, as I say, three cars, three men in a car, and me, I'll be in a pickup, I'll hold the goddamned thing together while I'm talking to the boss. We know where he lives, but I don't want to do it there. We hunt him on the roads. We move in hunter-killer teams. You get a sighting, we work the maps, we plot his course, we pick him up. Very professional. Like we are the fucking FBI. We get him and his pal on a goddamned country road, and then it's World War III. We'll show this *cabrón* something about shooting."

Twenty-one

NOW IT WAS HIS TURN to dig. He looked around, making certain. Yes, yes, this was it. The fallen loblolly, over there, snarled in moss, that was the first marker. The gray chunk of rock ten feet away was the second; he remembered it well, though it seemed to have worn over the years. Standing where he could see a notch in the high ridgeline of Black Fork Mountain through a gap in the pines was the third. Triangulating between the three, he knew: this was the spot.

Bob set himself, and with the same sure spade strokes that he had seen liberate the coffin that was not his father but some poor young man he attacked the earth. It fought him, but he was in a mood for a fight. The spade sliced and cut into the earth and lifted it; he began to sweat as he found a rhythm, and beside him a pile of dirt grew.

It was still early. He'd arisen before dawn, while the boy slept, and headed up this trail, a mile from his trailer. He used to walk it all the time with the dog Mike, but Mike was gone now. So Bob was alone, with the spade and the earth. As the sun rose it sent slats of light through the shortleaf pines and they caught the dust that his efforts raised, enough to make a man cough. He worked on, taking pleasure in the power of his movements.

It wasn't a coffin he uncovered. It was a plastic tube, nearly a foot in diameter, nearly four in length. Pulling it from the ground at last, he felt its considerable weight, even as its contents shifted a bit, but that was fine. He got it out on the ground and stood for a moment, breathing heavily. All around him it was quiet. His actions had scared the birds. No animals came around, and it was too cool yet for bugs.

He wiped his brow with his handkerchief. Then he put his boot on the cylinder to hold it steady and thrust the sharp blade of the spade against the cap of the cylinder, punching at the Loc-Tite bonds that sealed the capsule, until at last they gave. With his hands, he pulled the cap entirely off, then reoriented the cylinder so that he could get at its contents easier and began to empty it.

First came a Doskosil gun case. He opened it, flipped away the envelope of desiccant and took out a Colt Commander .45, dead black, with Novak sights and a beavertail-grip safety. He pinched back the slide to reveal the brass of a Federal Hydrashock; eight more rested in the magazine. It settled into his hand, almost nesting; he hadn't touched a gun in years. Thought he was done with guns. But in his hand the gun felt smooth and familiar, knowing almost. It fit so well; that was the goddamned thing about them: they fit so well. He cocked the hammer and locked the safety up; cocked and locked was the only way to go. Somewhere in here there was a holster too, and a couple of more magazines, but for now he only wedged the pistol, Mexican style, into the belt above his right kidney.

What came out next was a longer gun case, and when he got it out and opened, he saw a Ruger Mini-14, a kind of shrunken version of the old M-14, almost delicate-looking, light and handy. He seized the weapon, threw the bolt and clicked the trigger against an empty chamber. It was a carbine-style semiauto, capable of firing a 5.56mm cartridge that could chew through metal or men, depending. It looked fine too, though oily after three years underground. The film of oil and the packs of desiccant strewn about the tube had done their job.

He pulled out a last trophy, a canvas sack, and looked inside: four Mini-14 magazines, one of them an oversize forty-rounder, the Galco holster for the Commander, six boxes of .45 Federal Hydrashocks, five boxes of hardball 5.56mm and five boxes of M-196 tracer.

He sat back, then turned.

"Whyn't you come on down and fill in this hole for me?" he called.

Silence.

"Russ, you don't know enough how to move through the woods quietly. Come on out."

The boy came out sheepishly.

"I saw you go. I followed you. I heard the sounds of your digging."

"You shouldn't sneak around on an armed man."

"You weren't armed when you left."

"Well, I am now."

"What the hell is going on? You have to tell me. You owe me."

"What is going on is I want you to go home. This thing may get hairy. I was meaning to speak to you on it. Yesterday, I realized. I should have realized earlier."

"Bob, I'm not going. This was my idea from the beginning. I have to stay."

"I don't want to have to call your father and say, 'I got your boy killed for nothing.' "

"It doesn't matter about my father."

"Your mother, then. It would kill her."

"She's been killed before."

Bob said nothing.

Russ came over and started shoveling the dirt into the hole.

"I'm not giving you a gun," Bob said. "I don't have time to train you and I won't be around an untrained man. If there's shooting, boy, you just hit the deck and pray for the best."

"I will."

"Well, we'll see how it goes. I'm sending you home at the first sign of heavy weather. This ain't a picnic. Ask your father. He'll tell you. It's about as goddamned scary as it gets. Now let's move out. You carry the ammo. It's the heaviest."

They walked down the path. It was a fine morning, with the sun now up and blazing through the pines; between the shafts, Russ could see the green heights of the Ouachitas dominating the horizon. It was a quality of his mind that he was highly irony-conscious. Thus it provoked him that the scene was so innocent and sylvan, such an emerald-green panorama of natural goodness, and here he was walking with a heavily armed and very dangerous man, setting off on a mission that this man suddenly thought could end in violence. He shook his head. He was a *writer!* What was he doing here?

"Something funny?" Bob asked.

"It's just ridiculous," said Russ.

"Whatever it is, it ain't ridiculous," said Bob. "It may be dirty, it may be ugly, it may be evil. It ain't ridiculous and the people who put it together ain't funny. They're professionals."

"The sniper who killed your father?"

"He's just a little piece of it. He's working for someone else. Someone called the shot, someone laid it out, someone put it together very tight and solid."

"How do you even *know* there was a sniper?" Russ finally asked.

"It started with the bullet weights," said Bob darkly, as though he hated to explain to an idiot. "They recovered three bullets from my father. Two were 130 grains. One was 110 grains. The 130-grainers were clearly from Jimmy's .38 Super. But the 110? It's possible a third 130-grainer hit him and broke apart and only 110 grains' worth was recovered, but the goddamned list didn't say nothing about that. So that gets me thinking: where the hell does a 110-grain bullet come from? And what *is* a 110-grain bullet? Do you know?"

"No."

"Your father would."

"Fuck him."

"It's a carbine bullet. M-1 carbine, handy little job they used in World War II. Underpowered, but sweet-handling."

"Okay. So? What would the significance of that be?"

"I'll tell you when I'm ready. The next thing was the grocery store job. Forget why. Don't worry about why. Just look at the job: too clever. The right grocery store, the right time of day, very

professional. Jimmy was a small-potatoes car thief. How'd he figure on that so quickly?"

Russ said nothing.

"Then the getaway. Even you got that one. How'd they get sixty
miles south, through all them roadblocks? You could write it off to
luck, I suppose, unless you looked at it carefully. They had a lot of
other luck that day too. How'd they get so damned lucky? On the
other hand, it wouldn't be a thing to load that car in a semi and
haul it down here. You'd sail through. Trucks sail through all the
time."

Russ said nothing.

"The .38 Super. It's a pro's gun, a criminal's gun. It's a man-
killer. Bank boys love them, mob hitters, that kind of thing. Seems
very goddamned odd the best man-shooter in the world just happens to show up in Jimmy Pye's hands the day he gits out of jail."

Russ nodded.

"Then the shooting site," Bob said. "I'm a professional shooter. I
kill people for a living, or at least I did. And if I'm setting up a
shot, that's how I'd do it. You have to be high, because the corn
gets in the way of a level shot. He's in the trees, maybe a hundred
yards away, in a stand. His job is to watch. The setup is to have
Jimmy Pye kill my father with the .38 Super. But whoever's pulling the strings, he has to worry if Jimmy's quite the man for the
job. And Jimmy wasn't. So there has to be another guy there, just
in case. Shooting slightly downhill at a sitting target on a windless
night. It was an easy shot," said Bob.

"It was at night. *It was at night!!*" shouted Russ. "Could he see in
the dark?"

"Yes, he could," said Bob. "That's why he was using the carbine
and not a ballistically better weapon. Remember the rattlesnake?"

"The snake?" Why did this strike a note of familiarity with
Russ? Who had spoken of snakes? But then, yes, he remembered.
The old man had mentioned somebody named Mac Jimson shoot-
ing a snake on the road. He said he'd never seen anything like it.

"Snakes are cold-blooded night hunters, but they have some
advantages," Bob explained. "They're sensitive to heat. That's how
they hunt. They're sensitive to infrared radiation, in other words."

"I don't—"

"Infrared," Bob said. "Black light."

Russ swallowed. Infrared? Black light?

"Infra is light below the visible spectrum, the light of heat. It has certain military applications. If you radiate heat, you radiate light in that wavelength and you have an electronic device that can amplify it, you can see in the dark. Or you can put out a beam in that wavelength and you can see it in such a device. Ours was called the M-3 sniperscope, pretty much state-of-the-art in 1955. It was a scope and an infrared spotlight mounted on a carbine. Worked best on clear, dark nights. He puts out a beam. He watches my daddy in that beam. My daddy never knows a thing. One shot. Only the snake knew. It felt the heat; it has pit organs in its skin, heat receptors, and when the light came onto it, it stirred, rattled. Then it did what a hunter would do. It went *toward* the source of the infrared. That's why it crossed the road, no matter all the cops. It was hunting the sniper."

"But you can't *know,*" said Russ. "It's all abstract theory. There's no real proof."

"Yes, there is," said Bob. "The bullet hole in my father's chest. It was .311 of an inch, which is the diameter, with impact beveling, that an M-1 carbine bullet would make. Jimmy had a .38 Super. Its diameter would be a little more than .357. Bub had a .44 Special, which hadn't been fired. My father *was* killed in the dead of night by a .30 carbine bullet."

"Jesus," said Russ.

"You see the whole thing was about killing my father. I don't know why. My father must have *known* something, but there's nothing in his behavior that last week to suggest anything unusual was going on. But these guys maneuvered very cleverly. Stop and think: They investigated Earl and found his weakness, his soft heart for a white trashy punk named Jimmy Pye. They got to Jimmy in jail, made him some kind of offer so good he had to take it and sell out everything he had. They set up a grocery store job guaranteed to make Jimmy famous, even to the little bit about him stopping for a hamburger! They moved him downstate; he got in contact with Daddy to surrender. They had access to a state-of-the-art piece of hardware and a military shooter who knew what the hell he was doing, just in case. Thorough, professional, very well thought out, all contingencies covered. All to kill one little state trooper sergeant in rural Arkansas in a way that would appear to be open-and-shut. Put the body in the grave, say the prayers and walk away from it."

Russ said, "And it's still going on. The exchanged headstones. Duane Peck."

"Yes, it is."

He nodded.

"Only the snake knew," repeated Bob. "It was hunting the sniper. Now I am."

It came down to a telephone. There was no telephone at Bob's trailer so after he and Russ ate and changed and Bob locked the Ruger and its ammunition in the Tuf-Box bolted across the back of his truck, they got in and headed not into town but to the Days Inn, where Bob rented a room—for its phone and its privacy.

Jorge, leading a convoy of hitters, got to Bob's trailer forty minutes after they left. The truck was not in sight.

"Goddamn," he said.

He went back to the men in his unit. He left one man in the trees across from the trailer with a pair of binoculars and a phone; he assigned the remaining vehicles to begin to patrol on preselected routes in Blue Eye and greater Polk County, in search of the truck, a green Dodge, one unpainted fender, Arizona plates SCH 2332. The instructions were simple. They weren't to make contact or even follow. Instead, they were to phone in; Jorge himself, with telephone consultations with the boss, would try and determine where Bob was headed. The idea was to set the ambush well in advance and spring it with the whole team, in the coordinated way they had agreed upon.

Unawares, Bob started his hunt with a call to the Pentagon, Department of the Army, Archives Division, Sergeant Major Norman Jenks.

"Jenks."

"Say, Norman."

"Bob Lee, you old coot! What the hell, you still kicking around?"

"I seem to be."

The old sergeants, who'd first met on Bob's second tour when he led recons up near Cambodia while assigned to SOG and Jenks had been S-2 staff, chatted for a bit in the profane language of retired senior NCOs. But eventually Bob got to it.

"Need a favor."

"Name it, Coot. If I can do it, I'll do it. I'm too old for them to do anything to me now."

"And too top-heavy," sergeantspeak for having won too many combat decorations.

"Yeah, well," said Jenks. "Go ahead, pard. Shoot."

"You remember you guys had a gadget called a goddamned Set No. 1/M3 20,000 Volt?"

"That piece of shit? My first tour the ARVNs were using 'em. They were old then, and they was supposed to be fungus-proofed but whoever said they was never saw the fungus in Nam. That shit'd eat you for lunch!"

"Yeah, it was old by the sixties."

"It was really World War II vintage. Based on some piece of German gear an OSS team brought back after the war, as I recall."

"Well, anyway, I'm looking at the year 1955. Suppose a fellow had a need to use a night-vision setup in 1955 and he was in West Arkansas. How'd he get a hold of one? Where'd they be? Were they issued widely to troops? Would they have been, say, up at Campbell with the 101st Airborne? Would they have been at Bragg with the 82nd? Or maybe they were up at that ballistics development lab in Rhode Island? I'm just trying to get a feel for how common they was and how close to West Arkansas. And who was their expert? Who advocated them? Who trained on them and knew them? My feeling is, you couldn't become proficient without training."

"You couldn't. It was like looking into an aquarium. The gooks never did figure it out. Anyhow, when do you need this by?"

"If it came yesterday, I'd be late."

"Damn, Bob, what the hell this all about?"

"It's a deal I'm working on with a writer."

"Oh, a book! It'll be a best-seller, I can guarantee you. You gonna tell him about An Loc?"

"I might."

"Okay, I got a light schedule today and a newbie spec 4 just assigned; I'll get this boy right on it. Number?"

Bob gave him the number.

"You hang tight. I'll see what we can dig up."

He hung up.

"Now what?" said Russ.

Bob opened his wallet and peeled out $300.

"I want you to take the truck and head up one exit on the Etheridge Parkway. That's the Y City exit. I seem to recall a camping store up there. You go up there and buy two sleeping bags, a Coleman lantern, some Coleman fuel, some changes of underwear, toothbrushes, the works. Remember the fuel, the damn lantern don't work without it! We're not going back to my trailer for a spell."

"What are you talking about?"

"It's good to change your base of operations every once in a while. We been at the trailer a week. We'll move somewhere else for a couple of days or so."

"But I *had* a sleeping bag. At the trailer. I *had* underwear. I *had*—"

"Now, don't get yourself lathered up. Man, you start to squeal like a pup every goddamned time. We'll leave that stuff there. If anybody like a Mr. Duane Peck takes a look, he'll see it and figure we're due back at any time. Got it?"

"You are paranoid," said Russ.

"Para-what?"

"Never mind."

Russ left. Bob lay back and rested. He gave Russ time to drive off, then left the room and went down the hall to the pay phone and called his wife collect.

"Well, hello."

"Well, howdy, stranger," said Julie. "Thought you'd married a movie star and headed for California."

"Not this boy. No sir. Ah—"

"Ah—I know that tone. You're about to tell me something I don't want to hear."

"Sweetie, it's nothing. It just is going to take a bit longer than I thought. Maybe another week or two."

"Are you having a good time?"

"It's been interesting. I went to his grave. I had a moment with him. We been going through records. It's very educational. Saw Sam. That sort of thing."

"How is he?"

"Old. Older. I don't know, he goes a little strange now and then. I'm worried about him."

"We're all older."

"How's my baby girl?"

"She's fine. Misses her daddy."

"I'll be home as soon as possible."

"You're not in any trouble, are you?"

"Nothing I can't handle."

"You love trouble. That's your problem."

Bob bought a Coke and the Little Rock paper and went back to the room. About two o'clock the phone rang.

"Hello?"

"Down-filled or polyester?"

"Huh?"

"Do you want down-filled or just simple polyester? For the sleeping bags? Maybe it's too warm for the down-filled. Incidentally, I had to go all the way to Booneville. That camp store was closed."

"Polyester is fine. And a cooler. Fair enough?"

"Gotcha."

He hung up to more silence in the room and the minutes ticked by. At last the phone rang. It was about 3:30.

"Hello."

"Bob?"

It was Sergeant Major Jenks.

"Yes sir."

"All right, I got some info for you. You guessed right pretty much about the M-3s. At no one time did the army have on its TO&E more than two thousand of those units. They was damned expensive, they was hard to operate and they was delicate, so distribution was mainly to elite units; they never handed 'em out to the troops at the company or platoon level. Hell, you couldn't even buy one at the PX! Dispersion was mainly to special forces units in Europe, to the big airborne divisions at brigade or regimental S-2 level, to 4th Army in Washington State and the 3rd Mountain Division up in Alaska. The heaviest profusion of them was to 9th and 23rd Infantry on the DMZ at the 38th parallel in Korea. Another complement went to the Jungle Warfare School in Panama. Just what you'd expect."

Damn, Bob thought.

"Okay, fine, Norman, I—"

"Wait a sec, ain't done yet. Don't *this* beat all? According to our records, three such units were transshipped from the Panama Zone, the Jungle Warfare School, to Camp Chaffee, Arkansas, in late June of 1954."

Bob waited a second.

"What for?"

"Well, one of the problems with the goddamned things was simple: no doctrine. They were not effectively used in Korea because nobody had thought much about the best methods of deployment and there was thought about junking the things altogether. Then a brilliant young first lieutenant wrote a paper on night-vision tactical doctrine which he submitted to the *Infantry Journal,* where it got published and he got noticed. So he finds himself TDY Camp Chaffee, where he's put in charge of what they're calling the Experimental Night Tactical Development Program, code-named BLACK LIGHT, where they run a lot of night-fire operations trying to figure out the best way to deploy the thing, while also working with ways to refine it. They got some R&D types, they got some intel boys, maybe even some Agency boys in it."

"It sounds like a black operation. The technology would be useful for a hell of lot more people than company commanders with perimeters to defend."

"You got that right."

"Give me a name, Norman."

"I thought you'd ask for one," said Jenks. "And I got a hell of a name for you. Preece."

"Preece!" said Bob.

"Yep. That's where the whole army night-sniping program began. With BLACK LIGHT and First Lieutenant, later Major and now Brigadier General James F. Preece, retired. Jack Preece."

Bob nodded. The name took him way back.

"Tigercat."

"Tigercat. That's the one and same guy."

"You got an address for the general?"

"I went to the computer for you, Bob. You never heard this from me, which is why I am calling from a pay phone in Arlington."

"Fair enough."

"He's now CEO and director of research for an outfit called JFP Technology, Inc., in Oklahoma City."

"What's JFP Technology?"

"One of those small unmarked buildings that's really skunkworks for nasty toys. Their specialty is sound suppressors and night-vision equipment for the world's armies and SWAT teams. Our Delta guys use their stuff and so do the SEALs. That's what Tigercat gets you in the civilian world."

Norman gave him the number.

"Thanks, Norman," said Bob, then hung up. He waited a second, letting his head clear. Tigercat was the code name for the 7th Division Sniper School in Vietnam, where the army ran its snipers through and taught them the doctrine. Of course there was a problem: army doctrine was different than marine doctrine. Not worse, not better, just different. And it worked, or at least the kills said it did. Army snipers ran up far higher numbers in Vietnam than marines did.

So was it an interservice thing? The fact that there was not a lot of love lost between sniper communities in the two services, either then or now? Maybe. Maybe not. Bob didn't know. What he did know was that Preece's Tigercat turned out a number of first-class shooters very quickly; and in no little time, the army snipers were putting bodies in bags all over Nam. Yet even the army was a little awkward about this triumph; its huge and efficient P.R. machine never made a thing of it, no books came out of it, none of its high scorers ever became known to the public as had he and Carl Hitchcock. It was . . . well, it was different.

The door opened and Russ walked in.

"You want me to unload the truck?"

"Just a minute," said Bob. "Now you listen to me."

He dialed the number as Russ sat across from him. After a bit the phone was answered by a young woman.

"JFP Technology," she said.

"Yes, hello, I'm calling for General Preece."

"May I ask who's calling?"

"Yes, my name is Gunnery Sergeant Bob Lee Swagger, USMC, retired. I was familiar with the general's operations in Vietnam; he might be familiar with mine."

The phone went dead for a bit and then, "Gunnery Sergeant Swagger?"

"Yes sir, it is."

"By God, as I live and die, the real live Bob the Nailer. I never thought I'd have the pleasure. You did a hell of a job of work in country."

"Thank you, sir. Just the job the Corps gave me."

"You may not realize this, but do you remember when you won the Wimbledon Cup in '71 after your second tour?"

"Yes sir, I do."

"Well, I came in third!"

"My God!"

"Yes sir. You had it that day, Sergeant. Nothing threw you. Not the wind or the sun or the mirage. You shot through everything."

"That's our good Marine Corps training, sir!"

"Sergeant, you don't 'sir' me, all right? I'm retired now. All that's behind us. What's on your mind?"

"Well, sir, I've signed up to do a damned book. 'I was there,' that sort of thing."

"That'll be a hell of a book. I can't wait to read that one. The things I heard about the An Loc Valley."

"Hell of a fight," said Bob. "Anyhow: I'm working with a young writer and he's got me convinced we ought to do what he calls context. You know, background, the big picture, how it all fits together. So I thought I'd have to describe the marine sniper program in those days. And he wanted to look at the whole damned thing. Army sniping too; give it the grand overview, he says. Well, sir, I thought you'd be the man to talk to."

"Gunny, you know a lot of that is still classified. And the army never went public with its snipers in the way the Corps did. Too damn liberal in Washington, I suppose."

"Yes sir."

"Off the record?"

"Hell yes, maybe you could just point us in the right direction."

"You in town?"

"I'm actually home in Arkansas. Eight hours away maybe. Could drive up tonight."

"Get here tomorrow morning. Let me see. Hell, I have a meeting with Sales. Oh, fuck, I'll shift it. Jean, call Sales, tell them we'll have the meeting tomorrow afternoon!"

"That's it," said Bob. The general gave him an address.

"See you tomorrow."

Bob hung up.

"Let's go."

"Now?"

"I ain't getting any younger."

Some nights it was good and other nights it was beyond good, into some kind of great. Tonight was great. When he was done and when she had given him the ritual compliments, he rolled over and went downstairs. The huge house on Cliff Drive was more or less quiet except for the shiftings of his sleeping children. The light snapped off and she went to sleep. He poured himself a glass of Jim Beam, walked out on the patio and saw, far below, the winking runway lights of the airfield. He took a sip of the whiskey and enjoyed for just a second the illusion that everything was fine in his empire.

Then the beeper in his bathrobe pocket began to vibrate. Red checked the number and saw that it wasn't goddamned Duane Peck at all but instead the number of Jorge de la Rivera's phone. Quickly he dialed.

"So?"

"Sir, ain't got nothing. Goddamn been up, down and around this place. Left a man at his trailer, just picked him up, ain't seen nothing all day. Maybe they gone."

Red thought a bit.

"You want us to book time in a hotel, sir?"

"No, no, that would look odd, ten men in three cars and a truck pulling into a Holiday Inn all at once. No, head back up here, get back to the farmhouse. What, by the parkway that's only an hour."

"Yes sir. We hunt again tomorrow?"

"Ah, let's wait on that. Get 'em some good sleep. No fucking around. When we need 'em, we'll need 'em fresh and fast."

"Yes sir."

Red waited a second, then called Duane Peck's number.

"Hello? Who is—"

"Who do you think this is?"

"Yes sir."

"Where are you?"

"I'm outside the old man's house, just like you said. He did the craziest things today. I swear, this old man's lost it. He—"

"Make a report after I'm off the phone. Listen, Duane, tomorrow, first thing, you go in uniform to every motel, every restaurant, every gas station, every camp store there around Blue Eye and you see if anyone's seen Swagger and the boy. They've disappeared. We have to find them, fast."

"Yes sir. Instead of the old man?"

"For now, yes. Then you call me. You get something, you call me immediately, you understand?"

"Yes sir."

Red hung up, finished the bourbon and went to bed in a foul mood.

Twenty-two

SAM WOKE IN A FURY, but he couldn't remember about what.

His anger, unmoored, floated about blackly in his mind, looking for a target.

"Mabel!" he screamed. "Where's my goddamned coffee?"

Then he remembered that Mabel had been his secretary in 1967, for seven months, before she quit and went off to have a nice, quiet nervous breakdown. He thought she'd died sometime in the eighties, but he wasn't sure.

Mabel's untimely death did, however, mean one thing: no coffee. So he got up, struggled to find his glasses—nope, they hadn't taken them yet—and straggled through the house until he found the kitchen. Somehow he got some coffee going; some things a man never forgets. The coffee perking, he bumbled back to his room, got himself showered and dressed, though he had to wear a white sock and a blue sock, and headed back for the coffee.

Fortunately, the mail had come. Unfortunately, it was from 1957. He struggled to put two and two together for a while, unable to comprehend why this letter was lying out here on the dining room table, lavender, in neat, precise womanly penmanship. He looked at the signature. Lucille Parker. Who the hell was Lucille Parker?

Then, of course, he had it: it blasted into his mind.

"Goddamn woman!" he bellowed. *"Goddamned woman!"*

He grabbed his car keys, there on the vestibule right next to his meerschaum pipe and his sunglasses and—

His meerschaum pipe!

Where the hell did that come from?

Anyhow, he grabbed it and raced out to his Cadillac in the garage. He fired her up and backed out. Evidently, his neighbors had mischievously placed their garbage cans in his driveway, for there came a clatter and he looked up in his rearview mirror to see them rolling in the street, spewing their contents everywhere. Why would they do such a stupid thing?

He drove toward Niggertown.

West Blue Eye, it was now called. You couldn't say nigger anymore. You couldn't even say Nigra. It wasn't allowed.

The streets seemed to fill. People were staring at him and he wasn't sure why. He felt like the Queen of the May on some float in a parade. Horns were honking, children screaming. What the hell was going on?

Suddenly a patrol car, its siren blaring, its flasher pulsing, shot by him, in pursuit of some miscreant. But oddly, the car forced him to the side of the road.

A tall, lanky, pale-eyed man got out, spat a wad on the ground and approached.

"What's the story, Mr. Sam?"

"Who the hell are you?" Sam wanted to know. He read the plaque on the pocket: PECK, it said.

"Duane Peck, Mr. Sam. You know me as well as you know your own name."

"I don't know no such goddamned thing. What the hell do you want?"

"Mr. Sam, that was a traffic light you went through back there and you almost hit two cars, and some people had to run to get out of the way. You must have been doing sixty."

"I'm in a hurry, goddammit. What is this all about?"

"Well, sir, I'm just a little worried about your safety and the safety of the public."

"You gonna give me a ticket?"

"No sir, no need. If you tell me where you're going, I'd be

happy to follow you, make sure you keep your speed down and all. Or maybe you'd best let me drive you. That's all."

"Why, I never heard of such a thing. Peck, get out of my goddamned way or I'll call the sheriff and you'll spend the rest of your life on night shift. Do you know who I am?"

"Everybody knows who you are, Mr. Sam. Sir, I guess you can go on now, but I am going to follow you, so there ain't no problems, all right? You make sure you obey them traffic lights, do you hear?"

Sam muttered something black but Peck had already headed back to his car. Arrogant sumbitch! Sam remembered when all deputies treated him like a Caesar.

Peck finally pulled away and Sam started up again. He was very careful not to drive fast and to obey all the traffic signs. No one honked at him, although he did honk at one goddamned lady who took her goddamned time getting across the street with her baby. What did she think, she had the entire right of way for as long as she wanted?

He rolled over the tracks and down the dusty streets of Nig— . . . of west Blue Eye. These people still lived like Bantus. Why didn't they clean up? They wanted to be full citizens, they could at least keep their grass trimmed. No excuse for it, none at all.

But in his anger he also felt sadness: they were so sad. Who would take care of them? Who would direct them? Why did they *always* misbehave? Couldn't they see that wasn't the way. He shook his head.

He passed the church and the shell of mansion that had once housed Fuller's Funeral Parlor but was now a ruin, and in time he came to the house of the address, which was still trim and nice and had flowers on the trellis. He parked in the street and two little Negro children came up and watched him with those big eyes they had.

"Go on, shoo, get out of here!" he waved them aside, and stepped up the wooden steps to the porch.

He banged hard on the door.

A woman in her forties answered, looked at him quizzically.

"Did you write this?" he demanded.

She took it and looked at it.

"Sir, I was five years old when this was written. It's from Mrs. Parker."

"Let me talk to her."

"Sir, she does not live here. Who are you?"

"You don't know me? Everybody knows me. I'm Sam Vincent, the county prosecutor."

"No sir, I do not know you."

"You must be new in town."

"I have lived here for five years."

"Damn! I can't believe you don't know me."

The woman shook her head, and a certain expression came across her eyes. He knew the thoughts that ran through her head began with the words "White folks" and went on to chronicle something that she found utterly unknowable about Caucasians. But he didn't care.

"Well, where is she?"

"Where is who?"

"Mrs. Parker."

"Sir, do you really think *any* black person knows the whereabouts of every *other* black person?"

"Well, I wouldn't know about that. Never thought about it much. I want to help her. That's why I'm here. She wrote *me,* don't you understand?"

"You say you the law?"

"Yes, I am, in a way. But I'm not here to arrest a colored person. It's about her little girl. She—"

"Oh," said the woman. "Yes, I know. We don't never forget *that.* You wait here."

She disappeared and then came back in five minutes.

"She's at her other daughter's. Out in Longacre Meadows, the development."

It never occurred to Sam that Negroes could buy homes in Longacre Meadows, a fairly nice residential development east of Blue Eye, where Connie Longacre used to live.

"Do you have an address?"

She gave it to him.

"I'm sorry for being so loud," he said. "I didn't mean anything by it."

"Oh, Mr. Sam," she said, "I wasn't here, but Sheila"—now, who the hell was Sheila?—"told me how you tried that white man Jed Posey for beating poor Mr. Fuller to death. No white man ever tried a white man for hurting a black before."

It had cost Sam an election and a job he loved more than any other.

"Oh, that," he said. "He deserved the chair. I tried to get it for him but the state of Arkansas wasn't about to execute a white man for murdering a black one in 1962. At least he's still in the penitentiary, rotting to hell slowly. Death would have been better, but rot has its place in this world."

"Somewhere, I believe you trying to be a good white person. I hope Jesus is with you."

"He's probably busy today, but I do thank you for the thought."

Sam drove east out of Blue Eye down Arkansas 88 with an odd feeling. Goddamned Duane Peck went with him the whole way and Sam tried to concentrate on not speeding and staying on the right side of the road, a task built on the assumption that he knew which side of the road to drive on in the first place, which he did, usually, unless he forgot, as now.

Duane honked and Sam looked up to see an automobile coming right at him. Fool! Why didn't he turn? Then he saw *he* was on the wrong side of the road. Had they changed that recently? Agh! Filling with rage, frustration and anguish, he moved back where he belonged. The driver gave him the finger! Now, whatever for?

Eventually, the town fell away. There seemed to be a pleasant space of country, then he passed the double pillars of rock and Cyclone fence that led to Mountaintop, as Boss Harry's place was called, another ruin now that that goddamned ambitious son of his was running for President and hardly came back to Arkansas at all and when he did he stayed in Fort Smith, not down here in Polk.

Then he felt not a shock, but a terrible melancholy, and he remembered why he'd stopped coming this way. It was when they tore the old Longacre place down, once such a grand house where old man Longacre lived and where his son, Rance, had come with his new bride, Connie, in 1932 and where Connie had raised her son and buried her husband and then buried her son and his young wife, and then lent her cottage to Edie White Pye and soon enough buried Edie. Then when the county took the child and wouldn't let Connie keep it because she was no relation, and it was taken off by Pye people and then seemed to disappear, Connie, her heart broken for the very last time, seemed to finally give up and acknowledge that Arkansas somehow wasn't really meant for her, though she loved it so.

Where had Connie gone? Back to Baltimore? He thought so. Connie wouldn't tell him.

He had driven her to the bus station that last day, after she'd closed the house.

"It's such a beautiful state," said Connie. "And the men are so strong: Rance, of course. And my son, Stephen. And Earl, poor, beautiful, brave, doomed Earl. And you, Sam. You're such a man. I don't think I'll find your like in the East."

"Connie, you don't have to go, you know."

"Yes, I do. If I lose another man out here, I might not recover."

She was still beautiful and Sam had loved her secretly for many years.

"I'm sorry I couldn't get the boy for you."

"Poor child. He'll grow up without knowing his father."

"Well, that's one thing I don't care to worry about," said Sam. "He's better off not knowing Jimmy."

She just looked at him and something passed behind her eyes but whatever it was, she let it slide.

"I'm sorry," he said. "About the hearing. I thought the judge would understand."

This was the custody hearing: the child she had named Stephen after her own son and which she had raised for three months as Edie languished, and which she had held and comforted and loved when Edie had then died, was to be given to the Pyes. They named it Lamar and took it from her and drove off in a beaten-up old truck, a gaggle of tough-as-nails men and gristly women.

"The state paints with a broad brush," she said. "It believes in family and in kin. I agree with that just as broadly. Occasionally, however, it makes a mistake. Oh well. If they love him, he'll be fine, I suppose."

Sam didn't see much love in that brood, but he didn't say anything. The bus pulled in. Miss Connie, of course, was rich; she didn't have to take a damn bus. But she was also without airs, and if the bus was good enough to the poor white and black people she had loved and loved her, she would take it.

She smiled brokenly and climbed aboard while the driver loaded her considerable luggage into the compartment. He watched her as she found a seat. The bus shivered as the driver put it in gear and just as it lurched into motion, Connie turned and their eyes met and Sam made a little twitch of a smile and she smiled and disappeared forever. He always wondered: suppose he'd yelled, Connie, don't leave, goddammit, stay with me. Connie, I love you, don't go, please, we will work it out.

But he hadn't and knew he'd done the right thing. He was married with three children and a pregnant wife; what could be done about that? Nothing. So Connie drove away on the bus and that was all there was to it.

Where her house had been there were now fifty houses and the tasteful sign before them, where once the Longacre mailbox had hung, read LONGACRE MEADOWS, A SUBSIDIARY OF THE BAMA GROUP, and the houses were white and looked spacious and well lived in, though they were spread with such rigid orthodoxy on the gridwork of new streets that nothing seemed spontaneous or alive, quite.

Sam turned in, watching damned Duane Peck turn in behind him, but soon forgot about the deputy as he tried to negotiate the dazzle of cutely named streets. It was almost more than he could handle: he felt sucked into a vortex of houses that looked *exactly alike*. When did this happen? he wondered. But by a religious miracle, the only one he'd ever witnessed in his eighty-six years, he happened upon Barefoot Boy Garth, as the street was preposterously called, and soon enough came upon a house hardly different from any other with the address 10567. How on earth could there be ten thousand other houses on this little lane? Anyway, he pulled into the driveway and sat for a second.

Now, when perhaps he needed it most, a blessed wave of clarity washed across him. He felt focused, alive, intense; he knew exactly why he was here and what he had to find out. He got out and went and knocked on the door. A young black woman answered, her eyes hooded in hostility.

"Yes?" she said.

He was a little nonplussed: most people in these parts called him "sir" axiomatically, possibly because they recognized him and possibly out of respect for his age.

"Ah, I'm looking for Lucille Parker."

"What for?"

"It's old business. About a letter she wrote me."

"You're not some cracker segregationist Bible thumper here to tell her the Lord took her other daughter."

"Ma'am, I'm a graduate of Yale Law School and Princeton University. Though I respect the Bible, I'd never thump it. It is about Shirelle, yes, but I don't believe God had anything to do with it."

"You're Mr. Sam, then. Go on back," said the woman. "We heard you'd come around. Mama's waiting for you."

She led him through the neat house—Sam was amazed that Negroes lived so nicely; when had this happened?—and out back where the old lady sat on a lawn chair, under a scrubby little tree. The chair was a frail, almost gossamer thing, possibly bowed in strain; she was immense, serene and queenly in her bulk, sitting in her best purple clothes, sagacious and calm.

"Mrs. Parker," he said, "I am Sam Vincent."

"Mr. Sam," she said. "I remember you from the trial."

"Yes, ma'am. I remember you too."

"No, you don't," she said. "You never once looked at us or cared about us colored folks at all. You never talked to us or anything. Nobody ever visited us; we got us a phone call from someone at the Coroner's telling us Shirelle's body could be picked up. That's all we ever got from anybody."

"Ma'am, I ain't going to lie to you. In them days, we hardly thought of colored people as human beings. It's the way it was. I was the man I was and now I'm the man I am. But if I say I remembered you, I did: You wore a black dress because you were in mourning still. You wore a white hat with a camellia atop it and a veil. Your husband wore a dark suit; he wore horn-rim glasses and walked with a limp, I believe from a combat wound in North Africa. I came about this."

He handed her the letter.

"Yes."

"I can't ever remember seeing it. I think a secretary must have put it in the file."

"Because it wasn't important."

"Ma'am, if I'd have seen it, I'd have probably put it in the file too. It doesn't have any evidence in it."

"Only one white person ever told me the truth," said Mrs. Parker. "That was Earl Swagger. He was a fair man. The day that man got killed was a sad day for this whole county. But Mr. Earl said he'd find out what happened to my baby. And I know if he'd a lived, he would have, fair and square, no matter what or who."

Sam tried to be gentle.

"Ma'am, we found out what happened to Shirelle. Reggie Fuller killed her. And he paid for it. It's a closed account. Nowadays, accounts don't get closed so fairly. But we closed that one."

"No sir," the old lady said. "I *know* that boy didn't do it, just like I said in the letter."

Sam looked at the letter. She was quoting herself almost verbatim all these years later: "Mr. Sam, I know that boy couldn't have killed my Shirelle," she had written in 1957, a week before the execution.

"Mrs. Parker, everything scientific matched. I swear to you. I may not be no civil rights Holy Roller, but neither am I the kind of man who would railroad evidence."

"I don't care what the evidence said. That boy Reggie was over to my house when my Shirelle disappeared. He was in the house. He talked to me about her. He looked me in the eye. God would not let him look me in the eye and say he missed Shirelle if the night before he had killed her."

"Mrs. Parker, I have been around murderers my whole life. Black or white, they are wired different. They can look you in the eye and tell you that they love you and make you believe it, and when you turn your back, they hit you over the head with a claw hammer and take your watch and drink your blood and forget about it in the next second. They ain't *normal,* like you and me. A lie don't carry no weight with them at all."

"That may be true, sir, but Reggie wasn't like that. Don't you understand?"

"Ma'am, facts is facts."

"Mr. Sam, Mr. Earl said the detectives would come talk to us. No detectives never did. What you call it when you solve a crime? What Columbo does."

"Columbo is a made-up man. Investigation. You call it investigation."

"You never did no investigation. You found your shirt, you found your blood and you electrocuted your nigger boy."

"He was guilty. Who would go to so much trouble to frame a boy like that?"

"The man what killed my baby Shirelle and has been walking around laughing about it all these years."

"Madam: think about what you're saying. A man would have to find Reggie, break into his house, get his shirt, take it to the site of the murder, dip it in your daughter's blood, rip the pocket off, plant the pocket in your daughter's dead hand, return to Reggie's house, break in again, hide the shirt under the mattress. Now, who would do such a damned crazy thing? If he does *nothing,* we only find the body and there ain't no other evidence to point to a suspect. Without that damned pocket and that bloody shirt, there ain't no evidence, ain't no case, ain't no nothing. There's only a dead girl."

She didn't blink or look away but faced him square.

"I *knows* all that. But . . . he did have the time. It ain't like there's some limit on the time he had, like a single night. He had four full days between the time he killed my girl and Mr. Earl found the body. It could have been done."

It was the damn TV! Everybody thought they was Columbo or

Matlock or some such and when people's loved ones got killed, there always had to be some *meaning* in it. Sam looked into Mrs. Parker's crazed old eyes: she'd been fulminating on this over the decades. She'd invented a goddamned *conspiracy* about her daughter's death. No one wanted to face the squalid, simple, irrational truth, as here: a colored boy lost control and smashed her poor little daughter to death with a rock.

"Mrs. Parker, it don't never happen that way. It just don't."

"Mr. Sam, I see in your eyes what you thinking. You thinking, crazy old colored woman, she be blaming a *white* person. Every last thing, it's all the *white* man's fault. It's *race,* like all the colored, that's all they think about. That's what you thinking, right?"

She regarded him with fierce, brilliant eyes.

"Sister, I—"

"You is, isn't you? Tell me!"

He sighed.

"I suppose I am. There are some things I cannot overcome. Some suspicions about y'all. I haven't grown as I should have."

"Then let me tell you something surprise you. I *don't* think a white man done it. I think a colored man did."

This threw Sam. It was the last thing he expected. The old woman had him foxed something powerful.

"What you mean, there, sister?"

"In them days, the one thing we told our girls, and I must have said it a hundred times to Shirelle: you don't *never* get in no car with a white boy. White boy only wants one thing from you and you don't want to give it to him. He may be friendly, he may be nice, he may be handsome, he may have the devil's ways to him. But he only want *one* thing, girl, and if you give it to him, he hate you and all the black boys find out and *they* hate you, but they goin' try and git the same off of you and really be angry if you don't give it. So I *know* she don't get in no car with no white man. Some colored man done this to her."

Sam blinked, confounded. The old lady was *smart.* Not white smart, fancy sentences smart, but somehow she knew things: she had seen into the center of it. He'd known many a detective sergeant who wasn't as sly as this.

"Mr. Sam, you the smartest man in this county. You smarter even than old Ray Bama or Harry Etheridge and his son, you smarter than Mr. Earl. You got his boy, Bob Lee, off when the whole U.S. govmint say he was a killer. You got Jed Posey to spend his black evil days in prison. Now you a old man and I a old woman. We both be gone soon. Cain't you please just look at that case again? Just so's when you goes you knows you done your job as hard at the end as you done it through the middle."

"Well—"

He thought about it. His was a life of certitude. He was an absolute believer. He hated revisionism, hindsight, detached examination, the whole spirit of equivocation and ironic ambivalence which had become the American style in the nineties. He *hated* it. Goddamn Nigra woman wanted him to become what he hated.

But . . . there was time. She was right. It was not technically impossible. Why anyone would do such a thing was beyond his imagining, but it was, in the technical sense, by the laws of the physical world, possible. And the bit about the black man being the one who did it—that was so interesting.

As pure mystery, as pure problem of the intellect, it goaded him powerfully.

"My mind ain't what it once was. It gits foggy. It clouds up with anger. I can't find my socks. Seems like people hide things on me. But if I git another clear day like today, I will look at the case records again, or what of them remain. I will look, but don't you expect nothing. I can't have you expecting nothing, Mrs. Parker."

"God bless you, sir."

"Now, don't call me sir. Call me Sam. Everybody else does."

Twenty-three

IT WAS THE FOOTBALL DREAM, a late variant. Lamar Pye and Russ's father, Bud, were at his football game. It was 1981 and Russ was eight; he was not a very good football player. In fact he'd only played that one year.

Lamar said, "I think that damn boy's got too much gal in him."

"He ain't no athlete, that's for sure," agreed Bud. "You should see his younger brother. That little sucker's a studpuppy. You can't hardly git him to quit."

"I like that in a man and in a boy. When they don't quit. Old Russ here," Lamar explained, "not only do he got too much quit, he don't even got no start."

The two old boys laughed raucously on the sideline, and it seemed that everybody there was staring at poor little Russ, waiting for him to screw up.

It didn't take long. Because he was too small to play the line and not fast enough to play the backfield, he'd been stuck at a position called linebacker. It involved a lot of football knowledge for which he just had no gift and the coaches were always yelling at him for being out of place or slow to react. He was never, ever comfortable. When he charged the line, inevitably a pass zinged to the exact place he'd just abandoned; when he stayed put against a pass, someone blasted through the line and veered through the hole he was supposed to plug. It was a terrible season and he yearned to quit because he wasn't born with that coolheaded instinct his younger brother possessed in spades, but was, in truth, a spaz.

"Come on, Russ, stop 'em," yelled his dad.

"Come on, Russ, you can do it," yelled big old Lamar, ponytailed, charm, charisma, big white teeth, big sickle in his hands which he was sharpening with an Arkansas stone, running it with goose-pimply grinding sounds up and down the wickedly curving blade.

Russ was so intent on them that he missed the start of the play and when he finally snapped to—the coaches were yelling his name—it seemed that a big black kid on the other team had juked to the left then broken outside and was already beyond the line of scrimmage with no one near him but poor Russ in his weak-side linebacker's slot.

Willing himself to run, Russ found a surprisingly good angle on the running back and zoomed toward him. But as he approached he saw how big the boy was, how fierce with energy and determination, how his legs beat like pistons against the ground, and in some way Russ's ardor was dampened. Though everyone was yelling "Hit him low" he hit him high. Briefly, they grappled and Russ had the sense of bright lights, stars maybe, the wind rustling and then blankness.

When he blinked he was on the ground, his face mask having grown a fungus of turf, his whole body constricted in pain and as he turned, he could see through the ache behind his eyes the runner continue his scamper down the sidelines, borne by cheers from the crowd, until he crossed the goal line to be festooned with garlands and ribbons.

He tried to get up but Dad and Lamar stood over him.

"Russ, hit him *low,*" his dad said with contempt.

Lamar lifted the sickle. Its blade picked up a movielike highlight from the sun. He was Jason, Freddy Krueger, the guy in *Halloween* all combined into one. He laughed loudly.

"Sorry, boy," he said, "but you shoulda listened to your daddy. Nut-cuttin' time!"

Whoooshhhh! The blade descended.

Russ awoke in a cheesy hotel room in Oklahoma City, his mind filled with shards of glass, pieces of gravel and infinite regrets. Someone *was* hacking at him, but no, it was the door, being pounded.

"Russ, come on," someone was yelling, "you're late again, goddammit. It's time to go."

Oh. It was his *other* father, Bob Lee Swagger, one more true man to find disappointment in him.

Russ got himself out of bed.

"Isn't that illegal?"

"Not if you have it displayed."

"But it isn't displayed."

"My, my, if it didn't just fall off the gun rack here."

Bob pointed to the empty gun rack above the seat in his truck. Behind the seat, he had just slid the Mini-14 in its gun case, plus a paper bag with three loaded twenty-round magazines and the immense forty-rounder, a curved thing that looked like a flattened tin banana. "What cop is going to give me a hard time? This here's Oklahoma."

"That isn't legal," said Russ. "My dad catches you with that, you'd go to jail."

"Well, I'd never mess with your old man, so you'd best come up with a way to talk him out of it," Bob said, sliding the .45 Commander in its holster behind the seat too, along with the extra magazines.

"I don't know," said Russ. "This is getting hairy."

"It gets hairier. You drive."

They climbed in. They were in the parking lot of the Holiday Inn, getting ready to call on General Jack Preece, of JFP Technology, Inc.

"What was that address again?" Russ asked.

Bob told him.

"I think it's near the airport," he said.

"Go to it, Junior."

They drove in silence for a while. Then Russ said, "You'd better brief me on some stuff."

"Why?"

"If you and I are supposed to be doing a book on sniping and it turns out I don't know shit about it, this guy is going to kick us out on our butts and we get nothing."

"So what do you want to know? 'What's it feel like?' I used to get asked that a lot. 'What's it feel like?' "

"What's it feel like?"

"Smart-ass punk kid."

"All right. Why do you hate him?"

"Who, Preece?"

"Yeah."

"I don't hate him. He's a fine man."

"You hate him. I can tell. Even behind the famous Swagger reserve, you hate him."

"He was a fine officer. He ran a superior program. His people got hundreds, maybe thousands, of kills. They saved the lives of hundreds, maybe thousands, of American soldiers. He's a fine man, a patriot, probably a father and a Republican. Why would you say I hate him?"

"You hate him."

"Well . . . it's just a thing. You wouldn't understand it. I'd say it to another sniper and to no one else. What I said to you earlier, that's what's important. He's a fine man, a great officer."

"You have to tell me. I can't get through this if you don't."

Bob paused. He wondered if he had the skills to articulate what lay at his heart. Or the energy. Damn this kid, with his smart-ass ways and his penchant for always coming up with a question that was pretty damned good.

"If you do write a book, you *cannot* put this in it. Ever. Do you understand?"

"Yes sir."

"I don't want it said, Bob Lee Swagger, he had hard words for an American soldier who in good faith and out of duty and honor risked his life for his country. I won't have that. That's shit. That's what's killing the country."

"I swear."

"Then I tell you this now, and I will never hear of it again."

"Yes sir."

"It's about killing."

Russ said nothing.

"In war," Bob said, "death comes in three forms. Usually, it comes from far off, delivered by men who never see the bodies they leave behind. That's how we done most of our killing in Vietnam. The B-52s did the most, man, they'd turn that goddamn jungle into pulp and chew up everything for a square mile. And artillery. On the ground, the artillery does most of the killing. The king of battle, they call it. You may not like it, but that's how it is."

"Yes," said Russ.

"Second is in hot blood. Firefight. You see forms moving, you fire. Some of them stop moving. You may never see them up close, you may never know if you got a hit or not. Or you may: you see the little fuck go down, you see the tracers cut him up, that sort of thing. What's going on is really fighting. It's you or him. You may not like it, but goddammit you do it, because if you don't, you're the one goes home in a bag."

"Yes, I see."

"The third and last form is cold-blooded killing. That's what we do. We, being the snipers. We put a scope on a man from a half mile out and we pull a trigger and we watch him go still. Nothing pretty about it, but I would say it's necessary. I *believed* it was necessary. I know it makes people nervous. You're death. They call you Murder, Inc., and God knows what they say about you behind your back. They think you're sick or nuts or something, that you enjoy it."

"That's what you did."

"I did. But still, distinctions can be made. Somehow distinctions *got* to be made. I didn't shoot women or children and I didn't shoot anyone that wasn't out to kill me. If someone has a hard time with that, well, tough shit. I was a *hunter*. It's called fair chase. You go into the jungle or along the paddy breaks. You hunt your enemy and you try and find a position where he can't get you. You take him down. You hit him, you get fire. We lost a lot of men. We had rewards on our heads. The VC put ten thousand piasters out for me and eventually a Russian bastard claimed it, but that's a different story. What we did was war. Find and destroy the enemy. Shoot him. Try and go home. Finish the mission.

"Now, the army . . ."

He paused. Something in him recoiled at this; but he had to get it out.

"Different doctrine, developed first at this Project BLACK LIGHT and then deployed through Tigercat, the 7th Infantry Division Sniper School. What they'd do, they'd night-insert four-man teams into a zone, three security boys with poodle shooters and one sniper with a rifle. They liked to do it just after a sweep. So Charlie was out and about, and feeling safe. He thought he owned the night. The shooter had what they called their M-21, which was an M-14 7.62 NATO rifle—.30-caliber, Russ—worked over and accurized by the Army Marksmanship Unit. It carried a suppressor—since you been to the movies, you'd call it a silencer—and a night-vision device, an AN/PVS-2, called a Starlight scope. So these boys set up in the jungle and they just wait; the sniper's on the scope, the other guys have night-vision binocs. They pick something up and the sniper moves into position. He puts the scope on them. It's like they're moving through green water, but he's got them out to eight hundred yards. The gooks never knew what hit them. They couldn't get a read on the sniper's hide because there was no sound. They couldn't believe he could see them, but through the scope, bright as daylight, he could put them down. Lots of kills. It was easy. One boy got a hundred fifteen kills in about five months. They was getting six, seven kills a night. Were they hitting soldiers? Hell, from eight hundred yards out on a Starlight, who the hell can tell? If they're moving at night, I guess they're soldiers, but maybe they were kids going to the john or families trying to move at night so they wouldn't get bounced by our Tac Air. Who knew? Then, at 0700, a chopper evacs the team the fuck out of there and it's back to base camp for pancakes and a good night at the body-count factory."

"I see," said Russ. "You don't—it wasn't—"

"I don't know. I haven't sorted it out yet. But it's different."

"It isn't war," said Russ, "and I'll say it if you're reluctant. It was straight execution work."

"Yeah, well, you hide that. You got me? You hide that, and don't be so quick to judge unless you walked in the man's shoes. Now, this is how it's going to work. I'm going to tell him how much we-all in the Marine Corps *admired* the army way of doing things. They got so many more kills than us. Damn, don't that beat all. Get him to feeling all puffed up."

"He'll know you're bullshitting."

"Like hell he will. He's a general, ain't he? He's used to being buttered up. He'll want his place in history set straight. He'll want to show us some hardware. Son, I was a sergeant in the Marine Corps for fourteen years. I know how these birds work."

"There," said the general. "There, do you see them?"

He did. The phantasms rose in the green gloom, two, three, then four, dancing ever so softly, their movements fired by incandescent phosphors in the tube of the device, which was a Magnavox thermal sniperscope. It was the latest thing, a lens that truly penetrated the darkness. No living thing could pass unnoticed in its view through the night.

The figures danced and one of them came at last to the red dot reticle in the center of the view.

"Go ahead," said the general. "Take them."

It was too easy. Bob was welded to the scope and felt the stock against him, his finger on the trigger. It was some kind of M-16, only swollen, enlarged. His hold was rock-solid and the weapon itself secured against the sandbags beneath it; he pressed the trigger and the rifle spoke once with a sound somewhere between a cough and a sneeze, or maybe a hiccup. There was no recoil, no sense of having fired, yet the action cycled and an empty shell was jettisoned and the first target went down. He moved the red dot ever so slightly and fired again: same thing. Twice more.

"End of mission," said the general, snapping on the lights that filled a long shooting tunnel off of this sandbagged position. "Let's see how you did."

He turned to a computer terminal and punched in a command. The computer answered immediately.

"Superb shooting," said the general. "Exactly as expected. You

X'd the bull's-eye on the first two cleanly, you broke a line on the third and you X'd the fourth again. Four kills. Elapsed time, 3.2 seconds. Recorded noise, ah, under one hundred decibels, about the sound intensity of someone firing a BB gun."

The general reached over and hit a switch and the thermal scope died; Bob set the rifle, which looked oddly distended with the huge gunmetal-gray tube atop it, on the sandbags; he looked downrange at his targets and at the end of the tunnel, saw flattened metal silhouettes, clearly on some kind of uneven conveyer belt that gave them the lurching movement of human beings on patrol.

"How do you heat them?" said Bob.

"Essentially, you were shooting at a common household appliance. You just got four toasters. Or, rather, their heating elements. Congratulations."

"There's no infrared-light source on this piece," Bob said.

"No sir," said the general. "We're beyond that. We're beyond even ambient light, the Starlight scopes. That's passive infrared; no infrared beam and it doesn't need illumination. The problem with the ambient-light pieces was that they didn't work in total darkness, they didn't work in smoke, fog or rain, they didn't work in daylight, even. They were limited. The Magnavox collects all the infrared energy from the target scene by a single-element silicon aspheric lens. The emerging convergent beam is horizontally scanned by an oscillating mirror and then focused on a vertical linear array of sixty-four lead solenide detector elements which traduce the IR energy into electrical signals. Each detector's output is fed to a high-gain pre-amplifier. The signals from the sixty-four pre-amplifiers are then multiplexed to a single composite video signal. The composite video signal is then amplified and applied to a miniature cathode-ray tube that is viewed through the monocular eyepiece. It's MTV for snipers."

"Pretty goddamned slick," Bob said. The box did in fact look like a television set, a long rectangular 6×6 tube with the huge round eye up front for a screen, leading back to the eyepiece.

"Well, we've come a ways. The Germans used to shoot at concentration camp prisoners. That's how they tested their first-generation *Vampir* sight. We shoot at decommissioned toasters."

"Can the boy try it?"

"No, that's all right," said Russ.

"You sure, son?" asked the general.

"It's fine," said Russ.

The general turned back to Bob. "It's not just that the thermal sniperscope is the highest refinement in the night-vision electronics. But what we sell is a whole system. We wholesale from Magnavox, we mount it to the rifle, we manufacture our own suppressor, we pack it into a kit, and we provide trainers and a constant technical hot line and emergency system. That's not an M-16."

"It felt heavier than one."

"It's a Knight-Stoner SR-25 in .308, shooting a subsonic load. And our JFP MAW-7 suppressor. Unbelievably silent, accurate, lethal, isn't it? Muzzle blast is caused by high-pressure gases suddenly escaping from the end of the barrel as the bullet exits. Reducing the pressure results in less sound generated. We reduce the pressure by increasing the volume for gas expansion, reducing the gas temperature, delaying gas exit by trapping and turbulence. Damn, it's a good unit!"

"Yes, it is," said Bob.

"Nothing like your old 700 Remington?"

"I'd hate to be matched with my old rifle against a fellow with that outfit."

"You wouldn't have a chance. The night belongs to the man who can see through it. Imagine the kills you could have gotten in combat with this outfit."

Bob rose; the demonstration was over.

"Come on back," said the general. "We'll talk in my office."

Jack Preece was a stocky man, with the short neck that was common to many championship shooters; he was handsome and rather slick, with a mane of silver hair and a smooth way about him. He radiated confidence and charm; his skin was tan and his teeth, capped, were white and perfect.

He led them back from the firing range through workshops where the system—the Knight rifle, the night-vision device, the sound suppressor—was being assembled into kit form, a single plastic case, after assembly, zeroing and disassembly, for shipment at no doubt a pretty penny to the elite marksmanship units of the world—Delta, various special forces units, SEAL Team Six, a Ranger battalion, the FBI's HRT, various big-city SWAT units.

"That Knight rifle gives us an enormous advantage over even the M-21s. We can get minute-of-angle accuracy out of a semiauto; we can get second or third shots without breaking the shooter's spot-weld with a bolt gun's accuracy. Bob, the days of the bolt gun are over. By the decade's end, all the world's elite sniper teams will be shooting semiauto."

"I think I'll keep mine awhile," said Bob, and the general laughed.

He ushered them into his office, a small paneled warren, one wall of which was filled with marksmanship trophies from a hundred forgotten high-power rifle championships the world over, as well as photographs of men with rifles standing or kneeling around a trophy, each with a fancy target rifle in his hands. Bob glimpsed and read a shooting history etched on brass plates: Interzonal U.S. Army Champion, 1977; Panama Games, Standing Rifle, 1979; NRA High Master; Alabama High Power, Sitting Champion, 1978; and on and on.

"No Wimbledon Cup up there," said the general. "My best year, you took it. Nineteen seventy-one."

"Sir, if I'd have known you had a gap in your trophy case, I'd have dropped a shot or two!"

The general laughed. "It's all shit, of course. But I have customers in here all the time. It impresses them. Now, what's on your mind, gentlemen?" He lit a cigar and leaned back in his chair comfortably, as if looking forward to a good time.

"Sir," said Russ, "I've been hired to coauthor Bob Lee Swagger's story for the Presidio Press in San Francisco. We wanted to at least touch on the wider shape of the story: that is, American sniping in Vietnam as programs and how they affected the war. There's not a lot of data on the army's, yet I understand the army snipers got much higher kill rates than the marines."

"It had nothing to do with the quality of men," said the general with an executive's practiced smoothness. "At the senior noncommissioned officer level, the American services all have extremely talented and motivated individuals. The marines have stayed wedded to marksmanship as the core of their service; that's fine, as history has proven out time and again. The army has been charged with staying at the cutting edge of ground combat technology. That was my job. That's where Tigercat came from. We started in the early fifties trying to develop a technology that would give the night to the American sniper."

"The M-3 sniperscope," prompted Bob.

"A piece of junk," said the general, expelling a large curling cumulus of smoke. "Bulky, clumsy, awkward, with a distressing propensity toward showing the vegetation more clearly than the enemy. So heavy it could only be mounted on a light rifle like the puny carbine. But . . . a start."

"Yes sir," said Bob. "No doubt, if we'd have had your gear in the Nam, we could have kicked ass big-time."

The general wasn't really listening.

"Do you know what the difference between the marine and the army sniper programs was? I mean, speaking frankly. I love the spirit of the marines, but our kills were *so* much higher. Do you know why?"

Russ inwardly blanched. He knew this was the last thing Swagger would want to hear from this grinning, self-promoting baboon.

"No sir," said Bob evenly.

"The marines somehow couldn't commit at the conceptual level to the idea of technology. At some fundamental level, they believed still in the romantic notion of individual heroism. They somehow refused to enter the modern age. You marine snipers were like World War I pilots or cowboy gunslingers, going off on your own to do battle with the enemy and taking him out one-on-one. We believed in team spirit, sophisticated technology and body counts. Our body counts were *so much* higher. We saw through to the heart of it: it was about killing the enemy, not dueling him. And our sniper teams moved in and left nothing but step-ons. When we put a V.C. down, we didn't count it until the next morning we could put our boot on his chest. We called them step-ons."

"Yes sir," said Bob chastely, nothing showing on his bland face.

"I sure wish I'd had a chance to work the jungle with that kind of equipment."

His piece said, the general returned to the technical and the arcane.

"The M-3 was a great advance over the M-2 system of World War II, yet in Korea the troops hated it and the army itself didn't really understand or follow up. It was my idea to run the thing through a night-battle wringer and try to develop doctrine. Fortunately, somebody read my idea in *Infantry Journal* and I was given a chance to practice what I'd preached. We called the project BLACK LIGHT and ran it out of Camp Chaffee, where we tried to devise some data for night operations with vision devices. We were stuck with the goddamned M-3s. But at least we were able to *show* the R&D boys what was necessary in a night-combat environment. No one really knew until that time. They'd just copied the German hardware."

"Tell us about BLACK LIGHT."

The general launched into a long and somewhat self-serving account of the project, and it soon developed that the problem with him wouldn't be getting him to talk but getting him to shut up. His chatter soon evolved into performance, soliloquy, ultimately a one-man show, punctuated by theatrical blasts of smoke. He looked like the god of war, Mars himself, sitting there under his reasonable gray hair as the clouds swirled and he gave pronouncement. Much of his presentation seemed to turn on obscure issues, like trying to find the right number of men that stayed within command parameters and yet were adequate to provide security for the shooter. Months were spent determining if six or eight or ten were better, and the ultimate choice was four, given that the sniper himself could do double duty in a firefight with a greasegun. Night command vocabulary was tested; night map reading was examined and night navigation; radio techniques were explored. The shooting was a relatively late part in it.

"About '55 we got to the shooting."

"What did you use for targets? The Germans used people, you said."

"On the record? On the record, heat-generating targets were

not mandatory, because we were only beginning to understand the principle of ambient light, that is, passive night vision. We used the M-3's active infrared, that is, an infrared searchlight. We could have shot at anything. But there was a ballistic component to the project which mandated load testing on living organisms. Off the record, we shot sheep and goats. Cattle would have been preferable because their respiratory system most resembles humans, but I had no stomach for trying to bring down a steer with a bullet that at its best generated muzzle energies somewhere between a .38 Special and a light .357 Magnum."

On and on it went, through the construction of the units, problems with the clamps that secured them, difficulty with the webbing that supported, and so forth and so on. Russ thought he'd doze.

"I'm just curious," said Bob finally, and Russ knew that he'd played out the whole long hand, nursed the man's vanities and ego, gotten through the bullshit lecture on "individual heroism vs. team spirit and body count" to get to this point at last, "what sort of administrative control could there have been on the units themselves? Was it standard infantry arms-room administration; was it more stringent? Who actually *controlled* the units? The actual M-3s?"

"Technically, I did, though the true administration of the project fell in the hands of my first sergeant, whose name was Ben Farrell. Very good NCO. Killed outside Da Nang in '64."

"Who controlled the arms-room keys?"

"Well . . . what does this have to do with anything?"

There was an awkward moment.

Then Russ said, "The truth is, we think there's a movie potential for this book. And the reason I wanted to talk about night vision was that I had an idea for a funny scene. Young soldiers break into the armory and steal some night-vision devices. They use them to spy on a WAC encampment, some girls with nice tits. Tits and ass. That's the kind of wacky stuff the movies love."

"Oh, Lord," said the general. "Why don't you just make it up? What do you need my help for?"

"Sergeant Swagger insisted that everything be at least based in reality."

"Well, I can assure you nobody used *our* hardware to spy on WACs and if you knew anything about the WACs of the fifties, you wouldn't want to spy on *them* either."

"We could make it nurses," said Russ. "Would that be better?"

The general made a face of disgust. "Hollywood," he said. "No, it's impossible. There were only two arms-room keys. Three, I assume the base commander had one but he paid us no mind. We had our shop, our barracks space and use of three range facilities and various field assault courses. The only two keys were controlled by First Sergeant Farrell and myself and he was a Prussian in the discipline department. No one used those weapons without our permission or knowledge. Which means no one used them, period."

Bob veered away from the point.

"Did you find the units equally effective?"

"No," said the general, relaxing somewhat, and expelling a long whoosh of dark smoke, and went on to explain the difference in the units, the difference in the lots of ammunition, the difference in the three carbines themselves.

It went on like that, Russ pretending to keep notes, Bob prodding with gentle questions, up to and including the general's astonishingly successful stewardship of the Tigercat Sniper School, the record number of kills racked up once the mounting problems for the Starlight on the M-21 were solved, and so on.

Late in the afternoon, Bob circled in for another pass.

"Could we just get back to BLACK LIGHT one more time, sir?" he asked.

"Certainly, Sergeant," said the general.

"We agreed, the young man and I, that this book would be better if there were some personalities in it. So I'm thinking: there at Chaffee in '54–'55: any outstanding personalities involved? How big a team was it? Who were they?"

"The usual. Good men. Toward the end, representatives from Varo Inc. and Polan Industries, who ultimately got the initial Starlight scope contracts. Some civilians TDY from Army Warfare

Vision at Fort Devens. You know, I have a picture. Is that interesting to you?"

"Yes, sir. Like to see it."

"It's over here, on the wall."

He led them to the wall and pointed the picture out. Like the others it was a mixed group of civilians and soldiers standing and kneeling; Preece himself, much thinner but somehow rawer, crouched in the front row, holding the carbine with the huge optical device mounted. He wore army-green fatigues with his name on a white name tag and one of those goofy turret caps that were issue in the fifties. The men around him were doughy, unimpressive, unmemorable: they looked like NASA flight controllers, faintly ridiculous in the casual clothes of the era, mostly short-sleeved white shirts with slacks and lumpy oxfords.

"I should have had them write their names down," the general said with a laugh. "I only recognize a few. That's Ben Farrell. That's Bob Eadings, of Polan."

"Who's that one?" asked Bob, pointing to a kneeling figure at the edge of the photograph, a young man with a certain pugnacious set to his square, blocky head, who looked strong beneath his clothes and had a set of fiercely burning eyes.

"That guy," said Preece. "Lord, I remember him. He was from Motorola, I think. He was only on the project for two weeks but it happened to be the two weeks we took the picture. I cannot for the life of me remember the name."

"Were all these men shooters?" Russ asked.

"No, not really. Ben Farrell was a very good shot. Not exceptional, but excellent."

"Who did the shooting? Was it a team?"

"Oh, there was only one shooter," said the general, exhaling a long flume of smoke like a dragon's breath. "Me."

After they had gone, the general sat very still for a time. His cigar burned out and he didn't touch it. He didn't call his girlfriend or his daughter or his divorced wife or his lawyer or any of the men on his board of directors or his head engineer or any of the old boys in his sniper cadre.

Finally, he got up, opened the cabinet behind his desk, took out a bottle of Wild Turkey and poured himself a tall glass. He sat, looking at it for a time, and then reached for it, noting, as he drew it to his lips, that his hands were still shaking.

Twenty-four

SOME DANG DAYS a fella couldn't win. Duane, going on just a few hours' sleep after having spent all day yesterday bouncing around Polk County on the tail of old Sam, plus answering a few unavoidable police calls, was bushed; but he was up and at it early this morning, on his ordered sweep across all the commercial establishments he could find along the Etheridge Parkway corridor.

Yet he struck pay dirt early enough.

Goddamn, he thought, when the Indian day-clerk woman at the Days Inn at Parkway Exit 7 said yes, an older man and a younger man had checked into a room yesterday at around ten. Was there anything wrong?

Duane puffed and acted like some sort of important investigator, and pretty much bullied the poor woman—she was foreign, with some kind of fucking *dot* on her head, so what difference did it make?—into giving up the whole story. They'd checked in at ten, the boy disappeared for most of the afternoon, the man made long-distance phone calls all day and they'd left about six in a truck loaded with sleeping bags and, technically, still had a contract on the room, at least until checkout time, noon.

She remembered, because usually they don't rent rooms before one, but the tall man had insisted.

Duane asked to see the phone records, though he didn't have a subpoena. Fortunately, the woman was too stupid to know or too indifferent to care. In his notebook, he wrote down the numbers in his big silly handwriting, like a child's.

He thanked her, helped himself to a free cup of coffee and by ten was on the phone.

He gave his report to the answering machine, including the numbers, then sat back waiting for praise. It didn't come.

The phone rang.

"Peck, where are you now?"

"Well, sir, uh, I'm in the parking lot of the Days Inn."

"Git back down to Blue Eye. You stay with the old man today, you understand? You let me know what he's up to."

That was it: no nice going, nicely done, good job, just get back on the job.

Damn, you couldn't *please* some folks.

Red Bama had experts everywhere; that was one of the pleasures of being Red Bama. So he called one, a communications specialist formerly of Southwestern Bell who handled telephone problems for him, and inside half an hour had a make on the phone calls Bob had made.

One was to the Pentagon, the office of Army Historical Archives. The other was to a firm in Oklahoma, called JFP Technology. It took another couple of calls to get to the product line and meanings of JFP Technology.

When he did, he whistled.

Fucking Swagger was *smart*. He was inside this deal already, and getting closer and closer to secrets so carefully and professionally buried over forty years ago. This was a powerful antagonist, the best that had come against Red in many a year.

Next, Red made a call to a lawyer he knew in Oklahoma City, a good man who was, as they say, in the life. The lawyer, for a not unsubstantial fee, was quickly able to hire a licensed private detective, and on a crash basis the detective set up a surveillance at JFP after establishing, in the parking lot, the presence of a green Dodge pickup with an odd unpainted fender, license number Arizona SCH 2332.

The lawyer reported back to Red, who took a bit of a moment

to appreciate what he'd brought off—*I found you, you tricky bas-tard!*—and then issued further, and very specific, orders.

"I want one thing and one thing only. Just the time they leave that office as determined from an observation site as far away as possible. I *do not want,* and let me say that again because I love the sound of my own damn voice, I *do not want* any tail jobs or moving surveillance. Nobody's to follow. This boy is too tricky," he told the lawyer. "I don't know what kind of men you got in Oklahoma City—"

"Good men, Mr. Bama."

"Yeah, well, not *that* good. This boy is very, very smart and he has instincts for aggression you would not believe. I guarantee you: he will see any kind of tail you put on and if he does, every damn thing upcoming will fall apart. Is that understood?"

"Yes sir," said the lawyer.

"The time is very important. Meanwhile, I will think this thing through," said Bama, "and if I need your services I'll call you back. I will expect you to be available."

"Mr. Bama, you've never talked to a more available man."

"They do grow 'em good in Oklahoma City, then," Bama said.

He put down the phone in his little office, took another sip of rancid bar coffee and then felt something very strange upon his face.

By God, it was a smile.

He was *happy.* He was as happy as he'd been in, say, years. Other than the success of his children, nothing filled him with more delight than a good challenge. And, oh boy, was this Bob Lee Swagger proving out.

He tried to apply his purest intelligence to the problem.

The key was what time they left that visit to JFP. If they left soon, they could easily make it back to Blue Eye before dark, which was not good, because he didn't think he could manipulate his elements and set up what he had in mind fast enough. *And everything had to be in place.* If they came back later, it would be a night drive. He didn't like that at all. He did not want to set up an after-dark hit. Too tricky on the open road. In the city was a different matter, but on the open highway, in the country, at night with a tricky bastard like Bob Lee Swagger, it got real iffy and if the thing fell apart, who knew when he'd get another chance?

So: hope they spend another night in Okie City and come back in the morning. That gets them into the area around midafternoon, which would give him plenty of time.

So: assume they'll come back to Blue Eye from Oklahoma City tomorrow. Next question: which route would they take? Any normal man would do the normal thing, the dogleg: take U.S. 40 like a shot over to Fort Smith, then veer south on the parkway that Hollis had named for his daddy down to Blue Eye. Or maybe, out of sentimentality, Bob would pass up on the new road and choose the slower, more awkward Route 71; his father had died on that road, maybe he would too. But he doubted Bob would feel that sentimental. Bob's nature was essentially practical; sentiment was for late at night, when the day was done.

Red wished he knew how they'd got there in the first place; Swagger wasn't the kind of man to come the same way twice. He pored over the map, wishing he had something more expressive, more revealing. He wanted data, information, numbers, facts, he wanted to drown himself in them.

He saw quickly enough that there were really only two other routes into Blue Eye. Both were more or less direct east-west roads, though much smaller than the Fort Smith route. Both involved dropping down from U.S. 40 to McAlester, then heading east on a two-lane blacktop to Talihina. Shortly thereafter, they diverged: One, Oklahoma 1, followed the crest of the Ouachitas from Talihina fifty-seven miles into Arkansas, where it turned into Arkansas 88. It would be a high road, a couple of thousand feet up, with plenty of visibility. It was called, combining the names of the towns on either of its ends, the Taliblue Trail, and the state had designated it as a beautiful road, with mountain vistas on either side. He had driven it himself in a Porsche he once owned and had a goddamned great old time.

The other road, Oklahoma 59, crossed Oklahoma 1 at about the halfway point, then became Route 270 as it cut east and ran parallel to 1/88 on the valley floor beneath it, eventually linking up with 71 a little above Blue Eye. He realized that was the road off of which Bob's Blue Eye property lay, where the man now had his trailer. Maybe he'd go that way and set up again at his trailer. *That* was the logical way. Or was it?

He looked at it: very simple. High road or low road. He didn't have enough people to play it both ways, at least not under the mandate of maximum firepower.

High road or low road?

And then he knew the answer.

He's a *sniper*. He's a *shooter*. He works by seeing. His whole life is built on seeing. The input he gets from the world is all visual information, which he processes and from which he makes his decisions. He sees and he likes to see things a long way off. He doesn't like surprises. He likes to *be* the surprise.

The high road.

A plan formed in his mind. Three cars and a truck, coming from different directions, snaring Bob in the middle, ramming him off the road, burying him with full automatic fire. Ten men firing full automatic in the first second after the crash.

The phone rang.

"Hello."

"Sir?"

It was the lawyer in Oklahoma City.

"Yes?"

"They just left."

Ray looked at his watch. Jesus, it was after five. They weren't going to drive home tonight. He'd won!

"Good work."

"Sir, we found the rooms they rented. The Holiday Inn, near the airport."

"I told you—"

"Very discreet, Mr. Bama. No direct inquiries were made. We were able to get into the chain hotel computer directories. They reserved their rooms for two nights. Checkout time ten A.M. tomorrow."

"Good work," said Bama. "Are you looking for a job?"

"Mr. Bama, I'm very happy where I am."

"The check is in the mail, then."

"I know your word is good."

"It's good in every city in this country," Red said, hanging up. He quickly dialed Jorge de la Rivera.

"Yes?"

"The team is ready?"

"Yes sir. All stood down, relaxed. The girls you sent over went over real nice. They all been fucked or sucked, they all been fed, their weapons are cleaned."

"Here's how it's going down. It'll be tomorrow, midafternoon, on Oklahoma 1, about ten miles east of the 259 crossroads. It's called the Taliblue Trail. Nice high mountain road, not heavily traveled, should be nice and private and wide open. You site your cars in opposite directions and let him get in the middle, then you close in on him so he's got no place to run. You'll want to take him off the road and get the guns working overtime right away. You want to bury him. You've got the advantage of both surprise and firepower."

"It sounds very good. *Muy bueno.* Easy to do. We get him for you. But sir—how will we know he's coming?"

"Oh, I'll let you know over the radio. I'll be watching."

"You're going to get involved in this, Mr. Bama?"

"You can't miss me," he said. "Just look up. I'll be the one in the airplane."

Twenty-five

SAM WOKE IN A FOG after a dreamless but restless night. He had the nagging feeling that something important was scheduled for today. Was he due in court? Did he have to file a motion? Was some defense lawyer deposing him for an appeal? But nothing snapped into clarity and the goddamned maid had forgotten both the coffee and to pick up. That woman was getting sloppier and sloppier. He had half a mind to fire her, but he couldn't remember her name. Then he remembered that he did fire her—twelve years ago. Then he remembered Mrs. Parker.

That was the woman he should have fired. When did the colored get so uppity? They had no respect anymore. It was a case of the rules simply eroding away until nothing was left but chaos and anarchy. Then he remembered little Shirelle.

He got up, straggled through a shower and got dressed, remembering his undershirt, forgetting his underpants. It went on like that for several hours: he felt a deep and mournful pain that he was not all there, he *knew* he was not all there, but somehow he could not get out of the track, which was a kind of infantile literal-mindedness, an unwilled concentration on petty things. He wanted to cry: Where did my mind go? Who took my mind?

Finally, a squall of clarity blew in by midafternoon, and everything popped briefly into place. He felt sane, cool, smart again. Taking advantage, he quickly went to his basement and remembered that he had originally committed to discovering his brief to the Coroner's Office on the Earl Swagger shooting for Bob Lee Swagger. But that would have to wait. This was *so* much more interesting. He seized the file that he'd looked at the day before and this time he really bore down, sliding through the documents with a professional's easy authority, examining the case against Reggie Gerard Fuller.

It held together. It might not hold together today, when the evidentiary rules were much tighter and the fact that Reggie's initials were RGF and that those initials were found on the pocket crumpled in Shirelle's hand might not constitute probable cause for a search warrant. But it sure as hell did then, as even Judge Harrison confirmed. Sam had a moment of pleasure: I did it by the book, by God. I don't have to look back and be ashamed that somewhere I took a shortcut, I cut a corner, I faked this or that or lied about the other: no sir. The law was the law. The law was always right.

And the law looked at the shirt and the blood and Reggie's absence of an alibi and said: Reggie Gerard Fuller did it.

He was satisfied. What else could he do? He had no other files. The actual evidence was burned in that damn 1994 fire. Nothing else could be learned.

But then . . . oh, little niggle of doubt. Little qualm, little tremor, little twitch.

He thought back on that night and his actions. What cast the longest shadow over the case was the RGF initials. Once they'd identified RGF—done, really, before he'd put his full concentration on the matter—the case developed a peculiar momentum that could not be stopped. It was such a fat, huge piece of evidence, like a proverbial eight-hundred-pound gorilla, that it sat anyplace it wanted to. It shaped all thought, all interpretation, all investigation; it became the central organizing principle of the case, a perceptual reality that could not be avoided.

In fact, Sam had even played that one out straight. He'd spent one whole day with Betty Hill, the town's switchboard operator, going through the phone listings to ascertain if just possibly there wasn't another RGF, of any color or sex. There wasn't. He'd gone to the town registry looking for other RGFs who might not be on the phone list. He'd gone to every motel in a hundred square miles looking for another RGF in the area. No such thing.

That RGF: that was the monster.

It occurred to Sam: Suppose there was no RGF? Suppose we never found that RGF? Would we have ever tied the killing to Reggie? No, he thought not. If it weren't for the dying girl's spasm and the angry boy's fury, the case might never have been solved.

But then he thought: Imagine an investigation *without* the weight of that discovery, that wasn't misshapen or guided by it, that progressed quite naturally and led where it led, if anywhere. Of course he couldn't imagine such a thing: RGF made that impossible.

Little tingle, little tremor, little buzz. Where did it come from?

What was he feeling?

He couldn't pin it down: nothing. Forget it.

Then he had it.

Earl.

Earl Swagger had discovered the body. Earl had investigated the crime scene. Earl took notes. Earl made observations and suggestions. All of it untainted, or untouched, or unseduced by the mighty power of the RGF initials pointing the finger right straight into the heart of Reggie Gerard Fuller. Earl was dead before they ever linked anything to Reggie Gerard Fuller.

Too bad Earl hadn't lived long enough to . . .

Another bell went off in Sam's old mind. His son, Bob, had brought Earl's notebook. And some other effects. With that fool boy, Rusty, Rufus, whatever. The notebook. Whatever was in the notebook was put there without any knowledge of Reggie Gerard Fuller.

Only trouble was: where the hell was the notebook?

The old man was on a goddamn toot. Duane had never seen him like this. His gears had slipped or something. He was literally destroying his house from the inside out.

Duane had worked his way around back of the proud old dwelling on Reinie Street, which sat under a canopy of elms and maples with its stately porch like the house that Andy Hardy lived in, and peered in through the windows. Though it was not yet dark, the old man had turned on all the lights. One by one, he was emptying the insides out of every drawer, every closet, every box, every cupboard, every vase in the house. He had cracked, finally. He was in a frenzy, jabbering insanely to himself.

After doing the downstairs, he moved upstairs. Though Duane could no longer see him, he took a chance and opened the door. Inside, he could hear crashes and dumpings and things being thrown against the wall and curses.

"Goddamn sumbitch, where the goddamn hell *are* you?" came the screams, as from a desperate man, a man close to an attack or something.

Mr. Bama wasn't going to have to worry about this old guy. He'd end up doing himself in before the moon rose. A vein would pop, he'd be a lump in a body bag for the Coroner's Office.

Duane called in a report, but there was no immediate answer. Where the hell was Bama?

You old worthless goat. You dying old bastard, you brainless worthless old dog, you ain't good for nothing. Ought to put you down. Take you out and put a bullet behind your ear. Only merciful thing.

Sam looked about him. The house was ruined, smashed, destroyed. The rooms where his children played, the room where he had loved his wife, the room where so many Thanksgiving dinners had been eaten, the room where so many Christmases had been celebrated: all gone, all lost, all ruined, all wrecked and for what, for nothing, because he couldn't remember where he put the goddamned notebook.

Only the garage remained.

He was full of despair. How had he gotten so old and feeble, so infirm? He hated and loathed himself: he—prosecutor, man of the law, war hero, deer hunter, father, husband, lover, American: how had all that gone away and he come to this current state of nothingness? His daughter had told him it was time to move in with them or if he wanted into an apartment or even a home and his eldest boy had said no, Pop's all right, but now he thought she was right. He could—

The office!

You old goat! You *never brought it home!* He remembered now—Bob had handed it to him at the office and he'd locked it in the safe.

He looked around for his coat, but the only thing he could find immediately was his wife's pink bathrobe from years back. He threw it on and, miraculously, found his keys. He stepped into the garage, fired up the Cadillac and backed out with a shriek and a lurch, hitting something—he wasn't sure what.

He drove and a new fear assailed him: the combination. Did he know it? Could he remember it? Or was it gone like so much of the past?

He felt a whimper, or possibly a sob, rise from his chest, and felt enfeebled by the task ahead. He lacked all confidence. He was over, finished.

But after parking and somehow getting up the steps, unlocking the office and walking through the waiting room into his lair, a mercy came from on high, and as his fingers flew to the ancient lock, he saw the numbers before him big as daylight and in a second he had the vault open and the cardboard box out.

He took the treasure to his desk, clicked on the light and stopped for just a second to fill his pipe with tobacco. Lighting it, he drew a hot burst of smoke into his mouth, felt it buzz, then expelled it, and for just a second was back in the good part of his life, in command, a man of respect and power, not a cornpone, backwoods Lear raging on the moors of Polk County.

The box held but two objects and then he remembered that Bob and Rusty-Rufus-Ralph-whatever had taken the third, a manila file with some yellowed newspaper clippings in them. No matter: what was here was what counted, not the book of old traffic and speeding citations but the notebook, Earl's jottings from early July 23, 1955. It bore a brownish streak across the cover, like one of those flings of paint that Jackson Pollock was so famous for; and the edges of half the pages inside were brittle with the same brown substance.

Sam drew back. Earl's blood. As he lay dying, Earl must have bled in the car on the notebook. With a shudder, he opened it.

The shock hit him first of all: for ten years, as they'd collaborated enforcing the law, Sam had read reports that Earl filed and the man's handwriting was as familiar as his own—then forty years of nothing. Now here it was back again, in its familiar loops and whorls, its orderliness, its occasional underlinings, its occasional misspellings. The blood, the writing: it was as if Earl himself had suddenly walked into the room, so overpowering was the sense of his presence.

Another little shudder went through Sam as he tried to enter into Earl's mind. Earl, how did you work? What was your style? Investigators all have styles, little things that are important to them, that they recognize as they try to bring order to chaos. What was Earl's? He tried to remember. Then he remembered Earl's bench in his basement, with every tool in its place and a place for every tool. Earl had no need for the creativity of chaos; he believed in putting things in order.

His mind would work thus: Site. Body. Evidence. Conclusions.

No, no, no, it wouldn't. He'd make conclusions after every section. Then he'd list the conclusions at the end, adding them up. That's how he'd do it; that's how he always did it.

First up, a drawing of the body, in exactly the posture that Sam remembered seeing it the next day, with dotted, diagonal lines orienting it toward landmarks ("tree," "rock") and distance estimations. Earl had also scratched in some kind of cross-hatching behind the body and identified it as "shale wash," adding in parenthesis "no tracks."

Hmmmm. Sam thought about that. It was a new detail. What kind of original site investigation had been done? He tried to remember. He himself hadn't gotten there till late the next afternoon, after all that with Earl's death, and he'd been sleepless and irritable as well as depressed. He remembered a lone deputy telling him the state police forensics people hadn't shown up and that lots of people from the town had come out to see the dead nigger girl. So evidently, there wasn't much site investigation, other than Earl's. The crime scene was hopelessly contaminated.

He turned the page, to find CONC—Earl's comments on the

site. It said only "Body moved? Dumped where no tracks could be found?"

Body moved? This was new. Body moved? Why would Reggie have—

But then he remembered: Reggie *hadn't* been uncovered yet. No one would ask why Reggie would move the body, just as later investigators would not trouble to think about the body being moved, since they already had Reggie.

He turned the page: the body itself.

There were descriptions of the various violations worked on poor Shirelle, including scrapes and abrasions visible in the "private area," as Earl had so demurely called it. He also described a "grayish cast to skin, suggesting passage of several days" and "some bloating." He looked at the killing wound: "Looks to be a massive hematoma in the right frontal quadrant of the skull" and noted nearby "rock smeared with blood as possible murder weapon."

But then something strange: "Cause of death? Maybe not blow; swelling and bruising around throat area suggests strangulation?"

Sam sat back. Also new to him: strangulation.

Where was *this* coming from?

Maybe Earl was mistaken. On the other hand, when the coroner looked at Shirelle, another two days had passed: possibly she'd swollen more and the swelling and bruising on her throat weren't as visible. Or possibly, because Reggie was already in custody and there was a good deal of blood already in evidence, nobody looked that carefully at the body.

What was the significance of the strangulation?

Sam sawed away on this one and then had it. If he strangled her, there wouldn't be no blood. Or not much. Yet Reggie's shirt was stained fairly extensively with Shirelle's blood.

Sam didn't like this one damned bit. Then he thought: Reggie strangles her. He's not sure if she's dead. He smashes her with the rock.

Yes, that would explain it.

But it was a raggedness, an awkwardness, an uncertainty, where before there had only been absolute confidence.

His pipe was empty. He scraped the cake out with his keys, then refilled it, lit and sucked. It gurgled, burning too hot, wet and harsh, a sure sign he was agitated and somewhat diluting the great tobacco rush. He looked about. It was dark now, quite still. He got up, went to the window and looked out upon a small town at night, lit here and there by a window radiating heat and light, but generally still. The only thing he could see was a sheriff's car parked down the street. Was it that goddamned Duane Peck? What the hell could he want? Was Sam now so feeble he needed full-time supervision?

He went back to his desk.

Wasn't this a goddamned fine kettle of fish? How long was this going to last? The old goat was completely wacky. Now he was at his office. Duane looked at his watch. It was nearly nine. He'd been on the go since seven that morning, this on three hours' sleep off of yesterday's roaming.

Only one thing to break the monotony; middle of the afternoon there had been some kind of dustup on the radio, some kind of big gunfight over on the Taliblue Trail in Oklahoma, about forty miles away. He couldn't make any sense of it, Oklahoma Highway Patrol shit, and calls for originally ambulances and fire trucks but then coroners but it was none of his business.

Now he was just waiting. From where he was, he couldn't see much—just the light beaming out of the old man's office from the window. The old man had come to it a few seconds ago, sucking on his pipe, and stared for a bit. Then he'd gone back.

Duane wasn't quite able to see the old man, which had him worried. He was parked parallel to the curb, across the street and down a bit. So he got out of his car and walked into the square, passed the statue of General George F. James, the Iron General of Vicksburg, who'd actually been born in Polk County, though he died in a brothel in Savannah, Georgia, at the age of eighty-one surrounded by painted harlots, and went and stood on a bench at the far side. Standing so, with his binoculars, he could see the top of Sam's body as the old man bent over whatever he was examining. He was working away steadily, and he looked to all the world like Perry Mason except, of course, for the pink bathrobe.

Sam looked at the drawing. It appeared to be a window on a one-story, rounded building with a single line drawn from the top edge of the window to an inscription, and here his penetrations into the mysteries of Earl's handwriting ceased. "Reed dept.," it seemed to say. Now, what the hell could that mean?

He looked at it: a mystery. What was the building, what was the department of reeds? He searched his memory for a forty-year-old hint, but couldn't come up with a damned thing. He looked again at the drawing. Maybe it wasn't a building, maybe it was a television set. But in 1955, there weren't but ten televisions in all of Polk County. Maybe it was a drive-in movie screen, but the nearest drive-in movie screen was and always had been the Sky-Vue in Fort Smith, where Sam sometimes took his children.

His pipe puffed dry. He turned it upside down and smacked it into the ashtray, dumping the shards of ash. He looked around for his pouch, working slowly, enjoying the ritual and the cleansing effect it had on his mind. He was going to pack the 'baccy into the bowl when he remembered to clean the cake, but he couldn't lay a hand on his keys—they were across the room, he remembered—and so with his thick, horny thumbnail he scraped gunk off the bowl and wiped it on his pants. There, that cleared the bowl. He scrunched a wad of tobacco into the pipe, clenched it between his old teeth, lit a match and drew it to the bowl. He sucked in and watched the suction take the flame, draw it into the pipe and, ah—blast of smoke scented with the forest. Such a—

His fingernail!

His fingernail wore a crescent of ash deposit under its edge.

He looked again at the drawing: it was the girl's fingertip, her nail. The line ran from the rim of the nail to the inscription, which he now realized said "Red dirt," not "Reed dept.," for the period after dirt was a minor imperfection of the paper, not from Earl's pen.

Red dirt under her nails.

But there was no red dirt at that point off U.S. 71. Wasn't now, wasn't then.

Red dirt means she was killed somewhere else, yes, and brought here.

Red dirt means—Little Georgia.

He turned the page; at the top, under conclusions, Earl had written "Little Georgia?"

Little Georgia was a patch of red clay deposit not off Route 71 north of town but off 88, northeast of town, just before Ink.

If Shirelle had red dirt under her nails, it could mean that's where she was killed. But so what? Who would move her twelve, fifteen miles? What would be the point?

Still, Sam could see how unimportant the red dirt under the nails would have been to a coroner who already knew that Reggie Gerard Fuller had been arrested and charged with the murder. Or maybe it wasn't red dirt. Maybe it was blood, from Reggie. But there had been no forensic material of that nature entered.

Sam cursed himself. Maybe he hadn't pushed hard enough. Maybe he should have forced the coroner to do a bang-up job and not miss a trick. Why had he been so *sure* it was Reggie?

Well, because of the pocket, the blood match, the—

But more, because of a limit to the imagination. It was, after all, 1955. The world was a straightforward place, with a straight-shooting President, a known Red enemy with the hydrogen bomb, and white people and colored separate and apart. Nothing was mixed up; everybody knew where they stood. Things were what they seemed.

Now all this that was going on with Reggie and Shirelle? Nobody could really have imagined it. There wasn't room in the American mind in those days for such imaginings. They came later, after the murder of JFK, after Vietnam and Watergate; that's when people began to see conspiracies every damned place.

Because once you admitted the idea of conspiracy, the world changed. Paranoia ruled; there were no limits. There was no certitude. That is what he hated so much about the modern world he had helped create: it beheld no certitude.

For if there was a conspiracy involving the death of Shirelle

Parker, a poor Negro child in the West Arkansas of 1955, who knew where else it went and what else it contained? And for the first time, Sam began to see that it might also, though he couldn't understand how or why, involve the strange behavior of Jimmy Pye and the death of Earl Swagger. And if, furthermore, it involved a black man, on the basis of the fact that no colored girl would have gotten into a car with a white man, then things had gotten dense and complicated to no end. It was like some terrible modern novel, of the sort that Sam couldn't read: twisted, crazy, paranoid, ugly, cruel.

He knew he was onto something; it scared him, it exhilarated him, it made him angry, it made him sad. Quickly, he jotted some notes on a big yellow legal pad, so he wouldn't forget, but he knew he wouldn't forget. He felt dynamic, forceful, brilliant.

By God, he thought, I will get to the bottom of this and Earl's son and that damned boy Rusty will help me.

Duane Peck called in and made his report.

"Sir, I don't know, but this old guy's onto something. He's all excited, I can tell. He discovered something and I don't know what. He's been looking for something for three days, and by God, now he's found it. What should I do?"

The call came almost immediately. Bama sounded downcast, depressed, angered; a bad day at the office?

He made Peck go through it again, very slowly, he considered and then he told him what to do.

Twenty-six

THEY STOOD on a little yellow hill under the blinding sun. Off to the east, like a white-walled city from a fairy tale, lay some intricate structure, with towers and mansards and subbuildings: McAlester State Penitentiary. Off to the west, simple rolling Oklahoma countryside. Here there were markers, bleak and unadorned.

"So that's it?" Bob asked. "You brought me all this way to see this?"

"Yes, I did," said Russ. "That's what became of Jimmy Pye's only son. That's what remains on this earth of what happened July 23, 1955."

The inscription simply said, "Lamar Pye, 1956–1994." A few feet away lay another one. "Odell Pye," it said, "1965–1994."

"His cousin," said Russ. "Jim Pye's brother's boy. A hopeless retardate. Belonged in an institution, where no one would bother him. You see what the Pye blood got the two of them."

"Russ, I just see two gravestones on a bare hill on a little bit of nowhere in Oklahoma. It's like Boot Hill in some goddamned cowboy movie. It don't mean a thing."

"It's just so obvious," said Russ. "Don't you see it? It's all here: murder, a family of dysfunctional monsters, the seed going from father to son. It's *The Brothers K* set in Oklahoma and Arkansas over two generations."

"Son, I don't know what the hell you're talking about. But if it helps you to come look at it and say, 'Yeah, he's dead, he's gone,' that's fine. Glad to oblige."

Russ looked at him sharply.

"You scream at night, Russ," said Bob. "Sometimes two, three times. 'Lamar,' you scream, or 'Dad, Dad.' You got a mess of snakes up there. You best get yourself some help. See the chaplain, we'd say in the Corps. But see somebody."

Russ shook his head. "I'm all right," he said. "I just want to get this thing done with."

"It ain't about you and Lamar Pye. Your daddy took care of that, all right? Lamar is in the ground, he's finished, it's over. That's your dad's present to you: the rest of your life."

"And his girlfriend was his present to himself. The end of the family, that was his present to himself."

"Russ, things aren't as easy as you make them. Nothing's that clear."

"It feels clear," said Russ bitterly.

"You going to be all right? This thing could go crazy at any second. Maybe you ought to stay here in McAlester, take the bus back to Oklahoma City. You could get your old job back, work on the book from there. I'd let you know what I eventually found out."

"No, this is my project, I invented it. We'll solve it together."

"Okay, Russ, if that's what you want."

They walked down the hill. A black inmate trusty waved at them.

"You find what you want?"

"Yes sir," said Bob.

"That was Lamar Pye's grave you stopped at, wasn't it?"

"Yes, it was," said Russ. "Did you know him?"

"Oooo, no," said the man, as if a taboo had been violated. "No, Lamar was not friendly toward the brothers. He was as mean as they come. Got to say this for him, though: he was a brave man. He stood up in the joint, and when it came his time, he went down like a man. He kilt two polices."

"Actually, he just killed one. The other one lived," Russ said.

"My, my, do tell," said the old trusty mildly.

They walked another fifty feet to the truck, finding themselves in some kind of depression in the land, so that down here the white-walled prison was not visible.

"You drive," said Bob.

Russ climbed into the truck, parked a few feet away.

"Shall we head back up to U.S. 40?"

"Hell no," said Bob, looking at a map. "We'll go back the scenic way. I got some thinking to do. We'll head down to Hawthorne and then over to Talihina. There's a real pretty road down that way, takes us back over the mountains to Blue Eye. The Taliblue Trail. You'll like it. We'll be home for supper."

Around noon, Red filed a flight plan that set him on a course of 240 degrees south-southwest toward Oklahoma City. It took him another half an hour to fuel up the Cessna 425 Conquest and ten minutes after that for a takeoff clearance, as American Eagle's 12:45 P.M. from Dallas into Fort Smith was landing. But at last he was airborne.

The plane surged upward as Red eased the stick back, seemed to catch a little thermopane and rushed even faster skyward. He leveled out at 7,000 feet, well below commercial traffic patterns, scudded southwest toward the green mounds on the horizon that were the Ouachitas. The first leg, all twenty minutes' worth, was easy flying; beneath him the land was a blue haze, rolling and vague, without true detail, not particularly revealing.

He loved to fly and was quite a good pilot: perfect solitude, the fascinations of the intricate machine that held him aloft with its clever compromise of dynamic forces and its endless stream of numerical data. Yet at the same time, as mechanistic an equilibrium as it was, there was still the wildness of the unpredictable, the sense of being a true master of one's fate. Also, it was for rich people mainly, and Red liked that quite a bit.

When he got ten miles north of Blue Eye, he dropped down to 4,000 feet and the details sharpened considerably; he had no problem picking up the parallel roads of 270 and 88 as they plunged westward from just above Blue Eye, which itself looked like a scatter of dominoes, blocks, cards and toys against the roll of the earth. As he flew west, the town disappeared and below him were just two roads cutting across the rolling mountains and valleys. Traffic on both of them was very light.

He leaned to his radio console, switched to the security mode in the digital encryption system and keyed in the code he'd selected from the 720 quadrillion possibilities, the same code selected in de la Rivera's radio on the ground; the radio was now secure from intercept.

He picked up the microphone, punched the send button and said, "Yeah, this is Air, come in, please."

The radio fizzed and crackled and then de la Rivera's slightly Hispanic tones came back at him.

"Yes, I have you loud and clear."

"That extender is working nicely," said Red, "I have you loud and clear. No trouble installing it?"

"No sir. One of the boys did army commo."

"Good. Position report, please."

"Ah, I have you visually, you just buzzed my position. I'm at the wayside just inside Oklahoma. I got a car with three men with me. I got my other two units about twenty-five miles ahead, right where 259 cuts across 1."

"What units are those?"

"We're just calling them Alpha and Baker. My car here is Charlie, I'm Mike."

"Alpha and Baker, you there?"

"Yes sir," came a voice.

"You got me visually?"

"I see you on the horizon. You're still a few miles away."

"Okay, I'm going to buzz to Talihina and back. That's where I'll be. When I get a visual, I'll confirm. Then I'll trail him into your range. When you see me, you'll know he's coming."

"Yes sir," came the replies.

Red dropped down a thousand feet. At his altitude, the cars on the mountain road were easily recognizable by type and color, though not by make. He was looking for a green pickup with one unpainted fender. Suppose he found one and directed it into the ambush and it was some Mexican family traveling from bean harvest to bean harvest or some group of tender young college girls going to the Little Rock Pearl Jam concert? He had a set of Zeiss 10×50 binoculars, the finest that could be found in Fort Smith on a crash basis, and from 3,000 feet up he found he could get a very solid up-close and personal view of the vehicle. There wouldn't be any mistakes.

He flew onward, enjoying the freedom and the sense of the hunt. Off far to the left and a thousand feet higher, he made out another flight, a Lear, obviously headed south to Dallas; there was no other air traffic. The road below was equally empty, though he made out a station wagon pulling tourists along the vividly beautiful road as it rolled along the crest of the green mountains, one of those ludicrous camper things, a couple of private automobiles and one black and white Oklahoma Smokey pulled off by the side of the road, on watch for speeders or merely dozing in the sun. He switched from his secure channel to the Oklahoma Highway Patrol frequency and heard nothing except the odd exchange between troopers somewhere in the area, nothing of note.

He passed over the 259 crossroads and the possibility of contact drew him ever lower, down to 2,500 feet. Maybe too low; he didn't need FAA complaints against his license. But there were no other flights in view. The road beneath him, bright in the afternoon sun, was a ribbon. Onward he flew, all the way to Talihina, spotting nothing.

He veered and headed back along the highway, now having risen to 4,000 feet, and raced back toward the ambush kill zone. He could monitor the road just in case he'd missed something, but there were no green trucks.

"Okay, boys," he said into the radio when he was in range, "so far I got nothing. You all okay?"

"We're fine," said de la Rivera.

"No police interest or anything?"

"Haven't seen a cop all day, sir."

He glanced at his Rolex. It was 3:30 by this time. Where the hell were they? It was beginning to look like a wash. He'd guessed wrong.

He used some left rudder, then dropped back down to 2,000 feet and began to zoom up the road, eyes peeled. The traffic had really thinned out by now. It wasn't—

Green vehicle.

He dropped a little lower.

Pickup truck.

He overflew it and got on the radio.

"I got a possible. Got a possible."

"Copy you, Air."

"Okay, let me just check this out."

He banked wide to the left, left wingtip falling, right rising, the world going giddily topsy-turvy as the two big engines drove the props through the air, and came around again level-out about a half mile to the right of the road and saw the truck ahead of him. He reached for the throttles, eased them back; the sound of engines racing could be heard for several miles and he didn't want to alert them at all.

Gradually, he gained on them, trying not to force it or rush or anything.

When at last he was nearly parallel, he set the plane on autopilot and drew the binoculars into position and diddled with focus.

Green pickup. Unpainted left front fender. Dodge.

Got you, he thought, exultant.

He applied a touch of right rudder, a little aileron, and gently banked to the right, settling on a course of 180 degrees due south. He held the course for one minute, loafing at eighty knots, looking innocent, putting distance between himself and the target. Two minutes. He drummed his fingers on his thighs. Two minutes forty seconds. Red could take no more. He quickly reset the trim tabs, increased the pitch and pushed the throttles forward.

As the revs came up he executed a hard climbing turn to the left, straining for altitude. He was sweating.

"Air to Mike, Air to Mike. Are you there, are you there?" he said, hoping he was still in range.

"Yes sir," said de la Rivera.

"I have them confirmed, about twenty miles west of the 259 cutoff. They're coming your way. ETA 3:55 P.M."

❑ ❑ ❑ ❑

"Here's something I thought of," said Russ. "A theory. Let me just throw it out."

Bob said nothing, just waited. They were cruising along the Taliblue Trail, a two-lane blacktop that ran along the crest of the Ouachitas and had just blown by the crossroads with Oklahoma 259. Ahead of them stretched empty road, gritty and dusty from poor upkeep here in Oklahoma. On either side, the mountain fell away, not a cliff but a steep slope; beyond, on either side, the valleys were deep and green; to the right, he could see the lesser ranges of the Ouachitas, the Jack Forks, the Kiamichis, the Winding Stairs. He heard something somewhere, on the far edge of his consciousness, that he couldn't quite place. He ignored it.

"Go ahead," he said.

"In the movies or in books, there's no such thing as coincidence. No one's going to pay to see or read about some guy who just finds something or something just happens to him."

"Forrest Gump shows that one's full of shit."

"No, no, I mean *normally. Forrest Gump* being an exception to the rules. You can't—"

"Russ, I was just joking. Don't you got no sense of humor anywhere?"

"Well," said Russ, thinking, No, no, he probably didn't. "Anyhow, in real life, however absurd and irrational, coincidence occasionally happens. And I can't help but notice you have an army night-shooting program that's trying to develop tactics around night-vision devices in roughly the same area as the one where your father got hit at night. Maybe it's not a conspiracy; maybe it's one of those insane, ridiculous coincidences."

"You saying Forrest Gump did it?" Bob laughed.

Russ breathed out his frustration.

"Now, suppose," he continued, "they had a patrol or something and they got lost, got turned around. And they're off post: and they watch this gunfight through the infrared scope where the details aren't clear. They watch as one guy kills two others. And then he gets in a car; he's going to get away. Maybe the sniper can't help himself: he pulls the trigger and that's that."

"Won't work," Bob said. "He was in a tree. Had to be, otherwise he couldn't have seen through the corn. And there wouldn't have been that slight oval shape to the bullet hole."

Russ nodded. He thought, *Goddammit! He thinks he's so smart!*

"Okay, okay. Now, maybe, well, you know the attitudes were different then, there was very little press scrutiny, they all thought they were on some kind of crusade against the communists. They *did* test atom bomb radiation, biological warfare, LSD and some other stuff on unwary civilians. Maybe it was some test: they had to shoot at a human target. So they're on the track of Jimmy and Bub because they know those're clean kills without problems. But there's a terrible mistake and your father's the one that gets hit."

"Not bad," said Bob after a pause, "not bad. Wrong, but not bad."

"Why wrong?"

"I'll tell you why. You remember that short little guy in the photograph, the one Preece couldn't remember?"

"Yeah."

"Couldn't remember, my ass. I knew that little prick. And anybody who knew him would remember him."

"Who was he?"

"His name was Frenchy Short. He was CIA all the way. A cowboy. On my second tour I was detached TDY to lead recon teams in liaison with the Agency up near Cambodia. The Frenchman was hanging around; it was an outfit called SOG, Studies and Observation Groups. Lots of very nasty boys. Frenchy had a little war going on in Cambodia with some mercenary Chinese called the Nung and a marine officer named Chardy as the XO. Frenchy thought he was Lawrence of Cambodia. He was one of those goddamned screwball showboat guys, the rules didn't apply to him, he was bigger than the rules, he was bigger than the service or the Agency. Hell, he was bigger than the fucking war. He just happened to work for us, but he'd have worked for anybody. It was the work he loved, not no cause. The point is, I put out the question earlier: who could put together the kind of operation fast and on the fly that connected the criminal world, Jimmy Pye, a well-planned robbery, a daring escape, and brought it all off with my father getting whacked as the end result and nobody knowing any better? Well, maybe two or three men in the world. One of them being Frenchy Short. That was his goddamned specialty. And there's one other thing."

"Yeah?"

"When I DEROSed out of SOG and headed back to the world, Frenchy drew me aside and asked me to ship him five hundred rounds of civilian ammunition."

"I don't—"

"He carried a Colt automatic in a tanker's shoulder holster over his tiger suit. I just assumed it was a .45, same as mine. No, it was a .38 Super. He told me how he loved the .38 Super, it had so much less recoil than a .45 for the same killing power, plus extra rounds in the mag. He called it a pro's gun."

"Jesus," said Russ.

"It's more than—"

But Bob stopped.

A plane. That was it. The sound of an airplane engine, steady, not increasing in speed, just low enough and far enough away, almost a fly's buzz.

"Go on," said Russ.

"Just shut up," Bob said.

"What is—"

"Don't look around, don't speed up, don't slow down, you just stay very calm now," Bob said.

He himself didn't look around. Instead, he closed his eyes and listened, trying hard to isolate the airplane engine from the roar of the truck, the buffeting of the wind, the vibrations of the road. In time, he had it.

Very slowly he turned his head, yawning languidly as he went along.

Off a mile on the right, a white twin-engine job, maybe a Cessna. Those babies went 240 miles per hour. Either there was a terrific headwind howling out of the east, or the pilot was hovering right at the stall speed to stay roughly parallel and in the same speed zone with the truck.

"It's more than coincidence," Bob said, "that you got the one man in America there who could do such a thing and that he's a great believer in the .38 Super, just what Jimmy was shooting. I smell Frenchy all over it. I think Frenchy threw it together, real smart, very fast, a fucking Agency home run the whole way. Not for the Agency, maybe, but for someone else. Someone powerful, that I guarantee you."

He glanced quickly out the window. The plane was turning lazily away.

"Yeah, well—it's okay? I mean, you tensed up there, now you're relaxed. Everything's okay, right?"

"Oh, every goddamn thing's just superfine," said Bob, yawning again, "except of course we are about to git ambushed."

"Air to Alpha and Baker," said Red, holding steady at 2,500 feet, running east, loafing again, dangerously near stall.

"Alpha here," came a voice.

"What about Baker?"

"Oh, yeah, uh, I'm here too. I figured he said he was here, you'd know I was here."

"Forget figuring. Tell me exactly what I ask you. Got that?"

"Yes sir," said Baker contritely.

"Okay, I want you in pursuit. He's about four miles ahead of you, traveling around fifty miles an hour. No Smokeys, no other traffic on the road. You go into maximum pursuit. But I am watching you, and on my signal you drop down to fifty-five. I don't want him seeing you move superfast, do you read?"

"Yes sir."

"Then step on it, goddammit."

"Yes sir."

"You hang steady there, Mike and Charlie. No need you racing anywhere, they are coming to you. I see intercept in about four minutes. I'm going to let Alpha and Baker close in, then I'll bring you and Baker into play, Mike. You read?"

"Yes sir."

He looked back along the road and out of the distance watched as two large sedans roared along the highway at over a hundred miles an hour, trailing dust and closing fast with the much slower moving truck.

"Oh, I smell blood. I smell the kill. It's looking very good. Alpha, I see you and your buddy closing. You just keep closing, you're getting close, okay now, slow way down. Mike, you and Charlie now, okay, you start moving out, nice gentle pace, about fifty-five, we are two minutes away, I got you both in play."

Someone inadvertently held a mike button down and Red heard strange things over the radio—some harsh tense scraping and what sounded like someone systematically turning a television set on and off. Then he realized: that was the dry breathing of men about to go into a shooting war and they were cocking and locking their weapons for it.

Words poured out of Russ as if he'd lost control of them, and he could not control their tone: they sounded high, tinny, almost girlish.

"Should we stop?" he moaned. "Should we pull off and call the police? Is there a turnoff? Should we—"

"You just sit tight, don't speed up, don't slow down. We got two cars behind us. I bet we got some traffic ahead of us. And we got a plane off on the right coordinating it. We are about to get bounced and bounced hard."

Russ saw Bob shimmy in the seat, but he could tell he was reaching to get something behind the seat without disturbing his upright profile. He looked into the rearview mirror and saw two cars appear from behind a bend in the road.

"Here's the first and only rule," said Bob steadily. "Cover, not concealment. I want you out of the truck with the front wheel well and the engine block between you and them. Their rounds will tear right through the truck and get to you otherwise."

Russ's mind became a cascade of silvery bubbles; he fought to breathe. His heart weighed a ton and was banging out of control. There was no air.

"I can't do it," he said. "I'm so scared."

"You'll be all right," Bob said calmly. "We're in better shape than you think. They have men and they think they have surprise, but we've got the edge. The way out of this is the way out of any scrape: we hit 'em so hard so fast with so much stuff they wish they chose another line of work."

Ahead, one and then a second vehicle emerged from the shimmery mirage. The first was another pickup, black and beat-up, and behind it, keeping a steady rate fifty yards behind, another sedan. Russ checked the rearview: the two cars were drawing closer, but not speeding wildly. He made out four big profiles, sitting rigidly in the lead car.

"Don't stare at 'em, boy," said Bob, as he overcame the last impediment and got free what he was pulling at. In his peripheral vision Russ saw that it was the Ruger Mini-14 and the paper bag. He pulled something compact from the bag; Russ realized it was the short .45 automatic, which he quickly stuffed into his belt on his right side, behind his kidney. He groped for something else.

Russ looked up. The truck drew nearer. It was less than a quarter of a mile away. It would be on them in seconds now.

"Where is it?" demanded Bob of himself harshly, fear large and raspy in his voice as he clawed through the bag. His fear terrified Russ more powerfully than the approaching vehicles.

What is he looking for? Russ wondered desperately.

Red watched as his masterpiece unfolded beneath him with such solemn splendor. It was all in the timing and the timing was exquisite. De la Rivera in the Mike truck, followed by the four men in Charlie, closed from the front at around forty miles per hour. Meanwhile, the Alpha and Baker vehicles, moving at the speed limit, steadily narrowed the distance between themselves and Swagger. They would be fifty or so yards behind him when de la Rivera hit Swagger's truck and blew it off the road.

"You're closing nicely, Alpha and Baker," he crooned. "You're looking good there, Mike."

They had him!

It would work!

Red pulled in his breath, felt his heart inflate and his blood pressure spiral.

De la Rivera was now taking over.

"Okay, *muchachos,* is so very *muy bueno,* let's be very, very calm now, let's stay calm and cool, I see you, Alpha, you're so very fine, let's do a quick double check on our pieces, make sure we got our mags seated, our bolts locked, our safeties in the red zone, let's stay *muy glace,* icy, icy, very icy, very cool, it's happening, oh, it's gonna be *so good* for all of us."

The vehicles were closing.

They had reached a flat, high section of the road, where the dwarf, ice-pruned white oak lay gnarled and stunted on either side, yielding swiftly to vistas on either side of other ranges.

"Now you listen," said Bob fiercely. "This truck's going to try and whack you. The split second before you pull even to him, I want you to drop to second and gun this motherfucker. That should carry us by his lunge and cut the two boys off behind us. Then I want a hard left, you rap the rear of his follow car, really mess him up, shake up the boys inside; you continue from that into a *hard left panic stop,* we skid across the road and come to rest in the shoulder on that side, so's we can fall back and get into them trees and down the side of the mountain if need be. Okay, you're coming out *my* side of the vehicle and you're breaking left to the front wheel well where you're going to cover. You take the bag. Your job is going to be to feed me magazines from the bag as I need them. You watch; when I pop a mag, you hand me the next one, bullets out so's I can slap her in and get back to rock and roll."

"Yes sir," said Russ, trying to remember it all, desperate that he would forget it, but amazed somehow that already there was a plan, and somehow also calmed by it. And Bob seemed calm too.

"You gotta stay calm, you gotta stay cool," said Bob.

"I'm okay," Russ said, and he was.

"Ah," said Bob, "here the goddamn thing is." And with that he withdrew something from the bag and Russ could see that it was a long, curved magazine, different from the others, with a red-tipped cartridge seated in its lips.

The truck was on them. It was happening right now.

"What's that?" Russ had time to ask as the universe unlatched from reality and fell into dreamlike slow motion. He heard Bob seat the magazine and with a *clak!* let the bolt fly home.

"Forty rounds M-196 ball tracer," said Bob. "We're fixing to light these boys up."

Red watched in full anticipation of his precisely choreographed envelopment, simultaneously banking to the left and adding power so that he could hold the spectacle beneath him as he circled around it, gull-like. He watched as the vehicles seemed to combine and it was almost magical the way he'd seen it in his mind and it was working out in reality.

But there seemed to be something . . .

It was happening so fast, there was dust, so much dust, he couldn't . . .

Confusion. He'd never seen a battle before except in the movies but in the movies everything was clear. That was the *point* of movies. Here nothing was clear, it was a helter-skelter, some new dance, a reinvention.

He heard them on the radio as it unfolded in microtime.

"Ah, no, goddamn—"

Whang! the jarring bang of metal on metal.

"Jesus, what is—"

"Look out, he's firing, he's—"

"Oh, fuck, we're on fire. Christ, *we're burning!*"

"I'm hit, I'm hit, oh, shit, I'm hit—"

"The flames, the flames."

BEOWWWWWWWWWWWWWWWWW—

A high-pitched scream pierced Red's ears as he banked around; he winced, shuddered, wondering what the hell that was, and when he saw the geyserlike surge of blazing gasoline, he knew the microphone had melted.

It was happening. The truck's fender with its cyclopslike headlight was as big as a house falling on him, but at that second Russ slammed the gearshift, punched the pedal and with a surprising giddy lightness, his own vehicle shot ahead and the oafish rammer missed, veered to correct and jacked out of control, tumbling savagely backwards amid a sudden huge blast of dust. Bob's left hand reached for the wheel and wrenched it to the left. With a tremendous jolt the pickup slammed into the follow car, rocked crazily and continued to spin around, hauling up a shroud of dust as it fishtailed, then came to a rest, crazily canted to one side, half in and half out of the roadside gully.

Through it all, Russ had the ghastly sensation of ghosts, as faces lit up by rage and surprise floated by in the follow car, so close yet so far away. He felt that he was looking at men under ice, in a different world, their mouths working madly, their eyes swollen like his mother's deviled eggs from so long ago. Then it all went to swirl and blur and vanished in the weird perspective of the canted windshield and the cloud of rolling dust.

He blinked.

Wasn't he supposed to be *doing* something?

"Out, goddammit," barked Bob, and Russ clawed at his safety belt, glad that he'd had it on, felt it fall away and began to slither across the seat after already vanished Bob and out the door. He remembered the bag, and felt the loaded mags rattling around inside as he disengaged from the vehicle, slid fast down the front fender of the truck to the wheel well, where Bob had already set up in a taut, hunched shooter's position. Russ couldn't dive for cover. He had to *see*.

When he looked over the hood, the spectacle stunned him.

Upside down, the black pickup had cantilevered onto the shoulder on the other side of the road in its own cloud of dust, cutting off that lane. The two cars following Bob and Russ had slewed to a halt behind it, just coming out of their own panic stops and skids. They appeared to have collided themselves, the rear one smashing into the front one.

The truck's follower had also slewed to a halt to avoid smashing into the destroyed truck. It was almost directly across the road from Russ. There was a moment of horrified silence. Inside the cars, men fumbled in confusion, trying not to shoot each other, trying to locate their target, which wasn't where it should be.

Then, from just behind Russ, Bob fired.

Even in the bright light of day, the tracers leaked radiance to mark their passage as they flew across the narrow distance. They were like phenomena in a physics experiment, ropes of incandescence as straight as if drawn by a ruler, unbearably quick, quicker than a heartbeat or a blink, illusions possibly. Bob fired three rounds inside a second low into the car directly across from him; what was he shooting for? Not men, for he was shooting not into the passenger compartment but above the rear tire and Russ—

Then the car was gone in a huge flash as the tracers lit up its fuel tank. The noise was a thunderclap, throwing feathers of flame everywhere as it seemed for one delirious second it was raining flame. All around them, the world caught fire; and a wave of crushing heat rolled against Russ. He heard screams in the roar, and a flaming phantasm ran at him but fell under the weight of its own destruction into the roadway.

Motion struck at Russ's peripheral vision and he saw that one of the follow cars had gunned from behind the topsy-turvy truck.

"Coming around, coming around," he screamed.

But Bob was shooting even as Russ yelled and the tracers flicked quick and nasty like a whipcrack and seemed to liquefy the oncomer's windshield; it dissolved into a sleet of jewels as the car lost control and went hard into the gully, kicking up a gout of dirt.

"Magazine! Magazine!" Bob screamed, and Russ slapped a twenty-rounder, bullets outward, into his palm and he sunk it into the rifle, freed the bolt to slam forward just as the third car came around, bristling with guns. But Bob took it cleanly, riddling its windshield with a burst of ball ammunition, and then held fire, emptying what remained of the magazine into the windows and doors as the car went by. The car never deviated, but sped by furiously, more as if it hoped to get away than do them any harm, and a hundred yards down the road it noticed that its cargo was dead men and it veered into a gully, lurched out surfing a wave of dirt and grass and came to a broken ending amid splintered white oaks.

And suddenly it was quiet except for the dry cracking of the wind and the hiss of the flames.

"Jesus, you got them all," Russ said in utter astonishment and devotion, but Bob was by him, .45 in hand. He'd seen something. Two men with submachine guns had extricated themselves from the wreckage in the gully just before them, and started up the little embankment. But Bob stood above them and got his pistol into play so fast it was a blur. Did they see him yet? One did, and tried to get his weapon on target but Bob fired so quickly Russ thought for a second he had some kind of machine gun, floating six empties in the air, and the two shooters went down like rag dolls. One was an immense man in an expensive jumpsuit with gold chains on. He lay flat, eyes blinkless and vacant as the blood turned his sweatshirt strawberry and an odd detail leaped out at Russ: he had a necklace of scar tissue as if someone had gone to work on his throat with a chain saw but only got halfway around before thinking the better of it.

Another moment of silence. Bob used it to change magazines. Russ looked around.

"Jesus Christ," he said. It reminded him of TV coverage of the Highway of Death out of Kuwait City after the Warthogs and the Blackhawks finished a good day's killing. Four wrecked vehicles, one on its back, one boiling with black, oily flame of petroleum products oxidizing into the sky, bodies and blood pools and shards of glass and discarded weapons everywhere.

"What do you think of that, you motherfucker!" Bob suddenly shouted, and Russ saw that he was screaming at a white airplane a half mile out low and banking away to the south.

"You got them all," said Russ. "You must have killed twenty men."

"More like ten. They were professionals. They took their chances. Now let's see if we done bagged a trophy."

Then he strode across the littered roadway to the ramming truck, upside down and half in the gully. The odor of gasoline was everywhere.

He opened the door and peered in. Russ looked over his shoulder.

Inside, in a posture of unbearable discomfort that signaled something important had broken, was a tough-looking Hispanic with creamy silver hair and an expensive suit over an open silk shirt. The angle of his neck suggested that it was broken. Pain lay across his handsome face like a blanket, turning him gray under the olive tones of his skin. His eyes were glazing and his breath was labored.

Bob pointed the .45.

The man laughed and his eyes came back into focus. He held a lighter in his left hand.

"Fuck you, man," he said. "I'm already dead, you cracker motherfucker." His voice was a little lilting with Cubano accent, an odd play of *ch*'s through it. "I flick my Bic and we all going to heaven."

"It won't blow, partner, it'll only burn."

"Fuck you," said the Cubano.

"Who's the man in the plane?" Bob demanded.

The man laughed again; his teeth were blinding white. He made a little move with his free hand and Russ flinched but Bob didn't shoot. Instead, both watched as the hand reached his shirt and, pausing only once or twice in pain, ripped it open. The brown chest was latticed with extravagant tattoos.

"What's that supposed to mean?" Bob said.

"I'm Marisol Cubano, you *norteamericano cabrón.* You *puta!* Fucking Castro couldn't break me in his prisons, man, you think I'm going to talk to some hillbilly homeboy?" He laughed.

"You are one tough customer," said Bob, "that I give you."

He holstered the .45.

"Let's go," he said to Russ.

"Hey," screamed the man in the truck. "I say this to you, motherfucker, you got some balls on you, my friend. You *cubano?* Maybe Desi Arnez done fucked your mama when your daddy was out fucking the goats."

"I don't think so," said Bob. "We didn't have no TV."

They turned and were back at their own truck when the Cubano ended his misery; the truck flared as it went and the heat reached Bob and Russ.

It was nearly dark when Red landed back at Fort Smith. He taxied the Conquest to the hangar and instructed his mechanic to secure it from the flight. He went to the parking lot where his two bodyguards, ever astute, ever loyal, ever dreary, waited in their car. He got into his Mercedes and drove home.

"Honey," said Miss Arkansas Runner-up 1986, "how did it go today?"

"Oh, it was all right," he said. "You know. Sort of unsettled, but all right."

Then he and his two youngest children watched a videotape of *Black Beauty,* a favorite of the kids', and, truth be told, a movie that he himself didn't find too irritating.

After the kids were in bed, he watched the news. The big story, of course, was the drug-dealer shoot-out only a hundred miles away in Oklahoma, on the Taliblue Trail. Ten men dead, four pounds of uncut cocaine recovered. An Oklahoma State Police spokesman said authorities were still trying to figure out what had happened, but the unburned bodies had all been identified as professional criminals tied to Miami, Dallas and New Orleans, with long records of violent felonies, and that conjecture at this time was leading in the direction of some kind of drug shipment ambush that got out of hand and ended up in a flat-out battle on one of Oklahoma's prettiest highways. "Thank God," the cop said, "no innocent people were hurt."

Only after the news was over and the kids were in bed did he step out of denial and face the reality: he was in big trouble. This guy Swagger was the best who'd ever come at him, and, at least in the ten years after his father had been killed, men came after him regularly and he'd beaten them all.

Now he knew he had to do something very clever, very subtle and extremely professional, or he would lose it all. He looked around at his house and thought of his kids from this marriage and the kids from his first marriage and wondered what would happen to them if this guy Swagger took him. It terrified him.

He had a drink and then another, and then the buzzer on his beeper sounded.

He called his number and got Peck's report.

Then he called Peck.

"He's gone now?" he asked.

"Yes sir. What should I do?"

"Peck, I *have* to know what he's onto. Can you get inside that office?"

"Yes sir," said Peck.

"Okay, I want you to break in and make careful notes of his papers. I want to know what he knows, do you understand?"

"Yes sir."

"I don't need any more surprises," he said.

He hung up. He would have gone to bed, but somehow Miss Arkansas Runner-up 1986, real tits or no, didn't seem to amuse him tonight.

Instead, he placed one more phone call and arranged for a quick blow job from a black crack whore. That expressed his mood perfectly.

Twenty-seven

H E WATCHED as the old man finally turned the light off and then, forty-five seconds later, emerged from the office, still in his wife's bathrobe, climbed into the Cadillac and drove off with a shaky squeal of brakes and too much acceleration.

Duane checked his watch. It was 11:45. He decided to give it another fifteen minutes, but only lasted seven before he started to drift off. He knew he was dangerously exhausted. So he got out of the car, walked down the street with his flashlight, throwing beams into crannies just as if he were on patrol investigating a prowler or something, then boldly pushed the door. Naturally, the old man had left it open. He stepped in and followed the flashlight beam up the stairs to the office. Dammit, *that* door was locked.

He reached into his wallet and fumbled with a plastic credit card. Like many policemen, he was skilled at some small criminal crafts that he'd picked up over the years, and it didn't take more than a few seconds' manipulation of the card and the doorknob before he popped the lock and stepped into the outer office. He strode quickly through it and into the old man's lair. The odor of pipe smoke still lingered sweetly in the air.

He went quickly to the safe behind the desk and pulled it gently; sometimes a man will snap his vault closed and not spin the dial and therefore not set the lock. But no, crazy old geezer that he was, old Sam had spun the dial and the lock was solid and beyond

Duane's abilities to penetrate. So instead he went to the windows and pulled the shades. Then he turned on the lights.

The place was a mess! The old bastard seemed to be on some mission of self-destruction: he was systematically trashing everything he owned or held dear. Papers were strewn about everywhere, one of the file cabinet drawers had been dumped on the old carpet.

Duane sat at the desk, littered with old files and reports. He paged through them. Hmmmm. Most seemed to have to do with 1955. There was a letter from some woman, which he slipped into his pocket. He shifted papers about and came across a report on a pretrial hearing, dating from July 29, 1955, for the case of Reggie Gerard Fuller on a count of first-degree murder. Hmmmm. What the hell was *this* all about? It probably had to do with the niggers the old man had been visiting. Why was he visiting niggers? What was he up to? Did it have anything to do with Swagger?

He noticed a legal pad. It wasn't written on, but someone had just torn the top page off of it, and the heavy inscription of a pen had been embossed in the texture of the paper beneath. He held it up to the light, shifting it, trying to find angles on it. Words, in old gnarled writing, began to emerge: Moved body? Little Georgia? Strangled?

Hmmmmm again.

He felt a smug little blast of triumph. Wouldn't Mr. Bama be pleased?

He heard a clatter of noise, the swift thump of feet and the door blew open.

"What the goddamn hell are you doing?" said Sam Vincent.

The old man drove home heavily agitated. His imagination foundered against one significant problem. Who on earth in 1955 in West Arkansas would have considered it worthwhile to engineer a great conspiracy to place the blame for the death of a young girl on an innocent black boy? What would be the point?

He could see no point. But he tried to break it down into parts and see how it fit together. And he kept coming back to one thing:

someone didn't want anybody to know that Shirelle was killed at Little Georgia. Little Georgia was the key.

The significance of moving the body had to be that there *was* evidence, somewhere, somehow, that linked the killer to Little Georgia.

If someone had found the body at Little Georgia, then by God, there was some obvious, physical link to Little Georgia which would have led inexorably to the killer. What could that have been? What would have placed someone at Little Georgia?

He tried to think what he could do to dig up the connection, what it could be. There had to be a document, or at least something prominent in the memory of someone easily accessible at the time.

Maybe a land-use permit.

Maybe a site examination, as from an engineer or an architectural firm.

Maybe a bill of sale.

He tried to consider all the documents that could relate to a piece of land or a section of the county.

Suddenly, he screeched to a halt.

Panic hit him.

Suppose he forgot this? Suppose it had vanished in the morning in that great black fog that rolled in across his mind so frequently? Home was still ten minutes ahead. The office was only five back.

He cranked into a U-turn, bumping up on a curb and crushing what had to be someone's bushes, and with a blast of acceleration headed back.

"What the goddamn hell are you doing here?" demanded the old man. "Who the hell are you, anyway?"

"Ah—Mr. Sam, it's Duane Peck, the deputy. I, uh, seen your lights on. I came up. Hell, you left the door wide open and the lights blazing. I'se just checking to make sure nothing was missing or that there weren't no prowlers."

The old man didn't blink or back down; he didn't retreat into confusion.

"The hell you say! I did no such goddamned thing. I turned my goddamned lights off and locked my office. What are you doing here, sitting at my goddamned desk like you own the place?"

Pugnaciously, he advanced. His shrewd old eyes ate Duane up. He saw that Duane was holding the tablet in his hand.

"What the hell are you doing with that?"

"Nothing," Duane said.

"You were snooping! You were spying! You damned spy, what the hell are you doing?"

Then his eyes knitted up into something tight and knowing.

"Who you working for? You working for *them,* ain't you, you no-'count piece of white trash."

"Sir, I ain't working for nobody," Duane said, rising awkwardly. Still the man advanced on him.

"You ain't working for the sheriff. No sir, I know the sheriff, and you ain't working for him. Who are you working for? You tell me, you trashy dog, or by God I will beat it out of your scrawny hide and hang you out to dry in the morning."

"Sir, I ain't working for nobody," Duane said, alarmed at the old man's fiery temper.

"Well, goddammit, you better believe we'll find out about that. Yes sir, we will get to the bottom of that."

He pivoted slightly to pick up the phone. He dialed 911.

Duane watched him, stupefied. It was happening so quick. He tried to think what to do. His mind was blank, a vapid, empty hole.

Would they make him tell about Mr. Bama? What about the money he owed, would he still owe it to Mr. Bama? What about his new job, and how well he was doing on it? What about working for Mr. Bama personally?

The flashlight rose in his hand, almost as if on its own will, and Duane brought it down with a thunderous thud on the back of the old man's neck. He felt the shiver of blunt instrument striking meat and bone and in the impact thought he heard or felt the sensation of something brittle breaking.

"Sheriff's Department," came the voice over the phone.

The old man stiffened, reached back for his wound and turned, his face black and lost, his eyes pools of emptiness. Duane smashed him again, this time where the neck met the shoulder, a powerful downward diagonal blow that made the head twitch spastically. The phone fell free and banged on the floor and the old man took a stricken step backwards, face gray, old tongue working pitifully in an old mouth, then toppled to the earth as his eyes rolled upward.

"Sheriff's Department? Anybody there?" Duane recognized the voice as Debbie Till's, the night-duty dispatcher.

He hung it up.

He was breathing hard. His knees felt weak. The old man lay still, but was still breathing.

Duane tried to figure what to do next. He could just leave, and they'd find him here and ascribe it to a prowler. But then there'd be an investigation. Suppose someone had seen his car parked outside?

Then he had it.

He wiped the phone off with his handkerchief, in case he'd left prints. Then he quickly turned off the lights, pausing to rub the switches with the handkerchief. He stuffed the tablet with the engraved words into his shirt. Then he hoisted Sam under his arms, feeling the old man's lightness and brittleness. The old man stirred weakly, then went limp. Duane hefted him, because he knew if he dragged him, he'd leave a trail in the dust, and got him to the head of the stairs. He paused for just a second.

This is what Mr. Bama wants, he told himself.

He took a deep breath, gathered his strength and then launched the old man into the air. Sam hit on the fourth step, shattering his teeth, and rolled, legs and arms flopping, down the stairwell, gathering speed and violence as he went, until he smashed to a halt on the downstairs doorjamb.

Duane breathed heavily.

He went back to the office, pulled the door shut and heard it click. He wiped his prints off the knob.

Then he went down the stairs, stepping over the body.

Twenty-eight

AFTER THE FIGHT, Bob bypassed Blue Eye and caught the Boss Harry Etheridge Parkway and took a straight shot north up to Fort Smith. He wanted to put as much distance as he could between himself and the shooting site.

"From now on, we operate as if we can be jumped at any time. Do you understand? They are hunting us. We only got out because the boss man didn't trust his troops and had to control the thing from the air and I saw the plane. Without that jump, I wouldn't have had time to make a plan and we'd be dead."

Russ nodded gravely, as if he understood, as if he were functioning normally. But he was not. He was still half in shock: so much carnage, so fast, so much noise, so much smoke.

"It was so . . . confusing," was all he could think to say. Then it poured out.

"I mean, my God, it just happened, the shooting was so loud, Jesus, the explosions, we were so *lucky,* the whole thing just went berserk, I never knew the universe could go so psychopathic, so twisted. Jesus, you were unbelievably calm. You were like *ice.* I could hardly breathe."

Bob wasn't listening; he was thinking aloud.

"And I want to stow this truck as soon as possible. It'll take the police two days' worth of forensic examination before they realize there was another vehicle involved and another weapon. Then they'll find our tread type and match the paint we left on that boy when we cropped him, and come looking for us."

"I don't think there's enough left of that car to get a sample of its *own* paint much less any of ours," Russ said.

"You can't be too sure. I'll long-term it at the airport and we'll rent a car. Next, I got to find that Frenchy Short."

It was six before they were checked into a Ramada Inn on 271 south of town, the truck hidden, and Bob set about finding Frenchy Short. First, he called a friend he knew at the Retired Marine Officers' Association in Los Angeles, a retired gunnery sergeant who ran the clerical section of the association, and quickly came up with the number of a former captain named Paul Chardy, whom Bob placed in memory as having worked with Frenchy at SOG. He dialed the number, in some town called Winnetka, Illinois, and got no answer until, after several subsequent tries, he connected around 8:30 P.M.

A woman answered the phone.

"Hello."

"Ma'am, I'm trying to reach Captain Paul Chardy, USMC, retired."

"May I ask what this is in reference to?"

"Yes, ma'am, he and I served together in 1969 in the Central Highlands. I'm trying to locate a third man both of us knew."

"One second, please." He heard her yell, "Paul, Paul, honey. It's some marine thing."

The voice came on.

"Hello?"

"Captain Chardy?"

"Well, no one's called me that in quite a while. I'm a high school basketball coach now."

"Sir, I don't know if you'll remember me. I NCOed up at Base Camp Alice near Cambo and briefed you when you came in country in August '68. I served with you for six months before I DEROSed home. My name is Gunnery Sergeant Bob Lee Swagger and—"

"Bob the Nailer! My God, yes, I remember you. You were the best recon team leader SOG ever had and when you went back for your third tour—well, Gunny, it's an honor to talk to Bob the Nailer. Hell yes, I remember."

"Thank you, sir."

"Thank *you,* Gunny. You had a hell of a war. You showed the rest of us how to do it."

"Sir, reason I'm calling, I'm trying to find another man in country with us. He was civilian, spook type. You were closer to him than I was. You and him ran a number of missions together as I recall."

"Frenchy."

"Yes sir."

"Oh, Christ, I haven't thought about Frenchy in years. Poor old Frenchy." Bob thought he heard something in the man's voice, some odd tone: regret, buried pain, the stirring of memories best left untouched in the darkness.

"Sir?"

"Well, Gunny, the Frenchman didn't make it. His adventures caught up with him."

Bob cursed silently.

"Frenchy was pure spook, that I'll tell you. He crammed several hundred lifetimes into one."

"Yes sir."

"Yes, well, he recruited me. I spent, well, it's not worth going into, a long story, not a very pretty one. After the war, I spent four years on an Agency contract and Frenchy was my case officer. I went back for a hitch TDY in '82. But Frenchy, well—"

He paused. Bob could sense the pain.

"I shouldn't tell you this. It's all off the record, you never talked to me. Frenchy was captured and killed by a Soviet GRU colonel in Vienna in 1974. Tortured to death. Not a pretty story."

"I'm sorry, sir," Bob said, and then had to ask the next question: "What happened to the colonel?"

"Somebody blew him out of his socks," said Chardy in a voice that said he didn't want any more questions asked.

"Can I ask you something?"

"Go ahead, Gunny."

"What was Frenchy Short capable of? Under orders, or not under orders, what would he do?"

Chardy thought a bit.

Finally, he said, "Anything. He was capable of anything. The truth is, even though they had his name on a plaque on the wall at Langley, Frenchy sold me to the Russians in 1974, when I was in Kurdistan. There were unpleasant consequences. He had no conscience. He was a great man who was capable of great evil, not that uncommon a combination. Whatever you think he did, he probably did. And worse."

"Did he ever say anything about a job in Arkansas in the fifties? An Agency scam, something very black involving infrared stuff."

"Gunny, he never talked about the past. And if you'd seen him operate, you wouldn't want to know about the past."

"Yes sir. Thanks very much."

"You okay, Gunny? You need help or anything?"

"No sir. I'm fine. You told me what I needed to know."

"Good luck to you, Sergeant. Semper Fi."

"Semper Fi, sir."

He turned to Russ. "Good man. But goddammit, now where we going to go?"

"What about—to dinner?" Russ said.

"Yeah, yeah," said Bob.

They went to the motel restaurant and sat down. Bob ordered a cheeseburger, Russ the tuna salad. But Bob wouldn't or couldn't talk. Russ had never known a man quite like this: he just locked himself off, still, almost in repose, his face dark and wary, his eyes alert, but a definite No Trespassing sign impressed in the set of lines. He only pretended to eat. Something about Chardy or Frenchy, or that lost war and the men it devoured, was dogging him, Russ guessed.

"Uh, I have an idea," said Russ.

"What?"

"I said, I have an idea."

"Lord spare us," said Bob.

"Frenchy Short is gone; you're not going to get anything out of the Agency, that's a given. So we have to move from what we've got. Our first principle: your father *knew* something. That's what got him killed. Well, my thought is that we should locate whoever is left of the people he spoke to on the last day. Not casually, but his friends. Your mother is gone. Sam, we spoke to Sam, he didn't say anything. But didn't he mention—"

Bob nodded.

"Miss Connie," he said. He remembered her too, from all those years ago: an imposing, beautiful woman, in her fifties, who came from the East and was married to and widowed by Rance Long-acre, the county aristocrat. She had a son: he died young too. She had a kind of doomed quality about her: everybody she ever knew or loved died. He had some memory coming home on leave back sometime in the early sixties, before the war, that someone—his mother possibly?—had told him she'd left and gone back. No, his mother was dead then. Sam. Sam knew her.

"She'd be in her nineties now," Bob said, "that is, if she's alive, if her mind hasn't gone, if we could find her, if she would talk."

"Maybe Sam would know where she went."

"He would have said something. I have the impression—I don't know why—that there may have been something between them but it ended badly. He never talks about her."

"Um," said Russ, digging into his salad.

"Damn, boy, don't you ever eat meat?"

"It isn't good for you."

"Hell, it didn't do me any harm. I'm fifty goddamned years old and I may live another two or three days if I'm lucky."

He smiled finally, and Russ saw that he was joking again.

"But it's a good idea," he continued. "It's a damned good idea. Maybe Sam will know, wouldn't that be nice. We'll call him to-night. Maybe he's found that coroner's brief or whatever it was."

They got back to the room and called, but there was no answer, and Russ tried ten more times.

"I wonder where that old bastard is," Bob said.

"Maybe he's got a new girlfriend," Russ said.

Finally, in the morning, somebody answered at Sam's.

The voice, vaguely familiar, confounded Bob.

"Sam? Uh, I'm trying to reach Sam Vincent."

"Who is this, please?" asked the man.

"Ah, my name is Bob Lee Swagger and—"

"Bob! Bob, it's John Vincent, Sam's eldest son."

John was a physician in Little Rock, Bob knew; and he also knew the tone of voice, that hushed, exhausted tone that communicated in its remoteness the bad news.

"Is something wrong?"

"Bob, Dad died last night."

"Oh, God," said Bob, who really thought Sam would live forever, like some magnificent old black-maned lion howling toothlessly at the moon. He felt the news as a physical pain, a loss of breath and stability. He sat down on the bed.

"What happened?" he finally asked.

"You know, Dad was slipping in and out of gears. Well, last night, he went to his office late on some fool errand or other, something in the way his mind worked. He was wearing my mother's bathrobe and no socks and two different shoes. He slipped and fell at the top of the stairs and broke his neck in two places. At least it was clean, and over in an instant."

"John, I owe my life to your father."

"He was a damned good man but you couldn't tell him anything. I pleaded with him to move in with us; there was plenty of room. He could have gone to any of his children. You know there was money for a nurse, a home, anything, but Dad was set in his ways."

Bob could say nothing.

"They found him at seven this morning. I got a call at seven-thirty and just got here. Lord, I don't know what got into him. He tore his house apart and he tore his office apart. He was looking for something."

Bob realized he was looking for that coroner's document.

"I just saw him a day or two ago. He was big as life and twice as mean."

"You know, he loved your father. He thought your father was the best man that ever lived. And he loved you, Bob. I'm glad you got to spend some time with him before it happened. The funeral will be in a few days, Friday, I think. And after, we'll hold a family wake. We'd really like to see you."

"I'll be there," said Bob.

He sat on the bed. Paint it black. Hello, darkness. Death was no stranger, he'd seen it come in many forms and shipped it out more than any man ever should. But this one hit him particularly hard. He sat and looked at the wall until the wall went away, replaced by a great nothingness.

In time, Russ came in from his room, dressed and ready to go, and asked what was wrong and Bob told him, then retreated back into his emptiness.

Nothing seemed to happen. Bob just sat there, lanky and still and sealed off. Who could tell what was going through his mind? Russ thought of Achilles in his tent, sulking, nursing his anger into a fury so pure nothing could stand before it.

"The funeral?" Russ finally asked.

"No," said Bob. "Not with people hunting us. That's sure where they'd look."

He shook his head. Then he said: "They took my father. *Then* they took his body, his memory. Now they've taken Sam."

"You think—"

"You saw Sam. Whatever he was, he was not infirm. He did not have balance problems. He would not fall down stairs. Someone pushed him. Because again, he found something out. He was looking for that coroner's report or something, he found it, someone was watching him, he had to be stopped. Some hero sent him flying down those steps."

Russ saw where they were: the place called paranoia, deep into the culture of conspiracy, where everything was a part of the plot, evidence of the sinister tendencies of the universe.

"He could have just fallen. He *was* an old man."

"He didn't just fall. Some men fall. Not Sam. You think I'm nuts? You think I'm making all this up? Tell me, sonny: they was hired gunmen with submachine guns trying to fry our asses in Oklahoma, wasn't they?"

"Yes, it's true. But to—"

"Where'd that goddamn deputy who was dogging us go? We

was dogged by that deputy. Then he disappears and the gun boys come onto the scene. So where's the deputy go? We won't go to the funeral but we will go to the wake. You nosy around, you see if anybody saw that deputy. That's your job. But he's just a little man. There's someone behind this thing, you mark my words, watching us, setting all this up. And I will by God find him and face him down and we'll see who walks away."

"Yes sir," said Russ, seeing that no headway could be made against the iron of Bob's rage.

"But the funeral ain't till Friday. Today's Tuesday. Today's the day you find Connie Longacre. You got that?"

Russ nodded. Then he said, "All right. I can do that."

Twenty-nine

"NO SIR," said Duane Peck. "No sir, not at all, sir. I never seen him. I went up there, I got what I could, what I just give you, and I got out. That was it."

Like many policemen, he was adept at lying; he had the liar's best gift: he could absolutely convince himself that what he was saying was the truth, convince his own respiratory system, and come eventually to believe it wholly. He didn't swallow or tremble, he didn't breathe raspily, or touch his mouth, he had no difficulty meeting anyone's eyes, his pupils did not get small and far away, his face color did not change.

"You had nothing to do with the old man's death, then?" said Red Bama. They were in the back room behind Nancy's Flamingo Lounge, where he had summoned Duane when he heard the news.

"No sir, did not. Hell, I wouldn't do nothing to a old man. I got respect for the old. That's what's destroying this country, sir. Lack of respect."

His face was perfectly passive as he spoke. His voice was calm, earnest, under control, his throat unfilled with phlegm. His heart beat dully.

"You can't be killing people when you decide to," said Red. "There's something called the law of unintended consequences. It brings everything down. Besides, he was such an *old* man."

"I swear to you," said Duane, "sir, I *swear* to you I had nothing to do with that."

"All right," said Red, wanting somehow to believe in him, but not quite yet doing so entirely.

"Sir, he had gone crazy. I told you how he tore his stuff apart. Going back to that office in his wife's bathrobe, falling down them stairs. Hell, it was a tragedy. The old gentleman needed looking after. It's a crime his damn family didn't do nothing for him, all he done give them."

Bama nodded.

He examined the exhibits before him—a scrap of a hearing report from 1955, a letter in flowery script from some woman named Lucille Parker, dated 1957, and a yellow tablet faintly inscribed with the impression of writing on a top page now missing—then looked back at Duane.

"Sir, if you hold that tablet up to the light, you can sort of make out what the hell it's all about. I see the word—"

"All right, Peck, that's enough. I want you back in Blue Eye, but doing nothing. You wait for me to contact you. Is that clear? You do not want to be eyeballing Bob Lee Swagger. You stay away from him for now. He may sniff something out on you. I may need you for him later, if I can figure out a way."

"Yes sir. Uh, sir, uh . . . about my gambling debts—"

"Forgotten, Duane. You're no longer working in the red. You're in the black. Don't blow it. The pay's five hundred a week, starters. Full medical benefits. Of course you keep your deputy's job; that's why you're worth anything at all."

"I bet I could git Bob Lee for you."

"Don't even think about it," said Red. "He'll know and he'll come for you. There are ten men fried to crisps on a highway who thought he'd be easy. Now go on, get out of here."

After Peck left, Red went over and filled a Styrofoam cup with the rancid bar coffee. It was an important time: he had to make some decisions.

He had to kill Bob Lee Swagger and kill him quickly. But firepower, the best professional killers, a dream team of hit men, had not worked. He realized now that sheer violence wasn't the answer; stealth was. Cleverness, planning, nerve, execution.

Again, by God, underneath his melancholy and his acid distaste for Duane Peck, he was oddly happy. Swagger. This guy was brilliant. He was the best that Red had ever come against, smart and brave and calm and resourceful. If many guns couldn't do it, what could?

Hmmmmm. Maybe one could. How else to kill a sniper but to snipe him?

In his orderly mind, he tried to list his advantages. First, though Swagger of course knew he was being hunted, he had no idea by whom or why, other than the general suspicion that it had something serious to do with issues of forty years ago which he was currently investigating. That gave Red the opportunity, really, for any kind of approach. And the more he thought, the more he realized that the key to today lay in yesterday. There had to be a way to put something before Swagger, something which beckoned him and which he could not deny, whose call he would answer even if he knew it might kill him. In that way, the cautious and wary man could be destroyed.

Red was in a curious state: he throbbed with creativity. He understood the shape, the values, the thrust of the project he was undertaking, he just did not yet know the details, the connections. Yet, really, the details could come later. It was the excitement of creation that overwhelmed him so.

He set to work. He had to understand *everything* about forty years ago. The past held the answers.

With that in mind, he went back into another room where an ancient wall safe lay. It held the treasures and secrets of his own father's empire. He had a moment here of sentimentality, as his fingers touched the worn old knob of the dial. He knew his father's fingers had touched it thousands of times. He thought of his father: that shrewd and disciplined man, self-taught and vast of insight, part tyrant, part genius, who came from nowhere. Really, that was the thing. The man came from nowhere. He was born dirt-poor and barefoot in a sharecropper's shack in Polk County in 1916, amid appalling conditions of nutritional deprivation, impoverishment, brutality and the general coarseness of life in that station and that time. He had been beaten savagely, which is why he never beat his only son. He had been laughed at and called hillbilly and white trash by the quality, who secretly feared him, as they feared all long-boned, pale-eyed members of the rural proletariat.

Yet he'd come up to Fort Smith in 1930, a fourteen-year-old boy, on his own because he was smart enough to see nothing could happen in Polk County and if there was a future, it lay in the city; he'd gotten a job as a numbers runner for Colonel Tyree, who ran the town then from a grand suite in the old Ward Hotel. It wasn't a big job, a comer's job, just a job running numbers for a criminal organization that would not mourn him for a second if he fell under the wheels of a train or was ground to pulp by the wagon teams that still dominated Garrison Street in those days.

But like the gift he passed onto his son, Red, Ray Bama had a talent for numbers, for lightning calculation, and understood that the secrets of the universe lay within. (None of Red's own children had such a thing, but then, bless them, they didn't *need* one.) He was wary and shrewd, and his rise was the classic American gangster's, which mirrored the Horatio Alger myths of the larger population: that in crime, as in industry, the hardest, most tireless worker and the shrewdest, most able calculator ended up the winner. He went from running numbers to running pawnshops to shylocking to managing casinos and cribs to investing; there were always three or four layers between himself and his violence, though three times assassins attempted to nail him. He trafficked in flesh but did not partake of it; he lent money but never borrowed it; he sold drugs but never took them, nor allowed anybody around him to take them. He understood the dynamic of the separate black and white populations. Though he was, even at some remove, a killer, he never committed other crimes, which some would judge more harshly: he was not a racist and did business with black gangsters, eventually taking over their rackets, not out of fear but out of trust; he was not a psychopath, and only killed when it was necessary; he never killed families or siblings; he never killed indiscriminately; he never tortured or brutalized. He was the last thing a redneck pauper should have been, an honorable gang lord, a gentleman.

But of late Red had been thinking that there was more to his father than his professional triumphs. It wasn't that he succeeded, eventually; it was that he had the imagination to conceive success in the first place and that the most precious gift he gave his only child wasn't a business or an inheritance or a network of connection, though all were nice. No, it was his . . . whole life.

As Red drove the highways in his Mercedes, he'd sometimes see himself, but in overalls, weighted down by hopelessness, toothless and scrawny, destitute of self-belief. He'd think: Except for Dad, that could be me.

His father's single bravest act had been to leave the country and reinvent himself as a city man. On the face of it, quite an accomplishment: no chums, nobody looking out for him, nobody easing the way, a scrawny poor-white-trash hillbilly from the remote Ouachitas, barefoot and unexposed to any kind of culture whatsoever, almost illiterate. Yet in a single generation, he was able to give his son a whole different world: a prep school education, four years at the University of Arkansas, exposure to ideas, possibilities, stimulations. His son never had to wake at four to slop the pigs or wake at five to bring in the wood to light the fire or work in the fields from dark till dark to chop enough cotton or plant enough corn so that the Man would leave a few kernels for the sharecropping family to live on. And his son's children, they were so far removed from that they couldn't even imagine it. To them, it was a bad movie called *The Beverly Hillbillies,* not funny at all, just about crude, backward, stupid trashy people.

I hope I'm up to you, old man, he thought. *I will sure as hell try and be equal to your legacy.*

Red's father died in a bomb blast out front of Nancy's in 1975; Red was working as a vice-president of what was then called Bama Trucking, Inc. His immediate response was not to mourn, but to prepare for the assault on his power, his position and his organization that inevitably followed the assassination of a boss. Yet, strangely, it never came, though some years later and some years after that, interlopers moved against him, both easily defeated.

Thus, the mystery of his father's death became a prime obsession of his. He had spent over $200,000 on private investigation trying to solve the mystery. Why, when Lieutenant Will Jessop, the Fort Smith homicide dick who had been assigned the case, retired in

'88, Red put him on retainer ($50,000 per annum) to keep up the investigation privately. Red himself had used all his underworld contacts through a variety of subterfuges and come up, after all the time, effort and money, with nothing.

The problem with the case was simply that it yielded only one answer to *cui bono*. That is, Red himself. And he didn't do it (though it had probably been said of him, he knew). Lacking a motive to sustain it, no other explanation made any sense. For example, no lieutenant of the organization benefited and no phone tap or private observation had yielded the slightest smattering of a clue; no out-of-towner gained anything from it. It could only be revenge for some long-ago act, but such deeds are usually messy and emotional, and this one had been accomplished with the most amazing efficiency, control and precision, the work of a true pro in the bomb business, suggesting access to higher levels of craft.

That's what Lieutenant Jessop said too.

"Red, this boy knew what he was doing. This was the best goddamned bomb that anyone ever exploded in Arkansas, that I'll tell you. He was a goddamned specialist."

In time all investigations run down, and Red's into his father's death did itself after a hard decade and a half. Red finally gave it up and tried to make peace with the gaping hole in his life, the fact that whoever killed his father, for whatever reasons, had gone unpunished and was laughing even now.

I tried, Daddy, he'd think, when the bourbon got to him late at night and all the kids were down, and Miss Arkansas Runner-up 1986 snoozed contentedly in her $500 peignoir, *I tried so hard.*

With that recalled melancholy heavy on his shoulders, he spun the dial and opened the old vault. The past was broken down by years in ledgers, long lines of figures recording inflow and outflow, all costs noted, all sums accounted for. Every third page or so was covered with notes of explanation. His father wrote in small, perfect hand, dispassionately recording details. In that way, in very short order, Red learned all there was to know—or all his father wanted known and recorded—about the last two weeks in the month of July 1955. He met remarkable people: a Frenchy Short, for one, and a young army first lieutenant at Camp Chaffee named

Jack Preece, but others too, a whole slew of clever, fast operators, men of zeal and commitment. Jimmy Pye was there, as well as boss cons and screws from the Bama organization in the Sebastian County Jail. And of course, Earl Swagger was there, and as he examined what lay before him, Red saw the logic behind what he had taken on faith, and marveled at the professionalism of all involved.

Of course one name was missing. It had to be, for it was not and could not be committed to paper; but Red realized instinctively what the ledger documented: the key moment in Bama family history, when the Bama gang ceased to be a gang and his father ceased to be a gangster, but in which it began its climb toward legitimacy, public power and glory and the bastions of respect and admiration it—he—now commanded.

Red poured himself another cup of coffee. He called the office, checked his voice mail, talked to his secretary. He called the Runner-up and told her he'd be late and she reminded him that his son Nick had a swimming meet that night and he said he'd go directly. He thought he'd get there by Nick's event, the 100-meter backstroke, as that probably wouldn't run until 9:30 and they could stop on the way back for barbecue.

Then he cleared his mind and began to study the documents that Duane Peck had procured. It seemed clear that they related to some other event of 1955, occurring almost in the same time period as the murder of Earl Swagger. What was the connection? No, wait: that wasn't important. What, rather, did Bob Lee Swagger and the boy *think* was the connection, for what they thought would guide how they behaved.

The one document was a preliminary report from the Polk County Prosecutor's Office on a bail hearing for one Reggie Gerard Fuller, Negro, seventeen, of such and such an address, Blue Eye, on a charge of murder in the first degree against one Shirelle Parker, Negro, fifteen, of such and such an address, Blue Eye. Shirelle must have been Lucille's, the letter writer's, daughter. The prosecutor, Sam Vincent—Red winced, thinking of Sam on those steps, an old man whose time was up—Sam was arguing that the crime was so serious that no bail be set and the defense lawyer, one James Alton of the County Public Defender's Office, pled nolo contendere to the prosecution request, so of course the suspect was held in lieu of bail.

So: a murder, presumably of a black child by a young black man, July 1955.

Then he read the letter itself: two years later, the mother of the murdered girl pleads with Sam to reopen the case because she claims that this Reggie could not have done it.

Strange? You'd think a mother would want vengeance, not justice.

Perplexed, Red consulted his Rolodex and came up with the name of assistant city editor of the *Southwest Times Record* and put in the call. He got voice mail, left a message and got a call back in seven minutes.

"Mr. Bama, what can I do for you?"

"Jerry, don't y'all keep all your old papers on file?"

"Yes sir. On computers since 1993, and over in the library before then on microfilm rolls."

"Good scout. Now, can you do me a half an hour's worth of digging?"

"Yes sir. You know I can."

"The kids okay, Jerry?"

"Just fine, sir."

"Where you going on vacation this year?"

"Ah, well, sir, we're thinking about Florida. Daytona Beach."

"Oh, Jerry, you know I own part of the Blue Diamond Resort on Sanibel Island. Very nice place."

"Yes sir. I could never afford Sanibel. Daytona's it for us this year. I've got to pay for braces and—"

"Jerry, you want to take the wife and kids to the Blue Diamond? A mile of beach. Three heated pools. Very nice rooms."

"Well, I—"

"Jerry. Nineteen fifty-five. July. A murder. Polk County. Shirelle Parker. Committed by a Reggie Gerard Fuller. I want to know everything about it and I want to know it fast. Got that?"

"Git right on it, sir."

"Jerry. You know my fax number. And Jerry?"

"Yes sir?"

"Ocean side or pool side?"

"Ah—well. Ocean side. The kids love the ocean."

"The last two weeks in August?"

"Well, that's *fine,* sir."

"You'll get the reservations tomorrow."

He sat back and waited. An hour passed. Then the fax machine began to hum and soon enough it had spewed out four dense hand-printed pages, a chronology of the Shirelle Parker case, running from the discovery of the body, the trial, the appeal and the execution.

He read it carefully, then a second, then a third time. The salient feature was that the body was discovered by Earl Swagger the day he died and the *Times Record* had a brief editorial in 1957 noting with pleasure the execution of Reggie Gerard Fuller and the closure of the heroic state policeman and Arkansas war hero's last case.

But that wasn't the last entry in the summary of the *Times Record*'s coverage. That came five years even later, with the information that a life sentence had been delivered against a white man named Jed Posey for the first-degree homicide of the father of convicted murderer Reggie Fuller, a former undertaker named Davidson Fuller, who had become stridently active in the West Arkansas Civil Rights Movement. It was the first time a white man had been convicted of first-degree murder against a Negro in the state's history, the report said, and the prosecutor, Sam Vincent, was to be congratulated for forging ahead with the prosecution even against death threats and the sure reality that in pressing forward, Vincent was dooming his own reelection, which would cost him a job he'd held for eighteen years.

Red chewed all this over. Obviously, Sam had come to the conclusion that there was some connection between the death of Earl and the death of the girl. Had he told them? Was it their idea? What did they know in the first place?

He didn't know. But something else he did have to know.

Jed Posey. What had happened to him?

It took a phone call to find out that after thirty-five years in prison, the old man named Jed Posey resided still on Cell Block D at the state penitentiary at Tucker.

Now, that was useful. That was *very* useful.

A plan began to form in his mind.

The more he thought, the more excited he got. I *like* it!

Thirty

H E WAS A LITTLE EARLY but it was better to be early. He'd worn better suits too, but when you buy a suit at the Fort Smith Wal-Mart at eleven o'clock to wear to an appointment at one, you can't expect to make the pages of *GQ*.

Can I do this? Russ thought.

Then he thought: Yes, I can do it.

Bob dropped him at 12:55. It was a nondescript building, sheathed with new siding that cut off all windows, promising fluorescent dankness inside. It wore the odd sign DONREY HOUSE over the single grim entrance. Certainly there was no old-newspaper feeling to it, and nothing in it harkened back to glorious old days when cigar-stomping or tobacco-chewing reporters smartassed or exaggerated their way into national reputations while having a hell of a good time.

No, the offices of *Southwest Times Record,* like the offices of most newspapers in America, looked as if they headquartered a smaller insurance company or a medical supply house or a catalog service.

He went into a foyer that was blankly efficient if unprepossessing and told the receptionist that he had an appointment at one o'clock with the city editor and the copy chief. He was asked to wait until a very young black woman came down and gave him a cool professional greeting and escorted him up. It was only one story and the trip took them through the newsroom—lit with bright fluorescents, as he had guessed, messy, filled with troglodytes and mutants sleeping or haphazardly cranking away at VDTs like chimps beating on toy pianos, *any* newsroom—and into the city editor's office. That's when he got his first surprise: she didn't make the introduction because there was no one there to introduce him to. Instead, she herself slid behind the desk.

Ah! What was the name again, oh yes, Longly, Longly, Longly. Claudia Longly.

She was looking at the résumé.

"How long were you at the *Oklahoman,* Mr. Pewtie?"

"A year. I started on the features copy desk and they seemed to like me and I became the assistant Lifestyles editor after six months."

"And you left . . . ?"

"Well, I had a great idea for a book and I didn't think I could do justice to both careers. So I left the *Oklahoman* two months ago to work on it exclusively; I'd saved a little money. The research got me here, and here I've been for three weeks now. But it's going to take longer and I'm running out of money. So I thought if you had copy desk openings, and you were interested, I could sign on. I *am* good on copy. I'm fast, I don't make mistakes, I'm pretty smart and I work hard."

"But it's not a career thing? You don't see yourself committing to a career on the *Record?*"

"Oh, to be honest, my main thing is the book. I don't want to lie to you. But if you offered me a position, I'd take it as a matter of course that I'd stay at least six months."

"You went to Princeton, I see."

"Yes. I was lucky, I got a scholarship. I was a superbrain in high school, but I got tired of the East and I felt I needed a change after two years. I did do an internship on the *Miami Herald.* I've got names and so forth for you to call if you want."

"Can I ask what the book is about?"

"There was an act of violence in Polk County in 1955 that had a direct bearing on a subsequent act of violence in Oklahoma that affected my family. My idea was to research and dramatize both of them and show how they were connected. I'm just having trouble running down people from 1955. It's going to take several months, not several weeks."

"I should tell you, if you were offered a position, it's a Guild paper. I'll give you a copy of the contract. We'd start you at the one year's experience mark. It would be three-fifty a week. You'd be on the morning rim, probably from four to midnight. We expect hard work, professionalism and a good attitude. I don't like a newsroom that talks too much."

"That's fine," he said.

"Well, let's go introduce you to Bruce Sims, our copy chief. We'll give you the test and we'll see how you do."

"That's fine, thanks very much."

Bruce Sims was a folksy older guy, about forty-five, with thinning hair and a newsroom pallor. He jawed with Russ for a bit, showed him around the newsroom, the cafeteria, the wire room, Don's office—Don, the managing editor, would have the final say—and then finally the library.

This is what Russ was waiting for.

"What databases are you into?"

"Nexus, Entertainment Data Service and On-Line Search."

"Cool. What about the phones? Just as I was leaving the *Oklahoman* they'd bought into a CD-ROM national service."

"Oh, yeah. We started that up, too. Phone Disc Power Finder."

"Yeah, I think that's what we had. Very useful."

By this time, they'd reached a little room off the corridor.

"You're ready?"

"Yes, I am."

"Okay, it's two-ten. I'll be back at three-ten."

"Swell," Russ said.

Bruce left the room and Russ started the test at 2:11. He finished it at 2:26. Of the 100 general information questions, he knew he had gotten 97 right, and only had to guess on the year of the Little Big Horn (he guessed 1873, and it was 1876), the percentage of the vote Upton Sinclair received for governor of the state of California in 1936 (45, right) and whether Willa Cather or Edith Wharton had written *My Ántonia,* and since he'd seen a movie based on a Wharton novel and knew that she was a New York kind of girl, he guessed Cather, right again. Then there was a badly written news story to straighten out which, once he got the lead into English, fell into place in a second. The last page was for a short personal essay on "Why I want to work for the *Record*" (ho-hum).

Then, glancing at his watch, he rose, took off his coat, loosened his tie and discreetly stepped out into the corridor. Nobody that he'd been introduced to was in sight. Trying to look as if he belonged, he went to a coffee urn in the newsroom and got himself half a cup in Styrofoam. He picked up a ballpoint and a notepad from an untended desk. He didn't look ahead but he knew his newsroom culture: everybody read everything, nobody paid any attention to anything.

He turned into the library, taking a quick peek to see that no one he'd been introduced to was here either. All clear. He went up to a desk that said "Information Service."

"Hi, I'm Russ, I'm new in Metro," he said, hoping they called it Metro, but what else could they call it? It was *always* called Metro.

"Oh, uh, hi," said a middle-aged woman, looking up over half-lensed reading glasses.

"I'm looking for some numbers. Could you run the CD-ROMs for me, please?"

She turned and opened a desk, where a stack of CDs in their little clear plastic containers were.

"Which section of the country?" she asked.

Key question. Bob had searched his memory that morning and came up with the idea that Miss Connie was from Baltimore, or Maryland anyway. He didn't know why he thought that; it was just an impression from some clue stored irretrievably in his head. But would she retire to Baltimore? Would she return after her twenty-five tragic years in Arkansas? Or maybe she did return and died there in the eighties. Maybe she did return until she got very old and then moved to Florida. Or Mexico. Or California. Or Arizona. Or—

"Northeast region. Maryland."

She selected a disc and they walked over to a large computer terminal on the adjacent desk. She loaded the disc into the tray, which with a hum absorbed it into the machine, which buzzed, clicked, flashed to life ("Phone Disc Power Finder, from Digital Directory Assistance, Inc.") and yielded a menu.

"Do you know how?" she asked.

"Sure."

"Call me when you're done."

He sat down and snapped through the commands until he got an entry prompt.

He typed "Constance Longacre."

The machine hummed and flashed and diddled, and in seconds, across its blue screen, in white, there traveled a list of endless C. Longacres, Constance Longacres, Conny Longacres, Connie Longacres; fifty-nine of them, spread between Maine and Virginia.

He scanned the list. Anyone could be her or none of them could be her. What could he do now, write down the fifty-nine numbers and call them, one at a time?

Well . . . what about something else?

He restarted, this time narrowing the field to Maryland. Only thirteen Longacres resided in Maryland. That was something. He could write those down. He did, in fact, in the notebook. Now he could call those thirteen and . . .

But he knew another capability of the CD-ROM; it could be entered via phone number or by street address or by institutional identity. Returning to the menu, he called up a prompt by institution. He typed "Nursing home" and narrowed the field to Maryland.

Clickety-click, whickety-whack. The screen flashed. Suddenly, it was alive with names and addresses, eighty-seven of them according to the helpful listing up top.

He examined the thirteen Longacres and found between them only five different exchanges. He wrote them down and cross-referenced to the eighty-seven listed addresses and numbers and came up with eleven matches. He compared each of the thirteen numbers with each of the eleven matches.

There was only one match.

"C. Longacre, 401-555-0954" and "Downy Marsh, St. Michaels, Md., 401-555-0954."

Russ took a deep breath.

He looked about. Nobody was noticing him.

There was a phone. He picked it up, dialed 9 to get an outside line, then dialed the digits.

The phone was answered.

"Downy Marsh."

"Yes, this is Robert Jones, I'm an attorney in Fort Smith, Arkansas. I'm trying to reach a Miss Connie Longacre."

"Mrs. Longacre is sleeping."

"Well, please don't disturb her. She's been named in a will out here, or rather *a* Connie Longacre, who lived in Polk County, Arkansas, between 1931 and 1956, has. I've been trying to track her down. Has your Mrs. Longacre ever mentioned living in Arkansas?"

"That's confidential information, I'm afraid."

"Well, I think she'd be upset if she didn't attend the reading. The sum of money involved is considerable."

"Mrs. Longacre is not a needy woman, Mr. Jones."

"I see. Well, with the money, there's news. News of the people she knew and loved for twenty-five years, and that she left cold for reasons that nobody has ever understood out here."

There was a long pause on the phone.

"She never talks about Arkansas. I only know she was there because her photo album is full of pictures of the country, and once I asked her. 'Oh,' she said, 'another lifetime. Far, far away. Arkansas, believe it or not.' And then I knew it upset her because that night she was crying."

"Thank you very much for the information."

"You won't hurt her?"

"No, ma'am. Not at all."

"She's been through so much. She's ninety-five now, and very frail."

"Yes, ma'am."

"And, of course, she's blind. Has been for ten years."

Giddy with joy at his triumph, Russ downloaded the machine and returned the disc to the librarian, and with a light step, hurried out the door. He ran smack into his new friend Bruce Sims, who looked at him in surprise.

Russ felt stupidity drain into his face but then said, in a frenzy of fake desperation, "Bathroom?"

"Not in the *library*! Down the hall."

"Thanks. The test is on the table. I'm all done. Sorry, but when you gotta go—"

And he took off running down the hall.

"—you gotta go," called out Bruce, laughing.

Russ went and hid in a stall for ten minutes, then made a big deal out of washing his hands. He emerged to find Bruce waiting.

"Sorry, I shouldn't have left the room. But I never went back—"

"That's okay, don't worry about it. I picked up the test."

"So when do you think I'll hear?"

"Well, can you give us a week or so? We'll look it over and see how it fits into our needs. Do you have a phone?"

"No, I'm sort of mobile now. Let me call you. A week?"

"Yes, that's fine."

They stopped to pick up Russ's coat and then were sauntering through the newsroom when Russ noted that nearly everyone had left their desks and gathered around a television set suspended from the ceiling near the wire room.

"Oh, God," said Bruce.

"Willie just called. I think this is it, Bruce," said someone rushing by. "If it is, meeting at three instead of four."

"What's going on?" Russ said.

"Come on, watch this, you'll find it amusing."

Russ followed Sims over to the mob of reporters and editors, mesmerized by an empty podium, a microphone and the dreary look of a banquet hall in a chain motel near the interstate. A label on the screen identified the setting: Etheridge Campaign Headquarters, Los Angeles, California.

"Go, C-Span!" somebody cheered.

Soon enough, surrounded by aides and accompanied by a handsome but remote woman, a thin man with silver hair and a professionally distinguished face approached the podium. He looked about sixty-five and wore one of those almost uniform-perfect blue suits, a red tie and a white shirt. There wasn't anything out of place; there wasn't anything interesting either.

The party reached the podium. There was shuffling, chatter, awkwardness.

"Two years and *still* not organized," said someone.

"What a hopeless wanker," someone with a British accent editorialized.

"Who the hell is it?" Russ whispered to Sims, even as the man's features were beginning to vibrate with recognizability, like a character actor who always plays the best friend.

"Holly Etheridge," Sims responded. "You know, former Senator Hollis Etheridge. He chose not to seek reelection two years ago and has spent the past twenty-four months running the most inept presidential campaign since Ed Muskie."

"Yeah, yeah, I remember," said Russ. "He's the one who built the road for his dad?"

"The Etheridge Porkway. Who says there's no free lunch in America? If you knew Harry and then Holly, you got very rich."

"My friends," said Hollis Etheridge, reading stiffly from a prepared statement, "and members of the press who have chosen to honor me with your attention. For years and years, my father had a dream. He dreamed that his only son would become President of the United States. It wasn't too much to ask for. After all, he had come out of the backwoods of Arkansas and become United States representative for thirty years. As far as he saw it, in this great land of ours, anything was possible and no dream was too large."

Russ thought he'd seen the guy on talk shows over the years. He was always a fill-in, a somewhat orthodox man in whose mouth English seemed a foreign language.

"One thing about old Holly," whispered Bruce salaciously, "he got more pussy than a toilet seat."

"I shared that dream," Hollis droned onward. "I worked ceaselessly to make it a reality. I gave up my position in the august body known as the United States Senate to make it come true. I raised money and went to banquets and gave speeches.

"But as my fourth-place finish in last week's California primary has made clear, that dream will not come true."

There were some audible groans from the audience, whom Russ gathered were campaign workers and true believers. Though what in Holly Etheridge was there to believe in truly, other than the practical craft of the professional politician?

"That, coupled with a third in New York, a third in Massachusetts and a fourth in New Hampshire, has made it clear that the party will seek another for standard-bearer and that my continued presence distracts from the message of the two from between whom you will choose the candidate."

He paused amid the groans.

"There goes *my* Pulitzer Prize," somebody said, to laughter.

"You were never going to win a Pulitzer Prize," someone else said. "You don't work for the *Washington Post,* the *New York Times* or the *Miami Herald.*"

"True enough," said the first. "I should have said, there goes my *fantasy* of a Pulitzer Prize."

His colleagues hooted. Someone threw a wadded-up ball of paper at him. Russ smiled. Journalists. Cynics, smart-asses, calculating everything as a career move first and history second.

"Shit," said Sims to Russ. "Little Rock had its time in the sun. We thought Fort Smith'd get a goose out of old Holly. But no way: too square, too slow, too orthodox."

"He could put No Doz to sleep," somebody else said, "unless he was chasing stewardesses."

"I heard his specialty was nurses," somebody else said. "He liked the uniform thing and the white stockings."

"Look at his wife," somebody else added. "I think she has a Dove bar up her ass."

The woman stood just behind the man with one of those painted-on smiles lighting up a face that was pure stone.

"Dotty, God," somebody said. "She makes Pat Nixon look like Mary Tyler Moore. She makes Pat look . . . *perky.*"

"A Dove Bar is the *only* thing she's ever had up her ass."

"And so," said Hollis Etheridge, "I hearby announce my withdrawal from the presidential campaign. I want to thank my wife,

Dorothy, Paul Osteen, my campaign manager, and all you loyal workers. You people worked like heck and I do appreciate it; now it's back to private life for this son of Arkansas. Thank you very much."

"Senator," a question came, "what will you do with your delegates? And your war chest? You still lead in money raised."

"That's to be determined at a later time in consultation with key members of my team," said Etheridge.

"He could still carry some weight," somebody said.

"He's over, he's finished," came a counterverdict. "Color him the *Jeopardy!* answer without a question."

"God bless America, and God bless the state of Arkansas," Etheridge said, then turned and walked stiffly away.

"We won't have Holly Etheridge to kick around anymore," some wag said.

"Hell, there wasn't enough of him to kick around in the first place," someone else added.

Thirty-one

IT HAD BEEN A GOOD DAY for the general. At eleven, he had finally closed a contract with Colonel Sanchez of the Honduran Army. Colonel Sanchez was *el comandante* of Battalion 316, the counterterror and -insurgency specialists, American-trained. Though the Hondurans had plenty of money to spend, the general could see no justification for pushing the No. 1 System, as it was called. The SR-25 with the Magnavox thermal sniperscope and the JFP MAW-7 suppressor was the most sophisticated system in the world but it was labor-intensive maintenance-wise and he doubted a third-world nation without a sophisticated technical culture would be able to maintain the units through heavy usage. And heavy usage was expected: the current guerrilla war showed no signs of abating and indeed was moving into the cities, where Battalion 316 and Military Intelligence rightly understood that a long-range precision night-vision sniping capability would prove invaluable.

After much hassling and wrangling, the general had finally convinced Colonel Sanchez that a system built around rebuilt army AN/PVS-2 Starlights mounted on state-of-the-art McMillan M-86s with the JFP Technology M14SS-1 suppressors was exactly what the doctor ordered. Twenty of the units would be in .308 Winchester, ten in .300 Winchester Magnum and ten in .223 Remington, giving Battalion 316 a great deal of tactical flexibility.

Of course JFP sniper cadre would field-train designated

marksmen in the usage of the weapons system and serve, for an interim time, as consultants and advisers vis-à-vis their deployment in the combat environment. The general had a talent pool of several ex-SWAT and Green Beret snipers who performed such tasks, and were damn well paid too, both in money and in the odd extra kill they could pick up.

The general and the colonel then went to lunch, demolishing mighty amounts of rare roast beef at one of Oklahoma City's finest establishments, and the general dropped the colonel off at his hotel, to prepare for the flight home. The general himself went to his club, where he played three quick games of squash with his lawyer and one of his board members. He took an hour in the steam room, showered and got back to the office at four. He expected to spend another two hours on paperwork and to begin work on a presentation set in a month's time for the German GSG-9 antiterrorist group; if he could snatch *them* from the jaws of Heckler & Koch and its blasted, overrated PSG1, it would be a wonderful feather in his cap!

He sat at his desk, and Judy, his secretary, came in with his messages.

"Anything important?"

"No sir. Your wife. She's waiting for her payment."

"Dammit, I *sent* that check," he said.

"Two calls from Jeff Harris at the FBI."

"Yes, yes. They may go night-vision. Wouldn't *that* be something?"

"A Mr. Greenaway, the procurement officer for the Cleveland Municipal Police."

"Oh, I'll get right on that one."

"Long-distance, Mr. Arrabenz from Salvador."

"That old pirate. Okay, I'll get back to him. In fact, you may as well start trying to put the call through now. It'll take hours."

"Yes sir. And Mr. Short."

The general thought he misunderstood.

"I'm sorry?"

"Mr. Short. He said it was about Arkansas. He said he'd call back. Frenchy Short, the name was."

The general nodded, smiled, thanked her.

She left the room.

The general sat there, finding his breath hard to locate in his chest.

It was coming back. Swagger, now this.

Goddammit.

He waited and waited. His technicians left at five, as usual, and Judy went home at six, but the general stayed in his office. Twice after Judy left, the phone rang; one was a wrong number and another a hang-up.

You bastard, he thought, nursing a glass of Scotch neat. You bastard.

Finally, at 8:27 the phone rang.

He snatched it up.

"Hello."

"Jack! Jack Preece, you old son of a gun, how the hell are you? It's your old pal Frenchy Short."

The voice was southern and arrived in a laughing tone of fake heartiness.

"Who are you?" Preece demanded. "You're not Frenchy Short. Frenchy Short is dead. He died in Vienna in 1974. I saw the Agency report."

"Details, details," came the voice. "How are you doing these days, Jack? That divorce still takes a pretty penny, I'll bet. Your daughter likes Penn, does she? Business is booming, isn't it? Battalion 316? *Excellent,* Jack. That's quite a healthy little shop you're running."

"Who are you?"

"I'm Frenchy Short."

"Goddammit, *who are you?*"

The man on the other end let him sweat for a few moments.

"Jack, you're right. Frenchy's dead. You might say I'm his heir apparent."

"What the hell is this all about?"

"Jack, Frenchy Short was the best thing that ever happened to you. You've lived a charmed life ever since you met him. You got the commands you wanted. You moved up through the ranks. You had clout, power, prestige. You ran that sniper school, the premier sniper command in the Western world. You've seen your night doctrines accepted by the army. You've got a chestful of ribbons and medals. You've become a wealthy man. Jack, you owe Frenchy Short a great deal."

"Stop bullshitting me. Get to the goddamned point."

"Here's the point, Jack. In 1955 you did Frenchy a big favor. You hit a shot for us that no one else in the world could have hit. It bought us all kinds of things. And it bought you all kinds of things. Now, forty-odd years later, that case has been opened again. Somebody's come hunting us. You have to take another shot. You have to put him in the ground. Night shot. Long-range. Your specialty."

"No," said Jack. "That is the one thing I regret doing. That man was a law enforcement officer who did no one any harm. He was a hero. That is the only shame I feel. I don't care what the consequences are."

"Jack, I forgot how brave you are. You won the Bronze Star, didn't you? All right, Jack, go noble on your old pal Frenchy Short. You say you'll face the consequences? You'll give it all up, your good name, your firm, your family? You'll endure the scandal? That's not what it'll cost you. No, no, if he comes for me, I'll make certain no matter how it works out, he gets your name, Jack, then he'll come for you. He's the best. There ain't no better."

"Swagger?"

"And how, ten feet tall and really pissed off. Still the best. Still is. Dusted ten pros the other day, maybe you read about it?"

Preece had, dammit.

"Jack, I'll give you to Swagger and he'll take you apart. Or I'll set him up for you. One shot, one kill."

The general was quiet. He looked around at his marksmanship trophies, his paneled office, his medals on the wall. If Swagger came for him it was over.

"Then I'm out?"

"For keeps. You go back to your life, I go back to mine."

"How?"

"Tomorrow you move out with your gear. You go to a farm way out on a dirt road on County 70, off of 71, just north of Blue Eye, Arkansas. It's way, way out, near a little place called Posey Hollow. Your contact will be a boy named Duane Peck. He'll get you settled in. Meanwhile, I'm working to set Swagger up in the woods. He's got to be drawn in slowly, carefully. It can't be rushed, but I'm thinking a few days, maybe a week. When it happens you'll have to move fast and quiet. I'll get you your shot. You better not miss, General Jack, or he will bury you good and deep."

"I never miss," said the general.

Thirty-two

BEYOND THE BRIDGE the land changed. It grew flat and plain and gave way, after a time, to perspectives over water, choked with reeds, huge vistas of almost colorless marshlands, broken here and there by clumps of trees. The water sparkled in the sun.

"There isn't this much water in the whole state of Oklahoma," said Russ.

They were on the Eastern Shore of Maryland, heading toward St. Michaels, which, a map suggested, was a small town situated on a promontory that jabbed out into the Chesapeake. It seemed like land only marginally reclaimed from the sea: the water winked at them from behind the trees or off beyond farm fields; or it lurked, black and still, in deep pools that lapped around the edges of dark trees that seemed to stretch off for infinity; or, finally, it was in the rivers and streams that lashed this way and that, like saber cuts.

"Wet," was all Bob could think to say.

"Maybe she won't see us," said Russ.

"Oh, I think she will."

"Do we tell her about Sam? It might upset her."

"Tell her the truth on all things. She was a damned smart lady, as I remember. Back in the days when nobody thought a woman was smart, they all said, Miss Connie is *smart*. That says a hell of a lot about her. I do believe all the men were half in love with her, my own father and Sam Vincent included."

"She's ninety-five," said Russ.

"I'll bet she's still as sharp as a bee's ass. You'll see."

They passed through St. Michaels, a town so quaint it looked as if it belonged in an antique store window, and then, off Route 33 still farther toward the Chesapeake, they saw a discreet sign, expensive and muted, that said DOWNY MARSH and pointed the way, without explanation.

Russ turned down the drive, came to a gate under overhanging elms. A guard stopped them.

"Visitors," Russ said, "to see Miss Longacre. Mrs. Longacre."

The guard, uniformed and black, nodded and let them pass.

It had to have once been the estate of a robber baron or steel or railroad tycoon. An asphalt road curled across land which grew tenuous as they progressed through the high, fluttering reeds, and then at last yielded to a crescent of garden and lawn scalloped out of the marsh, dominated by a brick mansion. The building was gigantic, monstrous, capped with a mansard roof, green copper in the sun, and festooned with balconies themselves intricate with wrought ironwork on many levels and multipaned windows: unbearable ugliness that spoke of the violence and inevitability of capital. Russ thought it was a relic from a nineteenth century full of black smoke and grinding engines, an arrogant eyesore that faced five miles of serene marshlands and beyond the shifty sheetglass calm of the bay. It had the look of a place where rich people came to die.

Russ pulled into a parking space marked VISITORS, noting that his was the only visiting car. Out on the grounds he could see ancient people hunched in wheelchairs, being guided about by black nurses or aides, whatever.

It was two in the afternoon. The sun was bright, the sky Windex blue. A vee of geese flew far overhead; an egret stood on one leg off to the side of the house, by a little pool.

"Let me do the talking," said Bob. "I think she'll remember me."

They walked in, both in suits, and felt their shoes crack on the linoleum in the hushed silence. There was no sense of the medicinal in here, but more the devotional; it felt to Russ like a religious space.

They came to a counter, where two well-dressed women suspiciously watched them approach.

"Hello," said Bob. "I'm wondering if it's possible to see one of your patients—"

"Residents," he was frostily corrected.

"—residents—named Mrs. Connie Longacre. I'm the son of an old friend."

"What is your name, sir?"

"Swagger. Bob Lee Swagger. Tell her I'm the son of Earl Swagger. She'll remember."

They sat and waited for the longest time, and finally a woman came.

"She is frail. But she's alert, coherent and tough. I can give you no more than half an hour. Try not to excite her."

"Yes, ma'am," said Bob.

She led them through double doors, back through vast rooms that were largely empty, and out on a veranda that faced the bay but from such elevation that one could see the lacework of islands and marsh and miles of blue water. The far shore was not visible, though in the distance green islands poked out of the waves.

The old lady sat facing the view in a wheelchair. She was swaddled in blankets. She wore dark sunglasses and most of the flesh had fallen from her face, revealing taut, powdery skin well fissured with wrinkles. But two bright dabs of rouge brightened her gaunt cheekbones and her hair, snow white, sat on her head like a pillbox hat.

"Miss Connie?" said Bob.

"Lord, I'd know that voice anywhere," she said brightly, turning. "I haven't heard it in forty long years but I hear it every night before I go to bed. He was a wonderful man, your father. Do you know that, Bob Lee? Most men are not wonderful, it has been my experience to learn, but your father truly was."

"Yes, ma'am. I wish I remembered him better."

"Did you ever marry, Bob Lee? And have children?"

"Yes, ma'am, finally. I met a fine woman, a nurse on an Indian reservation in Arizona. I look after horses now. We have a daughter named Nicole, Nicki. She's four. We love her a great deal."

"I'm happy. Earl deserved a grandchild. I wish he could have known."

"Yes, ma'am," said Bob. "Ma'am, I'm here with an associate, a young writer. His name is Russ Pewtie."

"It's a pleasure to meet you, Mrs. Longacre," said Russ.

"Here, take my hand, young man. I want to steal some warmth from you."

Russ put his hand out and she seized it fiercely, her fingers cold but still tight with strength.

"There. Now, Russ, you describe for me what is before me, please. I insist. I want to borrow your eyes. I'm told it is beautiful, but I have no way of knowing."

Russ bumbled through a description of the scene, feeling less than articulate.

But she was kind.

"You speak well," she said.

"He's a writer," Bob said.

"What is he writing? Is he writing your life story, Bob Lee? That would be an exciting book."

"No, ma'am. He is writing a book about my father and how he died."

"A terrible tragedy," said Miss Connie. "A terrible day. Worse than any day in the war. Worse in some ways than the day my son and his wife died. My son was a drunk. If you drink and drive in fast little cars, you must face certain consequences. So be it. But your father was doing a job important to the community and setting a moral example. He deserved so much better than a guttersnipe like Jimmy Pye."

"Yes, ma'am," said Bob. "We came to talk about that. About what happened that day. What was said, the timing of it, what you remember. Is that all right, Miss Connie?"

"May I ask why?"

"I just want to know how my father died," Bob said.

"Any son's right. Go ahead. Ask away."

"You saw him?"

"Yes, I did. He arrived at the cottage at about two. He made an awful deputy who was hanging around go away. Most men did what Earl told them; he had that way. But Earl was upset. He didn't show it, because your father was a man in control. He didn't say much, he did a lot. He was a still man, a watcher. When he spoke he had such a deep and raspy voice, just like yours. But he was bothered by Jimmy. He could not understand it. He *believed* in Jimmy."

"Why was that, do you suppose?" Russ asked.

"I look at the two of them, Jimmy Pye and Earl Swagger, and I see the two Americas. Earl was the old America, the America that won the war. When I say 'the war,' young man, of course I mean World War II."

"Yes, ma'am."

"With young people today, you can never be sure what they know. Anyway, Earl was sturdy, patient, hardworking, stubborn, very courageous. Jimmy was the new America. He knew nothing. But he was handsome, slick, clever, cute, and evil. He only cared for himself. His theory of the world put him at the center of it, that was all. He never cared even for Edie White except to have her and say to the world, no one else can have this beautiful thing. She was a lovely, lovely girl. Earl would not allow himself to face the truth about Jimmy. That was his flaw, his hubris. That's why it's tragedy, not melodrama."

"Did my father—what was he working on those last few days? Was there an investigation, a project? I have to know what he was thinking."

"I was only with him for a half an hour that last day, maybe less. Then I left and he and Edie were alone. I never saw him again; by the time I got back, she was sleeping. But . . . I do remember this. He had found a body that day, earlier."

"The young black girl," said Russ. "Yes, we've heard of that."

"Shirelle Parker, her name was. She was murdered. Your father was very troubled by the event. I could see him turning it over. I remember exactly what it was. He said he thought there were signs of 'monkey business.' What those were, he never elaborated."

"But from what I understand, there was no monkey business,"

Bob said. "A black youth was arrested the next day or two. Sam prosecuted. It was open-and-shut. The boy was executed two years later. That was all there was to it."

"Yes," said Miss Connie. "All there was to it."

"So my father was wrong," said Bob.

She turned and set her face outward, as if she were looking across the bay.

Then she turned back to face them.

"Your father was right. Reggie Gerard Fuller didn't kill her. I found that out many years later."

"Who did?"

"I don't know. But I do know what happened and why it happened. The night that girl disappeared there was a meeting at the church."

Russ remembered a note inside the notebook that Earl Swagger had left behind. "Meeting—who there?"

"In those days, the South was being prepared for the civil rights movement, which no matter what you might think, did not spring out of nowhere. For a decade, very brave young black ministers and young white volunteers traveled from church to church, where they tried to prepare the people for the dangerous work ahead. The night that Shirelle disappeared, there had been such a meeting at the church. Shirelle was at the meeting. So was Reggie. After the meeting, he drove people home in his father's hearse, people all over Polk, Scott and Montgomery counties. *That's* why he never had an alibi. He didn't drive Shirelle home because she only lived two blocks away."

"I don't—"

"The white man was a Jewish radical from New York. His name was Saul Fine. I believe he was a communist. He was later killed in Mississippi. He was taken out and shot by some young white men who called him a nigger lover. That night, he gave an impassioned speech to some of the younger people that the reverend believed in. Then they went home and Saul moved on. But when Shirelle was found, and Reggie was accused, he must have decided that if he told about the meeting, there'd be consequences.

It would get out that a revolution was being planned, that a communist northern agitator was down South stirring up the colored. White people would get upset, there'd be violence against the church, the whole thing would come apart. The Klan would ride again. White people were very frightened in those days, I recall."

She looked out and took off her glasses. Her eyes were still blue though now sightless and opaque. A tear ran down them.

"Your father was a brave, brave man, Bob Lee Swagger. He won the Medal of Honor and he never spoke of it to a soul. But he wasn't the bravest man I ever heard of. The bravest man I ever heard of was a nineteen-year-old Negro boy who sat still in the electric chair while they strapped him in, and then they killed him and he never made a peep. Because he believed in something. He didn't get any medals or glory. He never went to meet the President. He understood there were consequences to everything, and he faced them squarely and followed them where they led him. That's what Saul Fine had told them: People will have to die. The Struggle will cost in blood. Nobody will remember those who die. It is the simple, brutal process of progress."

She paused. "Nobody ever knew, except the people at that meeting and they couldn't tell. His mother didn't know, his father didn't know and not even many of the blacks in Blue Eye knew. Sam never knew. Sam prosecuted him and believed he was doing God's work. I believed justice was served. When I found out—this was in 1978, when I met George Tredwell, he was the black minister who traveled with Saul Fine in those days—I almost called Sam. But then I thought: What's the point? It would kill Sam to find out he'd made such a tragic mistake. So that was the only gift I ever gave Sam, as much as I loved him."

"It can't hurt him now. Sam died night before last."

"I thought I heard death in your voice."

"He fell down some stairs. He was eighty-six. Spry and tough."

"He was another good man. I have missed him so over the years. Was he on a case?"

"Yes, ma'am. Never really retired."

"Arkansas: it produced some terrible men. It produced Jimmy

Pye and Boss Harry Etheridge and his idiotic son, Hollis, who wanted to be President. Holly, isn't that what they call him? I believe it's a mistake to give a man a girl's name, always. He certainly paid his share of girls back too, I'm told. But Arkansas also produced Earl Swagger and Sam Vincent."

"Yes, ma'am."

"Have I helped?"

"Yes, ma'am, I think you have. We'll be moving along now."

"Now I have a question for you."

"Yes, Miss Connie."

"I'm not sure I have the courage to ask it."

"No one ever said Miss Connie didn't have no courage. You got us through Daddy's funeral."

"All right, then. The child. What became of the child?"

"I'm sorry I don't—" started Bob.

"She means Edie's boy. Edie and Jimmy's son."

"Yes. Lord, I wanted to save that child. I tried to adopt him after Edie died. Sam argued the case for me. I cared for that child for three months. He was so strong, so alert, so bright. But no court in Arkansas in the fifties would let a northern widow take over a newborn child from an Arkansas mother if there was family around. I named him Stephen, after my own son. They made me give him to Jimmy's people. It broke my heart. I never found out what happened to him."

Her question was met with their silence.

"Oh," she said finally. "He did not turn out well."

"The Pyes didn't care about him," said Russ, "and they beat him and the more they beat him, the worse he got. Eventually, he went into the reform school system. By age twelve he was an incorrigible. They finally sent him off to live with Jimmy's older brother in Oklahoma. He became . . ."

Russ paused.

"Go ahead, young man. I've buried enough good men so that I can take anything by now."

"He became a violent felon. He killed many people and traumatized many, many more. He did time in the state penitentiary, where he became even more violent. A career criminal, the worst kind of bad news. Lamar Pye, that was his name. A policeman killed him in 1994."

"Nothing good came from that day, did it?" said Miss Connie. "I hope there's never another like it. An evil day."

Thirty-three

THE HOUSES were all the same but Duane knew the address and he remembered what it looked like and didn't have any trouble. He pulled into the driveway. The street was a dream of America, an America he'd never, ever be a part of.

Niggers.

Niggers lived here and he lived in some trailer out beyond the interstate?

But he told himself to cool off, to dial it way down. He had to be smooth. That's what Mr. Bama had said: You got to be smooth, Peck. You're not going in there to kick ass and show them what a stud you are. You got to crawl and snivel. He quoted somebody called Neechee: That which does not kill you makes you strong, Peck.

So he took a deep breath, climbed out of the cruiser, tucked his hair up behind his Stetson, then walked up to the house. He took some pleasure in the fact that someone was nervously watching him from a window. They *still* get scared when the Man comes calling.

He knocked on the door.

He waited. Seemed to be scraping and jostling inside.

Finally, the door opened and a young black woman peered out at him. Her face was tight and she was scared. Peck liked that a lot.

"Y-yes?" she said.

He smiled. "Ma'am?" he said as charmingly as he knew how, "ma'am, I'm Deputy Duane Peck of the County Sheriff's Department. I'm here to talk to a Mrs. Lucille Parker."

"That's Mama. What is this in reference to, please?"

"Ma'am, I'm investigating the death of Sam Vincent, the former county prosecutor. He died night before last. That day, he came out here and talked to Mrs. Parker. I happened to see him out here. I'm just checking up to make sure everything's on the up-and-up. I know she's an elderly lady, ma'am, and I don't mean her no bother. Just got a few questions is all. Be over and out of here in a jiff."

"Just a minute," the woman said stonily, shutting the door.

The anger rose in Duane, like smoke. A nigger gal treating him like that! He has to stand in the hot sun! But he quelled it, telling himself to be cool, for this here goddamned thing was going to lead to a bigger job working for Mr. Bama permanent, and no one would treat him like white trash ever again. Neechee said so!

The minutes passed and eventually the door opened.

"Mama will see you. She's upset over the death of Mr. Sam. You go easy with her, you hear? She's eighty-two years old."

Duane walked into the house, astonished to find it so nice and whitelike. He'd always thought these people lived like pigs in a sty.

The woman—the daughter, he knew—led him through a living room to a back porch, where the old lady sat like a queen of the village, in regal splendor and glory.

"Ma'am, I'm Deputy Peck. Hope I'm not bothering you none, but we have to make inquiries. I'll try and be out of here fast."

She nodded.

"Ah, you know that poor Sam Vincent fell down the stairs of his office night before last and died?"

She nodded.

"Poor Sam," Duane said. "Anyhow it looks like a straight accidental death, but I have to ask a question or so."

"Go ahead, Deputy."

"Ma'am, did he seem agitated about anything? Was he in control of hisself? What was he talking about?"

"My daughter was killed in this town forty-odd years ago," said the proud old lady. "He prosecuted the boy they said did it. I had written him a letter about the crime some years back. He came by to talk about it, that's all."

"I see. But he was okay? I mean, he weren't in no *state,* what you might call it. So excited-like, he might fall or something. Balance problems. Did he have balance problems?"

"He was a good man. It seems like good people die around these parts and the bad ones just go on and on."

"Yes, ma'am, it do seem that way sometime. But he was physically all right, wasn't he? Is that what you're telling me."

"I don't think Mr. Sam would fall down no stairs, no sir," said the woman. "He was strong as a bull and very sharp and clear. I didn't see any evidence of balance problems."

"Yes, ma'am."

"His death is a terrible thing. He was a good man."

"I agree, ma'am. Old Sam: he was like a daddy to me."

"He was the only man in this state with the gumption to prosecute a white man for the murder of a black man. That took courage."

"Yes, ma'am," said Duane, trying to bite down his delight. The woman had brought him right to where he wanted to be.

"I looked it up," he said. "Jed Posey, convicted and sentenced to life in prison for the murder of Davidson Fuller, back in 1965. Beat him to death with a shovel."

The old lady shook her head. She was tracking the tangled coils back to the murder of her daughter Shirelle. Shirelle was killed, the law said, by Reggie Fuller, who was sentenced to death. Davidson Fuller, his father, lost *everything* trying to free his son but was somehow made strong by the ordeal and emerged in the early sixties as the most energetic and fearless of the civil rights leaders in Arkansas. He had stopped for gas out near Nunley and a terrible white man came out of a gas station and hit him three times with a spade, just for nothing, just for being black, then went back on the porch to drink a Cherry Smash until the police arrived. Mr. Sam couldn't get the death penalty but he got Jed Posey to spend the rest of his life in prison.

As if they both reached that destination simultaneously, their eyes met. And Duane gave her the news he'd been sent to deliver.

"D'ja hear they finally paroled that old boy Jed Posey?"

She looked at him in horror.

"Yep, he gets out today. They say he's going back to his brother Lum's cabin somewhere in the damn mountains. A shame a boy like that can't die in the pen, where he belongs."

He smiled.

"Well, thanks so much, ma'am. You cleared it all up for me."

Jack Preece opened the gun vault and stepped inside. It was a large vault, extremely expensive, with space in it for two hundred rifles. But there were only thirty or so, all ready for shipment, various of his products destined for the world's hot spots.

He tried to think it out.

Night shot. Infrared or passive ambient light? Range, two hundred yards or less. What to take? Match the weapon to the mission.

State-of-the-art, of course, was the Knight SR-25 with the Magnavox thermal sniperscope mounted and zeroed and a JFP suppressor, the No. 1 System. It was at this moment in time the best sniper rifle in the world. But the businessman in him looked at the one unit locked in the rack, the demonstrator. It represented an investment of about $18,000, for the rifle, the very expensive thermal scope, the suppressor and the complex array of armorer's skills to unify all the elements into the single system. There was always the possibility of a breakage or even a battlefield loss. Could he absorb that much of a financial bite? Worse, the gun was not wiped clean; it still bore Knight's serial numbers and the Magnavox unit bore the Magnavox numbers, both traceable to him. If by some twist of fate, he got out but the gun didn't and it was recovered by authorities, it led them straight to him, literally in a matter of hours. Of course he had his powerful allies in the intelligence and military communities, and the helpful mantra of national security could always be invoked, but that was much less powerful nowadays. You couldn't be sure it would work at all: newspapers had no commitment to a higher thing called national security, they hardly believed in the concept of the nation, much less security! His friends could only protect him so far; in the realpolitik of Washington, he could find himself served up fried and covered in gravy for somebody's Pulitzer Prize. So the Stoner was out.

He looked next at the rack of lesser semiautos. These were mostly recovered M-14s or Springfield M-1As, all in 7.62 NATO, reconfigured as the standard army M-21 sniper rifle of Vietnam, accurized and mounted with an ambient night scope, usually the AN/PVS-2 Starlight scope, and the JFP suppressor. Fine weapons, with a hundred custom tricks to make them shoot straighter and more reliably than off-the-rack 14s. But they had something in common with the Knight weapon: they were traceable to him, although there might be some salvation there, as the guns were older, had a much longer history and had come through many sources and via many avenues. That meant that the paper trail could be very complex, with dead ends and red herrings strewn throughout it, depending on the actual weapon. Would it be complex enough to protect him if the weapon was lost and then recovered? There was no way of knowing and he wasn't sanguine about living the next ten years of his life waiting for some government computer to kick out the serial number connection to him. Nix to the 21s.

Next were the bolt guns. These too came from a variety of sources, many of them civilian. All were basically the same rifle, the Remington 700, though they had been worked over by secondary contractors, in some case the Remington Custom Shop, some cases Robar, or McMillan or ProFiber, or individual custom gunworks, like Tank's Rifle Shop or D&L Firearms or Fulton Armory. Some had the night-vision device, one or two had lasers, one or two had simple Leupold police marksman scopes or Unertl 10x's, the marine choice. Again, the possibility of tracing these guns was present, though possibly not paramount, if he consulted the records and chose carefully. But another difficulty presented itself to this system: that was tactical.

Preece knew he'd be hitting two targets, Swagger first and then that kid. The bolt gun was a highly accurate system, as Swagger himself had proven in Vietnam and hundreds of SWAT and Delta or FBI HRU engagements had since proven; it was the quintessential exemplar of the professional's code: One Shot, One Kill. But it was not the system of choice for engaging multiple targets. There was that damned bolt throw after the shot, an inch up, three inches back, three inches forward, an inch down. Peter Paul Mauser had cooked it up back in 1892; it was a hundred years old. A good, trained rifleman could do it under a second and there was a time when Preece was as fast as anyone in the world. This was not that time. He didn't want to be throwing a bolt then looking for target number two; the whole thing fell apart if one of the targets made it out.

So he wanted a very clean gun, untraceable, he wanted a semiauto capacity, he wanted accuracy.

There was only one choice, really.

It was outmoded weapons technology, to be sure, but it had the great attraction of stepping out of the long tradition of black operations. He owned it more as a curiosity than as an item for sale. Who would buy something so antiquated? The Agency had evidently used it in Nam as part of SOG's Operation PHOENIX, the infrastructure eradication program that targeted high-profile V.C. suspects for assassination by special killer teams. Then it had gone God knew where, done God knew what for a number of years: if weapons could talk, then this one had the experience of a best-selling book in its sleek contours. Certainly, it had seen much action in South and Central America, perhaps even in Africa and Europe as well.

Preece had bought it sub rosa from one of his own sniper cadre, a man with much experience. One look into that man's lightless, hunter's eyes and at that flat dead face told the general that further inquiries were pointless. The man was facing his third divorce, needed to raise cash; he sold it to the general for $4,000, no questions asked, no papers given, nothing recorded. It was the weapon that never was, unless it was firing at you.

The piece was an M-16, firing the little 5.56mm round, but at its muzzle it boasted an old long, thin Sionics suppressor, the HEL-H4A model, and, by special mount, it wore the last operational American military infrared weapon sight, the AN/PAS-4. This was no ambient night sight, and still less a Magnavox thermal sniperscope, but it was miles better than the old carbine sniperscopes. For one thing, its battery pack had been miniaturized. Specs described it as "a battery-operated sight and aiming device consisting of an infrared light source, an infrared sensitive image forming telescope (4.5×) with integral miniaturized high-voltage power supply and a light source power supply (a belt-mounted 6 VDC rechargeable nickel cadmium battery)." The telescope assembly was thirteen inches long; the telescope and light source were approximately fourteen inches long; the entire sight assembly weighed about twelve pounds. It looked like a scope with a searchlight mounted atop it, awkward and crude but surprisingly easy to manipulate.

It had but one disadvantage: that light source. That is, it was active infrared, as opposed to the Magnavox's passive mode: it had to project a beam of infrared light from the light source to the target area for the sensitized telescope to pick up. In a technologically sophisticated combat environment such a system was inherently dangerous because for sure the enemy would have an infrared spotting scope through which his light beam would be a vivid indication of his locale, and countersniper measures would be undertaken with massive firepower. Thus it was better in the undeveloped portions of the world, Central America, Africa, West Arkansas.

He picked the weapon up, ran a quick battery check. Everything was fine. He snapped the charger back and released it, felt the weapon cock with a satisfying clack. The trigger pull was a dry, light snap, like a glass rod breaking. He set the weapon down and went at last to the ammo locker within the vault and selected six boxes of Ball M-193 5.56mm, confident that the night belonged to him.

Thirty-four

THE FUNERAL was in the late morning but they couldn't make it, because the Baltimore-Dallas flight and the hop via American Eagle to Fort Smith didn't get them back until about noon. But there was a wake to be held at Sam's old house at four, and, driving hard down the parkway, they knew they'd make it by at least four-thirty.

Russ drove; Bob was even more sealed off than usual. The sniper's stillness: part of the legend. His bitterness, his repressed anger, his sense of isolation—all a part of the same package. But behind those calm, dark eyes, Russ knew there was something going on.

"So what are you thinking?" Russ finally asked.

"That we just wasted a good solid day and that I'm out thirteen hundred bucks in tickets."

"I'll pay you—"

"It ain't that, I don't want your money. It was just waste. We are heading in a wrong direction."

"No sir," said Russ. "I honestly believe that there *has* to be a connection between the death of that child and the death of your father."

"You bonehead," said Bob cruelly, not even looking at him. "That's impossible. My father was killed the same day that girl was found. There's *no way* they could have set what they set up that fast. It was a four- or five-day operation, Frenchy working at his goddamned craziest. And second: there was *no way* anybody could have predicted that my daddy would find that body that day or any day. That was pure goddamn luck or whatever. Her mama came to him, and he went a-looking. Suppose he hadn't have found that body? He'd still be dead by 11:00 P.M. That body could have laid for weeks yet before someone came across it, and by that time it could have been so decomposed that it would take still more weeks before they got around to identifying it. No, what happened to that girl is a crime, and if poor Reggie Fuller died on its account, that is a pity and a sorrow, but it don't mean shit to us."

Russ still believed that there was some connection.

"It had to. What else could possibly have been going on in Polk County in 1955 that would have been worth setting up that elaborate conspiracy? Frenchy Short wouldn't just do something for—"

"That is right as rain," said Bob. "So here's what I think. I think my father was on some kind of investigative team or something the state police were running. Maybe it had to do with what was going on at Camp Chaffee. And somehow he found something out. And had to be stopped."

"That sounds like a crummy movie," said Russ.

"I know it does, and I don't even go to movies," said Bob grumpily.

"Well, maybe—"

"Slow down," said Bob, "and don't turn around fast."

A moment or two ticked by.

Bob slid his .45 out of the inside-the-belt holster which Russ hadn't even seen him put on.

"What the hell—"

"Easy, easy," said Bob.

Russ became aware of a van, blue, riding in the dead man's slot just where his mirrors couldn't track it.

The van suddenly accelerated and began to pull even.

"Don't look" said Bob, "and if I say go, you hit the brake *hard,* you understand?"

Russ swallowed, tasting pennies. They were back.

But the van kept passing them and Russ could no longer obey; his head sneaked sideways, where he saw, in the backseat, a very pretty little girl who stared intently at him. She stuck out her tongue.

"Shit," said Russ. "You had me scared."

"Maybe I am losing it," said Bob, sliding the pistol back behind his jacket. "I didn't see that boy pull up; he was in the slot. I got to be paying more goddamned attention."

"So what do we do next?" asked Russ.

"You're the Princeton boy. You tell me."

"Well," said Russ, and then he realized . . . he didn't know either.

The complexity that had been Sam Vincent was on full display in the odd mob that congregated at his house to mourn his passing, or possibly to celebrate it, or at least to get drunk at his expense. African Americans from the west side of the tracks, aristocrats from Little Rock, cronies from the thousands of hunting trips he'd taken, old boys who'd guided him, farmers who'd traded with him, politicians, police officers, children, bitter secretaries, opposing lawyers, corrections officers, even a few men that Sam had sent away. Each had a Sam story to tell, but the one that was making the rounds when Bob and Russ finally arrived and found parking—the street was thronged with cars, everything from Mercedes to forty-year-old pickups—had to do with the ultimate disposition of Sam's estate, itself quite large from a lifetime of extremely shrewd investing and trading. He'd been wisely sidestepping the estate tax by dispensing his wealth in $10,000-per-year chunks for a number of years to his children and even to his sons-in-law and daughters-in-law, divorced or not, second marriage or not, no questions asked, on the principle that anyone who'd had to put up with him in the family deserved a nice little present. He'd also already established trust funds for each grandchild worth $200,000 but only payable to educational institutions in the form of checks for tuition, food or housing. He left each of his fired or resigned secretaries $10,000 except for the one who'd become a drunk: she got $15,000. That left an untidy sum in the estate of $19,450.

"God, Dad," said Dr. John Vincent, Scotch on his breath (the bar was well stocked) and amazement in his voice, "he left $9,725

to the NRA's ILA fund and $9,725 to Handgun Control, Inc. I can
see him cackling when he thought that one up!"

"He was a good man," said Bob, who seemed in the crowd of
revelers the only one who was morose and still grieving.

"Oh, he was a mean old bastard," said the doctor, the eldest son,
the one who'd borne the brunt of his father's rages and praises.
"Smart as a whip, mean as a rooster. He whaled the tar out of us
when we were growing up. But by God each of us turned out. Two
doctors, a lawyer, a travel agent, an investment counselor and an
impressionist painter."

"Who's the painter?" Bob asked.

"Jamie."

"I thought he was a lawyer."

"He was, for ten years. Then he finally screwed up his courage
and did what *he* wanted, not Dad. I think Dad respected him for
it."

"He was a stubborn bastard," Bob said.

"Jesus. And tough. You know in twenty-two years at home, I
only saw him cry once. He didn't even cry when Mom died. He
only cried when your father was killed. I remember he sat downstairs all by himself when he got back. Must have been well toward
dawn. He sat down there and had a drink. I was awakened by a
sound I'd never heard. I snuck downstairs. He was sitting in that
old rocker there"—John pointed through the crowd to a threadbare old chair that had stood in the same spot for fifty years—"and
rocked back and forth and sobbed like a baby. He loved your
father. He thought Earl Swagger was the most perfect man ever
put on earth: hero, father, police officer, incorruptible symbol of
everything that was right and strong about America."

"I keep telling people: my father was only a man."

"Well, my dad didn't think so. Bob, I have to ask: what's going
on? I keep hearing things."

"About old crazy Bob Lee digging up some Confederate?"

"Yes. That. And suddenly you're here and there's a terrible
gunfight over in Oklahoma and ten men are killed. Never happened before you came back. Nothing connects you to it, but people still remember you went hunting a few years back, and two

boys came out of the woods in body bags. Old Dad saved your butt in a federal court."

"Nobody went into a body bag around me that didn't deserve to. It's just some old business. About my father."

"Did it involve mine?"

"I asked him to do some legal work for me. That's all."

"That's it?"

"My young friend over there. He come to me because he wanted to write a book about my daddy. No one remembers Earl Swagger, except maybe your father and old Miss Connie. He's dead, she will be soon. It seemed to me to be worthwhile. Better'n writing a book about me."

"Okay. You should know, people are asking. You walk alone, but you cast a long shadow, my friend. Now come with me, I have something for you."

They walked through the crowd, which in effect was a walk through the fragments of Bob's past. He saw Sara Vincent, Sam's eldest daughter, who had married twice and divorced twice; she was now the town's travel agent, prosperous and lonely. She alone of the Vincent kids did not have Sam's magnetism, though she'd once conceived an awful crush on Bob, and even now threw an awkward, hot-eyed glance at him. But she alone made eye contact; for the others, he knew, he was an embarrassment.

I killed men. I am the sniper. I am apart.

It was the crushing sense of exile that the killer feels, which sometimes makes him more of a killer. Everyone knew from the publicity three years back: Bob Lee Swagger, not just a drunken marine vet alone on his mountain, but a sniper, an executioner, a man-hunter, the man who reached out and touched eighty-seven somebodies. In Arizona, nobody really cared because that's who he was from the start, but here it had the effect of a scandal. They connected him with a past and wondered: Why him? What sets *him* apart? What does the sniper know that other men don't? What's it like to send a piece of lead and copper through somebody's head and blow his brains out? The pink mist effect: turn a man to colored rain. What's it feel like?

There was a girl once named Barb Sempler: he'd been on a date with her in high school but she thought he was too wild, a country boy. Wasn't her father a lawyer or something? Now she was oddly inflated, having picked up the forty pounds, her once beautiful features spread across the wide face. A boy over there, now fat and bald and well dressed, had once blocked him blindside on a football field and laughed about it until Bob had jumped him and the coach had pulled him off. He'd grown up to sell insurance, Bob to kill men. Strange. That woman. He thought her name was Cindy—ah, what, Tilford, that was it—and he'd gotten backseat tit off her one night in 1961. So long ago. Tit seemed like paradise. She was now slim and hard, where she'd been fat and dumpy. A divorcée, therapy, lots of aerobics. She smiled, scaring him. He yearned for his wife. He yearned to feel whole and connected again: father, family man, lay-up barn owner. Julie, YKN4, horses: he missed them, but also what they represented, which was the normal way, not the sniper's way. But they parted, to let him pass, to let him stand alone.

I am the sniper. I stand alone.

They reached the stairs, again the crowd parted magically, and they went down into the basement where Sam had had his office. John walked to the closet, opened it, took something off the shelf.

"I had to clean out Dad's office," he said. "Here, I think this stuff belongs to you. It was locked in the safe."

He held out a cardboard box: in it were his father's old notebook, with its brown blasphemy of blood, that old tablet of half-issued tickets.

"And this too," said John, holding out a sheet of yellow legal paper. "Dad had inscribed some notes. He seemed to be working on a case. Maybe it'll help you."

Russ was talking to an extremely pretty girl who seemed to know all about him, or at least to be very interested in him. It was slowly dawning on him that in this odd world he was a minor celebrity: the sidekick of the famous, mysterious, dangerous and—yes—sexy Bob Lee Swagger. He felt a little like Mick Jagger's gofer.

"So Princeton," the girl was saying, "why'd you drop out?"

"Oh, my mother and my father separated. I knew it would be

hard on my mother, so I didn't want to be twelve hundred miles away. I spent the last year in Oklahoma City, working on the *Daily Oklahoman*. That, plus the fact I didn't really like the East. I spent my life trying to get out of Oklahoma because I was too *good* for Oklahoma. Then I got to the *Ivy League* and the people seemed to be so, you know, *little*. They were fundamentally bigots. They viewed the world through such a perverted prism. Everyone outside was a redneck Nazi, anyone who owned a gun or was in the NRA or voted Republican was subhuman at worst and an amusing ignoramus at best. I just couldn't stand it. They didn't know *anything*. I somehow ended up working for a year on the *Oklahoman*, where I discovered that I fit in . . . *nowhere."*

"Oh, go on. I'm sure you'll find a fit. You're very bright."

"I *was* very bright. In Oklahoma, I was *so* smart. Then I got to New Jersey and I was just another toad on a rock."

She smiled.

"Aren't you some sort of writer?"

"The *unpublished* sort. Very glamorous."

"Are you going to write a book about Bob the Nailer?"

"No. Bob has secrets so deep ten years of therapy followed by ten years of torture couldn't get them all out. He's spent his life trying to live up to his father's ideal. And, unlike the rest of us, I'd say he made it. He wouldn't say he had, but I would. Anyhow, the book is reputedly about the dad. Earl Swagger was an extremely heroic man, killed in a shoot-out with white-trash scum, after winning the Medal of Honor on Iwo Jima. I had the idea of doing a long narrative on his last day, how it summoned up a whole slew of American pathologies. But all I've done is run around and get coffee."

"It sounds interesting. I like the idea of a symbolic episode: you learn so much about the macrocosm by evoking the microcosm."

"Wow," he said. "You must be an English major."

"I'm a junior at Vanderbilt."

"That's a good school."

"Thank you. I'm writing my senior thesis on Raymond Carrr-*rrr*," Russ not quite catching the last name.

Raymond? Writer? Begins with *C*, has *r*'s? Russ panicked. Had she said *Carver?* He'd never read any Carver. But maybe she'd said *Chandler.* That was much better. He hadn't read any Chandler either, but at least he could bluff his way through.

"The L.A. private-eye guy? Lots of neon, that sort of stuff."

"Yes, but so much more," she said, and Russ sighed with relief. "He could really tell a story. Maybe it's a southern thing, but I love it when you can just sink into a book's language. Will your book be like that?"

"Yes," said Russ, thinking *I hope.*

"How far are you?"

"Well, we're really still researching. Listen, I'm sort of mixed up. Who are you?"

"Oh," she laughed. "One of the grandchildren. You knew Grandpappy?"

Now he got it.

"At the end, I went with Bob to see him. He was a crusty old boy, I'll say that. He told me a thing or two."

"Crusty as they come. The original male tyrant king. But somehow, a necessary man," she said. "And sweet. Underneath. He was getting vague, though."

"We noticed. But there was something heroic in the way he fought it. He was an Arkansas Lear," Russ said, really pleased with the Lear remark, though he'd never gotten around to reading it either.

"Such a man. A tyrant, a ruler, but somehow, oh, I don't know, *necessary.* They don't make them like that anymore, do they?"

"No, they make 'em like *me,*" he said—she laughed—"and I agree it's a kind of a comedown."

"Oh, Russ, you'll do fine."

"You're . . . whose daughter?"

"My father is John, Grandpap's oldest son. He's a doctor in Little Rock, an internist. I'm Jeannie."

"The New York one? I heard someone call you 'the New York one.' "

"Oh, that. I interned last summer in New York at *Mademoiselle.*"

"Oh," said Russ. Shit, she was ahead of him!

"I just got coffee for assholes in too much makeup who'd done too many drugs and now did too much aerobics. Not helpful."

"It all helps. Or so they tell me."

"Have you picked up on the big scandal yet?"

"No, what's that?"

"All the blacks are scandalized. I just learned this from my friend Tenille. She's over there with her mother."

"I don't—"

"My grandfather won the Silver Star at the Battle of the Bulge but the bravest thing he ever did was prosecute a white man for the murder of a black man. His name was Jed Posey."

The name rang some kind of bell with Russ, but he couldn't quite nail it down.

"In 1962 he beat a civil rights leader to death with a spade in a gas station."

"Oh, yes," Russ said. "One thing about this, I'm becoming quite an expert on the Faulknerian substrata of Polk County, Arkansas."

"Faulkner would have won *two* Nobel Prizes if he'd been born here, that is if he didn't drink himself to death beforehand. Anyhow, Grandpappy prosecuted him and though he couldn't get the death penalty, Jed Posey went away for life."

"Yes?" said Russ.

"It cost Grandpappy the election and he was out of office for twelve years, after eighteen years in office. Finally, in 1974, he won again, and had eight more years. By that time, he'd turned into an anti-gun-control liberal, if you can imagine such a thing."

"Just barely," said Russ.

"Anyhow, they just paroled him. Jed Posey. Two days after Grandpappy died, they paroled him."

"Jesus," said Russ. "That's disrespectful."

"No," she said. "That's Arkansas."

But suddenly Russ wasn't there. It all fell away, the wake, the noise, the crowd, even impossibly bright and pretty Jeannie Vincent in front of him.

He saw that name somewhere in infantile print, but couldn't quite pin it down. Jed Posey.

It was part of a list.

Lem Tolliver.

Lum Posey.

Pop Dwyer.

Where?

"Russ? Are you going to faint?"

"Ah no, I just—"

He remembered suddenly. Jed Posey. His name was on the inside of Bob's father's last notepad. He was in the party that found Shirelle Parker. He and Miss Connie were the only two people still alive who'd spent time with Earl Swagger on his last day on earth, July 23, 1955.

"Do you know where this Jed Posey would be?"

"I don't—what's going on?"

"We have to find him. We *have* to!" he said, and thought he'd explain it to her, when Bob grabbed him suddenly and pulled him away from the young woman, with a look on his face like the war was just about to start and it was time to load the damned guns.

Thirty-five

SOMETIMES he even impressed himself!
    Red Bama sat back for just a moment and reflected upon the wondrous thing that he had brought off and how quickly he had snatched an apparent victory from the jaws of defeat.

He felt now like crowing loudly from the roof of Nancy's. The secret war he had been fighting was about to pay off.

His lawyer reported: the parole of Jed Posey happened with alarming alacrity. Posey himself was well prepared, initially by a screw whom Red controlled and then by a private detective in Red's employ: he had been told that he would be paroled and that in order to stay out of stir, he had certain obligations to the man (unspecified) who had arranged all this. He would be located in his old cabin, a mile or so off old County 70 at the foot of Iron Fork Mountain in the densest hardwood forest in Arkansas. By this time, Jed was an experienced professional convict, with over thirty years in stir: surviving and finally flourishing, he had become an adept liar, a shrewd manipulator, a vivid reader of human weakness, a tough, scrawny, tattooed old jail rat, capable of witnessing the most extraordinary violence without a wince. Other people's sorrow meant nothing to him at all; empathy had been milled out of him by the prison and, in fact, his favorite of all memories was the recollection of that blissful day in 1962 when he had stove in that nigger's head with a spade, then sat down and had a last Cherry Smash before cops arrived.

So it turned out freedom meant little to him; a chance to strike at the goddamned skunk-ass Swaggers was enough to get him happily through his old age.

His role was easily within his grasp. He was told that sometime in the next week or so, Bob Lee Swagger would come to him in the forest. Don't ask how or why, he just will; trust us. Your role, Jed, is twofold. First, simply step on a rigged floorboard that will send a radio signal. The second, keep him there until after dark or at least until twilight. You have no other responsibilities. In the daylight, Bob Lee is a formidable man. In the night, he is just another target.

Jed knew he could do this. Cackling evilly through his toothless gums, he thought he had a trick or two up his sleeve that would keep them boys busy for a time.

The sniper was the second part of Red's plan. Now located on a farm just on the other side of 70 in the charge of Duane Peck, Jack Preece had spent the past few days in night-fire exercises and Duane reported that at ranges out to two hundred yards he was extremely deadly. He regularly patrolled, both by day and by night, the terrain on which the engagement was slated; terrain familiarity, after all, was the sniper's best ally. When he was alerted that Swagger had arrived at Jed Posey's, he would move swiftly over the familiar ground to intercept. The access in and out of the draw in which the ratty old Posey cabin sat was through a narrow enfilade where a creek cut between two hills. Under combat discipline, of course, Swagger would never take such an obvious path; but he wouldn't be thinking in such terms, but merely be obsessed by the mystery he was trying to unravel. Plus, it would be dark, and going up or around the hills would be dangerous and time-consuming.

Preece set up his hide about 150 yards out, oblique to the left, with a good clear field of shooting, an arc of more than forty degrees. The M-16 didn't have much recoil. They'd come along into the cone of infrared light, bright as day, and he'd drill the man first, the boy second, one 55-grain ball round to each chest, velocity a little under 3,000 feet per second, delivering about 800 foot-pounds of energy. The man would be dead before the boy knew a shot had been fired; the boy would be dead before the man had begun to fall.

As this was explained to Red, he thought of it as an incoming simo in sporting clays, two birds coming right at you. You panic the first or second time, but you learn quickly enough to simply pull through the last bird to the first, shooting as the barrel covers up the bird. It's a shot that's quite easy to master but demands aggressiveness and confidence more than talent.

It was beautiful. It turned on Bob's predictability. He would learn that Jed Posey was free, for Red had seen to it that the black woman herself was told. He would think on it. He would investigate, and satisfy himself that it was not a trap. He would sniff, paw, hesitate, think, but in the end, because he believed, he would go forward. He had to. It was his nature to push on, heroic to the end, destroyed by his very heroism.

Only this last bothered Red a bit: the man, like his father, was a true hero, bold, smart, violent and aggressive. Such men were harder and harder to find; possibly Bob was the last one left in America, outside a few Army Rangers or Green Berets. Red respected heroism but he was not sentimental about it. If it came at him, it must be destroyed and what was accomplished must be preserved. It was that simple.

The phone rang.

"Bama."

"Mr. Bama?"

It was a Bama lieutenant who was officially on the books as a security consultant to Redline Trucking, but actually served as Red's troubleshooter in all aspects of communications that his enterprises demanded.

"Yeah, go ahead, Will."

"Sir, you know we broke down the calls from the motel out to the army archives and that JFP Technology place for you?"

"Yes, I do, Will. That was fine work."

"Well, sir, I got to thinking that if this boy is smart as we think he is, he wouldn't use a traceable phone for a private call."

"Uh-huh," said Red.

"He'd use a pay phone. So I dropped by that hotel yesterday and I took down the numbers of all the pay phones in the lobby."

"Yes," said Red, wondering where this was going.

"Then I designed a software program for the phone company mainframe—you know, I can still get into their system."

"Yes."

"And it turned out on one of them phones, there was a collect call to Ajo, Arizona."

"Hmmmm," said Red.

"So anyway, I backchecked the number to find the address. You said he was from Arizona. Well, sir, that's our boy's home. He's got a wife and a daughter there. You know, sir, I know how important this is to you. But you could now use that to strike at him. The wife, the little girl."

Red nodded. *"Excellent,"* he said. "You are one smart boy, Will. I am grateful and you will be rewarded."

"Thank you, sir. You want me to alert the boys?"

"I'll do that," said Red. "Don't you worry."

He hung up.

It was appealing: he could strike at the family. Now he really had him.

But it was a no-brainer.

He thought of his own little squirmers and the warm and safe place he'd made for them. No, we don't do families. It isn't about families. We leave the families out of it. The families aren't on the board.

He wasn't an idealist but—he just didn't do families. It was his only rule.

Thirty-six

BOB WAS STILL GRIM and freaky with paranoia. He radiated hostility and sat, hunched and tense, always silent, communicating in grunts. He didn't want to return to the trailer or get a set of motel rooms or anything to make them easy to find. They sat in the flicker of a Coleman lamp deep in the Ouachitas, the silence even more forbidding than usual.

"What's eating you?" Russ finally said. "You're pissed. I can tell. Something's going on."

Bob, typically, said nothing. He looked like Achilles again, and Russ thought how the severe planes of his face would fit so appropriately under the bronze of a fierce Greek helmet, scarred from much action outside the walls of Troy.

"You learned something," Russ said again.

Bob breathed out a wisp of vapor, like liquid anger, possibly enough to allow him to live another moment or two before the demons inside chewed him to pieces. He had an ulcer of anger like a gigantic leach sucking fluid from his soul.

"I ran into a neighbor lady," he finally said. "I couldn't get rid of her. And then she said, 'I wonder where that wonderful deputy is? I'm surprised he isn't here.' Seems our boy Duane Peck done been hanging out in Sam's neighborhood. She saw his car parked there two, three days running and later saw Sam driving 'cross town, Duane right behind. We gonna have us a chat with Duane real soon."

"You ought to reconsider that," said Russ.

"What for?" Bob demanded, flashing a Bronze Age glare at Russ.

"If you call him out and kill him, you're a murderer. What does that prove?"

"It proves that Duane Peck is dead."

"But it doesn't get the man or men who killed your father, for whom we both believe Duane works. You have to wait until Duane moves against you. Then you do him and it's righteous; nobody cares, you go home to YKN4 and Julie. Put your anger aside until it's time."

Bob stared out into the darkness. His eyes narrowed into something pale and bitter and Russ knew he was looking at the pure soul of a killer. It was the first time he'd ever recognized how much anger smoldered in Bob and what terrible things the man was capable of.

But Bob got himself under some kind of control.

"We'll deal with Peck when the goddamn time comes," he finally said.

"Good, because I have something to work on."

"What's that?"

Russ told him about Jed Posey's parole.

Bob wanted to know what she'd said. Where had the information come from? Was it tainted? Was it a trap?

Well, no, it seemed to arise spontaneously. Someone in the black community had found out about it. They weren't even *talking* about it to white people, but one of Jeannie's friends, a black student at Vanderbilt, had heard about it from her mother.

"How would the blacks find out?" Bob wanted to know.

"You know, they talk among themselves. A black prison guard tells his wife that goddamned Jed Posey has been paroled; his wife tells her sister tells her friend tells her husband tells his brother; it goes like a telegram; and down here they probably hear faster than anyone. It's how an oppressed community would survive; it would develop extremely refined communications and intelligence skills."

"But who *originally* found out? That's what I want to know. Where does it start?"

"I don't know. It's lost, I guess."

"It can't be lost," Bob said irritably.

"Do you want to go house-to-house knocking on doors in Blue Eye?" Russ said in exasperation. "Look, it's simple. This guy is one of two people left alive who saw your father on his last day. Maybe his testimony is important. They searched for Shirelle Parker. They were together for, near as we can figure it out, close to three hours. That's a long time. Maybe he can remember."

Bob just didn't like it.

"Why now? Why release him now?"

"He's been in prison since 1962. That's over thirty years. It was time. Do you want to go down to Tucker tomorrow and make inquiries as to why? Do you want me to call the paper"—the paper! Russ thought. What about that job?—"and see what their cop guy says? *Or* do you want to check it out tomorrow, go straight to Jed and find out what he has to say?"

It was like arguing with a stubborn old man. Bob never agreed or disagreed, he simply affected a blank look that stood for a strategic retreat while he reconsidered his options. Nothing ever budged him except himself and he only believed in things he could see or touch.

"We don't even know where he is," he said.

"I found Connie," said Russ. "I *will* find Jed."

"Fine," said Bob. "Get some sleep now."

Bob himself didn't get to sleep. Instead, he lay in the hissing light of the Coleman lantern, trying to settle down, put his furies in the far place and nail them to the floor. He was now looking through the materials that John Vincent had handed over: the old book of tickets, the blood-smeared notebook, now yellow and brittle with age, and, fresh, the yellow legal paper with Sam's notes on it.

He looked the notes over carefully. On the first run-through, it seemed clear that Sam was reinvestigating his father's last case. Why would that be important? Bob asked himself. What had started him? What could that have to do with anything? It puzzled him; he simply could not imagine a mechanism by which the two could be connected, since the time element was all wrong. The body of Shirelle was found on the day that Earl was murdered; there couldn't have been time to set something up based on Earl's discovery.

But on faith, he progressed. Sam seemed to be noting ways in which Earl's notes diverged from the later, official version of the crime.

Sam had written: "Body moved. What significance?" Then, underneath, in bolder pen strokes, "To disaffiliate body with site of crime!!"

Bob took this in. Sure. What would the point of that be?

He read on: "Fingernail: red dirt under fingernail!"

Would that be Shirelle's fingernail? And if so, what would the significance of *that* be?

But Sam himself had solved it. "LITTLE GEORGIA," he'd written in all caps. Then adding: "Must be authentic murder site."

Bob himself knew that Little Georgia was a red clay deposit a few miles west of town, a notorious place where teenagers went to neck, just over the town line and in the county. So what? *He'd* been there, even.

Then: "Mrs. Parker says: it would be a black boy. No black girl in 1955 would get into a car with a white boy." Then he'd written: "Damn!"

Bob saw why. Had Shirelle gone off with a white boy, some kind of conspiracy theory might actually work, particularly (though he couldn't imagine how yet) if it was leveraged into the plot against his father. But if she'd gone off with a black boy, nothing made any sense. For, of course, if the murder of Shirelle Parker was another elaborate conspiracy, who in the black community could possibly benefit, and who would have the resources to put together the elaborate plot by which Reggie Gerard Fuller took the fall?

That was the cruncher: Shirelle would not get in a car with a white person in 1955. Bob knew why too. Black girls wouldn't get in cars with white boys five years later. They probably *still* wouldn't because the white boy only wanted one thing.

He rolled over, still confused, and lay there trying to get to sleep.

❑ ❑ ❑ ❑

Bob drove around the town square six times. Russ had never seen him so tense; his eyes would not stop working the landscape, the terrain, the buildings, the mirrors; his muscles were tense and his neck so stiff and rigid Russ thought he'd break it off.

"You okay?"

"Fine, goddammit," said Bob, breathing harshly.

"There's no one here," said Russ. "It's small-town America, ten in the morning."

Bob didn't even listen or stop working security. Finally, he said, "Okay, you git in there and do your goddamned business and git out. No fucking around, no messing with the pretty women, nothing but work. You don't go to the bathroom, you eyeball anybody comes in. You pick an escape route."

"I hear you," said Russ.

"You don't ask for no help. You don't let anybody see what you're doing. You don't leave nothing behind. You find what you got to find and you fall back, watching your back the whole way."

"Man," said Russ, "you got it bad."

"I'll watch from out here," Bob said.

"You know—"

"Don't you doubt it for a second," said Bob. "They are hunting us."

Russ nodded and stepped out of the car. Of course he felt ridiculous: this living in the red zone, what Bob called Condition One— it took too much energy and passion, it left you breathless and actually, he thought, duller than normal. You were beyond paranoia, in some strange and squalid place, where that lady up there with the baby buggy could reach into it and pull an AK-47 or that friendly mailman could reach into his pouch and come out with a sawed-off shotgun. He couldn't live that way. No one could except some kind of nutcase.

So he put it out of his mind and walked the thirty-odd feet to the steps and bounded in. Nobody shot him; nobody even seemed to notice him.

It took a while but not forever. No phone books listed any Posey family but he requested the bound volumes of the weekly *Polk*

County Star for the year 1962, received the heavy volume in due course and paged through it until he came at last to the big news: COUNTY MAN SLAYS NEGRO, it said.

There, under the headline, which ran across the top of the page, was a picture of the glum and trashy Jed Posey, his cheeks sunken, his jaw clenched about a mouthful of tiny jagged teeth, his eyes baleful and dark, a Polk County Sheriff's Office ID number under his chin. There was an odd lopsidedness to his face as if it had been broken apart, then cemented together again imperfectly. Next to it was a picture of Davidson Fuller, a haggard black man in his sixties, with a short Brillo pad of gray for hair and the haunted eyes of a father still mourning his loss. Both pictures were inset upon a shot taken at the gas station soon after the police arrived, with a body supine next to an old truck, its top half covered by somebody's old blanket, but a raggedy track of black ran out from underneath, and Russ knew it was old Davidson's blood. He shuddered, then read the account, which gave Posey's address as County Route 70. He went to the county map and quickly found a RR 70—but was it the *same* 70? He looked around for someone elderly to ask but then recalled the Federal Writer's Project Guide to the States, from the thirties. The card catalog yielded a call number and he found the volume in seconds on the open shelves. He paged through, county by county, until at last he came to Polk and to a map that dated from 1938: yes, in the old days, that road was called 70.

Next he went to the filing cabinets for the county land plats and sifted through them. Again, luck or whatever was with him: the plats offered a much more detailed examination of the terrain and he found the area and looked at a map of the place. He found County Route 70, a straight line running perpendicular and east from 271, past Iron Fork Lake. It plunged deeper and deeper into map blankness like an arrow, a road that went nowhere except to the very limits of the known world. Civilization hadn't reached that far into the dark woods, evidently; not even any sewers appeared to have been laid. But that wasn't important; instead he looked at the words along the road marking local place-names. Way, way back—maybe twenty miles in—he came across a "Posey

Hollow," in what had to be the shadow of Iron Fork Mountain. The map there was blank except for the ominous word *Forest*. A squiggle denoted a rough road snaking inward toward nothingness.

As best as he could, he copied the directions down, drawing up a facsimile. Then he headed back outside, feeling good. He'd found him. That fast, that simple.

They drove the 271 until they reached the dirt road that was County 70, where a sign pointed toward Iron Fork Lake.

"There, there!" he shouted.

But Bob did not turn down it.

"Keep your voice down," he said.

He threw a U-turn when a gap in the traffic permitted and headed back to the closest town, which was called Acorn, where a slatternly convenience store sat in isolation behind some gas pumps across from a one-horse strip of dying retail outlets and a trailer post office. Bob pulled into the convenience lot.

"I need a Coke," he said, "come on."

They went in, and Bob took a plastic bottle of the soft drink from the glass case, got one for Russ, then went up to the counter, where a black woman watched them sullenly. He threw something at her that caused Russ to bumble into a movie-scale double take. A smile! A beaming, radiant, howdy-there smile.

She smiled back.

"Maybe you can help me," he said. "I got some friends supposed to come through from Little Rock to look at some hunting camp property. Damn, I may be lost. You seen any groups of strangers, city-looking boys, very careful types? Truth is, we're all Little Rock cops. You know that cop look: way the eyes is always traveling, way one guy is sort of hanging back, taking it all in, the way they don't talk loud and keep to themselves. You see my friends in here in, say, the last few days?"

"Mister, in hunting season you see boys like that all the time. I ain't seen a soul in months I don't know his mama and his papa and his brothers."

"No four-wheel-drive vehicles? Sunglasses, expensive boots, clothes look real new?"

"You ain't looking for no cops."

"No, I ain't, truth is. I am worried about these damn boys and would be grateful if you'd think about it a second."

"No sir, I ain't seen nothing like that."

"Okay, good work. Thanks." He left a five on the counter.

They walked back to the truck.

"Man, you are careful," said Russ.

"I am alive," Bob said, "and I goddamn well intend to stay that way."

They drove back along 271 to the dirt road, turned down it and began to pick their way along. Periodically, Bob would stop, get out and examine the dirt road for tracks. There were no fresh ones. They passed a lake far off to the right, flat pewter water against the green bulk of a mountain.

They drove and drove. The forest swallowed them, the canopy trees interlocking to block out the sun and the blue sky, as if they plunged through a green tunnel toward blackness. Every mile or so, Bob would pull over, get out, let the dust settle, check the road for tracks, listen intently. His persistence and his patience Russ found really deeply annoying.

Come on, he was thinking.

They crept past deserted farms, timbered or burned-out patches of field, the occasional meadow, but soon enough the forest grew denser, black oak and hickory and winged elm, a curtain of hardwood shot through with an undergrowth of bristly saw brier and yucca.

Finally, they came to a ragged track off to the right.

"That's it," said Russ. "If the cabin is here, it's back there."

But Bob continued on for at least a mile, then pulled off the road, sliding the car as deep in the woods as he could.

"It would be easier to walk down the road," Russ said.

"It ain't about being easier. It's about being safer."

He got out, waited again for the dust to settle.

"Bob, I—"

"Shhh," Bob cautioned. "Use your ears. Shut your eyes and listen."

Russ heard nothing. Bob concentrated for a good five minutes, waiting to discover if the far-off hum of a following car would announce itself. But nothing came. The world was quiet except for the occasional squawk of a bird and the quiet hiss of the wind in the trees.

"Okay," Bob said, looking at the crude map Russ had drawn from the land plat. "You're sure this is accurate?"

"It's almost a tracing," Russ said.

"Looks to me like the road trends back to the southeast. That would put the cabin a mile and a half in. We ought to be overland from it about a mile."

Bob shot an azimuth on a small compass he pulled out of his jeans, grabbed a pair of binoculars, and they set off into the woods. The forest absorbed them. It was dense and green, the light overhead filtering through the canopy, more like a jungle than Russ's idea of a forest.

Every so often Bob would shoot another compass angle, then veer crazily in an odd direction. It was soon enough gibberish to Russ; they seemed just to be wandering through the heavy woods in the heat, the bugs biting, the birds singing. He was hopelessly lost.

"You know where we're going?"

"Yep."

"You can get us out of here?"

"Yep."

"We must have come miles."

"We've walked about three, yeah. By beeline, we've come less than one, however. In the jungle you don't go nowheres in a straight line, 'less you want to be taken down."

Russ thought: he's been here before. He's taken men down before.

Look at him, he thought. A force of nature. Bob slid so easily and silently through the trees, his boots never slipped, he never stumbled or grunted, just maneuvered with the easy grace of the man who'd done it before. His face was blank, his eyes working the edges of the horizon, the demeanor utterly calm and concentrated. Leatherstocking. Natty Bumpo. Daniel Boone, Davy Crockett. Damned John Wayne, like his father, whom everybody always said looked like John Wayne. Soon the sweat showed on his blue denim shirt but Bob paid it no mind; he just kept on trucking, the grip of that .45 sticking out of his jeans above the kidney.

In time, they came to a creek, cool and dark, and swiftly flowing. Russ scrambled over the rocks and got a mouthful of the water, which tasted faintly metallic.

"You make too much noise that way," Bob said. "Cup it up to your lips and sip it. You never was a marine, right?"

"Not hardly," said Russ.

"Okay, let's go. It ain't far."

They cut across a path which ran between two low hills and appeared to lead to a clearing in the dim, overgrown trees ahead, but Bob never did things the easy way. Instead, halfway through that little draw, Bob took them off the path, through some heavy growth, and then broke onto the barer high ground under a maze of pines. Ahead, Russ could see the light of vista and openness. But Bob dropped to a low crawl and slithered ahead, coming at last to the edge and setting himself up behind a tree. Russ, feeling utterly like an imposter, did the same.

Two hundred yards below in a hollow by the stream sat the cabin. It was built of logs, low and primitive, with a woodpile, an outhouse, a feed trough for the pigs who scurried in a pen. A beat-up Chevy stood near it, rusted out, one fender gone to primer. Yet it had nothing of rustic Dogpatch, your quaint rural hamlet to it: instead it looked mean and squalid and impoverished.

"No phone lines," Bob said. "No goddamned TV aerial. No electric wires."

"Question," said Russ. "If he's just out of prison, how come the place looks so lived in?"

"He had a brother named Lum," said Bob. "The brother had a son, who also lives here. It's the son's work you're seeing, not old Jed's."

"Okay," said Russ. "So let's go see if he'll talk to us."

"No way," said Bob. "You stay here. You eyeball the place. You got another hour. Then the sun's too low to the west and it'll reflect off the lenses. You got a watch?"

"Yes."

"It's two forty-five. You eyeball it till three forty-five. What are you looking for?"

"Uh, anything that's out of the ordinary."

"How do you look?"

"Uh—" Completely new question. Russ flubbed around.

"Hard," he finally said.

"No, dummy. Divide it into quadrants. Thirty seconds a quadrant. Blink to black between, then move on. Follow the same pattern for ten minutes, then reverse it or change it around. Take frequent breaks and study the woods around. Use lens discipline. Never let them rise above the midpoint, you might throw a reflection. You're not looking for men and guns, because you won't see them and there's no point. You're looking for regular outlines. Nothing in nature is regular. If you see a straight line in the woods, you know something's off. Got it? One hour. Then put the glasses down and just go to regular vision."

"Where'll you be?"

"I'm going to circle around and see if I cut any tracks in the woods. I want to know if parties of men have moved through here to that damned place. If it's empty, and you haven't seen anything, then we'll go down."

"Okay," said Russ. "We're not going to get out of here until after dark."

"Don't you worry about that, Donnie. You just eyeball the place."

With that, he slid back and in seconds—the sniper's gift—had disappeared.

Who the hell is Donnie? Russ wondered.

Thirty-seven

JACK PREECE was working on budgetary projections for 1998, one of his most favorite things.

He loved the steady march of the numbers across the page, the semblance of order they brought to chaos, the inflow and outflow as his fortunes advanced. It answered some deeply felt need he had.

> Battalion 316, Honduras Army
> Salvadoran Treasury Police
> Detroit SWAT
> Baltimore County Quick Response
> FBI Hostage Rescue
> Atomic Energy Commission Security Teams
> Library of Congress SWAT
> Navy SEAL Team Six

It was amazing, really. Nobody had ever looked at it this way, but sniping was a growth industry. The explosion in terrorism in the seventies, its ugly reappearance in the nineties, the profusion of heavily armed drug cartels with paramilitary capacity, the specter of armed right-wing militias, the increasing liberal call for "sophisticated" (i.e., surgical or low-lethality) police operations, all added up to one thing: the precision rifleman and the gear and culture to equip and train him were a skyrocket for the nineties and the century beyond the millennium. He was surprised, come to think of it, that the *Wall Street Journal* hadn't done a story yet.

Every town, every city, every state, every agency, every country, needed the trained rifleman with the world-class equipment. Life was becoming psychotic. Rationality had broken down. Crushed and shattered by disappointment, political, domestic or economic, many men turned to violence. The workplace berserker, the family hostage taker, the organized criminal gang, the drug security goon squad, all heavily armed. Who would stop them? Not the patrol officer or the security dork, not enough training, not enough guts. No, it would be some replication of himself: a man with the coolness, the experience, essentially the will, to lie there in the dark and when the whole thing was going down, to do his duty. Trigger slack out, breathing controlled, absolute confidence in weapons system, not a hitch or a doubt or a twitch anywhere: the trigger goes back. A hundred yards away a small piece of metal driven at supersonic speeds enters the cranial vault, expands like a fist opening to hand, then spurts out the rear in a fog of pink mist. It's over.

He, Jack Preece, had seen this earlier than anyone and was now prepared to ride the wave to a better, a safer tomorrow.

"General?"

It was Peck, long-boned and pale-eyed and trashy as death itself, in his deputy's uniform, his gold badge shiny and bright.

"General," he said, "it's time. Signal just come through."

"Give me a sitrep, please."

"Huh?"

"Report on the situation, you idiot."

"Oh. Yes sir. They're there, they must be coming in. The old man got a good visual, else he wouldn't have sent it."

"Then let's saddle up."

Preece was already wearing his ghillie suit, a ghastly jumpsuit apparition painstakingly festooned with thousands of strips of camouflage cloth threaded through thousands of loops, giving him indoors the appearance of a great shaggy green dog that walked on two legs and had just stepped out of the swamp. But in the natural environment, it conferred an instant shapeless invisibility. He rose, feeling the swish of the strips, and quickly went to the bathroom.

Before him on the sink were four wide paint sticks, black, brown, olive drab, jungle green. He hated the masks some of the boys wore: too hot, and limited peripheral vision. He worked quickly in applying the combat makeup, diagonal streaks an inch wide. The darkness of the jungle ate up the pink of his face like a lion swallowing a pie: it was gone, that pink, bland, square, handsome mug behind which he faced the world and hid his inner nature. A warrior gazed back, ancient and fearsome, his white eyes preternatural against the jungle tapestry that muted his flesh.

He grabbed his boonie hat—the original, worn in Nam for the two years he commanded Tigercat—and raced outside, pausing only to pick up the cocked and locked Browning Hi-Power that slid into a shoulder holster under the ghillie. Duane Peck had a four-wheeled ATV fired up and a long plastic case which packed the weapons system tied across the handlebars.

Jack Preece climbed aboard and with a spurt of the throttle Peck gunned ahead. They had not used the vehicle at all in previous recons of the area but had plotted a path through the trees that would in ten minutes bring Jack Preece within a half mile of one of the hills that overlooked the creek and the path. The little vehicle ate up the distance, though Peck kept the speed moderate so there was no wailing engine.

They reached the destination and Preece dismounted, took the case and opened it. The M-16 with its gigantic eye atop its gigantic tube mounted to the receiver was a black shadow in the decaying light. The suppressor protruded from the gun muzzle like an elegant snout, a sleek cylinder fully a foot long. The metal was all Teflon-coated, lusterless and somehow dead to the touch. He bent, quickly attached the miniature battery pack to his belt, lifted the rifle and locked in a twenty-round banana clip with only nineteen cartridges, always a sound precaution when working with magazine-fed weapons. With a snap, he pulled back and released the charging plunger, loading and cocking the weapon, and thumbed the safety to On. He threw the support harness around his shoulder, rose and lifted it: less than eighteen pounds total, quite easily done.

"Get out of here now, Peck. You meet me at the staging area at midnight; if I'm not there, check each hour."

"Yes sir," said Peck.

The general turned and headed up the slope, hearing the low buzz of the engine as Peck's ATV lurched off and slowly faded away.

He walked for ten minutes and saw before him a broad, flat, needle-carpeted forest floor, broken by the vertical maze of the trees, lit at one edge by the setting sun on the other side of the clearing. He moved through it fluidly, advancing twenty or thirty feet at a time, then melting into the earth, and listening intently. He reached the edge and, placing himself beside a pine tree with the lowest possible profile, peered downward. He could see figures behind the window, speaking animatedly. It was hard to make out. Binoculars would bring them out, but the sun was just low enough to present the possibility of a reflection. Instead, he brought the rifle up and with a snap of his thumb first to light and then to scope, went to infrared.

The cabin, two hundred yards away, was a bit out of range for the reach of the searchlight, so he didn't get great illumination. The lack of total dark also eroded illumination. But he got enough: in the murky green light, he could see three figures. They seemed animated. Details were lost; one appeared to be tall and thin and could match up easily with the Bob Lee Swagger who had visited him two weeks ago. Another was the boy.

Do them, he thought.

Right now, why wait? Do them, be done with it. He could put nineteen rounds through the window in less than two seconds, and the .223, though not a powerfully heavy and accurate long-range round, was a true speed merchant and still offered more than 2,500 feet per second of velocity at that range. They'd be dead before they hit the ground.

But Jack was professional. You go by the plan, which you've rehearsed painstakingly. When you improvised, the law of unforeseen accident always took its toll.

He snapped the beam and the scope off and withdrew, snaking along the ground until he was lost in the trees. He stood then, and traced his way back along the ridgeline, making no noise, raising no dust. By the time he got to the hide, it was nearly full dark.

A thatch of plastic greenery which would never give itself over to dead brown and thereby reveal its position lay across it. Jack pulled it aside. The hide was not so much a conventional spider hole as a long narrow trench scooped out of the earth, deep enough to conceal a prone man, but easy enough to bail out of if the shit hit the fan. The dirt the digging had uprooted had been meticulously spread through the woods to attract no attention.

Preece slid into position, pulling the screen atop him. Quickly enough, he found a solid shooting position, bracing the weapon against the sandbag.

He went to infrared and instantly it all lit up before him in fishbowl green: the white winding ribbon of the path, the wavering wands of the vegetation, the lighter tonal quality of the rocks. The path passed before and below him a mere fifty yards away: that's where he'd take them, putting the reticle on the taller figure's chest, pumping one silent round out, then pivoting ever so slightly to the other figure. He'd done it a hundred times in practice.

He snapped the light off. It had a good eight hours' worth of battery but he knew he'd hear them as they came up the path and there was no sense wasting power. You leave nothing to chance in this business and the one thing he could not control was the length of time it took for the two targets to get into range.

He settled back, slipping the camo band back to reveal the face of his watch: 7:10. He guessed another hour or so. But maybe longer and he had to stay alert.

Preece was really more a visionary, a leader, an administrator, a trainer and a coach than any real sniper. But even in Vietnam he believed a commander should endure and face the same chances that his men did, if only to understand their problems more fully. Thus he went on the missions on a weekly basis. Over his two years, he'd accumulated thirty-two kills, none officially recognized, of course, because officers were not supposed to do such things. Still, the thirty-two men were all unquestionably dead. One night, he even got four in about two minutes. Incredible occurrence, incredible sensation.

But they say you remember your first kill best of all and that was true with Jack Preece. And as he lay there in the hide in the intensifying darkness and the night forest was beginning to come to life all around him, he remembered perching in that deer stand in the dark of another Arkansas forest (not far from here, less than twenty miles as the crow flies). He hated the weapon: impossibly heavy, with a huge infrared spotlight bolted underneath the barrel and a huge scope atop, and a huge battery pack on his back, its straps cutting into him, all this for a puny .30-caliber 110-grain full metal jacket that hit with just a little more force than a .38 Special. It was the good rifle, of the three working M-3 sniperscope units, and he had it loaded with the most accurate lot of ammunition. And, as Frenchy Short had explained, he probably wouldn't have to shoot. He was backup.

"Bubba, you got to do us a job," Frenchy Short had said to him. "We got us a goddamned bad-ass state cop who's acting as cutout to the Russians."

"Huh?" said then-twenty-four-year-old First Lieutenant Preece, still an unformed boy whose celebrity as the author of "Night Sniper Operations: A Doctrinal Theory" in the *Infantry Journal* was beginning to fade.

When he thought about it later, Preece recognized what a load of bullshit the story Frenchy sold him had to be. But to a twenty-four-year-old infantry officer seething with anticommunist bacillus as inculcated by the political culture of the year 1955, who worshiped Joe McCarthy and had just—dammit!—missed Korea, it made a kind of sense. And part of it too was Frenchy, who had that weird psycho's gift of utter conviction. Frenchy could sell Stalinism in the gulags. Frenchy had the odd chameleonlike ability of absorbing *your* personality, of becoming *you,* and so in effect entering your subconscious as he ground you down with furious and one-pointed eye contact, smothering, ass-kissing charm, and a bandit's utter ruthlessness.

"We thought we's years ahead of the Reds in IR," Frenchy, who was originally from Pennsylvania, breathed in the assuring tonalities of Preece's own South Georgia accent, "but goddamn, we're gittin' reports they got IR working on an experimental sniper rifle, combat-effective out to two hundred yards."

"Shit," the young man said.

"Now, you know they ain't that good and I know they ain't that good. How come they that good?"

"Spies," said Preece.

"You got that right. Seems this old-boy state trooper got his ass in a little gambling trouble, so some old Red Army spymaster sniffs him out and makes his ass a proposition—he's got to git inside BLACK LIGHT or he'll go down. So this old boy arrests a corporal on a fag charge and threatens to destroy his life. But the cop'll let him go if he supplies certain documents. CID got the kid's statement and the kid in the hoosegow. Now we got to send the Reds a message: this is what happens when you go against the U.S. Army. We don't take no prisoners."

If Preece believed it, it was because he wanted to believe it and because it was, of course, well known that Red Army intelligence had penetrated the entire establishment, lurked everywhere and was capable of anything. As Frenchy pointed out many times, "Them boys don't even b'lieve in *God* and once you give up your spiritual heritage you're capable of doing *anything*."

So it was that four nights later he found himself in the deer stand, watching a drama play out before him. As he understood it, Frenchy had gone to some lengths to set up an arrest scenario where the real shooters were to take the cop down. The point was to disguise the murder as a duty-related killing, so that only the Russians would get the message. It had to be done. It was duty. But suppose the pros missed? That was Jack's job.

He watched from the tree as the police cruiser pulled in, backed around, sited itself. Jack put the scope on the man, snicked on the IR unit and watched the dull scene spark to incandescence. The officer sat in his car; he looked sad, nervous. He took his hat off and rested patiently. At one point, he tested his searchlight. Jack had good elevation and saw clearly over the corn: but the corn was a problem because its leaves reflected too brightly in the iridescence. But still he knew: he could hit that shot easy.

In time another car pulled in. It sat across from the police car as the rogue officer put his beam on them. Two young men got out, one a James Dean clone, hair slicked back in a wavy pile, an insolent cigarette dangling from his lips, his jeans tight and sexy, and the other a doughy, sullen farm boy in a T-shirt. It was too far to hear distinct words, but the two youths had their hands up; the cop got out of the car. It appeared to be some kind of surrender thing. The cop was yelling instructions. The slicker boy threw something into the dust. Preece put the scope on it as it lay there and saw at once that it was a wrench, not a gun.

The heavy boy started across. Preece watched in grim horror. The night seemed to have stalled out. There was a terrible frozen moment and Preece at that instant utterly changed sides, his natural respect for the uniform and what it represented overriding the rational part of his brain.

He has a gun, he wanted to scream to the cop. He put the sight on the slick boy's chest and almost fired. Almost. Took the slack out.

Shoot!

No.

He lowered the rifle and realized he was sobbing. He watched; in the next second, the slick boy pulled his gun. The flashes lit the night but the sound of the shots was flat and far away. Dust rose as men ran and dodged. Preece raised the rifle again and in the green of the scope saw the sullen farm boy flat on his back, a big dark stain spreading across the glowing greenish white of his T-shirt. Dust or gun smoke floated in the air still. The cop was down by his car, reloading. The other boy had disappeared into the corn.

Stay put, Jack yelled in his head. *Call for backup. He isn't going anywhere.*

But the cop finished his reload and rose. Jack could see that he too was hit and he moved with the slow pain of a man locked into his duty by forces too broad to be understood by other men.

Stay put, Jack commanded.

But the cop was too bull-stubborn or proud, too much of a goddamned rare-as-hen's-teeth authentic American hero to stay put, and he sloughed along the edge of the dirt road, one arm dead, walking the slow walk of a man losing blood but not heart, some kind of fiend for duty. Jack lost him in the reflection of the corn. He put the carbine down and waited. The minutes dragged by. Jack heard yelling, voices again indistinct. Then the crackle and flash of shots from the corn.

It was silent. He waited. Near the car, a figure emerged from the cover of the corn. Jack watched, unable to identify him, until he at last recognized no single feature except the rhythm of the walk.

It was the cop, now so laden with melancholy he could hardly move. He made it to his car and sat sideways in the seat. He seemed to be fumbling with something. Then Jack saw him talking on the radio. He put the mike down. He waited and tried again. A third time he tried. He set it down. Then he stirred, as if popped by something. He seized it up, spoke animatedly. Then he put it down. He'd made contact.

The cop sat in the car.

Jack hoisted the rifle, flicked on the scope, and the beam of black light reached out to ensnare the policeman.

He put the crosshairs square on the center of the chest. The lawman was breathing heavily and seemed to be talking to himself.

Do it, Jack told himself.

He's a Red, he told himself, though he no longer believed it.

Do it, he again told himself.

The rifle grew heavy. The crosshairs wavered, came off the chest, rode down the leg to the ground.

DO IT!

He raised them until they quadrasected the square broad chest. The trigger broke and through the silencer the rifle spoke with a cough but no flash. There was no recoil, or hardly any. Jack saw the rifle bullet strike, saw the body jack with shock, then topple sideways and catch against the steering wheel.

He turned off the scope.

Jack put the safety on and slung the rifle. It was only a short climb to the ground, even with the monstrously heavy battery pack. He turned and was halfway down the hill on the other side when he heard the first siren.

❑ ❑ ❑ ❑

Voices.

Jack flashed back to the present.

He snicked the scope on.

They walked, talking animatedly, the tall man, the shorter boy. The optics were superb. They were big and clear as life, rushing down the forest path by the creek in the enfilade between the two low hills, now seventy yards distant, now sixty.

Jack's thumb pronged the silent safety to Off. He pivoted the rifle ever so slightly, ever so smoothly, tracking the large man, a green phantasm in the glow of the scope, lit by the infrared lamp atop. He felt the slack coming out of the trigger, as the crosshairs came onto the chest until in a magic moment they seemed locked there.

Thirty-eight

THEY CAME OUT of the woods into a sudden, late burst of sunlight. Russ felt liberated from the green gloom of the forest. Before them was the squalid cabin. Incongruous wildflowers lit up around its messy base and front yard.

"He's watching us," said Bob. "I can feel him and I just seen something move behind that window."

As they approached, a man semi-emerged from the doorway and stopped, hiding in the darkness. He observed them with ancient, embittered eyes. As they approached he dipped inside and retrieved a shotgun.

"Y'all git on out of here," he yelled, glaring. "This ain't no goddamned freak show. You'se on my property and you be gone or I'll give ya some buckshot."

Jed Posey had the look of a man whose life had been consumed in fury. He was scrawny, leathery and toothless, and the denim overalls hung on his frame, showing an old man's wiry body. He was nothing but sinew and hate. His bare arms wore the dapple of three and a half decades' worth of prison tattoos, and he had two tears inscribed in the taut flesh of his face, though his eyes were tearless and fierce. His hair was the prisoner's gray bristle.

"You go on," he said, bringing the gun up, "or I will by God blast you out of your goddamn boots and be damned."

"We have business," said Bob.

"We ain't got no business, mister. You working for the niggers?

Bet the goddamned niggers sent you down here. I'm telling you to stop, by God, or I'll send you to hell where I sent that goddamned nigger."

"We don't work for nobody," said Bob. "I am Bob Lee Swagger, the son of Earl Swagger. I'm here to talk about the day my father died, Jed. I don't care a damn about nothing else."

Jed lowered the shotgun. But the aggression that suffused his entire body and made it tight and shivery like a pointing terrier's diminished not a bit; his dark little eyes narrowed in anger and if possible he got even redder and tenser. He seemed to be breathing hard.

"Your goddamned father done socked me in the jaw," he said. "That's how come my face is broken. I've had forty years of pain on account of your sumbitch old man."

"If my daddy smacked you, Jed, by God, it was a smack you'd earned and I'll bet it was a smack you ain't never forgot."

Jed seemed to melt backwards a step. Something flashed through his little eyes, and told them yes, yes by God, no matter what had happened, Jed Posey had never forgot the day Earl Swagger broke his jaw.

"What you want?" he said. "All that's long time ago. Jimmy Pye kilt your daddy and your daddy kilt Jimmy Pye and his cousin Bub."

"I got some questions."

"Why the hell should I answer one goddamn question for a goddamned Swagger? Nothing in the law or nowhere says I got to talk to you."

He hawked a squirt of tobacco venom into the dust.

"No sir, you don't," said Bob. "But a old goat like you understands one goddamn thing. Money. You gimme an hour of your time, I'll give you twenty dollars."

"Twenny dollar! Mister, you must think I'm stupid. Twenny dollar! Cost you *forty* dollar, Swagger. For *forty* dollar I'll tell you any goddamned thing you want to know."

Russ started forward, but Bob caught him.

"I said twenty dollars and I *meant* twenty dollars. I don't bargain with scum. Come on, Russ," and he pulled the boy back and turned.

Russ shot him a what-the-hell look but Bob yanked him backwards and they turned and started walking back toward the woods.

"Goddamn you, Swagger, *thirty* dollar."

Bob turned. "I said I don't bargain with trash. You take what's on the table or I will leave the table and that's true today or a hundred years from today and you won't never make no twenty dollars."

"Goddamn you, Swagger."

"Goddamn me one more time, you old coot, and I will come up on that porch and knock in the *other* side of your face and finish my daddy's work."

"Let me see the twenny."

Bob pulled his wallet and removed a twenty.

Jed considered narrowly, as if he had a lot riding on the decision.

"You give me the twenty now."

"If you want to hang onto something, you hang onto your dick, you egg-sucking piece of trash. I'll hang onto the money until I am finished with you and *then* I will hand it over. You know no Swagger in these parts or any other ever broke his word or welshed on a bargain."

"There's a goddamned first time for everything," said Jed bitterly. "You come on, then. But you keep your distance."

Bob and Russ climbed the rickety steps into the dark dwelling. Russ was always amazed at how things diverged from his imagination of them, but this time he was absolutely correct. It was one grim big surpriseless room, rank with odor. A deer's shabby antlers were nailed to a crossbeam; the stove was old and stank of cold, ancient grease, the bed, a pallet in the corner, supported a scurvy nest of swirled blankets. One wall had been transfigured into Jed's hall of fame by the industrious use of thumbtacks as his front page from the paper had been pinned to the wood, where it was now yellow and crackly with age—COUNTY MAN SLAYS NEGRO, it said, uniting him and Davidson Fuller in journalistic immortality. The smell of unwashed clothes, dead animals, human destitution and loneliness hung everywhere in the thick air.

"Ah, could I have a decaf cappuccino and a mocha for my son?" asked Russ. "And the *chocolate* biscotti."

"Shut up, Russ," Bob said, as Jed's squirrelly little face fell into anger, "this ain't no time to be smart."

The old man threw down at an oilcloth-covered table, clinging to the shotgun, and Bob sat across from him. There was no place for Russ to sit and there wasn't enough money in the world to induce him to physical contact with that bed—*yccch,* he shuddered—so he just sort of leaned against the closest wall.

"Tell me about that day," said Bob.

Jed pulled a pack of Red Man from his pocket and stuffed some of the stringy tobacco in his mouth, did some manipulating with his tongue until he got it lodged between cheek and gum on the right side, where it bulged like a tumor. He smiled, showing brown gums.

"Ain't much to goddamn tell. They woke me in the Blue Eye drunk tank along with my brother, Lum, rest his soul, and that fat old deputy Lem tole me he had work detail. I'se so hung over, I didn't realize where we was until we got there. Let me tell you, Swagger, I wasn't in no mood to go horsing around in them hot woods lookin' for no nigger gal."

"What *happened?*" Bob said. "Talk me through it."

Jed looked around, spat at an overflowing Maxwell House can on the floor and then narrated a rambling account of the day, of the heat and dust of the forest even high in the mountains, of the agony of picking through the saw brier and the bracken, of the mosquitoes and other things that buzzed and bit, and the stench of the dogs, and the final thing, the girl.

"Shit," he said. "She was a ripe one, all blown up like b'loon. You could see her goddamned li'l mouse, tell you what. Just out there in the open. Now they show that stuff in the magazines. In them days, boy, you never saw no mouse. Heh, heh." He absently chortled in memory of the smoky pleasure of it and Russ saw a flicker of rage play across Bob's face, then subside.

"Why did my father belt you?"

" 'Cause he's a mean sumbitch is why," said Jed, not meeting Bob's eyes.

"My father was many things but he wasn't a bully. Why'd he hit you, old man?"

"I didn't mean no harm. I said a little something about riding the gal is all. Bastard. He had no cause to do that. She was a nigger gal and I was right. A nigger boy kilt her. I said so then and that's way it turned out. Then that nigger boy's daddy he go all around pretending to be some kind of big shot. Well, I showed him. I ripped open his skull with a goddamned spade. Best feeling I ever got, yes it was, by God, and worth ever damn day of prison. Niggers tried to kill me in prison, you know. Yeah, look at *this*."

He pulled down the strap of his overall and the bib fell, and Russ saw a long purple crescent of scar tissue, a witless smile of pucker, running from one nipple almost down to the appendix.

Jed's eye lit with yellow madness. "Niggers done that. Two hunnert and thirty-five stitches! Doc sewed me up like a burlap sack. But they couldn't bleed me out. No sir. I got more damn blood in me than a sloat pig on slaughter Friday. By God, not no niggers, not no Earl Mr. Fancy Medal Swagger done got the best of me, by goddamn!"

He sat back, spent, and awarded himself a recreational gob of tobacco juice which he launched like a missile in an arching parabola until it hit dead center in the can, raising a tiny mushroom cloud. Russ shuddered in revulsion and looked away. But Jed wasn't done. He looked up.

"I was right about the niggers too. I said, you give them people anything, next thing you know, they be shooting and fucking and killing all over the goddamned place. And they is too, ain't they? Niggers is fine in Africa. Bring 'em over here and look what good it done us. Niggers. They's the end of America, that's for damned sure."

Bob kept still through this tirade, as though he were waiting patiently for a dark storm to blow over. Then he said, "Tell me about my father. What was his mood? What was he doing? How did he act?"

"He was soft on the niggers, that was his problem," said Jed. "I could smell it on him. This little missing gal: hell, you'd a thought it was *his* little gal, not some nigger's. He was *sad.* Whole goddamned morning. That is when he weren't coldcocking me. I could take him in a fair fight."

"Not on your best day, you old dick. Ask the Japanese. They knew him well," Bob fired back. "Who did he talk to? What did he say?"

"Mainly, old Lem. And Pop Dwyer, who run the dogs. He liked Pop but he didn't like them dogs. I don't know why, but I could tell. He hung back from them dogs. But mainly, he was fuckin' around on me. Mr. High and Mighty. He's on my case like a bastard from the start," said Jed. "Didn't your old lady give him none? It was like he hadn't had nothing in weeks."

Bob just glared at him.

"So he runs us up and down the road and into the woods, goddammit, it was hot nigger work. All the time he's jawin' on me, like I say. And when he finds that damn girl, I hears him telling goddamn Lem to order all this fancy equipment. Teams, shit like that, from Little Rock. Like it was goddamned *important* or something. Hell, it were just a raggedy-ass nigger gal."

Bob took all this in evenly, his face drawn and remote.

"How did he know to look there? What led him to that spot? Do you recall?"

Jed's features knitted up in concentration. As if summoning a memory, he summoned up a gob of juice and fired it toward the can, missing by a wide margin. Russ noticed that the gobs were coming closer and closer to him.

"Something about a lady calling in saying she'd seen a nigger boy acting 'peculiar' four days earlier out by the Texaco sign. Yore damn daddy always poking his nose in other people's business. When he heard the girl was missing, he put 'em together and that's how he got us out there."

Bob nodded. It squared: the black boy, in local lore, would have been Reggie Fuller.

But it wasn't Reggie Fuller, because he was driving people home from the meeting in secret. But if it *was* a black boy who'd killed the girl, someone was doing an elaborate operation to frame Reggie. Why? Why? What possibly could there be to gain?

"Did he say anything about *other* investigations or matters?" asked Russ. "Was he consumed with anything else?"

"He's tired," said Jed. "That's all, tired. He always seemed tired."

"From what?" asked Russ of Bob.

"He didn't work no regular duty day," said Bob, recalling. "He'd be gone sometimes fifteen, sixteen hours a shot, sometimes two or three days. He'd work the mornings and the afternoons, maybe come home for a couple of hours at dinner, maybe take a nap. Then he'd go back out on the road, monitor the state police network, look for speeders, mischief, answer calls, that sort of thing. He worked like a goddamned dog."

Bob ended, letting it hang quiet in the melancholy air.

"Is that it, Swagger?" Jed demanded.

Bob just looked at him.

"That's all you wanted? Hah! That ain't worth no twenny dollar! You ain't got no more questions and I'm still hotter'n a firecracker."

He laughed, as if he'd won some great victory.

"You boys been here so long it's dark out! Ha! And what'd you learn? Nary a goddamned thing! Hah! You got my money, Swagger?"

Bob threw the twenty on the table.

"Have a party, Posey."

It was full dark and Russ felt both exhausted and liberated when at last he sucked in a lungful of air that wasn't tainted with the odor of bacon fat and stale sweat.

"We didn't learn much," he admitted, as they stepped off the porch.

"I told you we wouldn't," said Bob. "You keep trying to make this link between poor Shirelle and what happened to my father. You keep trying to do that but it don't work out in time or in logic."

"Well—" said Russ. But then he paused. "Consider this. First, coincidence. Is it logical that there would be *two* elaborate conspiracies engineered within days of each other in a remote backwater of West Arkansas? I mean, things like that hardly ever happen in real life. Doesn't it make some kind of sense to presume they were in some way connected, that there was only really *one?"*

Bob said nothing.

"Then consider," Russ said, "that although each conspiracy is *different* in terms of objective, they share the same mechanism or pattern. In both cases, there's two levels. The first, seemingly impenetrable, offers a plain and simple crime, complete to motives and very obvious clues. Jimmy and Bub Pye rob a grocery store; ten hours later they're confronted by Sergeant Swagger, who guns them both down and is killed himself. Open-and-shut. Shirelle Parker is raped and murdered twelve miles outside Blue Eye. Her hand conceals the monogrammed pocket of her killer. At his house, the rest of the shirt, smeared with her blood, is found. Open-and-shut. But in *both* cases, at the level of the most excruciating detail, the anomalies begin to assert themselves and if you go beyond the open-and-shut, you see that in each case some genius operator set it up—night infrared for your dad, moving the body from the site of the crime in the other case. Don't you see?"

"Consider yourself," said Bob. "The boy that killed Shirelle was black, you dope. Shirelle's mama told Sam she was raised so she wouldn't get in no car with no white boy. Now, you got to ask, if he's a black boy, who the hell in Arkansas in 1955 had the wherewithal to throw together a frame? For a black boy? Don't make no sense at all. If it were a white boy, maybe. But no: it was a black boy."

"Shit," said Russ.

"I'm convinced my daddy was investigating a crime and that's what got him killed. He learned something, something big, that powerful men wanted stopped. How else would they have had the resources? They had the CIA, an army sniper, state-of-the-art gear."

In exasperation, Russ shouted, "I am the son of a state police sergeant. My dad couldn't investigate an outhouse!"

"Shut up, we just passed our mark."

"What?"

"I'm counting."

"What?"

"Steps. Once we hit two hundred forty steps from that big boulder, we head off this goddamned path, veer to the left and begin our zigzag back. We move in units of two hundred forty of my long steps, hard left, hard right by the compass, and that gets us back to the car."

But Russ hadn't been paying attention. They had now reached the draw where the creek bed, off to the left, cut between the two hills. The trees loomed above them, more felt than seen. The wind gently pressed through them, filling the night with whispers. The dark lay like a blanket, suffocating Russ. A flash of paranoia illuminated a far corner of his mind; he thought of being alone out here with his hyperactive imagination, zero visibility, lost in some maze that wore an ancient cloak, alone completely. He would die.

Then he heard something terrifying: from close by, it was the raspy, dryly cracking rattle of a poisonous snake; it released an almost archetypal toxin of fear into his system.

Thirty-nine

THESE WERE DIFFICULT DAYS for Red. He could do so much and then had to let go, sit back and trust the others to execute his plan. He couldn't, as Amy had said of her father, indulge in his capacity to overmanage. He had to trust. Would Bob read the clues correctly? Would he show up as predicted? Would the damned Duane Peck be able to bring off *his* end or would the man's stupidity and impetuousness bring them down? Would Jack Preece hit the shots that needed to be hit? Would the old man, the scrofulous, nasty Jed Posey, hold together in a long session with Bob?

Ironically, of them all, Red trusted Posey the most: he was familiar with the type, the prison rat so hardened by a life lived at the extreme end of existence he'd been turned into some Nietzschean thing, a being so intense and one-pointed he hardly had any other life left him except the life of duty.

The other irony was that this whole thing even now, as it had for so long, completely delighted him. It was . . . remarkably fun. Such a clever plot, so astutely calibrated, based on such an intense analysis of Bob's character. Really, truly a masterpiece.

"Red, you're away."

That was Jeff Seward, first operating vice-president of Fort Smith Federal. The others in the foursome were Neil James, of Bristow, Freed, Bartholomew and Jeffers, Attorneys-at-Law, and Roger Deacon, of McCone-Carruthers Advertising Agency. It was the weekly golf foursome of the Fort Smith Rich Boys Club, at Hardscrabble Country Club off Cliff Drive.

And Red was indeed out and Jeff was indeed delighted.

His ball lay a long fifty-three feet from the pin. Between it and the hole was a wilderness of elevations, switchbacks, slopes and bare spots. It was the eighteenth hole: Red had shot low, standing at a 71, but damned Jeff, who had never beaten him, was standing at a 72 and had hit an uncharacteristically nice approach shot that had deposited him a few feet from the pin. His one-putt would put him out at 73; Red's two-putt would leave him at 73 also— *damn!*—and if he three-putted, a distinct possibility, he'd lose. The image of Jeff's smirk filled him with dark rage, which he enjoyed because it cut through the mesh of anxieties that he otherwise had suffered.

Jeff was an old friend and enemy; he'd played on the same Razorback football team with Red in the early sixties, and had at least kept up with him in the wife department, trading in an older model on a newer one every fifteen years, though he'd never reached—and never would—the beauty pageant level as had Red. They'd been in and out of business deals a dozen times and made at least four or five million off of each other's friendship and connection. But . . . golf was thicker than blood. Red did not want to lose.

He approached the ball and knelt to read the green. Around him the vivid beauty of the course expressed itself in full vertiginous glory, the most agreeable golf course in West Arkansas and better than all of the courses but one in Little Rock.

So Red looked across the ball into a treacherous maze of possibilities. He glanced at his watch. It was late. Suddenly, he felt a strange thing, a collapse of will. It was as if his warrior's spirit, which had sustained him these many years, had suddenly vanished. He didn't want to putt out. He wanted to lie down.

I am getting old, he thought.

He read the putt as a left-to-right crosser and knew it demanded courage above all else. It would seem to die a half dozen times, seem to quit and sputter or slide off into irrelevancy, would live a whole odyssey of adventures before it even got in the neighborhood of the cup. You had to hit it hard. You had to believe. You could not shirk or flinch or whine: go at it like a man and live or die, like a man.

"That would be a hell of a putt, Red," said Jeff.

"You wouldn't want a side bet, would you, Jeff?"

"Hmmmmm," considered Jeff. "Something in the neighborhood of—oh, a grand?"

"A grand it is, bubba," said Red, smiling wolfishly and setting himself up. "Did I ever tell you boys about the time I took three grand off Clinton? That's why he won't play with me no more!"

Damn!

The buzz of the vibrator on his beeper.

"Scuse me, gents."

He stepped off the green and took his folder from his caddie. He punched up the phone mail and heard Duane Peck's breathless voice: "Call me. Fast."

Red punched the number in.

"Mr. Bama?"

"Yes."

"It's working. I just dropped Preece off. The old man's got 'em in there. I'm holding now at the fallback point, waiting for Preece to dust them. By God, it's going to work! They're here!"

Red's heart filled with joy! He was so close and it would all be over: another threat to his empire and its little secrets defeated. Life, its own beautiful self, would go on and on and on: he'd put all his children through college and maybe, in a few years, when the Runner-up wore down, he'd gracefully retire her to some country mansion and get himself the actual thing he wanted more than anything: a true, authentic Miss Arkansas, young, hot and nubile. Wouldn't that beat all!

"Duane, you call me the second it is over, do you understand?"

"Yes sir, I do."

Red handed the folder back to the boy and remounted the green.

"Good news, Red?"

"The best."

"Another million for Mr. Bama," said Neil James, "and that means another twenty thousand in billing for me."

"Boys," said Red, "when the big dog's happy, *everdamnbody's* happy."

He addressed the putt, filled to the eyeballs with blazing confidence.

"Jeff, you want to make that five grand, even up?"

"Hell, Red," said Jeff, "I'se hoping you'd let me off the hook on the grand!"

Everybody laughed except Red, who bent into the putt and laid the considerable pressure of the Bama concentration against it, until he thought he'd explode. Then, almost reflexively, with a sharp rap, he struck the ball, wrists stiff, head down, shoulders loose, a perfect putt built on courage, iron determination and $100,000 in golf lessons over the years.

Like Xenophon's lost Greeks, it wandered across the Persia of the green, this way and that, up mountains and down into lush green valleys, seeming to die at least twice but always getting over the next crest on the apparent delusion that the sea lay ahead. At last it descended, bouncing and gathering speed, and hit the cup, spun with a whiskery sound—and halted.

"Damn," said Red.

"Five grand!" shouted Jeff.

"It may drop still," said Neil.

Red stared at the ball, balanced on the very equipoise between hole and green, seemingly riding on nothing more than the sprig of loam fighting the ball's weight and preventing Red from achieving yet another triumph.

"If a jet'd come along and a sonic boom would hit, maybe it would drop," said Roger Deacon. "You could probably call the air force on your phone, Red."

"Damn," said Red.

"You could explode another car bomb," said Jeff. "That might loosen it."

But Neil had the best idea.

"Order it to drop," he said. "It knows who you are."

"Damn right," said Red. "Everybody does."

He squinted, assumed the position of an especially pugnacious bulldog and issued his command: "Ball! Drop!"

Damned if it didn't.

Red sat around the nineteenth hole with his fellow Rich Boys, choosing a very expensive twelve-year-old George Dickel Tennessee bourbon as the night's poison, finding himself in a boisterous mood. He said he'd let poor Jeff off the hook on his thousand if Jeff would just pick up the tab. Jeff agreed and Red set out to drink a thousand dollars' worth of Dickel. He wasn't celebrating too soon: he was trying to get a certain part of his brain disengaged from the drama that was surely playing out seventy miles to the south even now, in a forest battleground.

If he let himself think on it, he was sure he'd die. His heart would go into vapor lock; he'd pitch forward in rigor mortis and they'd have to cut him out of his golf shoes. He'd end a joke: the total golfer who died in a bright red (his favorite color) Polo shirt and a pair of lemon-yellow slacks.

"You okay, Red?"

"Yes I am. Tell that gal: another round."

"Red, you are so generous with my money," said Jeff, though not bitterly. "Damn, I have to give it to you. You always squiggle out. I got you on the goddamn hook and presto, you're off it!" But it was said in something like respect.

"Many a man has thought he had me on the hook, only to find out the hook was in him," said Red, as the girl deposited another Dickel straight up before him. He took a hit: blam. Hot, straight and tough, just the goddamn way he liked it.

"Hey, Red, got a question for you."

"Shoot, son."

"Have you heard the Holly Etheridge rumor?"

"Every goddamn one of 'em."

"No, I mean *the* rumor."

"Which one would that be?"

"It's all over town. He's your friend, you'd know."

"He isn't my friend. He went to Harvard. He ain't hardly *ever* come back to the old stomping grounds. Hell, he went to prep school in Washington, D.C. St. Albans School, I think. He ain't no Arkansawyer, I'll tell you that. I know him some."

"They say he cut a deal with old Mr. You Know Who, the front-runner. He'd drop out early and work behind the scenes . . . and that would get him the vice-presidential nomination."

Roger Deacon pitched in with a comment. "We have been his local media buyers for eighteen years, and believe me, if Holly Etheridge were going on the national ticket, we'd know it by now. You have to buy into prime time early. It's too late otherwise."

"You ain't thinking right, Rog," said Red. "It ain't a senatorial race. The buy would come from national party headquarters and not in his name. You check, and I'd bet you'll see the parties already got money down on the time they need, through one of the big Little Rock shops."

"So it *is* going to happen, huh, Red?"

"Neil, I ain't heard diddly about old Holly. He's too busy trying to fuck every living female between Maine and Southern California. I think he's made it through Illinois and is just starting on Missouri."

"I don't think he's given up his national ambitions," said Jeff. "His daddy gave him an order, and one thing about Holly, he *always* obeyed his daddy. I think I ought to give him a call. He'll probably end up looking for a good chief of staff. Maybe I'll be moving up to Washington."

"Shit, his team is set," said Red. "I shot sporting clays with Judge Myers a few weeks back, and he's the boy with the inside track. But he didn't say nothing."

"Holly may surprise us yet," said Neil.

"We made a hell of a lot of money off that goddamn road he wanted to build for his daddy, though," Red said.

"Hear, hear," cheered the Rich Boys, for they too had made money, even at some remove, from the $90 million that the federal government had poured into Arkansas to build the Boss Harry Etheridge Memorial Parkway down to Polk County.

It went on that way until eleven, when Red finally broke it up. Toward the end, as the booze wore off, he found himself becoming morose and mean-spirited. The vibrator on his beeper had not gone off.

What did it mean? What was going on? It was so goddamned *perfect*.

He pushed aside his fears and went to the car, but for the first time in years, his two obedient, discreet bodyguards irritated him, though they were so steely efficient there was no cause for the annoyance. They just bugged him tonight.

He said, "I'm going to the lounge, not home."

"Yes sir," came the reply, untainted by human emotion.

He climbed into the big S-class and turned right, down Cliff Drive and back toward the city, instead of left toward his big white house overlooking the airport. At the halfway point, he called the Runner-up.

"Hello?"

"Beth, honey, something has come up. I've got to nurse one through the night."

"Sweetie, are you all right?"

"I am fine. And soon, I'll be finer."

"Are you sure?"

Dammit, even *she* was irritating him tonight.

"Yes! Yes, everything is fine. You know what I want you to do? Plan a vacation. A nice one, the whole family, both families, Hawaii, we'll rent out a goddamned island to ourselves. Your mother, even. All right?"

"Yes, Red, honey."

"Your brother. He can come too. That's my babe."

He hung up, crossing Rogers, turning in toward town, took his next right and followed the progressively seedier Midland Boulevard until at last he came to Nancy's. His parking place was wide open, as usual, and he pulled into it. As he leaped out, his two bodyguards seemed to materialize from nowhere and took up position next to him.

He threw open the door and about six dreary drunks and four dreary pool players looked over at his magnificence and withered in it; he blasted through, telling Fred the night barkeep just one word: "Coffee."

In his lair, he felt a bit more relaxed. Here at last was a world small enough and known enough to be completely dominated. He sat at his father's old desk. He felt comfortable. He set his folder on the green blotter before him and willed it to ring: *Phone! Ring!* But unlike the golf ball of late afternoon, it did not obey him. What adventures could it be concealing? What extraordinary battle, what act of profane violence, what deliverance or destruction?

He tried to shut it out by concocting a plan to implement if he were to fail utterly.

Swagger lives. Swagger kills both men. No, worse, Swagger captures poor Duane, who spills the beans about the Bama connection. What would Swagger do next?

He'd come after me, he realized.

He leaned out and gestured to his bodyguards.

"It is very possible," he said, "that a very tough man will be coming after me in the next few days. Not sure, but possible. Therefore y'all will need to be at your absolute tops. Understood?"

"Yes sir," said the talkative one.

"We go into Condition One, all the way. We'll need support teams, aerial surveillance, motion detectors, the works. I ain't going to give it up without a fight."

"We'll get him, sir."

Maybe, he thought, that would be better: face it, do it, get it over with. He and Swagger, man-on-man.

Then he laughed.

Swagger was too good. That would be suicide.

He looked at the phone.

Damn you. Ring!

But it wouldn't.

The hours leaked by. He read the papers, tried to work on his books, had a lot of coffee, watched some TV on a ratty black-and-white. He may even have dozed for a time, for it seemed that there was a moment when it was dark followed by another moment when the dawn was suddenly breaking. He went out, looked down the broad boulevard that was still lifeless. Odd, even a slum like north Fort Smith could look pristine and wondrous in the first wash of moist, dewy light. But he knew his sentimentality was phony, more a function of stress and exhaustion than genuine feeling.

Now he began to feel sorry for himself. It went with the territory, the long night nursing through a crisis that he himself was incapable of influencing at this point, one which he must fight with surrogates.

He mourned his father, that great man. He wondered again at the great bitterness of his life: who had killed him? He missed his two wives and his five children. He missed the boys at Hardscrabble, the men he hunted, fished, flew to Super Bowls and occasionally caroused with. He mourned his life: was someone going to take it away from him now? At least his children would know who killed him, more than he knew of his own father's death. He saw Swagger as a pale-eyed avenger, a figure of death, come to take it all away. Part of him yearned to fire both barrels of that expensive Krieghoff into Swagger and blow him to shreds. He calculated: two blasts of Remington 7½ from five feet, that's almost sixteen hundred pieces of bird shot delivered at over 1,200 feet per second, hitting him that close, before the shot column opened up into a pattern but instead traveled through space with the energy and density of a piston. Wow! Total destruction.

But in the end, he weakened. His warrior spirit was spent. His dick was soft and would never be hard. He needed sleep, he needed help.

He faced the phone. It was nearly seven.

I can take it no more.

I have to know.

He dialed Duane Peck's number. The phone rang once, twice, three times, and Red feared that catastrophe had occurred. His heart bucked in terror.

But on the fourth ring Peck answered.

"Yeah?"

"What's happening, Peck?"

There was a pause that seemed to last an epoch in geological time as ice ages rolled down from the north, then retreated, whole species were created and evaporated, civilizations rose and fell, and then Peck said, "It's over. Got 'em both."

"Goddammit! Why didn't you call me?"

"Ah—" began Duane.

"I told you to follow orders *exactly*. Don't you get that?"

"Yes sir," said Peck. "Sorry, I—"

"Is the general all right?"

"Yep."

His heart soared in gratitude and intense pleasure.

"Bury the bodies, get the general home and disappear for a week. Call me next week. I want a full report."

"Yes sir," said Peck.

Red snapped off to the dial tone, the most beautiful sound he'd ever heard.

Forty

R USS HAD AN INSTANT of clarity: he thought, I've finally done it. I've pissed him off so bad he's going to beat the
shit out of me.

For even as the snake's rattle registered in his brain, Bob had
turned and driven savagely into him, knocking stars into his brain
behind his eyes, taking his breath from him, forcing him in a wild
plunge to the precipice of the creek bed where he panicked at the
instant surrender to gravity. Yet through his fear as he fell, literally
in Bob's arms, toward the black cold water, he heard one other
thing.

This was the sound of a whip crack next to his car, for the air
was full of buzz and fury, a sense of presence that Russ couldn't
identify, for it had no real antecedent in his life. And as he fell
toward the water he also noted the appearance of explosions of
some sort, on the far bank, geysers of earth spouted upward, filling
the air with grit and dirt, but fastfastfastfast, so fast he couldn't
believe it and—

The water was cold. It knifed through him. He shivered like a
dog, breathed some in (it tasted like cold nickels in his throat), and
he fancied he saw black bubbles climbing until he broke free of
Bob and started to rise, but Bob had him again and smashed him
forward into the bank as three more silent blasts erupted into the
dirt above and seemed to turn the darkness gray with haze and
dust to the tune of three more whip cracks.

Russ had come to rest in the lee of the shallow bank. It was about a foot deep, a narrow gulch. The water cascaded over him, swift and numbing. He gasped for air and understanding.

"Sniper," hissed Bob. "He's up there on the elevation above the path. Infrared. The snake, Russ. I heard the snake."

All was silent except for the rush of the cold, cold water over their limbs.

"Fuck," said Bob. "Ain't he a *smart* one, though."

"Can you see him?"

"Russ, he's got *infrared*. He can see us. We can't see him."

Russ rose as if to peer over the lip of the bank, but Bob pulled him back.

"He can shoot your eyes out. He can see *you*. You can't see *him*."

"It was so close."

"What you heard was sonic boom. He has a silencer. You can't hear his muzzle blast."

It dawned on Russ where they were: no longer in the precincts of paranoia, where every living thing seemed a threat, but in the actual universe of hurt, where every living thing *is* a threat. This was it, then: the ultimate existential horror of the sniper's world— to be hunted in a dark forest by an invisible antagonist who could see you when you couldn't see him, who could fire without giving his position away and to be, yourself, unarmed.

Not unarmed: Bob had his .45 out.

"Can you get him?"

"Not likely. He don't have to close. *Fuck!* Smart motherfucker."

"Who is it?"

"What the fuck difference does it make?"

But then he knew.

"Preece. It's his specialty. *Goddamn.* So smart."

"Preece! How—"

"Don't think about that now. Think about where we are, what we got."

"We're going to die, aren't we?"

"I don't know."

"I don't want to die."

"Welcome to the club, sonny."

In the dark, Bob's features screwed tight in concentration. He looked both ways up the creek bed, threw himself into the problem, searching his mind to recall the terrain that lay between himself and the car, where he had a rifle.

"All right," he said. "Here's the deal. You work your way up the creek bed, about a hundred feet. You stay low, you stay in the water. He's scanning right now. I'm going to work my way in the other direction. In four minutes, when you're set, I'll make my move and try and draw him away. When I go, loudly, you go softly, back—"

"To the cabin?"

"No! There's nothing there but death. You back up into the woods and find someplace to go to ground. I don't want you moving in the dark. He'll find you. Remember: *it's a light.* A black light, but a light. If you ain't in the light, he don't see you. Then, in daylight, that rifle is more of a problem than a help. Here."

He gave Russ the compass.

"This'll get you through the woods. After first light, you make good tracks. There's a hill behind us, I don't want you going up it. You cut back around it. Then you head due west by the compass, and soon enough, maybe fifteen miles, you pass Iron Fork Lake; five miles past that, you'll come to 271. You call the cops, you tell 'em what's happening. Meanwhile, I'll try and make it back to the car and get my rifle. Then I'll hunt this motherfucker down and fucking *nail* him."

His face was a hard mask, set in stone and psychotic anger.

"He'll kill you," Russ said, the simple truth. "You don't have a chance against his stuff."

"It ain't the gun, sonny. It's the operator."

Preece felt neither rage nor panic. He did not curse his luck or wonder what could possibly have alerted the two and caused them, in some incredible way, literally to disappear as his first brilliantly placed shot rocketed toward them. He recovered quickly, but they spilled into the creek bed exactly as he reacquired them and his next four rounds puffed against the far bank.

In the circle of the scope, in the cone of black light, it was bright as green noon. There was some verdure reflection but not much: it was like peering into a tinted photographic negative, a soupy, almost aquamarine world brilliantly illuminated by the infrared searchlight.

He scanned up and down the creek bed, knowing that Bob would realize that to stay put would be to die. Bob would have to make some kind of move: it was his nature. Now, how would he go? The creek bed was like a narrow trench about three hundred feet long at this point, and only deep enough to sustain cover for about one hundred feet. He could snake out either end, or he could go over the top, fading into the woods. But that would take him straight against the incline of the far hill; he'd be staked out against the rise like a butterfly on a pool table.

No, Bob would go out either one end or the other, and that was the problem with Preece's system. It depended on a beam of invisible light, which gathered strength by focus. It was not powerful enough to illuminate both ends of the creek. Therefore, he had to scan continuously, covering the one, then the other—or figure out which one Bob would choose. It occurred to Preece to move lower down the slope to lessen the angle to the trench: in that way, he'd narrow the degree of muzzle arc he'd have to cover from one end to the other. But at the same time, suppose Bob moved when he himself was moving? Could he recover to shoot in time?

No. Stay put. Be patient. You have the great advantage. Do not squander it. Be strong, keep the heart hard. Keep scanning.

Then, at the far end of the trench, back toward the cabin, he saw a target. The cross hairs came onto him. Head shot, he thought. Very carefully, Preece began to take the slack out of the trigger.

Russ watched Bob slither away down the creek bed, totally animal now, feral, intense, driven. Bob was out of sight quickly in the dark, and he moved so expertly he made no noise. It was his gift: he vanished.

Now Russ was alone. A great aching self-pity came over him. He did not want to be here, he did not want to be alone in the dark, with a world-class sniper with world-class gear hunting him.

He looked up and down the creek bed, feeling the numbness of the cold eat into him, looking desperately for at least the energy to obey his meager instructions, which were only to position himself farther up the bed, wait for Bob to make his move, then slip away.

He moved tentatively along, discovering in his twenty-second well-fed year what every infantryman learns in his first week of duty: that crawling along the ground, particularly through mud and water, over rough stones with somebody trying to kill you, is quite unpleasant. It is in fact sheer misery.

Russ shivered as the water bubbled and frothed against his face. He slithered noisily through it, fighting for leverage, slipping occasionally. He scraped his numb fingers raw on the rocks. He was so *cold*!

At one point he lay, gasping for air. He looked back down the waterway and saw only the glint of the liquid and the claustrophobic walls of the creek bed. Ahead: more of the same. An immense depression came and sat upon his shoulders. He just wanted to curl up in a little ball and go to sleep. He wanted Mom and Dad and Jeff to tell him he was all right. He wanted to be in that beat-up little house on the outskirts of Lawton, with his fat old dad on the sofa watching football and drinking beer and his mother in the kitchen working like a dog and his brother just come in from hitting a home run, and he himself upstairs, reading Nietzsche or Mailer or Malamud or whomever, and feeling infinitely superior but also infinitely connected to them.

Fuck, he thought. I am turning into Dorothy. There's no place like home.

He clicked his heels together three times but it didn't work: he was still in the Oz of the Ouachitas, alone, with a wicked witch with a rifle trying to track and kill him.

He squirmed ahead another thirty or forty feet. Suddenly, he realized: I am out of creek bed. This is it. This is where I ought to be.

He gathered himself for a rush and someone spoke to him.

"Time for some cappuccino, motherfucker, heh, heh, heh."

It was Jed Posey, with his shotgun.

❑ ❑ ❑ ❑

Bob looked at his watch. The minutes hustled by. Three minutes thirty, three forty, three fifty.

From where he lay, half in and half out, he could see nothing, though to a sniper the dark itself has textures and may be read like a map. He knew where the hill was across the path because the black there was dense and impenetrable; there was enough illumination in the sky that he could read or sense the horizon at the top of the hill. To his left, the forest rolled away, essentially downhill, the path zigging off.

Bob knew he had about two hundred naked yards to go, uphill, then over the crest, moving through a screen of trees. It was too far. It was too damned far.

Fifty he might make, a hundred at the farthest reaches of luck. But two hundred to the point where he could fade into the forest past the crest and in its protection beeline north to intersect the logging road where the car was hidden: no, too far. Nobody would be that lucky.

Three fifty-five.

It was a lousy plan. It was a terrible plan. Why had he committed to it? He now saw it made better sense to go to hide right here, at this end. Then maybe, in the dawn, Preece or whoever would have to come and investigate. He might get into range with the .45 and Bob could take him.

But he hated that plan too. Preece would come at night, and he'd come with his black light blazing, and there was no place Bob or Russ could hide and he'd see them, cowering in the water, and from fifty yards out he'd do them both, easy as pie.

You have to move or you'll die.

He tried to remember. Was he this scared in Vietnam? Was he this scared *ever*?

Everyone thought he was such a hero, such a cool hand in the insanity of a gun battle. He didn't feel heroic. He felt like a little boy when Major Benteen comes and tells you your daddy is gone and the loss sits upon you and you face the universe totally alone.

I am alone, you think, and it scares you.

I am so alone, Bob thought: then he thought of his wife and his daughter.

I will get back! he thought, and with that he launched himself, screamed "Preece" loud as he could and started to run.

"You know what'd happen to you in prison, puppy? Them old cons'd use you like a gal. You'd be a gal, in prison."

Russ cowered at his feet, still in the rushing water, freezing, trapped.

"Please don't hurt me," he begged. It wasn't *The Wizard of Oz* anymore. It was *Deliverance*.

" 'Please don't hurt me,' " laughed Posey.

"I never did anything," whimpered Russ.

"Damn, ain't that the way it always happens?" said Posey, scrofulous and old, so rancid of odor that Russ could smell him even now.

"Bye, bye, Maryjane," said Posey, lifting the shotgun. "Here comes both bar—"

An interesting thing happened. As he was speaking, the upper half of Posey's head, that is, from the nose up, simply vaporized into a cloud of mist, as if it had been somehow squirted away by a giant atomizer. There was no sound, there was no agony or death spasm, it was simply that in a nanosecond a living man became a totally dead one, the instant rag doll, as Jed Posey imploded like one of those poetically rigged buildings where the explosives knock out all the weight-bearing girders and the thing dissolves downward into its own rubble.

So it was with Posey, who melted downward ("I'm melting," Russ thought incongruously, returning to Oz), spun and in a second had fallen with such loose-limbed thunder that when his crownless skull hit the ground, it sent a spray of brain gobbets and plasma spattering into Russ's face. It was raining brains!

Ycccch!

He bolted backwards and puked for several seconds.

Then he cowered in the water.

No way he was going *anywhere.*

Preece knew from Nam what it looks like on the green scope when you hit. He saw the exact second the shot hit the brain and blew it out, noted the instant of utter stillness that came across a body from which life has just been ripped. A white, glowing spume expelled from the stricken skull; the body fought the inevitable for a split second, then yielded to death and collapsed into the creek bed.

One down.

Bob?

Probably the boy.

At that moment came the call "Preece" from the other end of the creek bed and Preece cursed, recognizing Bob's tone in it, and pivoted swiftly to track the man down. But Bob was outside of the field of fire of the hide—*dammit!*—and Preece lost a valuable second deciding what to do and another one or two in the actual doing of it; with a stout elbow, he punched aside the plastic roof of the hide and sat upright, dragging the rifle with him. It took still more seconds to reorient as his target now lurked in the range of forest and slope just beyond the hill.

He brought the rifle to his shoulder and the scope to his eye and through its lens began to scan. He pivoted back and forth, in and out, listening intently, waiting for the device to yield a treasure, for surely Bob was out there, running crazily outward, toward the crest of the next low ridge.

Damn! Nothing.

He blinked, wiped his eye, reset the rifle and began again to pivot, now cursing that he had active IR instead of ambient-light or passive IR technology, for it made him dependent on the range of the IR searchlight atop his scope. He looked for indicators: wavering bushes, crushed undergrowth, dust in the air, all of which might signify that the man had come through.

Then he had him. Bob was zigzagging toward the crest, near it, but Preece had him, could see him, nearly two hundred yards out and at the ragged edge of the black light's ability to illuminate. He laid the crosshairs on the man, waited to take the tremble out of the sight picture until the reticle sat perfectly astride the shoulder blades and pressed the trigger.

❑ ❑ ❑ ❑

Bob ran like a crazed man, zigging this way and that, trending north toward the crest of a ridge. He ran blindly through the dark trees, beyond caring what came at him. Branches cut his face, slashed at his arms, snarly roots tried to bring him down, sending him spinning at one point nearly out of control. He ran in darkness, and all his wounds screamed at him. He ran in fear, and all his doubts began to yell at him.

He could not will his imagination to cease: he saw it, a man in a ghillie suit with a big, silenced rifle, superbly accurate, drawing a bead, taking the slack out of the trigger, sending a bullet through him. The sniper sniping the sniper. Something enraged him about this: *he* was the man on that end of the rifle, and now he was the man being sniped.

Oxygen debt clawed at him; shrapnel from an old wound seemed to have worked its way free; loose glass ground and clicked in his stomach.

He could see the crest line just a few yards ahead but the trees thinned and he hated his nakedness, his gunlessness, his terrible vulnerability. Just a little bit more and yet as he moved from the trees to the open area just at the crest, the huge weight of intuition clamped down on him.

If Preece was going to shoot, this is when he'd do it.

Involuntarily, Bob went to the earth.

Sonic booms filled the air. The sound clapped loud and when the rounds struck the ground, they yanked up huge gouts of dirt and he could hear the whine of ricochets spiraling away.

He's shooting, goddamn him, thought Bob, low to the ground and squirming desperately through the vegetation.

He crawled like a madman, for surely Preece would be scoping the area where he had to be.

Preece couldn't see him, but he could feel him.

Recon by fire.

Every three or four seconds, Preece put out a probing round. There was the close-by *crack!* and the earth suddenly erupted as a bullet tore into it.

Bob found cover behind a tree which might stop a bullet or might not. He crawled to his feet.

CRACKkkk.

A bullet struck nearby, filling the air with dust.

Behind him: *CRACK.* Another one.

Bob stood behind the tree, as still as he could hold himself.

WHACCCCKKKK.

Preece put a bullet into the tree; it exited an inch in front of Bob's face, spewing slivers of wood and bark as it blasted outward. He blinked blood away and saw lights flash as his optic nerves fired off. A tongue of pain licked through his brain.

Oh, Christ, Bob thought. He's seen me.

He stood very still.

Would the sniper fire again? If he fired again, the bullet would go through the tree and hit him. Would it have enough velocity to kill him?

Nothing could be done.

You just stood there, your ass on the line. If he fired again into the tree, the bullet would hit Bob and, yes, would kill him.

Please, he prayed. Get me out of here.

WHACCCCCKKKKK!

Another round tore through the tree; something stung Bob in the arm and made him flinch furiously. The bullet had torn through the dead center of the tree but, as bullets will by the alchemy of velocity, terminal energy, rotation and target density, had somehow deviated off the true and deflected enough to tear a furrow in an arm. It must have missed his body by a half an inch.

Would he shoot again?

Run, he told himself. Run like hell, get away from here.

But he knew if he ran he was dead.

CRACKkkk.

A bullet tore into the ground ten yards behind him.

The sniper fired again, farther away still. He was probing another area.

Bob heard a last shot, maybe thirty yards away.

How big was the cone of his light? Maybe not that big.

Without willing it, he broke for the crest.

CRACKkkkk.

The bullet broke the earth just to the right of him, kicking up a wicked spout. But he dove and launched himself, feeling achingly vulnerable, and landed beyond the crest as *CRACKkkk,* another round tore into the ground.

He was beyond the crest.

He was safe. He lay there, breathing hard.

Damn!

Preece thought possibly he'd hit him, but couldn't count on it. The reticle had been dead center as the man leaped over the crest but he had a memory, a sensation, that his trigger finger may have rushed, just enough to pull the aim off.

Now what?

One down, now what?

A certain part said: Disengage. It's over. You've lost the advantage. He knows you're hunting him, he can hide a hundred places and ambush you.

But another part reminded him that Bob had yelled his name and figured out who was coming for him. He would come again.

Preece decided: move forward aggressively, set up on and scan the ridge. You still have the advantage in the dark. You can overtake him in his flight and still get the nice clean shot between the shoulder blades.

He stood, removed the magazine and reseated a fresh one with nineteen more 5.56s in it. Time to go to work.

He moved out, at the trot, and swiftly traversed the two hundred yards to the ridgeline, and set up again. Very carefully he scanned the two hundred yards ahead of him. He could see no sign of Bob, but on a far crest line, where it should have been still in the night, a bush still quivered as if something had brushed it in blind panic.

He's on the run, thought Preece.

His past flared up before him, all his regrets, his mistakes, the terrible things he'd done, the shame he felt, his weaknesses, his failures, his rancid uglinesses. The forest was his own mind with all its crudities and barbarities, its insensitivities, its selfishness, its indulgences, its cruelties. He couldn't stop running and he hated running; he'd never run before in his life and now he couldn't stop.

Panic flared through him. He didn't want to die. He had a wife, he had a daughter, he had a life: now, after three tours and the terrible business in '92, *now* he was going to die.

Please don't let me die, he thought, abject and broken.

He crossed a ridge, dropped for a second. Had he been running mindlessly? Was he lost? Could he just drop and wait for the dawn and come out in a few days? He could get out, get in the rental car and speed away for Arizona. He could forget all this. The hell with it. What was the point? No matter what happened it wouldn't bring his father back.

He rose, ran again, directionless.

But no, not really: he knew he was trending due north, for that was the Dipper above and at its farthest point, the North Star, the lost man's only and truest friend.

He ran farther, through dense shortleaf pines, through tangled scrub oaks and briers and vines, up ridges, at one point through a creek. He fell once too, stumbling on a root that pitched him forward, scraping his hand, ripping his knee. He lay there, on the edge of exhaustion, feeling as ancient and as doomed as the Egyptians.

I am fifty goddamned years old, he thought, *and I ain't going to make it.*

But somehow he rose and kept going through the dark and dreamy forest, now up another ridge, now down another one. Ahead he saw a white, winding river, glowing ever so in the dark, and ran toward it, fled toward it, feeling the hot sweat race down his chest and neck, sensing his own hot smell rising, finding some kind of left-right rhythm that recalled the far-off cadences of a Parris Island drill field, and all the Jodie chants, how Jodie was fucking your girlfriend but he never had a girlfriend and how Jodie was the pride of your mama and your daddy, but both his mama and his daddy were dead. So who was Jodie anyhow, and why did he have it in so bad for poor marine recruits trying to master the intricacies of close-order drill on a pitiless South Carolina field, assaulted by men with leather lungs who tried to make them feel like maggots?

But Jodie came through here as then. Hating Jodie somehow liberated a last squirt of adrenaline from a secret gland store in his body, and he hit the river only to find it was a river of dust: it was the road.

He crossed it quickly, without a thought to security, suddenly realizing he was far enough ahead of his pursuer. He faded into the underbrush, following the road from twenty feet off it, gathering strength and passion with each step.

At last he saw it: a little brown rented Chevy. Would they have set up here? Were there more than one? No, there couldn't be. One man, a good man, hunted him, not a team.

He ran to the car, got the key out: opened the trunk.

He grabbed the Mini-14, flicked the scabbard away so that the gun itself was in his hands. Then he dug through the bag, thinking that he had one, yes, one more, and here it was, a last box of "Cartridge, 5.56mm, M-196 Tracer." He broke the box open and quickly threaded the rounds into the forty-shot magazine, twenty of them. Then he broke open another box, "Cartridge, 5.56mm, M-193 Ball," and slipped five in atop the twenty tracers.

He racked the bolt, felt a round feed. He was armed.

He knelt, put his fingers into the loam and came up with dirt, which he smeared abundantly on his face, to take the brightness off. There was a bandanna in the old bag too, and he tied it swiftly around his head, to keep the highlights of his still-blondish hair from glowing. He needed one more thing.

How do you fight infrared? What is infrared? It is heat. It sees heat. You have to fight it with heat. You have to fight its fire with your fire. At last he found the last thing: the gallon can of Coleman fluid for the lantern.

He picked it up, feeling its liquid-sloshing weight and terrible awkwardness, but that couldn't be helped.

He slammed the trunk shut.

All right, he thought, *time to hunt.*

Forty-one

PECK SAT IN THE FOREST, slouched atop the ATV in the dark. He was in the middle of a serious crisis of confidence. His imagination soared with negative possibility; he felt himself growing shaky, testy, rancid. He kept looking at his watch, willing the numbers to melt more swiftly into other, later numbers. But they were stubborn boys: they'd hardly moved a notch since the last goddamned time he'd checked, three minutes ago. This was going to be a long night.

He rested in a hollow, a few hundred feet off the trail by which he'd brought the sniper into his territory. Around him towered huge trees that leaned gently in the breeze. But he could see exactly nothing and had no sense of space or distance. The nearby trees yielded merely to textureless black. He felt like he was hiding under a blanket and at any second someone could sneak up on him and put a bullet into him. He didn't like it a bit.

He spat a gob into the undergrowth. He listened. His only connection to what lurked around him was through his hearing. He knew: no news is good news. The sniper worked silently. If Peck started hearing things, happiness wasn't just around the corner.

And so far, he had to admit, so good. He heard the whisper of air, now and then the scream of something small and furry dying before its time, the hoot of the occasional owl, but nothing metallic or mechanical. That was good. That was very good. He knew sound traveled miles in this place under these circumstances and his worst fear—Bob silently dispenses with the sniper and then comes hunting him—couldn't come true.

He dreamed now of a simple pleasure: a world without this Bob Lee Swagger. That was the world he wanted, because in that world, with the patronage of Mr. Red Bama behind him, he at last had found his place, his niche. No redneck deputy with little education, gambling debts, dental bills, zero savings and an amphetamine habit. No sir: he would *count*. He could have a nice woman, a *place*. He'd be part of what he had always seen as "it," meaning people who knew what to do, people with friends and possibilities, instead of, as he was now, a little man out on a limb all by his own lonesome, no one to catch him if he fell, no one to care. He was on nobody's agenda: he was just an angry white man, and if he didn't take care of himself, who would?

Thus, when the first sound arrived, he went into denial. He convinced himself it didn't come. He had heard nothing. It was some trick of nature, out to hornswoggle him. But then it came again, this time classifiable by direction: it was from the north and it was the sound of metal striking metal, familiar but still unidentifiable.

He fought a bit of panic: what was it? He tried to search through his memory and the only image that seemed to associate itself with the sound was ludicrously automotive. It sounded somehow like someone working with a car in some way, possibly opening a trunk, then throwing things around inside the trunk.

He waited, listening so hard he thought his brain would explode. How could there be a car nearby? And how nearby was "nearby"? Then he remembered the dirt road north of here, about half a mile. He knew that Bob and the boy would have come by car and would have parked somewhere before they moved into the forest.

He looked at his watch: 9:43 P.M.

Could Swagger have made it all the way back to the car in that time? He waited for the sound of an engine, to signify that whoever it was, was moving out of the area, leaving him to his own mission.

But then he heard, louder than anything before, the solid crunch of metal locking into metal. He knew it instantly: a trunk lid being slammed.

Shit and goddamn.

He suddenly felt achingly vulnerable. The ATV was out of the question: he couldn't be bopping around the woods on a four-wheeled motorcycle, generating noise and exhaust, easy meat for all and sundry. Instead, he dropped off the vehicle and quickly calculated the point where the noise originated and the point where the sniper hid and thought to intersect them. If Bob was moving around in the woods he would be hunting a sniper, not any old poor nobody-gives-a-shit-about-him Duane Peck, with a chance to make his way in the world.

He didn't want to do it, but sometimes, as Duane well knew, *wants* don't have nothing to do with it. He flipped off his hat and began to night-navigate through the woods. He drew his Glock, repeating to himself what that Neechee had said: that which does not kill you makes you strong.

Bob tried to recall the terrain. Why do you never pay attention to the things that become so goddamned important? But he willed himself to recollect, and had a memory of what he thought would work best if the plan he'd cooked up were to have a chance. Wasn't there a place he'd noticed on the left, maybe half a mile in, where the trees thinned for a bit, opened to a clearing, possibly left over from a logging operation some years ago at the base of a ridge. Or was that from some goddamned dream? Would he just bumble around until he placed himself before the sights of the sniper, who would nail the Nailer?

He tried to press that out of his mind. He tried to think: What will Preece do? Will he follow me? Yes, he has to: but how aggressively? He'll dawdle, scanning the woods, afraid to get too close for risk of an ambush, knowing that he's got all the advantage if he doesn't blow it with overaggressiveness.

That's what I'd do.

Now: how to draw him toward me.

There was only one answer. He drew the Mini-14 to his shoulder, aimed it pointlessly into the dark and fired three times fast.

The gun cracked and flashed, spitting empty brass, lighting the vault of trees that curved overhead, kicking ever so slightly. The noise was loud, and in its echo a few sleeping birds screamed or flapped airborne, uncorking a sense that the night had been disturbed.

Bob wondered: is he close enough to see the flashes?

He didn't know, but now he'd informed his antagonist that he was armed. On dead reckoning he started to move to the left, praying that up ahead, just where he dreamed it was, the clearing waited.

Preece heard the shots, three fast ones, much less than a mile away. Though they were flat taps, without texture or resonance, he knew by the whipping crack that followed in their wake that they were supersonic, and therefore rifle bullets, not pistol bullets.

It had to be Swagger. He'd gotten to his car, gotten a rifle. From the swiftness of the fire, a semiauto, not a full auto, for they weren't quite fast enough and didn't have the deadening mechanical regularity of a machine gun. It sounded like an M-16 or a Mini-14, nothing big like an '06 or .308.

But more: Bob had panicked. He thought he saw something move and ventilated it. Now he cowered breathlessly, afraid that he'd missed, probably afraid to go forward. He'd move laterally, knowing that whoever was stalking him would move toward the sound. Or he'd fired deliberately, to attract whoever was hunting him.

Didn't really matter: the solution was the same.

You move left or right of the source of the noise, then set up, anticipating a target to come to your new front. If he's moved left, he comes right to you. If he's moved right, he'll come around you. But he'll be making the noise.

Preece drew a compass from his pocket and shot an azimuth to a tree on a ridge two hundred yards away. He flicked on the scope and took a last scan of the area, looking for movement in the black light of the infrared. Nothing but the shimmer of vegetation.

He left his position and moved swiftly to the tree. Setting up on the ridge, he scanned again, this time for several minutes. Nothing. Ahead, through the trees, he saw another ridge. He shot another azimuth to another tree, and moved to it, not rushing, not making undue noise, feeling relaxed, confident and aggressive. He was the only one who could see in the dark.

At the ridge, he looked down: a clearing. The trees ended halfway down the slope and yielded to a kind of meadow or something, where perhaps once there'd been a forest fire or some logging operations. Hmmm. It scared him. In the forest, he was invisible, but out there, possibly an experienced man might read his darker textures against the texture of the grass and send a shot home, even without night vision.

This perplexed him. Maybe Bob was playing some extremely subtle game on him. Whatever, the trees cut off a good view of the ridge. After scanning for several minutes to convince himself that Bob wasn't hiding on this side of the clearing, he moved stealthily over the ridgeline and, keeping trees between himself and the clearing, moved down toward the edge.

He was almost there when *krak krak*, two shots lit off across the clearing and he could see the vivid flash, not a hundred yards away. Was Bob shooting at him? But no rounds came whipping through the trees, and the supersonic *whisssh-crack* of bullets overhead didn't sound. He dropped behind the tree, scooted back into a solid prone and quickly brought the rifle to his shoulder, simultaneously going to IR. The rifle rested on the girders of his bones, not the uncertain power of his muscles: it was solid, and the reticle didn't drift or wander.

In the green scope he could see it all: the high grass of the clearing, undulating in the breeze just like the corn, the blunt verticals that were tree trunks and . . . yes, there he was . . . the man.

Bob the Nailer. He was on the other side, about as close in as Preece was, moving back and forth, evidently trying to decide whether or not to move across the field.

Preece put the crosshairs on him.

Mmmm, no. No, it was a hard shot, because he was wandering

back and forth between the trees, visible for only fractions of a second between them.

What the hell was he doing?

Now that he'd fired, he'd know Preece would be on him, but he couldn't know Preece was already here. Had he gone mad? Had he flipped out?

Then it occurred to him that he was hoping his fire would draw Preece and that maybe he could lure him into the field and gun him down there, where he was marginally visible.

Sorry, Bob: I'm already here. I have plenty of battery time, hours more. I can just watch you and when you get impatient and step out from the trees, I can take you down.

It was that easy.

He watched now as the glowing man settled behind a tree. He kept peering nervously out. He was waiting for Preece.

I can wait longer than you, Bob. I'm not going anywhere at all.

Peck heard the first three shots from far away, a dry sound, almost like a tapping. He gauged that they came from his right. Slowly, he began to move in that direction, scuttling between trees, taking up a good observation position before moving on.

He moved across the night terrain steadily, growing in confidence. That was Bob shooting, but not at him. Had he hit Preece? He didn't think so. The shots had more the sense of panic in them than anything.

He moved through the trees from ridgeline to ridgeline, taking cover at the top of each crest and scanning beneath him for signs of movement. But he saw nothing.

He was halfway up another ridge when he heard *krak krak,* two fast shots, maybe a quarter mile off and over to his left still farther. He climbed the ridge and could see nothing. But instead of descending, he decided to traverse the ridge and moved along it for a bit, until at last he saw, what, light? No, not light: openness. There seemed to be a clearing or something ahead. He scurried along the ridgeline and at last came to rest overlooking the field. This should be where the shots came from. He had a feeling that if something were going to happen, this is where it would happen.

❏ ❏ ❏ ❏

Bob peeked around the tree. He had no indication that any human eyes or ears were within a hundred miles of him. He felt alone on the face of the planet.

No, he told himself. He's there. He's tracked me by the shots, he's seen me move among the trees, he's there. He's all set up. Right now he's in a good, solid prone a hundred-odd yards out, he's got this tree zeroed, he knows he's got me.

But there was no snake to announce the sniper this time. That's because there aren't snakes *everywhere* in the forest. He had gotten a snake in the draw. He wasn't getting one here. He'd used up his snake luck. It didn't matter. Preece was there. He had to be. There was no other place for him to be.

He looked at his watch. It was close to ten. That's when my father died, didn't he? At ten, after a running fight. Some guy in the trees a hundred yards out puts the scope on him, pulls the trigger and goes home to cold beer and rare steaks.

Well, let's see what happens this time.

He pulled himself out, darted quickly between the trees, back and forth, drawing the sniper's scope to him, until he felt the crosshairs. But he was relatively confident the man wouldn't fire, because the trees interfered with his sight picture. Why should he shoot between them, when in seconds his target would step out into the open?

How long would it take? How quick would he shoot? Would he shoot fast? Yes, he'd shoot fast. He'd be on him like a flash, put the crosshair center mass and with a champion's long-honed trigger control, fire in a second.

One second.

No, two seconds.

He won't rush. There's no need to rush. He has it all, right there before him, there's no need to rush.

Two seconds.

You have two seconds, he told himself.

Bob leaned the rifle against the tree and picked up the gallon can of Coleman fluid. With his fingers he explored the can until at last he found the bottom. He took out his Case XX pocketknife, pried open the blade. Quickly, holding the can upside down, he punctured its metal skin right at the bottom three times on each side. The sound of the blade plunging into the sheet metal had an odd thrum of vibration to it.

He tossed the can out beyond the tree, where it hit, tipped, but gurgled as the volatile liquid inside poured out of the holes and soaked into the brush. He seized the rifle, listening as the fuel chugged out. It formed a pool and its vapor began to rise in a palpable mist, its stench washing over him. It would linger for a second or two, a balloon of gas without a skin.

Time to go, he thought, and stepped out.

It felt so familiar.

It was so like the first time. He's waiting, a hundred yards away, for a man to emerge. Except not from the trees but from the corn.

The weather was almost identical, and so was the time. It had the ache of déjà vu to it.

He knew it was close to time. Bob couldn't wait any longer. He had to move.

In the scope, against the green of the infrared, Preece saw him behind the tree, fiddling with something, possibly checking his rifle. An odd banging came, metal on metal, signifying what? He watched as something was launched from the tree and landed with a thud beyond.

Now, what the hell was that?

He grew impatient.

Come on, marine, he thought. Let's do this. Let's finish it. It has to be done.

At last Bob stepped out into the black light, which was green in Preece's scope, faced him frontally and appeared to step toward him.

Got you, thought Preece.

He placed the crosshair dead center of the chest and felt the trigger begin to slide back of its own volition, encountering just a whisper of resistance as it pressed against the internal mechanisms straining for release. It was a five-pound trigger; he had two pounds of weight against it, then three, then—

It was all gone.

The black light wiped white in harsh incandescence. What the hell?

He blinked hard, involuntarily drew his eye from the scope and looked into the heart of fireball that vaporized his night vision, detonating his optic nerves, filling the eyes in his brain with pinwheels, skyrockets, illumination rounds of sheer wild color.

Bob stepped out, his rifle in his left hand, his .45 held behind him in his right.

Hold it, he told himself, smelling the vapors.

One.

Hold it again, he told himself, as the vapors rose around him.

He felt crucified. He was on the cross. There was no help.

He fired the pistol.

It bucked in his hand: its muzzle flash ignited the column of vapor behind him as he dropped it. He felt the *whooosh* as the darkness ruptured with a blade of light so fierce and radiant that it bleached the colors from the forest and the field even as it briefly exposed them. Starburst, nova, supernova, the universe ending in fire.

The heat rolled across him and he felt his back pucker and blister as he fell forward.

Across the clearing, like a dog's eyes caught in the full light, two lenses captured the radiation from the fireball and reflected it back at him. They were stacked circles: the lens of a light-amplifying scope and the lens of an IF searchlight. But still they were the eyes of a beast.

Bob fired over his sights, not through them, aiming out of instinct, following the illuminated trajectory of his first round. The tracer flicked fast and a little low, kicking up some dirt. In a nanosecond he corrected, fired again, the tracer skipping across the distance so fast, a whipsong of illumination, and it went to the eyes and struck between them.

Fire for effect, he thought. That's in the book of countersniper operations: locate, then overwhelm with superior firepower.

He jacked ten fast rounds into the eyes, the tracers snaking over the clearing and plunging into the position across the way, a sleet of light. He threw darts of light, bolts of light, missiles of light, as he burned through the rest of the magazine, a controlled burst, three shots a second, walking the rounds across the position where the now vanished eyes had proclaimed themselves. The tracers struck and sunk, or they bounced crazily away, like flecks of an exploding star.

He looked and all about him, fires burned.

But he was done.

Jesus H. Christ.

Peck drew back, astounded at what he saw before him.

A column of flame, like the detonation of a bomb, gushed upward through the trees.

Then in a second, someone was shooting tracers. They dashed across the field fast, low and ugly, snapping remorselessly at the base of a tree on the far side.

He had a terrible suspicion that Jack Preece was on the receiving end of the fireworks.

His night vision was shattered, but enough of it came back in time to see a dark shape rush from the tower of flames, cross the clearing and close on the far position and bend to probe a body.

It was enough.

Peck knew he was overmatched.

Time to get the hell out of there.

Bob found Preece in his ghillie suit, looking like a sofa that had exploded. He lay on his belly, and Bob almost put a shot into him, but held up. The body was still, the fingers relaxed.

Fuck you if you can't take a joke, he thought.

He turned the body over. In the illumination of the fires flaring across the clearing, he saw that the man had taken at least four or five shots in the head and upper torso. Blood everywhere, the face smashed and broken.

Bob flipped the body aside; Preece was the ultimate step-on. Bob knelt to examine the weapon and saw quickly that it too was destroyed. A bullet had smashed the scope and another had shattered the lens of the infrared searchlight.

Now it occurred to him he was illuminated in the firelight. Maybe there was someone else around.

He felt no triumph or power but only the emptiness of survival. He moved out.

Forty-two

NOW WHAT?

It was first light and the sun had begun to filter through the black trees, turning them gray and then green.

Russ stirred painfully. His limbs were numb from the water that had washed over them all night. He tried not to look at Jed Posey, whose skull had been evacuated and now seemed like a queerly semi-deflated balloon.

He had no idea what was happening. Sometime last night, the sky had lit up for a second or so, as something huge and hot burned fast; there'd been gunfire too: a batch of rounds tapping out, almost fast as a machine gun, he thought.

But since then, silence.

He remembered his instructions. Wait until dawn. The sniper's rifle is worthless in the light as well as awkward and heavy, so you'll be safe. Then strike out due west, moving quickly. Six or seven hours away is the road, U.S. 71. Get into town, call the cops, tell everything to everybody.

And what about Bob?

No sign of Bob.

Possibly Bob was doing all that shooting, possibly not. Russ couldn't imagine a world without a Bob in it. It somehow seemed impossible.

He pulled himself out of the creek and climbed up the bank. He searched for the compass in his pocket, found it, held it level and

let it orient itself. Then he shot an azimuth due west, picked a
landmark at its end and started out for it.

The woods, in the increasing light, were quiet, green and oddly
lovely. Something about the freshness of the morning dew, the
sense of a long and bloody night past and having somehow survived it. Wouldn't this make a terrific book?

He wondered if he had the strength to write it. Maybe not now,
but after a few weeks' rest. He had an image: he'd take that job on
the Fort Smith paper, get a little place and work hard in his off
hours on the book. Maybe he could go up to Nashville, to Vanderbilt, and see Sam's granddaughter Jeannie, who—

Something crushed into Russ, knocking him flat. He thought it
was Bob, rescuing him, but the iron strength applied against him,
pushing his face into the loam, and the sudden spasm of pain as a
knee drove into his kidneys told him no.

He struggled pointlessly, as the larger, stronger man dominated
him toward submission. Another knee thundered into his kidneys
and sent a rocket of terrible pain up his body. He couldn't see: he
felt something hard and cold against the flesh under his ear, and he
then heard a voice:

"You move, you fucking whelp, and I'll kill you right here."

It was Duane Peck.

Something snapped around his wrist and then around his other
wrist.

He was handcuffed.

"Come on, baby boy," said the deputy, pulling him up. Peck
looked crazed, splotched with sweat, his hair a damp mess, his eyes
wild with madness. "We're going to meet your pal."

Bob crawled from the brush at first light. He thought hard about
his own next move and saw that attempting to intercept Russ in
the forest was pointless. Instead, he decided to move back to the
car, escape the immediate area and set up somewhere on Route 71
where Russ would probably emerge around noon. Then they could
go get a good hot meal and return to base camp and figure out a
next move, whatever a next move might be.

He looked at his watch. It was about 6:30 A.M.

He had one subsidiary stop: to head back to the far side of the clearing, where he had to recover the Mini-14, a rifle that was traceable to him and whose spent shells would match the spent shells found on the roadside of the Taliblue Trail. That might lead to more explaining than he cared to do.

Warily, he looked around and in the gray but increasing light, could see nothing. There was no noise, except the occasional peeping of an awakening bird. A low mist clung to the ground, all the better.

He crawled from cover, reached back to check his .45 and then began to move low and zigzagging through the forest. Did he want to recheck the body?

No, he decided not to. If there was another man in the forest, one thing such a boy might do is set up there. He determined that there was no incriminating evidence at the body, nothing to connect him once he got rid of the Mini-14. The rifle was the important thing.

He approached from the southeast, slithered up to a fallen log and examined what lay before him. He could see no signs of human activity: only an undulating, wild clearing a hundred yards by a few hundred yards, crazed with knee-high grass and speckled with flowers. At the oblique, a scorched, blackened tree stood, where he had detonated the fireball. Lucky the forest was damp and the flames didn't spread. Very lucky. It was something he hadn't thought of in the craziness of the moment last night.

It's better to be lucky than good, he thought.

Carefully, he maneuvered around the perimeter of the clearing until at last he had returned to the site of last night's action. A few small fires still smoldered and he kicked them out. He stood in the core of the fireball: a blackened cylinder seemed to have been cut in the trees, but it would grow out quickly.

He went to the tree behind which he'd hid, and saw the rifle lying a few feet out in the high grass. He went quickly to it and lifted it. While he was out there, he collected spent shells and seemed stuck at nineteen, but then, remembering the sense of being pronged in the face by a shell ejecting straight back (it happens), he slid backwards and found the twentieth shell far from where the others had landed and, near it, the single .45 casing that had lit the fire. Shit, he'd forgotten that one. He stuck it in his jeans pocket. Then he remembered he'd fired twice more, to attract attention, back in the trees a bit. He moved back and had a little trouble at first, but then a glint of brass announced itself and he picked up one and, nearby, the other.

Shells at car, he thought: three of them. Pick them up too.

He took a quick look back. Across the way, he could make out very little of where Jack Preece lay. It occurred to him to bury the body, but he didn't have a shovel, he didn't feel like getting Preece's blood and DNA all over himself, and some forest animal would come along and dig it up, anyhow. If Preece was found, Preece would be found, and someone could have a field day coming up with a conspiracy theory as to how he got there and what he was up to. Some Johnnie would probably write another goddamned useless book on it.

He was set.

It was time to go.

He stood and began to move and then he heard something. Not sure what it was—a shout, a call, a squawk, something natural, something human?—he slid back, pulling out the .45, thumb rising to the safety, as the empty Mini-14 was now useless.

What the—?

He waited and it came again.

Yes, it was a human call, blurred and almost recognizable, from somewhere off to the left.

His eyes scanned the terrain.

He caught a flash of motion across the way, in the trees, and watched as it tumbled into focus, the awkward form of a man walking clumsily. He saw it was Russ, tumbling forward but yanked back, then pushed forward again. Bob made out the second man behind him, controlling him. It was Peck, of course.

Peck screamed again.

"Sniper! Come on and fight me, sniper, goddamn you."

Duane Peck saw his future in a second when the boy stumbled toward him. He would take the boy and through the boy take the sniper. In that way he would endear himself to Red Bama and the Bama organization and enjoy a life of respect, wealth, property and importance, everything he yearned for.

And the boy presented himself so easily, snot-nosed punk stumbling through the woods. Duane had subdued many prisoners in his time: the secret was leverage and meanness, one of which he obtained by surprise and the other of which he had always had, by genetics or environment. The boy captured, cuffed and pushed before him, he now had to determine how to handle Swagger. But it didn't take long to figure that out: the Glock had a hair trigger when you took the slack out of it; the muzzle held against the boy's head, the trigger gone back on itself as far as it could go, and he was invulnerable to any rifle shot, for a rifle shot would surely cause his finger to constrict and the boy would be dead too. That he knew about Swagger: he cared about the boy. He would not let the boy die.

He would draw Swagger to him, unarmed, and then simply shoot him. What could Swagger do? He could not risk losing the boy, that was his code, that was his weakness. It was the one thing that Duane knew better than his own name: attack through weakness. This was Swagger's; this gave him an advantage that neither the ten professional gunmen nor the night-vision-equipped marksman had. It was in fact the one advantage Duane Peck had always had and he knew it: he was willing to do the dirty work. He didn't have any illusions: he didn't mind the blood spatters and the screams. He could get through anything. He knew he could do it. He'd been spoiling for this chance his whole life.

He pushed Russ along savagely, not seeing him as human. He was full of rage and power, and felt at last he was coming into what was owed him for having put up with having so little for so long.

"Go on, you little fucker," he hissed, his mind foggy with anger. "You give me any shit and I will kill you right now."

"I—" the boy started, and Duane clubbed him hard with the gun, driving him to the earth, drawing a rivulet of blood down his neck and into his shirt.

He reached down and sank a hand into the boy's thick hair,

pulling his head back hard while putting his boot between the boy's shoulder blades, as if to break him on a rack.

"Yeah, you give me lip, you little bastard, and you will be sorry as a sack of shit."

He pulled the boy up to his legs and shoved him ahead.

"You moron," the boy shouted back at him, "he knows you killed Sam. He's been looking forward to this. He'll kill you dead cold."

Duane's breath left him; that wasn't a good sign. He felt adrenaline flare through him, and the urge to dump the boy, shoot him in the head and run like hell spiraled through the deepest and most frightened part of his mind.

But, no, goddammit, maybe the old Duane Peck, not the new one. This was it: his chance. Grab it and make it happen. Be strong.

"Git going, you little bastard," he hissed.

In what seemed like not much time at all, they reached the clearing. Duane held Russ close and looked about it. He could see nothing. Was Bob there? He didn't see him.

He shoved the boy ahead. They moved through the grass into the clearing. Duane started hollering.

"Come fight me, Swagger! Come on, goddammit, or I will kill this boy right here. Come on, you gutless asshole, come and fight me!"

But nothing happened.

"See, he's chickenshit," he said to the boy. "You say he's a man, but he ain't. He likes to kill people from a long way off and scurry away like a little toad. But when it comes to man's work, by God, his little dick gets small and goes away."

He paused.

"Come and fight me, sniper," he screamed again.

And then he saw that he was going to get his wish.

Across the way, he watched as a man emerged, tall and strong, and walked toward him with the slow and steady pace of a gunfighter.

"You're fucked," said Russ.

□ □ □ □

Bob had the .45 Commander cocked and locked over his kidney, not in the inside-the-belt holster, but wedged lightly between his jeans and his shirt, too delicately situated for vigorous action. It was set just so for one reason: to draw. He could see Peck hardly at all as he approached. Only Russ, his arms jacked tight behind him, was visible. The boy's face was pale with fear and he looked as if he were in great pain. Now and then Peck peeked around for a glance, but quickly retreated behind his human shield.

With a good rifle, Bob could have possibly hit the brain shot, but he didn't have one. He just had the .45 and he didn't like Peck's damned Glock with its tricky, dangerous trigger, its black snout pressed at the boy's temple.

It seemed to take forever, that long, slow walk through the grass across the clearing. The sun was shining through the trees. The birds were singing. The grass ruffled in the breeze. It looked to be a glorious, radiant Arkansas summer day.

Get in close, he told himself. *You get in close, then you get ten feet closer.*

He kept moving.

Am I fast? he thought. *We'll see if I'm still fast.*

"That's far enough," called Peck.

"What?" Bob said, taking another few steps.

"I said *hold it!*" Peck bellowed, the gun coming off Russ's head and toward Bob.

Bob stopped and raised his hands, and the gun went back into Russ's neck, just under the ear. Bob was five feet away, close enough to see the whiteness of the taut index finger as it rode the trigger right to the breaking point and the way the square muzzle actually plunged a quarter inch into the soft skin in the gap between the boy's jaw and his skull, just under the ear. Russ's eyes bugged like deviled eggs.

"Ain't this a pretty picture," Bob said.

"Fuck you, Swagger," said Peck. "You are checking out today, partner."

"Shoot him," said Russ through a throatful of gun. "Shoot through me and kill him."

"You shut up now, Russ," said Bob. "Peck, this here's between you and me, isn't it? Let the boy go. Let him run free. Then you take your shot at me and we will see who's the quicker man today."

"I got a better idea," said Peck. "I shoot him and then I shoot you and then I go home a big hero."

"Who you working for?" said Bob.

"You ain't ever going to find out," said Peck.

Now and then he'd lean out from behind Russ, and just a bit, say a two-inch slice of the side of his face, would be clear, but only for a second. Like many stupid men, he was quite cunning. He was not exposing anything for Bob to shoot at, assuming Bob could even get his gun into play fast enough.

"Shoot him," screamed Russ.

"I got some money," said Bob. "I been financing this thing off a killing I made in a lawsuit years back. Got sixteen thousand left, small, unmarked bills. Buried not far from here. What you say, Peck? That money for the boy. Then you and I have our business. Winner take all. Might as well get paid."

Peck considered. The money was a little tempting. But nothing would keep him from his idea of the good life.

"No way," he said. "Turn around. Turn around or by God I shoot this boy, then take my chances with you."

Here it was. If he turned, Peck would shoot him, shoot the boy. If he drew, he might be able to hit Peck before he fired but the odds were against it. But he had to move. The time had come. He looked at Russ, who had his eyes shut and whose face had gone gray: he'd made his peace, like many a soldier who's about to die will do.

So here it was.

"Keep them hands up," Peck was shouting, more and more insanely, gone now, lost in madness, "and turn around or by God I will—"

A telephone rang.

Incongruously, there in the middle of the clearing, with the sun rising, Russ choking to death, Bob with his hands up, Duane Peck playing his last and grandest hand, the telephone rang.

Peck leaned out in surprise and Bob saw the confusion in his eyes as he tried to figure out what to do, and then in just a split second his eyes involuntarily veered downward to look at the phone on his belt and by the time they came back they were surprised to see not Bob but a blur of Bob, a Bob whose hands already seemed to have a gun in them and were moving so quickly up his chest and leveling toward him that there was no way to make a measurement or take a picture, and Peck tried to get the Glock over on him to catch up but knew he never could.

The bullet hit him in the right eye, crushing through it, bounding through the cerebrum, opening as it went, and plunged to the dense tissues of the cerebellum. The impulse to fire was trapped forever in his nervous system, never reaching his trigger finger. He fell backwards stiff as a bronze statue, his knees so locked that when he hit he bounced. The Glock thumped into the grass.

Russ was stunned by blast, his face peppered by flecks of hot powder, and one eye was blurred and watery. His ears rang thunderously.

He turned and looked at Peck, totally defunct.

One word came to his mind.

"Cool," he croaked.

But Bob was already kneeling at the man and had pried the ringing folder phone off his belt. He looked at it in terror. How did it work?

"The button under the earpiece, push it!" Russ cried.

Bob's quick hand reached it.

"Yeah?" he said gutturally.

"What's happening, Peck?" came a voice that he had never heard, an Arkansas voice, not without its polish and charm, though now undercut with urgency. Bob's mind emptied at the question. Then he said, in a slightly better imitation of Peck, "It's over. Got 'em both."

"Goddammit!" bellowed the voice. "Why didn't you call me?"

"Ah—" Bob began, but the voice plunged ahead.

"I told you to follow orders *exactly*. Don't you get that?"

"Yes sir," mumbled Bob, trying to keep himself bland and simple. "Sorry, I—"

But the voice had lost interest and shot ahead to new topics.

"Is the general all right?"

"Yep."

"Bury the bodies, get the general home and disappear for a week. Call me next week. I want a full report."

"Yes sir," said Bob.

The phone clicked to dial tone.

Forty-three

NICHOLAS BAMA, fourteen, was dreading his biology test, because he hadn't really studied for it—or at least to the degree he was expected to. He had small gifts for certain things—math, for example—but not for biology.

And Mr. Bennington, St. Timothy's School for Boys' entire biology department, was known as a mean and nasty sucker, even in the summer semester, which was saved for boys who possibly weren't up to the relentless course as part of their five majors during the regular academic year.

So Nick sat with a combination of self-loathing and anxiety in the school's lab, as Mr. Bennington, a large man who peered at the world through flat pale eyes over the half-crescents of reading glasses, bore down on him like the bad news that couldn't be avoided.

The test was distributed.

A word flashed from the text that terrified him: pith ray. Now, what on earth was a pith ray? It seemed somehow to touch something he knew, someway, somehow, but . . . pith ray? He felt his mind purge itself of its few torturously acquired biological concepts, yielding a great empty void.

Yet suddenly there was a commotion and he looked up astounded to see the headmaster, Mr. Wilmot, and his stepmother, the beautiful Beth, Miss Runner-up 1986, as everybody called her behind her back, earnestly conversing with Mr. Bennington.

"Mr. Bama?" spoke Mr. Bennington in his best fake English accent. "Your services are required."

Nick turned the test over and obediently trotted to the front of the room, the immediate envy of all the other non–biology geniuses in the lab.

"Well, aren't you the lucky boy?" said Mr. Bennington imperiously. "Saved from yet another brush with distinction. Madame, take him, he's yours, is he not?"

Beth didn't know quite what to do in the face of this Continental hauteur, but she managed her best thing, which was a smile of such glacial, aching beauty that its failure to impress Bennington proved for once and all the man was homo, and she nodded to Nick and out they went.

"Beth, is anything wrong?" he asked. "Is Daddy all right?"

"Keep the long face up, hon," she said conspiratorially, "I told them he was in the hospital. He's as right as rain."

Beth ushered Nick through the signing-out-of-school process, down the dank, frosty corridors—"It looks like a morgue, Nicky," Beth whispered, and it would, to a girl who grew up in a town called Frog Junction, Arkansas—and out into the sunlight, where her gleaming black Mercedes S-class awaited. Nick could see that he was the last pickup: Beth's own twins, Timmy and Jason, were in the backseat, looking grumpy for having been pulled out of soccer camp, Nick's older brother, Jake, lounging in the front seat, his hair a thistly unshowered mess, as if he'd just been roused from his bed (he had), and his oldest sibling, Amy, pert and pretty and perfect, looked, as usual, pissed off at being hauled out of her job at the tennis club by a stepmother who was closer to her own age than her father's.

"What's going on?" Nick asked.

"Oh, you know your father. He called me at nine and said 'Get the kids. All of 'em! It's time for a party.' "

"A party?" said Nick.

"Yes," said Beth, "a party. That's what he said. You know your father and his ways."

They drove through town and in twenty minutes Beth had driven them up Cliff Drive to Hardscrabble Country Club, of which their daddy was majority owner. It was a vast, baronial building, red ragged stone and gabled windows, set on the highest point in a lush kingdom of golf course and tennis courts and swimming pools. The doorman ushered them in.

"This way, please," he said mysteriously. "Mrs. Bama, Jeff will park the car."

The whole unruly, unwashed mob straggled in, through the foyer and into the banquet hall, making odd sounds of confusion and alarm. What on earth?

What they saw astonished them.

The long table had a groaning buffet on it, all the styles of eggs in the world, sausages, pancakes, mounds of fluffy grits, fruits, pastries.

"Golly," said Nick.

And next to it: Nick blinked. This was the craziest thing his father had ever done. Next to it, a twelve-foot, fully decorated Christmas tree, heaped underneath with presents.

"Is everybody here?" his dad said, stepping out of the kitchen. "Come on, let's eat. Then we'll open presents."

"Uh, *hello?*" said Amy. "Earth to Daddy: It's August. I thought Christmas was in December."

"Oh, we'll have one then," Red said. "But I thought we'd have one today too."

"Red," said Beth, "when did you start planning this?"

"Believe it or not, less than three hours ago. I called the staff of the club to get them going, I called that Christmas All Year Round place out on Rogers and I called Brad Newton." Brad Newton was the owner of Newton's Jewelry, Fort Smith's most exclusive store, sole Fort Smith importers of Rolexes.

"But I—"

"Honey, you have no idea of the power of cash money. Now come on, y'all, let's dig in and then open our presents."

The family, all the kids, the new wife, the old wife, who showed up presently, and all the bodyguards, had themselves a fine old time chowing down, with the exception, of course, of Amy, the Smith freshman, who stood apart and would not participate because she considered such ostentatious displays of wealth and capital . . .

"Vulgar," she pronounced.

"I am vulgar," said her father, twitting her. "I admit it. Gauche, even. What about crude, overbearing, ostentatious, self-indulgent, selfish and boorish? But, honey, you have to admit: *vulgar* puts the food on the table. Lots of it."

"Daddy," she sniffed, "you are so gross."

Then it was time for presents.

"Each one of you," Red said, as he took command of the assembly, "each one of you *should* have a Rolex. Life is much better with a Rolex than without one. So the theme of today's Christmas-in-August celebration is: Rolexes for everyone. Even those of you who *have* a Rolex, now you have *two* Rolexes."

He walked among his children and wives with an armload of gift boxes.

"Let's see," he said, "I think this one is for *Timmy.* Oh, and what do we have here, we have one for *Jason.* And, I . . . think . . . this . . . one . . . is . . . for . . . *Jake.*"

At last he got to Nicholas.

"Now, Nick, isn't this better than biology?"

"Yes sir, it sure is," said Nick, gazing up at the loony tune who was his father.

"Go ahead," his father said, "open it."

Nick opened the package: yes, it was the Oyster Master Submariner with the day/date and the red and blue bezel.

"You wear that on biology field trips and you'll never get lost," Red said.

"Thanks, Dad."

"I just want *everybody* to be happy."

He gave each wife, Miss Third Runner-up and Miss Runner-up, a diamond necklace. They oooohed and ahhhhhhed appreciatively.

"Red, I don't know what you just survived," said Susie, his first wife, "but it must have been a honey of a fight."

"Sweetie, you don't know the *half,*" he said.

Then he turned to Amy.

"I know you've got one. This one is different."

"Oh, Lord," she said.

"Go on, open it."

She opened it. It was different. It was solid gold.

"How's that for *vulgar?*" said Red. "Let me tell you, they don't *git* more vulgar than that!"

"What am I supposed to do with this? I can't possibly wear it."

"Sure you can, honey. You're a Bama. You're the eldest daughter of Red Bama, you can wear anything you like. Or, if you want, since it's yours, you can do with it what you want: return it to Brad Newton and give the twelve thousand to the homeless."

"Well," she said, looking at it, "it *is* beautiful." She decided she'd think about it.

As he walked away to join his wives, Red looked back: well, well, well, wasn't that just a smile on the face of dour Ms. Amy?

Someone touched his arm.

"Mr. Bama?"

"Yes, what is it, Ralph?"

"Telephone."

"Ralph, I'm with my family now. It can wait."

"Mr. Bama, it's Washington. They say it's urgent."

Forty-four

I DON'T SUPPOSE nobody's hunting us now," said Bob. "Let's get some goddamned breakfast."

They pulled over at a Denny's on 271 just south of Fort Smith and went in. It was about eleven now. All the ejected shells had been picked up, the Mini-14 had been dumped in a deep and remote part of the black Arkansas River and they were an hour north of the Ouachitas. The bodies would be found when they would be found: maybe in days, maybe in months, maybe in years.

Russ was going on sheer adrenaline. He was out of the shock and numbness, which had been replaced by a burst of manic energy.

"I feel *great*!" he proclaimed. "Denny's! God, I never thought I'd ever be so glad to see a place in my life! I could eat a horse."

They ordered two big, solid breakfasts and reduced them to crumbs and grease slick. For Russ, life after a night as tense and dramatic as the one he'd just survived seemed especially poignant with meaning and sensation.

He turned to Bob.

"Twice you saved my life. You stopped us from getting sniped; you hit Peck in the head. Unbe*liev*able shooting! My God, I thought my father was a good shot. That was unbe*liev*able!"

"Shhh," said Bob. "Just relax. You've still got a gallon of adrenaline in you. In an hour, it'll dump and you'll feel like shit. We got to get you some sleep. And get them abrasions fixed. Russ, just for the hell of it, let me tell you this: you did good. Okay? Lots of people would have lost their heads out there. You did real good. Your old man would be proud of you, okay?"

Russ said nothing.

"Well, anyway," said Bob. "Next move? Before your adrenaline dumps, and you whack out on me, give me the next move."

"You're the genius."

"Okay," said Bob, "we beat the man again. We got to find the man now and bring the fight to him."

"Who's the man?"

"Hell if I know. I know he's there. I just don't know who the hell he is. Any idea?"

"No. The only people who could tell us are turning to fertilizer in the forest. We have nothing."

"Are you sure?"

"Best bet," said Russ. "Go back to Fort Smith. We have a few days when he thinks we're out of it, when he thinks he's won. We go back to the paper: I can get in and spend a day in the morgue. I can investigate the Fort Smith of 1955, where all this began. Maybe somehow I can—"

But Bob wasn't really listening.

"What's going on?" Russ wanted to know.

"We do have a prisoner," said Bob.

He held up Duane Peck's flip phone.

"And I think I know how to make him talk," he added.

They found what they needed in the Central Mall, off Rogers Avenue, a dark cathedral to consumerism. One of the hushed devotional niches in the long corridor was dedicated to cellular phones, pagers, faxes and other new-age information technology. They entered and in a second Bob had selected the wannest and palest of the young men there to chat with, soon snaring him in fatherly power and sheer Marine Corps sergeant charisma.

"Now, see, here's our problem," said Bob. "We were hunting in the woods, and we come across this here phone. Now I'm thinking, some important man needs this phone. I'd sure like to know how to return it to him. You have any ideas there, young man?"

The boy took the phone and examined it: a Motorola NC-50, the very latest and most expensive thing.

"Have you tried autodial?" asked the young man.

"No, and I haven't tried that redial either. Now, if I tapped that redial button, wouldn't that connect me with his last phone call?"

"It would," said the young man. "Why don't you just call and see what you get?"

"Hmmm," said Bob, "that *would* work, wouldn't it? Let me ask you another thing. You been working around phones long?"

"Ah, a couple of years," said the boy. "I'm sort of into phones. Very interesting stuff."

"Know what?" said Bob, squinting up his eyes as if he'd just come up with a hell of an idea. "Bet if I hit redial and you listened to them tones as the number played out, you could read them for us, couldn't you? You know the numerical values of the tones, right?"

The boy looked a little uncomfortable.

"I think that's against the law," he said.

"Is it?" said Bob. "Damn, I didn't realize that."

"It's just to return the phone, right?" said the boy.

"Yes, indeed. We definitely want to return the phone to its rightful owner."

The boy took the phone, held it close to his ear and pushed Redial.

The phone issued a bleat of beep music, a chatter of robot tones. Before the call could connect, he broke it off.

"Okay," he said, "it's an 800 number. Let me try again and concentrate on the last seven numbers."

He hit it again.

"I get 045-1643. Let me try it again."

The beeps poured out.

"That's it. 1-800-045-1643."

"What does that tell you?"

"Ah—nothing. I never heard of an 045 exchange. I never heard of an exchange beginning with a zero. It's not from around here. I never heard of that exchange."

"Do you have a CD phone disk?" asked Russ.

The boy nodded his head, really into it by now.

"Let's see what we get," he said.

This took a bit of time, but in a minute or so, at a computer terminal the young man had a phone-finder running on CD-ROM and quickly learned that the 045 exchange was wholly unlisted anywhere in the United States.

"What would that mean?" said Bob.

"Well, these disks have a lot of unlisted numbers on them, but ever since deregulation, private exchanges, private companies, private information networks have sprung up all over the place, only lightly monitored by the FCC. My guess is this is somebody's most private line, not immediately accessible to the public or maybe even to the government. It's just a very, very private number. I still say: just call it."

"Well, for now, we don't want to do that. Listen, thanks so much."

"Sure, not a problem."

They left the mall.

"It was too much to hope," said Russ. "He wouldn't have been so sloppy as to leave something at risk that would point the finger straight at him."

"Damn," said Bob. "What else do we know about this bird?"

"Well, he must be rich, powerful and connected. If he was able to get Jed Posey paroled, if he was able to put together a team of hotshots, if he was able to get Jack Preece on the job, he's got a lot of clout. He—he has an airplane!"

Russ wasn't sure where that popped out of; it just issued from his deep subconscious.

"He has an airplane," said Bob. "Presumably from around here. Now, if he's in the air the day of the big shoot-out, didn't he file a flight plan?"

"Yes, he'd have to."

"That's a public document, isn't it?"

"Uh, I think," said Russ.

"Now, whyn't we go out to the airport and see if there's some-way we can get into the FAA records for that day. Maybe on that flight plan, he's got to list a phone number. Maybe it's this one or close to it?"

"Goddamn," said Russ.

"Goddamn yourself, Russ. He has an airplane. You're a god-damned genius."

At the airport, Russ himself did the deed. He went into the FAA regional office, pulled his *Daily Oklahoman* press card and explained that he was doing a big takeout on civil aviation, particularly the conflict between private plane owners and the commercial carriers in crowded aviation corridors. He spent an hour taking notes as a droning administrator explained the government's position to him, two or three times in case he missed anything. Russ finally told the man that one way to do such a story would be to set it into the context of a single day in the American air (why hadn't he thought of this before?) and it might be nice to profile who was in the air at a given moment as a kind of cross section of the problem. He seemed to pluck a date out of his memory, which was in fact the date of the shoot-out on the Taliblue. He wondered if he could examine the records of that day and get in touch with some private plane owners who were aloft?

Again, the minutes ground by, but in time he had a thick file of flight plans fetched from the files, and he peeled through them, recognizing nothing, until at last he came to a Cessna 425 Conquest twin-engine job, CN13467, registered to Redline Trucking, whose pilot had filed for Oklahoma City that day, leaving at 10:25 A.M. and landing at 5:20 P.M. That was very interesting, but what really caught Russ's attention was the phone number that the pilot had listed on the plan: It was 045-1640, only three numbers off the mystery number and it had the strange 0 prefix.

Russ realized that Redline Trucking must lease or own a whole bank of 1600 numbers for its various enterprises, under a private 045 exchange, of which 1643 would have to be one. He looked at the pilot's name.

"Bama," he said the name aloud. "Randall Bama."

The next day, much rested after an eighteen-hour blast of sleep in a Ramada Inn south of Fort Smith, Russ and Bob went to the Fort

Smith Municipal Library, where they accessed all the information
that was in the record about Randall "Red" Bama of Fort Smith,
Bama Construction, Redline Trucking, the Bama Group Real Es-
tate Development, Hardscrabble Country Club, the Chamber of
Commerce (president 1991–93 and 1987–88), the Rotary, the Opera
Guild, and so forth and so on.

It explained a lot: how three carloads of professional shooters
and a deputy sheriff and a world-class sniper could be set up to
hunt them down. But did it explain enough?

They went back through the stacks and found as many refer-
ences to his father, the great and notorious Ray Bama (1916–75),
pawn king of Fort Smith, denizen of Nancy's Flamingo Lounge,
known compatriot of the big Little Rock and Hot Springs mob
and rumored mob kingpin with ties to Santo Trafficante and Car-
los Marcello in New Orleans and Big Jim Westwood in Dallas,
whose life was ended in a mysterious car bomb in 1975.

But by late in the afternoon, when they reached the end of the
research, they still had nothing but speculation which led them to a
certain conclusion: that somehow, someway, Earl Lee Swagger had
learned something about the old gangster and was therefore
targeted for elimination. But nothing in the last weeks of Earl's life
made any sense along those lines: he was a rural state police sergeant, a good one, but not an organized crime investigator or a
member, as far as could be determined, of any elite unit of investigators, county, state, federal or otherwise, that could be moving
against Ray Bama, then at the start of his burgeoning career.

And there was no accounting anywhere that suggested any connection to the death of Shirelle Parker, discovered on July 23, 1955,
the last day of Earl's life, by Earl himself.

At dinner that night, Bob said: "I think we should move against
him anyhow. He'll explain what he's up to at the point of a gun."

"Jesus," said Russ, "the guy's sure to be heavily guarded. He's a
gangster, for crying out loud, no matter how civic-minded and
philanthropic and visible. You just don't walk up and point a gun
at him."

So that seemed to be it.

"All right," said Bob, settling down. "We've still got more work.

We have to find someone in the state police in '55 and see what my father would have been doing where he could have known or learned something about Ray Bama."

Russ shook his head.

"I think you're *overvaluing* your father's profession. You want him to be some kind of superinvestigator hot on the big case, so that his death will have a lot of meaning. But the truth was, your father was just like my father: a rural state policeman. My father probably hasn't investigated two things in his life. He's not an investigator, unless he's detached to a special unit, and your father clearly hadn't been detached to a special unit."

Bob chewed this over.

"All right," he said bitterly, "you're the expert. What does a state policeman do? That's the most elementary question. I ain't ever asked it, I guess. What *does* a state policeman do? You tell me. Maybe that's the answer."

Russ thought.

"Well, he goes on patrol, he appears in court, he answers calls, he clears accidents, he reports to his barracks commander, he goes on training, he writes tickets."

He stopped, smiled.

"He writes tickets," he said. "If my father has done one thing over the past thirty years it's not hunt down Lamar Pye and his gang, it's write tickets. He probably wrote ten *thousand* tickets in his time."

The moment hung in the air. Bob had a sense of something before his eyes, something luminous and heavy, something palpable and dense, something big.

He looked at Russ.

Russ looked back.

"Something's on your face," said Russ.

"Ah—" Bob thought. "Tickets," he finally said. "Tickets."

"So? I—"

Then he too felt the touch of the breeze.

"In my father's effects. Remember?" said Bob. "A last book of tickets, half gone. Right to the end: he was giving out tickets."

Tickets, he thought: tickets.

Forty-five

"Pull!"

Incomers. They shot from the trap, a simultaneous pair, and rushed at him as if they were bound to destroy him.

But Red was together today. The Krieghoff barrel was a black blur as it rose through the lowest—he fired—and then moved, instinctively, a bit right and up through the highest—and fired again. The two birds detonated spectacularly against the green of the forest, powdered, literally obliterated, by the 7½ Remington charges.

"You are on a tear, Red!" said his companion.

"I am, I am," he said, pleased.

He'd hit thirty-eight straight. He hadn't missed. The expensive shotgun felt alive and beautiful in his hands, hungry to kill. It sought the birds as if liberated from all restraint, like a purebred, ferocious dog just off the leash, and gunned them out of the sky mercilessly, pounded them to puffs of orange powder.

"I feel good," said Red. "Next week, I'm taking the family to Hawaii. All of 'em. Both wives, all the kids, except goddamned Amy, who wouldn't go across the street to see me hanged, my guards, the whole thing. My first wife's *mother,* goddammit. The Runner-up's worthless *brother,* for God's sake. We'll have a great time."

"You've been through a lot," said his companion. "You want to be fresh for the fall."

"Yes, I do," said Red.

They walked through the forest to the next station. It was a beautiful day in West Arkansas and the trees towered majestically, green and dense against the pure blue sky and the surrounding mountains. The path occasionally yielded to openings where they could look out on the humps of the Ouachitas stretched before them, or, in another direction, to the flatter lands of Oklahoma to the west.

"It's good to be alive," said Red.

Ahead, his trapper scampered into the trap station and Red stood back as his friend took the next cage. Rising teal, far out, a tough one, a single, a following pair and a simo pair. As he set up to shoot, Red absently closed his gun, took out his choke wrench and changed his Improved Cylinder and Skeet I and screwed in Modified and Modified Improved for the longer shot.

His friend was shooting an expensive Perazzi and was an excellent shot, but not up to Red's standards today. He fired, took the single, but only one of the following pair.

"Just relax," called Red.

"I'm *too* relaxed," he called back.

"Pull," he called, and the two birds climbed out of the tree line against the blue sky; he followed and tracked them and fired, but only one vaporized.

"Damn!" he said.

"You have too much on your mind," Red said. "You have to be empty, Zenned out. You have to trust your instincts."

His friend laughed.

"Whenever I trust my instincts," he said, "I get into trouble."

Red went into the shooting cage, a little wooden gazebo that oriented him down a long yellow draw to a clump of bushes between two golden hills, slid a Remington into the lower barrel and set himself.

"Pull!" he commanded, and the bird announced its own launch with the *whang* of the trap arm, and soon rocketed into vision. With leisurely aplomb, Red followed it and dusted it.

Felt so good!

He ejected the shell, dropped two more into the chambers, reset himself. He gave himself a second to think out the sequence: see it, move, mount, shoot, follow through. He took a breath, looked for little indications of panic or doubt and found none.

"Pull," he shouted.

Whang the bird rose and he waited until it came to a dead rest, that wondrous moment where gravity and acceleration were in total equipoise and blew it away. He dropped the barrel a bit to pick up the rise of the following bird and there it was, there it was, he rose up and through it and squeezed and the bird was vapor.

Ah, he thought, a warm surge of pleasure. He'd never shot a 50. He'd had seven 49s, dozens of 48s, and hundreds of 47s and 46s, but never a 50. And he'd never been this close. And this teal simo was the last really tough shot. He had to get this shot and then it was downhill.

He broke the gun, watched the small mushroom of gun smoke rise from the chambers as each shell popped out, and threaded two more in.

He set himself, but didn't want to take too much time, because it's more than possible to think yourself out of a good shooting sequence. He liked where he was: loosey-goosey, ready, hot, fluid, quick and in the zone.

"Pull!" he called.

Nothing happened.

No *whang,* no birds, nothing.

Damn. He hated it when that happened. That's how you lose concentration. He made a mental note to chew out the trapper when the round was finished.

"Are you ready?" he yelled.

There was no answer.

He took the silence as assent, set himself again, wiped his mind and once again called, "Pull!"

Again: no birds.

"Mike," he called the trapper's name. "What the hell is going on?"

There was no reply.

He looked back to his friend and—

The vibrator on his pager buzzed against his hip.

Damn! That meant Peck was calling him. What the hell was *this* about? He thought about ignoring it, just shooting the round out, but how do you ignore it?

Call him, get it dealt with, then get back in the round.

He leaned the shotgun against the gun cage, stepped out.

"Have to make a call," he told his companion.

He dialed the message line, waited for it to connect, heard that he had one new message and then got the message.

"Call for the birds again," it said.

Fine, he thought, stepping back into the cage, picking up the shotgun.

Then his mind computed the significance.

A tremendous sense of unfairness came over him. He picked up the shotgun, gripping it tightly, but he could see nothing.

He set the gun down, looked back at his unconcerned partner and seized the folder off his own belt. He dialed Peck's number. He heard the phone ring in his ear . . . and twenty feet away.

He grabbed the gun and ran out of the cage, off to the left, and saw Peck's phone hanging from the limb of a tree, ringing.

"Peck didn't make it," said somebody.

He turned and saw his nightmare: the sniper, in full camouflage regalia, an ancient god of vengeance, his face not even human but a warrior's face lost in the swirling colors of the woods, his hair wrapped tight in a camouflaged bandanna, his eyes narrow and dark. He had simply stepped from invisibility into Red's life. He lifted a .45 automatic and pointed it straight at Red's face.

"Set the shotgun down, Bama, or I will kill you and you know I will."

Red set the shotgun down.

"Guards," he screamed. *"Guards!"*

"They're tied up two stations back," said the man. "It wasn't their day."

Red turned.

"Swagger," he said, because it was all he could think to say.

"In person," said Bob, then pivoted to point the gun at Red's friend.

"This has nothing to do with me," said the man. "I don't see a thing. I'm not involved in this at all."

"Then drop that gun or I will drop you, sir. I am not here to fuck around."

The Perazzi fell to the ground.

"You may think I'm frightened of you, Swagger," said Red, his face narrowing in fury. "But I'm not. Guys have come at me before. And if this is the day I check out, fuck you, because my family is taken care of and my children love me. So fuck you, Swagger, you do what you have to."

"You got some balls, Red, that I'll say," said Swagger.

"Talk to him!" screamed the companion. "Negotiate with him. Make him an offer. This doesn't have to happen."

"You shut up," said Bob to the man. "I have a boy a hundred yards out there with a .308 right on your chest. You shut up and sit still until I talk to you."

The man went silent as if struck. The idea of the rifle on him chilled him out and he sat as if to move one inch in one direction would earn him a bullet.

"Now, Red," said Bob, "I do want you to talk to me. Why'd your father kill my father back in 1955?"

"Fuck you and the horse you came in on, Swagger. I have allies. I have people who know I was gunning for you. If you kill me, they'll hunt you down and take you out."

"Well, maybe that's a fact. But it won't mean no never mind to you, Red, that I guarantee you. Now, you going to answer me or do I have to shoot a kneecap off?"

"Who's kidding whom?" said Red furiously. "You don't have it in you to shoot my kneecap off. You're a soldier, not a goddamn torturer."

"Talk to him!" screamed the terrified companion. "Tell him what he wants to know. Make him a deal. A cash deal."

"Fuck cash," said Red. "He's not a cash boy." He looked at Swagger, his eyes burning with furious contempt and rage.

Finally, he said, "All right. I'll tell it once. Then it's over. Then you do what you have to do."

"Talk," said Swagger.

"Your father was looking to buy some land. He had been examining plots in the Polk County Deeds and Claims Office and he'd learned that something called the Southland Group had bought up most of the land in Polk County. Because he was curious, he'd investigated and found out what nobody was supposed to know: that Southland was a dummy corporation owned by my father and a man named Harry Etheridge, a U.S. congressman. They'd funneled thousands into it, with the idea that Etheridge would push through a parkway or highway and open up that part of the country for development. It would be worth millions. Your father bumbled into the information. He was the only one who knew of the secret, powerful, *very profitable* link between the Etheridge and the Bama men. It was the linchpin of my father's power and position. Your father had to be stopped. So the congressman and my father put together a plan that turned on some contacts we had in prison and they recruited a kid named Jimmy Pye, just due out. They told him if he did it, they'd set him up in Hollywood. He wanted to be the next Jimmy Dean. But we were worried he wasn't good enough, so Harry Etheridge, who was on the Intelligence Oversight Committee, called in a CIA chit and got a case officer named Frenchy Short to ramrod a secondary plan through. The backup shooter nailed your dad and nobody was the wiser. End of story. Sorry, but business is business."

"And that's the truth?"

"As I live and die. Now fuck you, do what you want."

"Guess what, Red?"

"What?"

"You're wrong."

There was a long moment of silence. Then Red turned and stared at the sniper.

"Fuck you."

"No, fuck *you,* because you're wrong. You been played like a yo-yo and your daddy too."

Another long moment.

"Yesterday," said Bob, "I'd have believed that. I'd have blown you away and gone home a happy boy. But not today."

"What are you talking about?" said Red, his eyes narrowing in concentration.

"It ain't about land. I bet if you wanted to you could pull that story apart real easy. I bet the dates don't match, the money don't match, it don't quite work out. It's what you were told, it's what got your family involved, but it ain't quite right. It's a cover story. Not only because my daddy loved his own land and wasn't about to move for nothing."

"What's it about, then?" said Red.

"It's about a boy who didn't want to pay his speeding ticket."

There was another long pause as Red looked Bob up and down, his rage somewhat tamed by curiosity.

"What are you talking about?"

"On July 19, 1955, at 12:28 A.M. my father issued a speeding ticket to a nineteen-year-old kid for traveling eighty-two in a fifty zone near a spot on Route 88 between Blue Eye and a town named Ink called Little Georgia. What my daddy didn't know was that the reason that boy was speeding was because he had just raped and murdered a little black girl named Shirelle Parker, fifteen years old, at Little Georgia, which was a red clay deposit.

"He'd picked her up in Blue Eye on the way back from a church meeting. And why'd she git in the car with a white boy when her mama had told her *never* to get in no car with a white boy? Because that was a civil rights meeting, and she'd met a white person who believed in her and believed in her struggle. So she'd learned *not* to hate white boys and it got her killed."

Red stared at him.

"Who was the kid?" he asked.

Bob said, "A Harvard kid. Raised in Washington, D.C. The son of a powerful politician. Himself loaded with ambitions." Then he turned and pointed at the man on the bench.

"Him," he said.

Red turned and faced his friend, the son of his father's friend. "Hollis?"

Hollis Etheridge stood.

"Hollis, you? *You?*"

"He's lying," said Hollis.

"He went home in a panic and told his father. His father being Congressman Harry Etheridge, Boss Harry Etheridge, and being the sort of man he was, he couldn't see his boy's life being ruined by a little mistake with a black gal. So he moved quickly through his sources and came up with Frenchy Short, who moved the girl's body to get it away from Little Georgia and set up a frame on the lightest-skinned black boy he could find: a boy named Reggie Gerard Fuller, who was executed for the crime.

"The problem was the state trooper. They could get the ticket out of the court records but they couldn't get it out of the trooper's mind and they knew the trooper would put two and two together. They knew from the start they had to kill the trooper, but in some way that didn't look suspicious and didn't invite close examination of the trooper's last days, and for which there was a ready explanation and a convenient killer.

"That's how Jimmy Pye, the next Jimmy Dean, and Jack Preece, the sniper, come into it. All for him. For the next Vice President of the United States."

"There's no proof," said Hollis. "It's all lies. All political figures are used to rumors like this. You'd be laughed out of court. Red, it's nonsense. It's nothing. He doesn't have a thing."

"I have this," said Bob.

He held up the old book of tickets.

"Your signature. The time, the date, the place. Any crime lab can authenticate the age of the ticket and the age of the ink. It's just as good now as it was then: it puts you at the site of the murder at the time of the murder. It'll put you in the chair today just as it would have forty years ago. And this time, your goddamn father ain't around to pull strings. And if my father'd had another day, he'd have seen the connection and put you on the row."

He lifted the gun and pointed it at Hollis's handsome head.

Hollis bowed.

"Please," he said.

"You know how much evil came out of that night? You know the people who died? You know the train of destruction you set in motion? You know the lives ruined, the lives ended, the lives embittered because of that night? Why? Why? Did she laugh?"

"I didn't mean to," he said. "She started to scream. I had to stop her from screaming. I never meant to."

Bob lowered the gun.

"My friend is a newspaper reporter," he said. "We'll go to the paper and publish this. We'll get the case reopened. There's been enough killing."

He slipped the .45 back into its holster and turned to face Red Bama, who now held the loaded Krieghoff.

Through the lenses, Russ watched Red Bama pick up the shotgun from a hundred yards out. He watched the man raise the shotgun, watched its barrels pivot lazily.

Do something! he told himself.

Involuntarily his fingers closed on a trigger. But there was no trigger. He had no rifle.

Why didn't you give me a rifle! he screamed to Bob Lee Swagger, his eyes glued in horror to the binoculars. *I could have done it!*

"Red, thank God," said Hollis.

"Yes," said Red, "thank God," and he fired both barrels, one two, fast as they could be fired.

The No. 7½ shot hit its target; it didn't have time to open or spread but delivered an impact similar to that of a nineteenth-century elephant gun, a tremendous package of weight and velocity and density; the first charge literally eviscerated the chest, the heart and lungs, the spinal column; the second hit just above the mouth and destroyed the skull, all the facial structures, the features, the hair. The body was punched backwards and came to sprawl in the bushes.

Gun smoke hung in the air.

Russ, watching from a hundred yards away, bent and puked.

"Nice shooting," said Bob.

"It'll cost me a million dollars," Red said, "to straighten this out. And it's the first fatal accident in the history of sporting clays." He shook his head. "He would have been Vice President, you know. It was set. He might very well have been President."

"Everybody has to pay. It was his turn," Bob said.

"Yes," said Red, "but do you know why I did it? To save me the trial? To save the humiliation? To save the legal fees? To avenge that poor girl, because he broke the rules and hurt a child? Maybe. But the real reason is that I now realize he not only killed your father, he killed mine. My father must have been the only man alive who wasn't an Etheridge but who knew the secret. And when Boss Harry died, son Hollis got to worrying about that. So: there you have it. Did we pay our fathers back for what they did for us? Not really. But I'll say this, Swagger: we sure as hell tried."

"Damned right," said Bob.

But Red had a last surprise for him.

He looked up, his eyes narrowed in sly concentration.

"And I know you think you're much smarter than I am, because you figured all this out and I didn't. So I give you that. But I have a surprise for you too."

Bob looked at him.

"When you go home, I want you to say hello to Julie and YKN4 for me."

There was a long moment.

"My family?" said Bob.

"The pay phone. We tracked your collect call. I had your wife and daughter, Swagger. I could have used them to get at you. You made a mistake."

Bob saw how it could happen.

"But I don't do families. That's my policy. Now you have no more business around me and mine and I'll have none around you and yours. You evened your scores, I evened mine. It's over, it's finished, it's done. We are free men, right?"

"That sounds like a deal to me," said Bob.

Forty-six

S TATE POLICE INVESTIGATORS descended on the accident scene in their legions, along with hundreds of media
types, and for a few days, the little sporting clays range in West
Arkansas was the most famous site in America, leading all the
network news shows. The newspapers were full of the Etheridge
tragedy. A grand jury was swiftly empaneled by Sebastian County
prosecutors.

But by the end of the week, no true bill of indictment was voted
and prosecutors announced their acquiescence to the inevitable
ruling of accidental death. There just wasn't any evidence to the
contrary: Red Bama clung to his story, and his two bodyguards and
the trapper, all of whom had witnessed the event, confirmed his
account. He'd just loaded the Krieghoff when his cellular rang,
and he turned to step out of the constricting cage to get it off his
belt, momentarily forgetting that he held the loaded shotgun, and
he banged the stock against the cage and somehow the gun fired,
although investigators could not get the gun to duplicate the accident in the ballistics lab. But that is the tragedy of the firearm: so
enticing, so alluring, so beguiling, so damned much fun is the gun,
and yet when a mistake is made with it, the consequences are
beyond all scale to the act itself. A man grows confused with a gun
in his hand, turns and bumps and *boomboom!* The end of a promising and already distinguished career.

Editorials appeared nationwide, lamenting the decease of Hollis

Etheridge, former two-term senator, respected legislator, beloved husband, son of one of the most powerful politicians the state of Arkansas had generated, but a man who insisted on making it on his own, not riding his father's coattails. He was the kind of American who had done so much to help so many. His party's leaders issued proclamations; flattering posthumous profiles ran in all the big magazines and on TV shows; in the Arkansas State Legislature, a bill was introduced to rename the parkway now called solely after his father the "Hollis and Harry Etheridge Memorial Parkway," and it passed within a week, though no money could be found in the budget to remake the signs so that will have to wait until a better year.

As for Red Bama, after the grand jury refused to indict him, he joined his family in Hawaii for the remainder of the summer. They had a wonderful time, and returned in the fall, fit and tan and rested. His children prosper, even poor Nicholas; Amy is planning on Yale Law School and wants to go to work as a prosecutor and Red has told her he can arrange it and she still sniffs at him. But occasionally she wears that gold Rolex. He is, after all, her father. He is still married to Miss Runner-up but rumors persist he has been seen in out-of-the-way clubs with an actual Miss Arkansas of early nineties vintage.

Bob and Russ left Arkansas that very afternoon; they drove all night, after turning in the rental car and paying a healthy fee to get the green pickup, much battered, out of the airport parking. Late that afternoon, they were in Oklahoma City, where Russ still had his apartment in an old house.

Bob pulled up outside it.

"Okay, bub, here you be," he said.

"God," said Russ, "I can't believe it's over."

"Over and done," said Bob. "Or as done as it can be."

"Jesus," said Russ.

"You're a great kid, Russ. You write that book. I know it'll be a success."

"I never really got enough. Not enough facts, not enough documentation. But it turned out to be exactly as I thought it would be, didn't it? A profound endorsement of the genetic theory of human behavior. Good fathers, good sons. Bad fathers, bad sons, straight down the line. Like a laboratory experiment."

"Write it as a story."

Russ wondered: a story? Then he realized Bob meant as fiction.

"You mean as a novel?"

"That's the ticket. Make up the names, change the locale, that sort of thing. All them Johnnies do it, no reason you shouldn't."

"Hmmmmm," said Russ. That's a good idea." It *was* a good idea.

"And let me give you one last piece of advice, all right?"

Russ said, "Okay."

"Make peace with your father. *You'll* be a lot happier. *He'll* be a lot happier. He's your only father. You only get one. I'd give anything for another few minutes with mine."

Russ laughed cynically. Then his bitterness came washing over him.

"Yeah, well," he said. "Your dad was a hero. He was a great man, a great American man. They don't come any better. But my dad's just a man. He's an asshole. He finally gave in to his selfishness. That's all there is."

Bob was quiet for just a second and then he said, "You know, you're a very bright kid. You were right on so many things. You were right about the Parker crime and how important it was. I was wrong, dead wrong. You were so smart, you saw so much, you were quick and brave. You'd make a hell of a marine."

"I—"

"But you missed something, Russ. You missed something big."

Russ turned. What could he have missed? What surprise was left?

"What are you talking about?"

"Ask yourself this: if the child who became Lamar Pye was born nine months after Jimmy's death . . . *when* did Jimmy get his young wife pregnant?"

Russ paused, considering.

"He never made it back to Blue Eye," said Bob. "My father

stopped him in that cornfield. Edie Pye never saw her husband alive from the last time she visited him in jail a month earlier."

Russ shook his head. What did . . . ? Where was this going?

"I think Miss Connie might have figured it out, but she was the only one. If she did, she didn't let on."

"I don't—" Russ began.

"Oh yes, you do," said Bob.

Russ looked up at Bob.

"My daddy was alone with Edie that last day for at least an hour. He liked her a lot. She liked him a lot. Later, when he left to go for Jimmy, he told me about two kinds of bad. Bad evil, where you decide to do wrong and say fuck it, and bad mistake, where you want to do the right goddamn thing but it gets clotted up and confused sometimes and before you know it, never meaning to, you done made a mess. He was talking about himself."

"You're saying . . . ?"

"That's right, Russ. Big bad old Lamar Pye? He was my brother."

Forty-seven

RUSS DIDN'T STOP having Lamar Pye dreams right away; in fact, two weeks after he got back, he had a terrible one, the worst yet, a screamer, full of Lamar, shotguns, this time Jeannie Vincent thrown in, his hero Bob's gun empty and not shooting, a real monster. But as the weeks passed, the space between them seemed to widen and then one day in late September he'd been so busy with his arrangements and his goodbyes, he suddenly realized it had been almost a full, clear dreamless month.

So he knew it was time for the last thing.

It was a small house, much smaller than he expected, and he checked twice to make sure he had the address right. But he had. The day was beautiful, now chilly with the coming fall, but very clear, and the constant Oklahoma wind pushed through the trees, shaking them dry of leaves.

Russ got out of the truck and went up to the house, climbing up the porch and going to the front door.

I feel like an idiot, he thought.

But he knocked anyway, and after a bit, the door opened—it was still the Midwest and people opened doors without looking out first—and a young woman stood before him. She was in her late twenties, strikingly attractive, thin, with a spray of red freckles on her whitish skin and a crop of reddish-blond hair.

"Yes?" she asked.

"You're Holly?" he said.

"Yes. I'm sorry, who are—"

"I'm Russ."

She still looked blank. She was not getting this.

"Russ *Pewtie*," he said. "My dad lives here."

"Russ! Russ! Oh, God, Russ, I didn't recognize you, it's been so many years and you were a teenager. Come in, come in, he'll be so *happy*!"

She all but pulled him into the house, which was modest but clean and had a lot of books and gun magazines around. Little indicators of domestic intimacy irritated Russ: a *Lawton Constitution* TV guidebook, a pair of Nike running shoes, his father's by the size, a table with a checkbook and a stack of bills where someone had been paying what was due, a frame displaying a batch of decorations from the Oklahoma State Police. But he pushed the anger and the pain away.

This is the way it is, he told himself.

From somewhere deeper in the house came the sound of a football game.

"Bud, Bud, Bud honey, guess who's here?"

"Goddammit, Holly," came his father's irritated voice from the sunporch where the TV evidently had been placed, "it's the fourth quarter. Who the—"

"Bud, it's Russ."

"Russ!"

His father came booming out of the doorway and stood there, huge and looking more like John Wayne than ever. His hair was shorter, but just as gray, and he'd lost that pallor and grimness that had been so evident when he'd been recovering from his wound several years back, Russ's freshman year. He no longer seemed halting or confused.

"Oh, Russ, it's terrific to see you," he said, beaming, his face flushing with pleasure.

"Hi, Dad," said Russ a little sheepishly, feeling fourteen again.

"This is making him so happy," said Holly, crying a little. "He just said to me, Oh, gosh, I'd like to see Russ again."

"Holly, get the boy a beer. No, get the man a beer, Lord how he's grown and toughened up. I talked to your mother on the phone: she said you were going back to school."

"Vanderbilt. In Tennessee."

"That's a good one, I hear."

"It's real good. It's better for me because it isn't so *eastern.*"

"You think you're going to stay in the newspaper business?"

"Well, sir, I'm going to give it a try. I'm majoring in English, and I've got some projects in mind."

"Is that why you were in Arkansas?"

"Yeah, you won't believe this: I decided to try and write the life story of Lamar Pye," he said. "So I went back there and looked into his background. He had quite a background."

"Russ, why? Why? He was a violent scumbag. He lived as he died. He hurt people."

"Yes, I know, Dad, and I wanted to know why."

"Did you find out?"

"Yes," said Russ, "I did. It has to do with family. Anyway . . . how've you been? You look great! What've you been up to?"

They talked for three hours.

The sun hid behind pale clouds. The day was gray and dreary. In the distance, the prison showed white, the only source of radiance in the grim day; as always, it looked exactly like it was what it wasn't, a magic city, an enchanted castle.

The tall, thin man climbed the scruffy little hill. Around him, the Oklahoma plains rolled away toward the horizon. He walked among the grave markers, seeing the names of felons long forgot, bad men who'd done terrible things and now lay unlamented in this forgotten parcel of America. The ever-present wind whistled, kicking up a screen of dust that swirled across the ground and between the gravestones.

At last he came to the one he'd been seeking.

"LAMAR PYE" was all it said. "1956–1994."

"That one," somebody said. "That was a bad one."

Bob looked and saw the old black trusty who'd been here before, when Russ showed him the spot.

"Wasn't you here a few months back?" the trusty asked, his face screwing up in the effort to remember.

"Yes, I was," he said.

"You was looking at old Lamar then too, right?"

"We came to see Lamar, that's right," he said.

"We don't get many people stopping by. You was the only one ever came to see old Lamar. I'd remember if there were more. Nope, you and that boy the only ones."

Bob looked at the gravestone. There wasn't much to see, just a flat stone, overgrown and dusty, showing the wear of wind and dust and time.

"A bad, bad boy," said the trusty. "The worst boy in the joint. Lived bad, died bad. Bad to the bone. Bad at the start, bad at the finish."

"He was a bastard," Bob said. "No one could deny that."

"Pure evil," said the trusty. "I do believe God sent him to us to show us what evil is."

"Maybe so," said Bob, "but from what I understand, someone did a good job of beating it into him. I'd say men put the evil in him, not God. It's what happens when you don't got nobody pulling for you or nobody who gives a damn about you."

The old black man looked at him and didn't know what to say.

There was the sound of other vehicles and both men turned as a tractor with backhoe began to lumber down the prison road, followed by a long black hearse.

"What the hell?" said the trusty.

Bob reached into his jacket and pulled out a document.

"Here. I'm supposed to give this to the supervisor but he's not here so I guess I give it to you."

The old man opened the document with a puzzled look, fumbled with some glasses and tried to make sense out of what was there.

"It's an official exhumation order," Bob said. "We're taking Lamar back to Arkansas. He's going to be with his father."

The old man's eyes were filled with incomprehension, but no further explanations came.

Bob turned and headed down the hill, where his wife and daughter stood waiting.

Acknowledgments

T HE AUTHOR would like to issue particular thanks to Weyman Swagger, who gave especially of time and effort. Then John Feamster, of *Precision Shooting*, pitched in with another large chunk of help.

Other friends were involved as well, notably Bob Lopez, Mike Hill, Lenne Miller, my brother Tim Hunter, and Barry Neville. A whole slew of people were of great help in Arkansas, including the three antique dealers in Fort Smith, who helped me find maps from the fifties, and the librarian who dug out the microfilm of the *Southwestern Times Record* for July of 1955. In fact, the people of Arkansas were unfailingly kind to me in my peregrinations in that state.

Peter R. Senich's *The Long Range War* was invaluable in explaining the difference between Army and Marine sniper programs in Vietnam, though it should be emphasized that any judgments made on those programs are mine and not his.

Two other points should be made. Polk Countians and other Arkansans will recognize that I've yielded to the godlike temptation to create and destroy at my own whimsy. For example, I've created the Harry Etheridge Memorial Parkway out of whole cloth; I've also disappeared the town of Mena and dumped the wholly fictitious town of Blue Eye, with a far more tragic racial history, in its place.

Second, the author hopes that some readers recognize that *Black*

Light is the third in what amounts to a trilogy, following on his last two novels, *Point of Impact* and *Dirty White Boys*. I've made a good-faith effort to reconcile this book with the other two, where it was possible; alas, in some cases, as where I placed the same event on different days in each book (duh!), it was not.

Finally, the author would like to thank his brilliant agent, Esther Newberg, for enthusiasm, shrewd judgment and unflagging support; his first editor at Doubleday, David Gernert, for *his* enthusiasm and support; and his second editor at the house, Bill Thomas, for picking up the project and running with it.

Naturally, none of these good people is responsible for any mistakes or failures of nerve, taste and character in the book; those rest with me entirely.

ABOUT THE AUTHOR

Stephen Hunter was born in 1946 and graduated from Northwestern University in 1968. After two years in the Army, he began work at the *Baltimore Sun*, where he is now film critic. This is his seventh novel. He lives in Columbia, Maryland, with his wife and two children.

BMKH